FIRST BITE

Without warning the vampire was flowing forward and Shay found herself trapped in the corner with his hands on either side of her head. "You are mine."

His face was so close that she could see the flecks of gold in the midnight eyes. Easily sensing her flare of desire Viper stilled above her, his fangs lengthening as his own body reacted.

Her eyes widened. "Don't."

With a slow, relentless motion his head began to lower. "You fear me drinking your blood?"

"I don't like being a meal on wheels for anyone."

His cool lips skimmed her mouth before brushing her cheek. "There are many reasons for a vampire to share blood. Trust, friendship, love . . . lust."

Her heart crashed against her chest as a dark heat spread through her body. He was touching her with nothing more than his lips, but already a flutter of excitement was rushing through her.

It had been so long.

The satin of his hair tickled her nose as his mouth stroked down the curve of her neck. He smelled of expensive cologne and something far more primitive. Something starkly male.

His mouth lingered on the frantic beat of her pulse before his tongue traced the large vein in a wet path back up her throat . . .

Books by Alexandra Ivy

WHEN DARKNESS COMES

EMBRACE THE DARKNESS

DARKNESS EVERLASTING

DARKNESS REVEALED

DARKNESS UNLEASHED*

Published by Zebra Books

*coming soon

Embrace the Darkness

Alexandra Ivy

ZEBRA BOOKS
Kensington Publishing Corp.
www.kensingtonbooks.com

ZEBRA BOOKS are published by

Kensington Publishing Corp.
850 Third Avenue
New York, NY 10022

All Kensington titles, imprints, and distributed lines are available at special quantity discounts for bulk purchases for sales promotion, premiums, fund-raising, educational, or institutional use.

Special book excerpts or customized printings can also be created to fit specific needs. For details, write or phone the office of the Kensington Special Sales Manager: Attn. Special Sales Department. Kensington Publishing Corp., 850 Third Avenue, New York, NY 10022. Phone: 1-800-221-2647.

Zebra and the Z logo Reg. U.S. Pat. & TM Off.

First Printing: November 2007
10 9 8

Printed in the United States of America

Chapter One

The auction house on the outskirts of Chicago didn't look like a cesspit.

Behind the iron fences the elegant brick structure sprawled over the landscape with a visible arrogance. The rooms were large with vaulted ceilings that boasted beautiful murals and elegant chandeliers. And on the advice of a professional, they had been decorated with thick ivory carpets, glossy dark paneling, and hand-carved furniture.

The overall atmosphere was the sort of quiet hush that only money could buy. Lots and lots of money.

It was the sort of swanky place that should be peddling rare paintings, priceless jewels, and museum artifacts.

Instead it was no more than a flesh market. A sewer where demons were sold like so much meat.

There was nothing pleasant about the slave trade. Not even when the trade was demons rather than humans. It was a sordid business that attracted every decadent, demented slime ball in the country.

They came for all sorts of pathetic reasons.

Those who bought demons for mercenaries or body guards. Those who lusted after the more exotic sex slaves. Those who believed the blood of demons could bring them magic or eternal life. And those who purchased demons to be released into their private lands and hunted like wild animals.

The bidders were men and women without conscience or morals. Only enough money to sate their twisted pleasures.

And at the top of the dung heap was the owner of the auction house, Evor. He was one of the lesser trolls who made his living upon the misery of others with a smile on his face.

Someday Shay intended to kill Evor.

Unfortunately it would not be today.

Or rather tonight.

Attired in ridiculous harem pants and a tiny sequined top that revealed far more than it concealed, she paced the cramped cell behind the auction rooms. Her long raven black hair had been pulled to a braid that hung nearly to her waist. Better to reveal her slanted golden eyes, the delicate cast to her features, and the bronzed skin that marked her as something other than human.

Less than two months before she had been a slave to a coven of witches who intended to bring Armageddon to all demons. At the time she had thought anything was preferable to being their toady as she helplessly watched their evil plotting.

Hell, it's tough to top genocide.

It was only when she had been forced back to the power of Evor that she understood that death was not always the worst fate.

The grave was really nothing compared to what waited for her beyond the door.

Without thought Shay struck out with her foot, sending the lone table sailing through the air to crash against the iron bars with astonishing force.

From behind her came a heavy sigh that had her spinning to regard the small gargoyle hiding behind a chair in the far corner.

Levet wasn't much of a gargoyle.

Oh, he possessed the traditional grotesque features. Thick gray skin, reptilian eyes, horns, and cloven hoofs. He even possessed a long tail he polished and pampered with great pride. Unfortunately, despite his frightening appearance, he was barely three feet tall and worse, as far as he was concerned, he possessed a pair of delicate, gossamer wings that would have been more fitting on a sprite or a fairy than a lethal creature of the dark.

As if to add to his humiliation his powers were unpredictable under the best of circumstances, and his courage more often than not missing in action.

It was little wonder he had been voted out of the Gargoyle Guild and forced to fend for himself. They claimed he was an embarrassment to the entire community, and not one had stepped forward when he had been captured and made a slave by Evor.

Shay had taken the pathetic creature under her protection the moment she had been forced back to the auction house. Not only because she possessed a regrettable tendency to leap to the defense of anyone weaker than herself, but because she knew that it aggravated Evor to have his favorite whipping boy taken away.

The troll might hold the curse that bound her, but if he pressed her far enough she would be willing to kill him, even if it meant an end to her own life.

"*Cherie,* did the table do something I did not see or were you just attempting to teach it a lesson?" Levet demanded, his voice low and laced with a lilting French accent.

Not at all the sort of thing to improve his status among the gargoyles.

Shay smiled wryly. "I was imagining it was Evor."

"Strange, they do not greatly resemble one another."

"I have a good imagination."

"Ah." He gave a ridiculous wiggle of his thick brow. "In that case, I do not suppose you are imagining I'm Brad Pitt?"

Shay smiled wryly. "I'm good, but not that good, gargoyle."

"A pity."

Her brief amusement faded. "No, the pity is that it was a table and not Evor smashed to pieces."

"A delightful notion, but a mere dream." The gray eyes slowly narrowed. "Unless you intend to be stupid?"

Shay deliberately widened her eyes. "Who me?"

"Mon dieu," the demon growled. "You intend to fight him."

"I can't fight him. Not as long as I remain held by the curse."

"As if that has ever halted you." Levet tossed aside the pillow to reveal his tail furiously twitching about his hoofs. A sure sign of distress. "You can't kill him, but that never keeps you from trying to kick his fat troll ass."

"It passes the time."

"And leaves you screaming in agony for hours." He abruptly shuddered. *"Cherie,* I can't bear seeing you like that. Not again. It's insane to battle against fate."

Shay grimaced. As part of the curse, she was punished for any attempt to harm her master. The searing pain that gripped her body could leave her gasping on the ground or even passed out for hours. Lately, however, the punishment had become so brutal she feared that each time she pressed her luck it might be the last time.

She gave a tug on her braid. A gesture that revealed the frustration that smoldered just below the surface.

"You think I should just give in? Accept defeat?"

"What choice do you have? What choice do any of us have? Not all the fighting in the world can change the fact we belong—" Levet rubbed one of his stunted horns. "How do you say . . . lock, stock, and jug . . ."

"Barrel."

"Ah, yes, barrel to Evor. And that he can do whatever he wants with us."

Shay gritted her teeth as she turned to glare at the iron bars that held her captive. "Shit. I hate this. I hate Evor. I hate this cell. I hate those pathetic demons up there waiting to bid on me. I almost wish I had let those witches bring an end to all of us."

"You will get no arguments from me, my sweet Shay," Levet agreed with a sigh.

Shay closed her eyes. Dammit. She hadn't meant the words. She was tired and frustrated, but she was no coward. Just the fact she had survived the past century proved that.

"No," she muttered. "No."

Levet gave a flap of his wings. "And why not? We are trapped here like rats in a maze until we can be sold to the highest bidder. What could be worse?"

Shay smiled without humor. "Allowing fate to win."

"What?"

"So far fate or destiny or fortune or whatever the hell you want to call it has done nothing but crap on us," Shay growled. "I'm not going to just give in and allow it to thumb its nose at me as I slink into my grave. One of these days I'm going to have an opportunity to spit fate in its face. That's what keeps me fighting."

There was a long silence before the gargoyle moved to stand near enough so that he could rub his head on her leg. It was an unconscious gesture. A quest for reassurance that he would rather die than admit.

"I am uncertain I have ever heard such an inelegant speech, but I believe you. If anyone can get away from Evor, it's you."

Absently, Shay shifted the horn poking into her thigh. "I'll come back for you, Levet, that much I promise."

"Well, well, isn't this touching?" Abruptly appearing before the iron bars of the cell Evor smiled to reveal his pointed teeth. "Beauty and the Beast."

With a smooth motion, Shay had pressed Levet behind her and turned to regard her captor.

A sneer touched her face as the troll stepped into the cell and locked the door behind him. Evor easily passed for human. An incredibly ugly human.

He was a short, pudgy man with a round, squishy face and heavy jowls. His hair was little more than tufts of stray strands that he carefully combed over his head. And his small black eyes had a tendency to flash red when he was annoyed.

The eyes he hid behind black-framed glasses.

The thickly fleshed body he hid behind an obscenely expensive tailored suit.

Only the teeth marked him for the troll he was.

That and his utter lack of morals.

"Screw you, Evor," Shay muttered.

The nasty smile widened. "You wish."

Shay narrowed her gaze. The troll had been trying to get into her bed since gaining control of her curse. The only thing that had halted him from forcing her had been the knowledge she was quite willing to kill the both of them to prevent such a horror.

"I'll walk through the fires of hell before I let you touch me."

Fury rippled over the pudgy features before the oily smile returned. "Someday, my beauty, you'll be happy to be spread beneath me. We all have our breaking point. Eventually you'll reach yours."

"Not in this lifetime."

His tongue flicked out in an obscene motion. "So proud. So powerful. I shall enjoy pouring my seed into you. But not yet. There is still money to be made from you. And money always comes first." Lifting his hand he revealed the heavy iron shackles that he had hid behind his body. "Will you put these on or do I need to call for the boys?"

Shay crossed her arms over her chest. She might only be half Shalott, but she possessed all of the strength and agility of her ancestors. They were not the favorite assassins of the demon world without cause.

"After all these years you still think those goons can hurt me?"

"Oh, I have no intention of having them hurt you. I should hate to have you damaged before the bidding." Very deliberately his gaze shifted to where Levet was cowering behind her legs. "I merely wish them to encourage your good behavior."

The gargoyle gave a low moan. "Shay?"

Shit.

She battled back the instinctive urge to punch the pointed teeth down Evor's throat. It would only put her on the ground in agony. Worse, it would leave Levet at the mercy of the hulking mountain trolls Evor used as protection.

They would take great delight in torturing the poor gargoyle.

As far as she knew their only pleasure was giving pain to others.

Freaking trolls.

"Fine." She held out her arms with a furious scowl.

"A wise choice." Keeping a wary eye on her, Evor pressed the shackles over her wrists and locked them shut. "I knew you would understand the situation once it was properly explained."

Shay hissed as the iron bit into her skin. She could feel her power draining and her flesh chaffing beneath the iron. It was her one certain Achilles' heel.

"All I understand is that someday I'm going to kill you."

He gave a jerk on the chain that draped between the shackles. "Behave yourself, bitch, or your little friend pays the consequences. Got it?"

Shay battled back the sickness that clutched at her stomach.

Once again she was going to be placed on the stage and sold to the highest bidder. She would be utterly at the mercy of some stranger who could do whatever he pleased with her.

And there wasn't a damn thing she could do to stop it.

"Yeah, I got it. Let's just get this over with."

Evor opened his mouth as if to make a smart-ass comment only to snap the fish lips shut when he caught sight of her expression. Obviously he could sense she was close to the edge.

Which only proved that he wasn't quite as stupid as he looked.

In silence they left the cell and climbed the narrow stairs to the back of the stage. Evor paused only long enough to lock her shackles to a pole anchored in the floor before moving toward the closed curtains and slipping through them to face the crowd.

Alone in the darkness Shay sucked in a deep breath and tried to ignore the rumblings of the crowd just beyond the curtain.

Even without being able to see the potential bidders she could feel the presence of the gathering demons and humans. She could smell the stench of their sweat. Feel the smoldering impatience. Taste the depraved lust in the air.

She abruptly frowned. There was something else. Something that was subtly laced through it all.

A sense of decaying evil that sent a chill of horror over her skin.

It was vague. As if the being was not truly in the room in full form. More like a looming, intangible presence. An echo of foulness that made her stomach clench in fear.

Swallowing back her instinctive scream she closed her eyes and forced herself to take a deep, steadying breath. In the distance she heard Evor loudly clear his throat to command attention.

"And now, ladies and gentlemen, demons and fairies, dead and undead . . . it is time for our main attraction. Our *pièce de résistance*. An item so rare, so extraordinary that only those who possess a golden token may remain," he dramatically announced. "The rest may retire to our reception rooms where you will be offered your choice of refreshment."

Despite the lingering certainty she had just been brushed by some malignant gaze Shay managed a disgusted grimace. Evor was always a pompous blowhard. Tonight, however, he put even the cheesiest ringmaster to shame.

"Gather close, my friends," Evor commanded as the dregs of bidders were forced to leave the room. To be granted a golden ticket a person or demon had to carry at least $50,000 in cash on them. The slave trade rarely accepted checks or credit cards. Go figure. "You will not wish to miss your first glimpse of my precious treasure. Do not fear, I have ensured that she is properly chained. She will offer no danger. No danger beyond her perilous charm. She will not rip your heart from your chest, but I do not promise she will not steal it with her beauty."

"Shut your mouth and open the curtain," a voice growled.

"You are impatient?" Evor demanded, his tone edged with anger. He didn't like his well-practiced act interrupted.

"I don't have all night. Get on with it."

"Ah, a premature . . . bidder, a pity. Let us hope for your sake that it is not an affliction that taints your performance in other areas," Evor sneered, pausing to allow the roar of coarse laughter to fade. "Now where was I? Oh, yes. My prize. My most beloved slave. Demons and ghouls, allow me to introduce you to Lady Shay . . . the last Shalott to walk our world."

With a dramatic motion the curtain disappeared in a puff of smoke, leaving Shay exposed to the near two dozen men and demons.

Deliberately she lowered her gaze as she heard the gasps echo through the room. It was humiliating enough to smell their rabid hunger. She didn't need to see it written on their faces.

"Is this a trick?" a dark voice demanded in disbelief. Hardly surprising. As far as Shay knew she truly was the last Shalott remaining in the world.

"No trick, no illusion."

"As if I'd take your word for it, troll. I want proof."

"Proof? Very well." There was a moment's pause as Evor searched the crowd. "You there, come forward," he commanded.

Shay tensed as she felt the cold chill that warned her it was a vampire approaching. Her blood was more precious than gold to the undead. An aphrodisiac that they would kill to procure.

With her attention focused on the tall, gaunt vampire, Shay barely noticed when Evor grabbed her arm and used a knife to slice through the skin of her forearm. Hissing softly the vamp leaned downward to lick the welling blood. His entire body shivered as he lifted his head to regard her with stark hunger.

"There is human blood, but she is genuine Shalott," he rasped.

With a smooth motion Evor had placed his pudgy form between the vamp and Shay, shooing the predator away with a wave of his hand. Reluctantly the undead creature left the stage, no doubt sensing the impending riot if he gave in to his impulse to sink his teeth into her and drain her dry.

Evor waited until the stage was cleared before moving to stand behind his podium. He grasped his gavel and lifted it over his head. Ridiculous twit.

"Satisfied? Good." Evor smacked the gavel onto the podium. "The bidding starts at fifty thousand dollars. Remember, gentlemen, cash only."

"Fifty-five thouand."

"Sixty thousand."

"Sixty-one thousand."

Shay's gaze once again dropped to her feet as the voices called out their bids. Soon enough she would be forced to confront her new master. She didn't want to watch as they wrangled over her like a pack of dogs slavering over a juicy bone.

"One hundred thousand dollars." A shrill voice shouted from the back of the room.

A sly smile touched Evor's thin lips. "A most generous bid, my good sir. Anyone else? No? Going once . . . Going twice . . ."

"Five hundred thousand."

A sharp silence filled the room. Without even realizing what she was doing Shay lifted her head to stare into the crowd jamming the auction floor.

There was something about that silky dark voice. Something . . . familiar.

"Step forward," Evor demanded, his eyes shimmering red. "Step forward and offer your name."

There was a stir as the crowd parted. From the back shadows a tall, elegant form glided forward.

A hushed whisper spread through the room as the muted light revealed the hauntingly beautiful face and satin curtain of silver hair that fell down his back.

It took only a glance to realize he was a vampire.

No human could so closely resemble an angel that had fallen from heaven. And fallen recently. Or move with such liquid grace. Or cause the demons to back away in wary fear.

Shay's breath caught in her throat. Not at his stunning beauty, or powerful presence, or even the flamboyant velvet cloak that shrouded his slender form.

It was the fact that she knew this vampire.

He had been at her side when they had battled the coven of witches weeks ago. And, more importantly, he had been at her side when she had saved his life.

And now he was here bidding on her like she was no more than a piece of property.

Damn his rotten soul to hell.

Viper had been in the world for centuries. He had witnessed the rise and fall of empires. He had seduced the most beautiful women in the world. He had taken the blood of kings, czars, and Pharaohs.

He had even changed the course of history at times.

Now he was sated, jaded, and magnificently bored.

He no longer struggled to broaden his power base. He didn't involve himself in battles with demons or humans. He didn't form alliances or interfere in politics.

His only concern was ensuring the safety of his clan and keeping his business profitable enough to allow him the luxurious lifestyle he had grown accustomed to.

But somehow the Shalott demon had managed the impossible.

She had managed to linger in his thoughts long after she had disappeared.

For weeks she had haunted his memories and even invaded his dreams. She was like a thorn that had lodged beneath his skin and refused to be removed.

A realization that he wasn't sure pleased or annoyed him as he had scoured the streets of Chicago in search of the woman.

Glancing at his latest acquisition, he didn't have to wonder if Shay was pleased or annoyed. Even in the muted light it was obvious her glorious golden eyes were flashing with fury.

Clearly she failed to fully appreciate the honor he was bestowing upon her.

His lips twitched with amusement as he was returning his attention to the troll standing behind the podium.

"You may call me Viper," he informed the lesser demon with cold dislike.

The red eyes briefly widened. It was a name that inspired fear throughout Chicago. "Of course. Forgive me for not recognizing you, sir. You . . . ah . . ." He swallowed heavily. "You have the cash upon you?"

With a motion too swift for most eyes, Viper had reached beneath his cloak and tossed a large packet onto the stairs leading to the stage.

"I do."

With a flourish, Evor banged the gavel on the podium. "Sold."

There was a low hiss from the Shalott, but before Viper could give her the proper attention, there was the sound of low cursing and a small, wiry human was pushing his way through the crowd.

"Wait. The bidding is not yet closed," the stranger charged.

Viper narrowed his gaze. He might have laughed at the absurdity of the scrawny man attempting to bully his way through towering demons, but he didn't miss the scent of sour desperation that clouded about him, or the blackness that darkened his soul.

This was a man who had been touched by evil.

The troll, Evor, frowned as he regarded the man, clearly unimpressed by the cheap, baggy suit and secondhand shoes. "You wish to continue?"

"Yes."

"You have the cash upon you?"

The man swiped a hand over the sweat clinging to his bald head. "Not upon me, but I can easily have it to you—"

"Cash and carry only," Evor growled, his gavel once again hitting the podium.

"No. I will get you the money."

"The bidding is over."

"Wait. You must wait. I—"

"Get out before I have you thrown out."

"No." Without warning the man was racing up the stairs with a knife in his hand. "The demon is mine."

As quick as the man was, Viper had already moved to place himself between the stranger and his Shalott. The man gave a low growl before turning and stalking toward the troll. Easier prey than a determined vampire. But then again, most things were.

"Now, now. There is no need to become unreasonable." Evor hastily gestured toward the hulking bodyguards at the edge of the stage. "You knew the rules when you came."

With lumbering motions the mountain trolls moved forward, their hulking size and skin as thick as tree bark making them nearly impossible to kill.

Viper folded his arms over his chest. His attention remained on the demented human, but he couldn't deny that he was disturbingly aware of the Shalott behind him.

It was in the sweet scent of her blood. The warmth of her skin. And the shimmering energy that swirled about her.

His entire body reacted to her proximity. It was as if he had stepped close to a smoldering fire that offered a promise of heat he had long forgotten.

Unfortunately his attention was forced to remain on the seeming madman waving the knife in a threatening motion. There was something decidedly strange in the human's determination. A stark panic that was out of place.

He would be an idiot to underestimate the danger of the sudden standoff.

"Stay back," the small man squeaked.

The trolls continued forward until Viper lifted a slender hand. "I would not come close to the knife. It is hexed."

"Hexed?" Evor's face hardened with fury. "Magical artifacts are forbidden. The punishment is death."

"You think a pathetic troll and his goons can frighten me?" The intruder lifted his knife to point it directly at Evor's face. "I came here for the Shalott and I'm not leaving without her. I'll kill you all if I have to."

"You may try," Viper drawled.

The man spun about to confront him. "I have no fight with you, vampire."

"You are attempting to steal my demon."

"I'll pay you. Whatever you want."

"Whatever?" Viper flicked a brow upward. "A generous, if rather foolhardy bargain."

"What is your price?"

Viper pretended to consider a moment. "Nothing you could offer."

That sour desperation thickened in the air. "How do you know? My employer is very rich . . . very powerful."

Ah. Now they were getting somewhere.

"Employer. So you are merely an envoy?"

The man nodded, his eyes burning like coals in their sunken sockets. "Yes."

"And your employer will no doubt be quite disappointed to learn you have failed in your task to gain the Shalott?"

The pale skin became a sickly gray. Viper suspected that the sense of darkness he could detect was directly related to the mysterious employer.

"He will kill me."

"Then you are in quite a quandary, my friend, because I have no intention of allowing you to leave the room with my prize."

"What do you care?"

Viper's smile was cold. "Surely you must know that Shalott blood is an aphrodisiac for vampires? It is a most rare treat that has been denied us for too long."

"You intend to drain her?"

"That is none of your concern. She is mine. Bought and paid for."

He heard a strangled curse from behind him, along with the rattle of chains. His beauty was clearly unhappy with his response and anxious to prove her displeasure by ripping him limb from limb.

A tiny flicker of excitement raced through him.

Blood of the saints, but he liked his women dangerous.

Chapter Two

Shay cursed the shackles that held her bound to the pole.

She cursed Evor, the greedy, remorseless son of a bitch.

She cursed the strange human who smelled of that foul evil she had sensed before.

And most of all she cursed Viper for treating her as no more than an expensive party treat.

Unfortunately the worthless cursing was all she could do as the clearly crazed human waved about his knife.

"She's mine. I must have her."

The vampire never flinched. In fact, he stood so still that he appeared more dead than alive. Only the cold power surging through the air warned there was something stirring beneath the beautiful façade.

"You intend to battle me with no more than a hexed knife?" he demanded.

The man swallowed. "I cannot defeat a vampire."

"Ah, you are not quite so stupid as you look."

The tiny eyes darted about and Shay felt everyone tense. The man was desperate enough to try battling his way through a vampire. When he moved, however, it was not toward Viper but instead toward the gawking Evor. With astonishing skill he had his arm around the troll's neck and the knife pressed into the flabby skin of his throat.

"I will kill him. As long as he holds the Shalott's curse she will die as well." His gaze remained trained on Viper, no doubt aware he was far more dangerous than any other demon in the room. "She will do you no good if she dies before you can drain her."

Shay sucked in a sharp breath. She wasn't afraid to die. But, by God, if she were going to her grave she didn't want it to be while she was shackled to a pole and helpless to fight back.

Viper didn't move but his power was filling the room like an icy wave. The air stirred the silver strands of his hair and billowed the velvet cape.

"You will not kill her," he said in tones that made a shiver run down Shay's spine. "I do not believe your employer would be pleased if she is brought to him as a corpse."

The man gave a wild laugh. "If she ends up in the hands of another, I'm worse than dead. She might as well go with me."

"So does your employer desire her, or fear her?" Viper murmured, smoothly moving forward. "Who is he? A demon? A sorcerer?"

"Stop or I will kill her."

"No." Viper continued his flowing stride. "You will drop the knife and walk away."

"You can't glamour me with your eyes. I'm immune to mystical crap."

"Fine, then I will have to kill you."

"You can't—" The words of warning were still upon the man's lips when Viper had him by the throat and tossed him into a nearby wall.

For such a small man he managed to make a hell of a racket when he hit the paneling and slid to the floor. Astonishingly, however, he was back on his feet and reaching beneath his baggy coat in the blink of an eye. Clearly he was more than a mere human. No doubt a wizard with enough magical talent to offer some protection.

Lifting his hand, he clutched what looked to be a small rock. Shay frowned. She had lived with the witches long enough to know the crystal held a powerful spell.

"Viper."

She called out the warning without knowing why. What did it matter who won the battle? Was being nightly drained by a pack of vampires preferable to whatever the unknown monster might have in store for her?

In the end it didn't matter.

Even before his name had tumbled from her lips, Viper was leaping to the side and allowing the blast of black magic to strike the far wall. Flames crawled over the paneling and with cries of panic the wealthy guests began scrambling for the nearest door. Magical fire was the one thing that was as deadly to demons as to humans.

"Get the fire extinguishers, you fools," Evor cried, flapping his pudgy hands with growing panic. "I'm going to lose everything."

The mountain trolls reluctantly lumbered to battle the flames, but Shay's attention remained glued to the duel between the vampire and the increasingly desperate man.

Viper was on his feet, his black cloak flowing about him as he stalked in a half circle about the man.

"The spell that protects you will not keep me from ripping out your throat," he said in silky tones. "Are you that anxious to die?"

"Better my throat ripped out than what my master would do," the man rasped as he lifted the crystal and released the power toward the vampire.

Once again Viper smoothly moved aside to allow the blast to hit the podium. It burst into flames and Evor squawked in horror.

"Over here. Bring the extinguisher over here," the troll cried.

There was another blast and Shay fell flat on the floor, only her quick reflexes keeping her from being toast.

A low growl filled the air and Shay lifted her head to watch as Viper launched himself toward the terrified man. The hairs on the back of her neck stirred at the sight of his features honed to a stark, deadly mask and his fangs lengthened to kill.

He was no longer the beautiful angel but a lethal instrument of death.

The man screamed as Viper's teeth sank into his neck. The scream became a gurgle as the blood trickled down the man's throat and dripped onto the ivory carpeting. He was a heartbeat from death, but with futile desperation the man lifted the knife to stab the vampire in the back. Over and over the blade bit into Viper's flesh.

Shay winced. Although the knife couldn't kill a vampire it still had to hurt like a bitch.

There was another ghastly gurgle and Shay deliberately turned her head. A part of her was grateful not to be handed over to the looming evil that still tainted the air, but she preferred not to watch the vampire enjoy his midnight snack.

Especially when she might very well be breakfast.

There was a thump as the man was allowed to drop to the ground then the faint swish of fine velvet.

"I would suggest that you take better care of who you invite to your little auctions, Evor," the vampire drawled. "Black wizards are never good for business."

"Yes . . . yes, certainly." Dry washing his hands the troll glanced about the room. The flames had been put out, but there was no salvaging the podium or the paneling on the far wall. Or the ivory carpeting that was now stained with blood. The elegant ambiance had taken a definite blow. "I offer my most sincere apologies. I cannot imagine how he managed to get through my security."

"The question is not how. It is obvious he had help from a very powerful master. The question is who the master might be, and why he was so determined to get his hands upon the Shalott."

"Ah . . . well, I don't suppose it matters now." Evor gave a nervous shrug.

"Unless his master comes to search for him."

Evor's eyes flashed red. "You think he will?"

"My talents do not include reading the future."

"I must move the body." The troll shot a glance toward the lifeless body. "Perhaps I should burn it?"

"Not my problem." Viper shrugged his indifference. "I will take my property now."

"Oh, of course. Such confusion." Nervously searching his pockets Evor at last came up with a small amulet that he held out to the impatient vampire. "Here you are."

Holding the amulet in his long, slender fingers Viper regarded the troll with a lift of his brows.

"Explain."

"As long as you hold the amulet the Shalott must come when you call her."

The midnight gaze slid toward Shay. She stiffened at the smoldering satisfaction that glinted within it.

"So, she cannot escape me?" he murmured.

"No."

"What else does this do?"

"Nothing. I fear you shall have to control her on your own." Evor dug in his pockets once again to extract a heavy key that he handed to Viper. "I would suggest you leave the shackles upon her until she is safely locked in a cell."

Viper's gaze never left Shay's tight expression. "Oh, I do not fear controlling her," he said softly. "Leave us."

Evor gave a smooth bow as he motioned toward his goons. "As you will."

Careful to collect the money still laying on the stage, Evor hustled the trolls before him and left the room. Once alone Viper moved to kneel before Shay who was still crouched beside the pole.

"Well, my pet. We meet again," he murmured.

Ridiculously Shay felt her breath catch. My God, he was so beautiful. Eyes as dark and beguiling as a velvet night sky. The features chiseled by the hand of a master craftsman. The spill of silver hair that shimmered like the finest satin.

As if he had been created for the sole purpose of pleasuring every fortunate woman who crossed his path.

The urge to reach out and touch those perfect features and discover if they could possibly be real shuddered through her.

Shay discovered her hand actually lifting when she caught herself. Crap. What was wrong with her?

This . . . treacherous rodent had just bought her lock, stock, and barrel, as Levet would say.

She wanted to stick a stake in his heart, not discover if he could deliver on the pleasure he promised.

"I would say it's a pleasant surprise, but it isn't," she muttered.

"Not pleasant, or not a surprise?"

The silken words spread over her skin making her shiver in response. Even his voice was created to make a woman climax on the spot.

"Guess," she gritted.

He arched a brow that was several shades darker than his hair. "I would think you would be a bit more grateful, pet. I did just rescue you from what I suspect was a very grim future."

"I am not your pet, and my future is hardly less grim with you."

"You do not yet know my plans for you."

"You are a vampire. That's all I need to know."

He reached out a slender hand to touch the curls that had come loose from her braid to trail over her cheek. A cool rush of power swept through her body making her stomach clench with sharp pleasure.

Damn vampire.

"You believe we are all the same?"

"Vampires have been after my blood for a hundred years. Why should you be any different?"

His lips twitched with amusement. "Why indeed."

She pulled back only to be halted by the shackles that dug painfully into her wrists.

"Did you know I would be here when you came?" she demanded.

There was a momentary pause before he gave a nod. "Yes."

"And that's why you're here?"

"Yes."

"Why?"

"Obviously because I wished to have you."

That pang of disappointment returned to stab through her heart. Stupid, stupid, stupid.

"Even after I saved your life?"

He tilted his head to one side to allow the long silver hair to trail over his shoulder.

"Saved my life? Perhaps."

Shay widened her eyes in shock. "What do you mean, perhaps? Edra intended to kill you. I took a spell blast meant for you."

He shrugged. "Certainly you prevented a nasty wound, but it is impossible to determine if it would have been a killing blow."

"You jackass," she breathed, beyond caring that she was now his slave and utterly in his power. "I saved your life and yet you came here to buy me."

"Was there another among the bidders you would have preferred?"

"I would have preferred to kill you all."

His soft chuckle floated on the air. "So bloodthirsty."

"No, I'm sick of being at the mercy of every demon, monster, witch, or freak who has the money to buy me."

He stilled as the midnight gaze searched her flushed face. "Understandable, I suppose."

"You understand nothing."

His faint smile remained, but for the first time Shay noticed the lines of strain around his magnificent eyes.

"Perhaps not, but I do understand that I am in no humor to battle you this evening, pet. I have been injured and I need blood to recover my strength."

Shay had nearly forgotten the stab wounds he had received during his battle with the man. Not that she particularly cared at the moment.

She didn't like his mention of blood.

"And?"

The amusement returned to his eyes as he easily read her unease. "And while I prefer to escort you to my lair in a civilized manner, I can keep you shackled and drag you there kicking and screaming. The choice is yours."

She refused to show her relief. It was only a matter of time before she became an unwilling donor.

"Some choice."

"For the moment it is the only one you have. What is it to be?"

She glared at him before at last sticking out her arms. There was no point in fighting the inevitable. Besides the iron rubbing against her skin was hurting worse than she wanted to admit.

"Take off the shackles."

"I have your word that you will not attempt to fight me?"

Shay blinked in surprise. "You trust my word?"

"Yes."

"Why?"

"Because I can read your soul." He held her gaze with ease. "Your word?"

Well . . . crap.

She didn't want him to know that once she gave her word she would never go back on it. It gave him yet another hold over her.

For a moment she refused to make the pledge. How could she live with herself if she didn't at least try to put a stake through his heart? She did have her pride, after all. But as he continued to stare at her with that unnerving stillness only a vampire could pull off, she heaved a grudging sigh. He was prepared to remain in that precise position for an eternity if necessary.

"For tonight I will not attempt to fight you," she said through gritted teeth.

He smiled at her grudging promise. "As good as I'm going to get, I suppose."

"Damn straight."

Viper found a smile tugging at his lips as he escorted the Shalott from the auction house to his waiting car.

He wasn't at all sure why he was pleased.

He had come to the auction because he couldn't get the

beautiful demon out of his mind. He didn't have a clue what he intended to do with her. He had only known he couldn't allow anyone else to own her.

His plans, however, hadn't included a battle with some minor dark wizard, or pissing off a powerful enemy that would no doubt want revenge, or being treated like some bloodsucking monster by his very own slave.

So why the devil was he smiling?

His gaze lowered to watch the angry twitch of Shay's hips as she walked in front of him. Ah, yes. Now he remembered.

A lick of pure desire curled through his stomach.

The scent of her potent blood was enough to make any vampire hard and aching. She perfumed the very air with lust. But that was not what captured and held his attention.

It was her exotic beauty, the manner in which she moved with that liquid grace, the fierce determination that shimmered in the golden eyes, and the danger that swirled about her like a cloud of enticement.

She would never be just an easy lay. Her lover would never know when he kissed her whether she would wrap her legs around him or rip his heart out.

It added a delicious dash of excitement that he hadn't felt in far too long.

With his eyes still transfixed by the gentle sway of her hips Viper was forced to step to the side as Shay came to a sharp halt in front of the gleaming black limo.

"Is this yours?" she demanded.

"For my sins."

She forced a smile to her lips, but Viper could feel her wariness. She seemed more disturbed than impressed by his blatant display of wealth.

"Nice."

"I like to live well." With a smooth motion Viper pulled the door open and motioned with his hand. "After you."

There was a tense beat, and then with a tilt of her chin, Shay was climbing into the dimly lit depths.

"Holy crap," she muttered beneath her breath.

He smiled as he settled in the seat across from her. The car was a work of art. Plush white seats, polished satinwood, moonroof, built-in wine cabinet, and plasma TV.

What more could a discerning vampire desire?

Waiting until the car smoothly purred from the curb, Viper pulled out two crystal glasses and poured them a generous measure of his favorite vintage.

"Wine? It is a particularly exquisite burgundy."

She took the glass only to sniff at it as if she feared it might be poison. "I wouldn't know the difference if you had brewed it in your bathtub."

Viper hid his smile by taking an appreciative sip of the wine. "I see I shall have to introduce you to the delights of fine living."

The golden eyes narrowed. "Why?"

"Why what?"

"Why would you bother? It can't matter to you if I appreciate expensive wine or mile-long limos."

He gave a small shrug. "I prefer a companion who possesses a bit of sophistication."

"Companion?" Shay gave a short, humorless laugh. "Me?"

"I did pay a great deal of money for you. Did you believe that I intended to hide you away in some damp cell?"

"Why not? You can drain me as easily in a damp cell as anywhere."

Viper sprawled with elegant ease in his seat, wincing slightly as his injuries protested at the pressure against them. They would be healed within a few hours, but until then they would be a painful reminder of his most recent battle.

"It is true that I could make a fortune off your blood," he murmured, regarding her tight expression over the rim of his glass. "Vampires would pay any price for a taste of your potent elixir. However, I have no desperate need for more wealth, and for the moment I prefer to keep you to myself."

"Your own private stock?" she rasped, folding her arms over her stomach.

"Perhaps," he murmured in distracted tones as he reached

into a small compartment beneath his seat and removed a small ceramic pot. "Hold out your arms."

She predictably stiffened, her breath catching in horror. She had made it clear that she considered sharing her blood with a vampire a fate worse than death.

"What?"

"I said, hold out your arms."

"Now?"

"Now."

Her jaw worked as she glared at him with fury. Viper held out a slender hand, calmly waiting.

Long moments passed before she muttered a low curse and thrust out her arm.

"Here."

Grasping her forearm in one hand he used his other hand to scoop out the pale green cream from the ceramic pot and carefully began to smear it on the red and blistered skin of her wrists. The wounds from the iron shackles would scar unless proper care was taken.

"What are you doing?" she asked.

"There is no need for you to suffer. I have no liking for witches, but not even I can deny they know how to brew a hell of an ointment."

A frown touched her brow as he reached to tend to her other wrist.

"Why are you doing this?"

"You're injured."

"Yes, but . . . why do you care?"

Viper met her gaze steadily. "You belong to me now. I take care of my own."

Her lips thinned, not entirely happy with his explanation, but her muscles relaxed beneath his gentle touch and she didn't try to pull away. Not until he lifted her wrist so he could press his lips to her raw skin.

"No, please," she whispered, "I . . ."

Without warning her eyes widened, and with a powerful

movement that caught him off guard, she had pulled free of his hold and had her hand pressed to the window.

Viper tensed at the sudden danger in the air. "What is it?"

"The darkness from the auction house," she whispered. "It's following us."

"Get down," he commanded, once again reaching beneath the seat. On this occasion he pulled out a sleek handgun.

There was a sudden thump as the limo was hit from behind and Viper muttered a low curse. He wasn't concerned they would wreck. The car had been built to withstand a small nuclear bomb. And, of course, his driver was a vampire. Pierre's reflexes were the best he had ever seen. Not to mention the fact he was immortal.

The perfect chauffeur.

But he would have the heart of anyone stupid enough to so blatantly attack him.

Leaning sideways Viper slowly lowered the smoke-tinted window. A gust of air whipped through the interior, stealing the comforting warmth. Fall had descended without mercy, leaving a chilled edge to the night.

Behind them a large jeep was continuing to accelerate in a futile effort to run them off the road. Even at a distance he could tell that there were two passengers, and that they were both human.

"Give me one."

Startled by Shay's soft demand Viper turned to regard her with a narrowed gaze.

"You know how to use a gun?"

"Yes."

Keeping his gaze locked on her wide eyes he reached beneath the seat to offer her a handgun similar to his own. With startling efficiency she measured the balance of the gun in her hand, before smoothly flicking off the safety.

He would wager his finest ruby it was not the first occasion she held a gun.

Not precisely reassuring.

At least she wasn't about to accidentally shoot off her foot, or worse his own, he wryly acknowledged as he rolled down the opposite window.

"Aim at the tires," he commanded, leaning out the window and steadying his hip against the door. He paused, sighted, pulled the trigger, and took out the front tire with one shot. On the other side of the car Shay sprayed a line of bullets, at last puncturing the other tire. The pursuing car pulled hard to the right and Viper managed a shot through the side window, hitting the driver although it was impossible to tell if it was a kill-ing blow.

The car plunged off the road and Viper sent his thoughts to Pierre who was already slowing the limo. He wanted those men. He wanted them in his clutches to drain them of every last thread of information they might possess.

And then he intended to just drain them.

Whoever, or whatever, wanted his Shalott was proving to be more than merely a pest.

He needed to know precisely what he was up against.

The thought had barely crossed his mind when the skidding car rammed into a light pole. He muttered a curse, and then an-other as the car promptly exploded into a ball of flames.

Well, devil's balls.

Didn't that only happen in the movies?

Folding himself back into the car he gave a rap on the di-vider. On cue the limo sped easily into the darkness.

Viper watched as Shay lowered herself back in her seat. Closing the windows he held out his hand for the gun. There was only the faintest hesitation before she placed it in his hand and Viper bent down to place both guns in the hidden cabinet.

Settling more comfortably against the leather he flashed her a faint smile. "Not bad."

"It pulls right."

His smile widened. "Yes, I know."

Her eyes slowly narrowed. "You thought I might turn it on you?"

"Was it not a temptation?" he demanded.

"A gun can't kill you."

"The bullets are silver and would have at least caused me damage."

Her eyes glittered with the unspoken warning that she wanted to do far more than cause mere damage.

"You said that you trusted me."

"I have not survived so many centuries without realizing that I can occasionally be wrong. I fully embrace the motto 'better safe than sorry.'"

She tossed herself into the corner of her seat, yanking at the long raven braid that was draped over her shoulder. She had been angry when he had demanded her pledge not to offer him harm, annoyed that he had easily read her noble spirit. Now she was angry that he remained cautious.

Part demon or not, she was as contrary as any woman.

"If I wanted to hurt you, I wouldn't need a gun," she muttered in low tones.

Chapter Three

Shay wasn't entirely stupid.

She knew that baiting a vampire under any circumstances was dangerous. Like playing Russian roulette with a fully loaded pistol. Especially when she was completely and utterly at his mercy.

But while every sense might warn her to keep her mouth shut and disappear into the butter soft leather seat, her raw pride simply refused to listen.

Beyond being a vampire Viper was everything she disliked.

He was too beautiful, too obscenely rich, and worst of all, too brashly confident of his own worth.

That grated worst of all.

Deep within her she envied that cool, stately arrogance. Even if she lived a millennium she would never attain such a sure belief in her own worth.

She was a mongrel. Half demon and half human. She didn't belong in either world. And never would.

The vampire settled back in his seat and regarded her with a steady gaze.

"A fascinating discussion, pet, and one we will no doubt explore in depth at some point. But for the moment I prefer to concentrate on who, or what, is so desperate to get their hands on you."

"I don't know," Shay retorted with complete honesty. She didn't have a clue who was after her. She had spent her life in the shadows, never drawing attention to herself. It had been her only means of survival.

"No bitter past owner?" he demanded.

"Besides Evor who holds my curse, Edra was my one and only owner." Her lips thinned with annoyance. "Until you."

"No past lover who might hold a grudge?"

Stupidly she felt her face warm with embarrassment. "No."

"No past lover?" His lips twitched with ill-concealed amusement. "Or none who would hold a grudge?"

"None of your damn business."

"It becomes my business when someone tries to kill me."

Shay gave her braid a furious tug as she glared into his perfect face. "Then take me back to Evor."

"Never." Without warning the vampire was flowing forward and Shay found herself trapped in the corner with his hands planted on the seat on either side of her head. "You are mine."

His face was so close that she could see the flecks of gold in the midnight eyes. Her heart threatened to halt.

Partially out of fear. And partially . . . well, hell, she might as well be honest. Partially out of sheer lust.

She didn't have to like him to want to rip off his clothes and pull that magnificent male body on top of her. He was a sexual invitation from the tip of his silver hair to the toes of his hand-crafted leather boots.

She would have to be dead not to want to wrap herself in his potent beauty and sate the aching need she had endured for more years than she cared to admit.

Easily sensing her flare of desire Viper stilled above her, his fangs lengthening as his own body reacted.

Her eyes widened. "Don't."

With a slow, relentless motion his head began to lower. "You fear me drinking your blood?"

"I don't like being a meal on wheels for anyone."

His cool lips skimmed her mouth before brushing her cheek.

"There are many reasons for a vampire to share blood. Trust, friendship, love . . . lust."

Her heart crashed against her chest as a dark heat spread through her body. He was touching her with nothing more than his lips, but already a heady flutter of excitement was rushing through her lower stomach and her nipples hardening to tight peaks.

God, it had been so long.

The satin of his hair tickled her nose as his mouth stroked down the curve of her neck. He smelled of expensive cologne and something far more primitive. Something starkly male.

His mouth lingered on the frantic beat of her pulse before his tongue traced the large vein in a wet path back up her throat.

A stab of panic raced through her and her hands lifted to press against his chest.

"Viper."

"At this moment I don't want your blood, pet." His lips brushed her skin sending a jolt of pleasure down her spine.

"Then what do you want?"

"Everything else."

Shifting his head he captured her lips in a kiss that shook her to her very toes.

Oh, Shay, don't think about the taste of those male lips. Or the promise of his hovering body. Or the heat already swirling through the air.

A ridiculous, not to mention an impossible task, she admitted as the kiss deepened.

His mouth was not harsh, but there was a hungry demand that had her own lips parting in helpless response.

A soft moan escaped her throat as his slender fingers cupped her face. Damn and damn. Her entire body was stirring to life beneath his silken expertise.

With gentle insistence his tongue parted her lips to slip within. Her eyes slid shut and she tentatively allowed her tongue to tangle with his. Even worse, the hands she had lifted to ward him off now clutched at the heavy cloak, unthinkingly pulling his long frame to cover her own.

Since the moment she had encountered this vampire weeks ago he had invaded her dreams and made her remember sensations better left forgotten. Now she was paying for her weakness in not having banished those treacherous desires.

His hands softly skimmed from her face down her neck. His touch was as light as a butterfly's wing. So light that she barely even noticed when his fingers trailed low enough to slip beneath the tiny harem top to cup her breasts.

Not until his thumbs rubbed over the sensitive nipples. A small cry was torn from her lips.

"Viper?"

He swept his mouth over her cheek, his fangs scraping her skin but never drawing blood.

"Shhh . . . I won't hurt you."

"Are you going to bite me?"

"I had something else in mind at the moment," he huffed.

She shivered in response. Growling low in his throat Viper allowed his body to press her own into the soft seat, his knee nudging her legs apart to allow him to settle against her with shocking intimacy.

It was the hungry joy at the feel of his erection pressing against her that at last jolted her out of the daze of sensual pleasure.

By the flames of hell, what was she doing?

She had barely been Viper's slave for an hour and here she was battling the urge to rip off his clothes and guide him into her.

She might be in this man's power, but that didn't mean she had to be a willing victim.

Did she have no pride at all?

Sucking in a deep breath she attempted to gather her lost senses.

"No," she at last rasped.

It was a mere thread of sound, but it was enough to make Viper stiffen above her.

"What did you say?" he demanded against her lips.

Her body shuddered in disappointment as she forced herself to press her hands against his chest in silent denial.

"I said no."

She was prepared for him to laugh at her weak protest. Or at the very least ignore it.

She was his slave and he was in a position to do whatever he wanted with her body.

Besides which, she had never met a man yet who didn't think that a *no* was just a *yes* waiting to happen.

Astonishingly, however, the elegant form was lifting off her with fluid ease. Shay blinked as she watched him settle back in his own seat with cool composure. There wasn't even the faintest tremor of his slender fingers as he picked up his wine-glass and lifted it to his lips to reveal he had been at all affected by the last few moments.

"You . . ." Straightening Shay impatiently brushed away the handful of curls that had strayed from her braid. "Why did you stop?"

He regarded her over the rim of his glass. "You said no. I assumed that meant no, did it not?"

"It did, but . . ."

"I'm a vampire, not a monster."

"You say potato, I say potato . . ." she muttered.

"What?"

"Does it matter what I want? I'm your slave."

He abruptly set aside his glass. "But not my whore. Not ever."

Her eyes narrowed. He sounded sincere. But then, he was a vampire. Deception was perhaps their greatest skill.

If they couldn't enthrall you with their eyes, they would enthrall you with their gilded tongues.

"So all I have to do is say no?"

"That's all you have to do."

"I don't believe you."

The dark eyes flashed at her blunt accusation, but the ivory features remained unruffled.

"That is your choice, of course."

Her hand reached for her braid as she regarded him with wary distrust.

It was a trap. It had to be.

"If you don't intend to force yourself on me then why did you buy me?"

His lips twisted with sardonic humor. "Ah . . . the sixty-four-thousand-dollar question." Shay frowned but before she could probe him further, the car came to a silent halt. Viper held out his hand as the door to the limo was pulled open. "We have arrived. Shall we?"

Viper hid his amusement as Shay warily inspected the kitchen with its gleaming appliances and plain wood floor. Her gaze lingered on the gingham curtains and handwoven rugs before shifting to the copper pots that hung above the heavy butcher table.

The two-story cottage was beautiful, with what the real estate agent had claimed was a cozy warmth, but it could hardly compare to most of his residences.

When he had purchased the place his only interest had been in finding an estate that was secluded and easily defensible. After a handful of centuries every vampire needed a home where he could get away from it all and let down his hair.

Or more importantly his fangs.

Slowly turning to face him Shay frowned with obvious disbelief. "This is your home?"

Viper tossed aside the heavy cloak and followed it with the tailored jacket. He was left standing in a sheer linen shirt and leather pants.

He smothered another smile as Shay grudgingly allowed her gaze to stray over his body. Their time in the limo had revealed that she was not indifferent to his touch. And that she was as warm and passionate as any man could desire.

Soon he intended to have her warm and passionate beneath him.

And on top of him, to the side of him . . .

"One of them."

"How many do you have?"

He shrugged. "Does it matter?"

"I suppose not."

With slow measured steps he began to walk toward her, not at all surprised when she began backing away. She might be attracted to him but she would never allow an easy seduction.

It would be a tantalizing dance perfectly suited to entertain a jaded vampire.

"You were hoping for something a bit more grand?"

She grimaced at the thought. "God, no."

He continued to back her down until she came up against the refrigerator. "I have any number of mansions that I use to entertain, but this is my private retreat. I prefer to be alone upon occasion."

"We're alone?"

His gaze deliberately swept over her tense features before lowering to the barely there outfit. When he had first seen Shay attired like a harem slave he had wanted to rip out Evor's heart.

In the privacy of his own home, however, he could not deny it held a certain appeal.

"There are guards upon the grounds and I have a human housekeeper that comes during the day, but for the most part we shall have the house to ourselves." His attention turned to the full curve of her mouth. "A delicious thought, is it not?"

"Delicious is not the word I would use."

He shifted until his body was fully pressed to hers. "You would rather be surrounded by hungry vampires? That could be arranged."

Her breath caught and the pulse in her neck thundered. "Stop."

He touched her cheek. "You'll have to move, pet."

"What?"

"You're leaning against the fridge. I can't get to my blood."

"Oh."

With flustered haste she dodged around him, a faint flush touching her cheeks.

Viper pulled out a container of blood and swiftly emptied it. Then he reached for the numerous bags that had been left by his housekeeper. He set them on the counter and began to open them.

"I didn't know what you preferred so I had my housekeeper order out. There's a bit of everything. Chinese, Italian, Mexican, and the more mundane fried chicken. Take what you want."

"You already had this ordered?" Her eyes widened as she glanced over the bounty spread across the counter. "How could you possibly know you would be able to outbid everyone at the auction?"

Viper glanced down her slender body, a tantalizing heat pooling in his lower body. "I always get what I want. Sooner or later."

The golden eyes flashed with fire. "Spoken like a true vampire."

His bloodlust sated, if not his physical lust, Viper leaned against the cabinets.

"That's quite a chip you have on your shoulder, pet." He folded his arms over his chest. "Why do you hate vampires?"

She reached to pluck an egg roll from a nearby carton. "Beyond the fact they have tried to drain me since the day I was born?"

"Vampires aren't the only demons who crave your blood. Your dislike seems a bit more personal."

Silence descended as she ate the egg roll and then a wonton. Viper remained silent, simply waiting for her to confess the truth.

Another egg roll disappeared before she at last heaved a sigh and regarded him with a hostile frown.

"Vampires killed my father."

Bones of the saints. That certainly explained her aggressive dislike. And placed another hurdle directly in his path to seduction.

"I am sorry."

She gave a restless shrug. "It was a long time ago."

"You were raised by your mother?"

"Yes."

"A human?"

"Yes."

She was deliberately keeping her emotions hidden, but Viper

had been reading the body language of his prey for centuries. It was what predators did best.

"She kept you hidden from the demon world?"

"As much as she was able."

"Did you pass as a human?"

It didn't take skill to read the anger that rippled over her beautiful features.

"You asked me why I hated vampires and I told you. Now, can we change the subject?"

Viper smiled as he straightened from the counter. He had an eternity to explore Shay's secrets.

It was just one of many explorations he intended to conduct.

"Eat your dinner. I have a few phone calls to make before dawn."

Pausing only long enough to trail a finger over her soft cheek Viper moved toward the back of the house and the small study. He had not forgotten that there was something out there intent on stealing his Shalott.

That was unacceptable.

He intended to do whatever was necessary to track down the mysterious enemy and put a swift end to the danger.

Chapter Four

The house built on the bluffs of the mighty Mississippi was pleasant enough.

Like most farmhouses in the Midwest it was a plain, two-story structure, with a wraparound porch and sharply angled roof. In places the white paint was peeling and the gutters drooping, but some might claim it only added to the rustic charm.

Surrounding the house, the gently rolling yard held a handful of outbuildings. And, of course, the land was well populated with a number of ancient ash and oak and dogwood trees.

At a glance it offered the simple warmth of most houses in the area. The sense that a stranger passing by would be welcomed with a smile and a warm meal.

But only at a glance.

Any strangers unfortunate enough to pass close to the farm would find no smiles awaiting them, and the only warm meal would be themselves.

Thankfully, it was isolated enough to prevent most stray sightseers, and the locals had long ago learned to cut a wide path around the place. It was rare the heavy silence was disturbed by more than birds.

The location of the house was no accident. Beneath the rolling hills were hidden a series of caves that stretched for miles. There were a hundred local legends connected to the caves. Some claimed that they had been used by the Under-Ground Railroad. Some said that they had been the hideout of Jesse James. And others still that they had been used by smugglers who preferred the river to transport their ill-gotten goods.

None of the stories were true, of course. The caves had been home to demons since long before the first settlers had ever arrived.

In the deepest of the caves a slender imp with a cascade of golden curls peered into the scrying pool.

He appeared out of place among the bleak rock. With his satin green robe the color of spring moss that matched his eyes, and the delicate gold leaves that he had weaved through his curls he shimmered with an unearthly beauty.

An imp meant to rule a summer glade not the dark bowels of the earth.

Still, for the moment the darkness served him well enough.

He waved a slender hand over the pool to bring an end to the visions it revealed. Above him the shadow filled the cave with a fierce, choking anger.

"Your wizard has failed," the shadow rasped the obvious.

"So it would seem, my lord." Rising to his feet Damocles carefully brushed the dirt from his robe. "I did warn you that Joseph was not at all reliable."

"He was a fool and a lickspittle, but the fault was not entirely his own, was it?" The shadow seemed to thicken. "If I were a suspicious man I would wonder why you did not send my envoy with sufficient funds to bid on the Shalott."

A faint smile touched the imp's handsome features. It was not that he was indifferent to the pulsing danger in the air. Only a fool would believe that the shadow could not reach out and strike him dead. Or worse. But he had spent nearly a century becoming indispensable to his current master. For the moment he was secure enough.

"You wound me, sir," he protested, his fingers toying with the delicate chain that hung about his neck. "I could hardly have known that the vampire would make such an outrageous bid. Besides, would you truly have me hand over half a million dollars in cash to any servant? For all of Joseph's pledge of loyalty I do not believe even he could have withstood the temptation to . . . what do they say . . . take the money and run?"

The angry hiss scraped against Damocles delicate ears.

"He knew that if he ran I would have killed him."

"Of course, but greed is rarely logical."

"So now we do not have the Shalott and worse she is in the hands of a vampire."

The imp gave an innocent lift of his brows. "Surely that is good news? You have considerable power among the clans. Can you not simply demand that this Viper hand the demon over to you?"

"Idiot." An unseen hand struck Damocles across the face. "I cannot reveal my interest in this. It would only cause the sort of speculation and questions I have sought to avoid. There must be no hint I am connected to the Shalott until I am healed. If my enemies knew how weakened I have become . . ."

Damocles felt blood running down his cheek but he did not so much as flinch. "That shall never happen, my lord. Not so long as I am at your side."

"Oh yes, my sweet imp, such loyalty," the voice mocked.

"It is as deep and endless as the sea."

"More like as deep and endless as my coffers."

The imp offered a half bow. "We all have our weaknesses, do we not?"

"Bah." The shadow stirred with a restless impatience. "I want that demon. Awaken your pet."

Damocles straightened, his thoughts racing at this most unexpected turn. He prided himself on preparing for every eventuality. On reading the future with uncanny skill.

He was never caught off guard, never unprepared.

On this occasion, however, he had to admit that his cunning wiles had failed him.

Most annoying.

"My pet?" He lightly touched his golden chain. "Surely not yet, my lord? It is bound to stir unwelcome attention. I have several—"

His words were choked off as a pressure encircled his throat and cut off his air.

"Have you forgotten who is master here, imp?"

Black flecks were dancing before Damocles's eyes before the pressure at last eased and he was allowed to suck in a lung full of air.

A fury raced through his blood but with the ease of long practice Damocles lowered himself to his knees and bent his head as was expected of a proper servant.

His plans could be altered. He was nothing if not resourceful.

"Of course not, my lord. It shall be as you desire." He slowly lifted his head. "Still, there is no guarantee that there will not be casualties."

"What do I care as long as it is not the Shalott?" the shadow demanded.

"The vampire—"

"A necessary sacrifice."

Damocles deliberately paused. "Necessary perhaps, but I do not believe your Ravens will be so understanding."

That painful hiss echoed through the cave. "Which is why they shall not learn of my plan. Is that clear?"

He hid a smile. At least he need not concern himself with that meddling band of jackasses. They had done their best to interfere in his plots and schemes and he had promised himself a proper punishment. He was very good at punishment.

But not now. Not yet.

"Perfectly, my lord. Indeed I shall go along to ensure that there are no unfortunate mistakes."

"A wise decision."

Damocles slowly rose to his feet, his thoughts racing. "But first I believe I shall pay a visit on the troll."

There was a suspicious pause. "Why? He is meaningless."

The imp smiled. "Not so meaningless. He holds the curse that binds the Shalott."

"So?"

"If he dies, she dies. I think it would be wiser to have him in our care to keep him out of the hands of our enemies."

"Yes, yes, of course," the shadow rasped. "I should have thought of that. We cannot risk having that troll running loose. Anything could happen to him."

"I will attend to him personally."

"Good." The shadow stirred with a harsh sigh. "I must rest."

Damocles offered a low bow. "Certainly, my lord. Conserve your strength. Soon enough you will be strong and whole once again."

There was a brief silence. "Damocles?"

"Yes, my lord?"

"You will send me what I need tonight?"

The imp hid his smile of satisfaction. "I have everything prepared."

"You must take care. If the Ravens . . ."

"I will be the soul of discretion."

"Good. Now go before you are missed."

With one last bow Damocles was moving through darkness. There was a direct path to the upper caves, but he was wise enough to avoid it. He was well aware that the damnable Ravens devoted a great deal of effort to keeping track of his movements. It pleased him to be able to slip past their spies with such ease.

He had reached the narrow path that would lead to his own private caves when a shadow abruptly loomed before him. He didn't have to wait for the form to step into the flickering light of the nearby torch to know who blocked his path.

Only one possessed the arrogance to regard him as if he were a bit of filth stuck to the bottom of his boot.

"Hold, Damocles, I would have a word with you."

Damocles regarded the tall, fiercely handsome vampire with a taunting smile.

"Ah, if it isn't Sir Tall, Dark, and Gloomy. What's the matter? Did you weary of frightening the rats in the cellars and come in search of more elusive game?"

The bronzed features remained impassive. Nothing seemed to touch the leader of the Ravens. Not insults. Not threats. Not even blatant flattery.

A fact that annoyed the hell out of Damocles.

"Where have you been?" the man simply known as Styx demanded.

Damocles gave a lift of his brows. "I have been performing a small task for our master."

"What task?"

"Obviously that is between me and my master."

A cold flare of power washed over Damocles as the towering demon took a step forward.

"I could have the truth from you if I desired."

"And I could sprout wings and fly to Paris if I desired," Damocles mocked. "If you want the truth seek it from our master."

"I seek it from you. Tell me why you sneak through these tunnels like a thief."

The prickles became downright painful but Damocles determinedly ignored them.

Only the strong survived in these caves.

"I have been sworn to secrecy. Would you have me break my oath?"

The Raven gave a disgusted sound. "As if an imp would know anything of oaths and honor."

Damocles could have told him that he held his oaths more dearly than anyone would ever know. Instead he leaned against the wall and inspected the golden thread on the cuff of his robe with arrogant indifference.

"Did you seek me out to offer me tedious insults or did you have a purpose?"

The lean, harsh features tightened. "Much against my wishes the master has charged you with retrieving the Shalott. So far you have done nothing more than offer empty promises. Where is the demon?"

Damocles shrugged. "There has been a minor setback, but there is no reason to fear. I shall soon have her in my grasp."

Without warning Damocles found himself flat on his back nursing a bruised jaw. The blow had come so swiftly he hadn't had a chance to avoid it.

"I have no trust in you, imp, and even less liking. Your

arrival at our door was a dark omen that has brought nothing but grief. Produce the Shalott or I will have your head."

Without a backward glance Styx was sweeping through the darkness and leaving Damocles to wipe the blood from his mouth.

Alone Damocles allowed a smile to curve his lips.

It was always a good day when he could provoke the bloody Prince of Ice to lose his temper.

He intended to ensure there were many, many more such days.

Chapter Five

Waiting until Viper had left the kitchen Shay gathered the cartons of food and breathed in deeply of the delicious scent.

Damn but she was starving.

For the past weeks she had barely eaten enough to keep a bird alive. Evor enjoyed his tiny tortures and he thought it grand fun to watch her scrambling across the floor to gather the handful of crumbs he would toss through the bars of her cage.

And as much as she hated accepting anything from the vampire, she couldn't resist the temptation spread before her.

Starting with the boxes of Chinese food she had managed to polish them off, and most of the fried chicken, when her captor strolled back into the room.

Viper gave a lift of his brows at the sight of the empty cartons but, thankfully, he refrained from commenting on her gluttony.

"If you want to leave a list for my housekeeper I'm sure she'll be able to keep the kitchen stocked with any food you prefer."

Shay glanced over the piles of food. "She's already stocked it with everything but apple pie."

"I'm sure the apple pie could be arranged."

Shay didn't doubt it for a moment. The housekeeper seemed the type to go over and above the call of duty.

The question was whether the woman did it out of a sense of loyalty, or out of fear.

"Does she know that you're a vampire?"

The full, sensual lips twitched in amusement. "The bags of blood filling the refrigerator usually give it away."

Smart-ass.

Her eyes narrowed. "Most humans refuse to believe in demons. Or if they do believe they are terrified of them."

"Her family has served me for a number of centuries," he explained. "In fact she has four sons who work at my various businesses."

"A regular dynasty."

He gave an elegant shrug. "It simplifies matters."

"I bet."

His expression was curious as he studied her tight features. "You sound disapproving. Does it bother you that I hire humans?"

It did bother her, but not in the manner that he thought. "In my experience humans and demons don't mix."

He moved until he was standing directly before her. He gently tucked a stray curl behind her ear.

"That's not entirely true, pet," he said softly. "You've experienced the most intimate mixing of human and demon. A mixing that created you."

She resisted the shocking urge to rub her cheek against his lingering fingers. "That was . . . different."

He tilted her chin up to meet his searching gaze. "How was it different?"

"Neither of my parents intended to fall in love."

A slow smile curved his lips. "Does anyone?"

A tingle raced over her skin and Shay inched away. Space seemed a good choice when dealing with this unnerving vampire.

Lots of space.

"My father was preparing to leave and join the other Shalotts when he discovered my mother being attacked by a pack of werewolves," she tried to explain. She had heard the story told by her mother a hundred times. Always with that sad, yearning expression that revealed her mother still mourned the loss of her husband. "He saved her life and then took her back to his home and helped to heal her."

"And fate did the rest?"

She gave a jerky nod. "Something like that."

"Were they happy together?"

His probing was beginning to touch those raw nerves that she didn't want touched.

"Yes. They loved each other very much."

He ignored the edge of warning in her voice. Of course. Instead he allowed his gaze to slowly roam over her barely covered body.

"And they created you. I would say that the union of human and demon was clearly a match made in heaven."

She licked her dry lips. Either someone had just set a fire in the kitchen or the heat of his gaze was actually tangible.

"It was hardly heaven for my father to be shunned by his people, or for me and my mother to be forced into hiding."

"If they were happy what did it matter?"

She bit back her sharp words. Why bother? He was a vampire. He had never known a day of fear or uncertainty in his immortal life.

"I don't want to talk about it."

He paused before giving a slow nod of his head. "Very well. If you are finished with your meal, I'll show you to your room."

The egg rolls suddenly felt as if they weighed a hundred pounds in her stomach.

She was well acquainted with the rooms offered to a slave. Dark dank holes with iron bars. It was one thing that never changed no matter who was her current master.

"Now?"

He regarded her with a hint of curiosity. "Is there something else you wish to do?"

Eat broken glass. Stab a knife in her eye. Throw herself off the roof.

"I thought I might look about the house." She casually shifted from his looming form. "It is after all to be my home." Her lips tightened. "At least for now."

"There will be plenty of time for that tomorrow. Surely you must be exhausted?"

"I require little sleep."

A small, worrisome smile played about his mouth. "What a pleasant coincidence, I require little sleep myself."

Consumed with thoughts of a dank cell Shay was unprepared when he glided forward and scooped her from her feet.

Tucked closely to his chest Shay roundly cursed her inattention. She might not be capable of vampire speed but she could have done more than stand there like a gaping trout.

It was amazing what a well-placed kick or blow to the throat could do to even the most determined male.

"What are you doing?" she gritted.

With annoying ease, Viper moved toward the nearby doorway.

"You said you wished a tour."

"I can wander about on my own. There is no need for you . . ."

He hoisted her high enough so he could meet her gaze squarely. Just for a moment Shay struggled to breathe.

It wasn't just his stunning beauty. Most vampires were beautiful. How else could they so easily lure their prey? But there was something compelling about those midnight eyes. Something that threatened to stir sensations she definitely didn't want stirred.

"There is every need, my pet," he murmured in silken tones. "Now do be quiet and let me perform my duties as your host."

Shay grimly averted her gaze. She had never believed it was possible for her to ever be enthralled or seduced by a vampire, no matter what his powers. She had hated them her entire life.

Now, she wasn't nearly as certain as she should be.

"Do you make a habit of carrying all your guests around?" she muttered as she battled the most ridiculous urge to squirm in his arms.

"You are my first and only guest."

Her gaze shifted back to his elegant features. "You're lying."

His brows arched. "Why do you say that?"

"I can't believe a man like you would be willing to leave his harem behind."

"A man like me?"

"A vampire."

"Ah. I'm sorry to disappoint you, but I'm currently harem-less." The midnight eyes flashed their magic. "Unless, of course, you are volunteering?"

The prickling excitement inched over her skin and pooled in the pit of her stomach. Dammit. She had never been so intensely aware of a man. Certainly not a man who had the bad taste to be a vampire.

It was freaking annoying.

Time for a distraction.

"You've truly never had any guest here before?"

The midnight gaze held a knowing amusement. One that made her want to take a poke at that long, perfectly aquiline nose.

"I come here to be alone."

"Then why—"

"Ah, the living room," he firmly intruded, as if it was his turn for a distraction. "You will notice, I hope, the fine bay window that offers a stunning view of the lake. The wooden floors are polished oak that is native to the estate, as is the wood for the hand-carved staircase. There is something terribly fascinating about the stone of the fireplace, but I must admit that I did not pay particular attention when the real estate agent was torturing me with her endless spiel."

She had a brief glimpse of a shadowed room that seemed to consume an enormous amount of space. Oddly, even in the dark and with a muted sense of vastness there was a feel of warmth to the room.

No. She gave an unconscious shake of her head.

The feeling of warmth was not the room, but the entire house.

As if those who had lived here had made it truly a home and left behind the echoes of their happiness.

Lost in her ridiculous thoughts it took a moment to realize that Viper had not turned toward the nearby doorway that led further into the house. Instead he was climbing the wide sweep of stairs.

Crap.

Whatever his promises of not forcing himself upon her she didn't trust him.

He was a vampire.

Enough said.

"Surely that isn't all the rooms on this floor?" she demanded.

"No, but they are not nearly so intriguing as the rooms above." His voice was the same velvet midnight of his eyes. Just as magical.

Damn him.

"I wish you would put me down. I'm perfectly capable of walking." And running. And locking herself in the nearest room.

"I like the feel of you close to me." He reached the landing and turned into the first door on the right. He paused only long enough to touch the switch on the wall before continuing into the center of the room. "Here we are."

Holding herself stiffly, she studied her surroundings. She wasn't sure what she expected. Whips. Chains. Shackles bolted to the wall.

Instead she discovered a room that possessed the same welcoming warmth she had sensed from downstairs.

"This is your bedroom?" she demanded, regarding the large four-poster bed with its thick quilt and hand-carved dresser that held a vase of fresh daisies.

She could think of nothing less suited to the elegant, sophisticated vampire.

Oddly his face became an unreadable mask. Even the midnight eyes were guarded.

"Actually it is yours."

Her heart forgot to beat. "Mine?"

"Do you like it?"

"I . . ." She licked her dry lips. Suddenly the soft, charming room was more frightening than any amount of chains or shackles. "Why?"

He studied her expression with that unnerving intensity of a predator. "Why what?"

"I'm your slave. You can do anything you want to me. Why are you treating me like some sort of privileged guest?"

"It is because you are my slave that means I can treat you in any manner I think fitting."

She closed her eyes against the power of his gaze. "Please, just tell me what you want from me," she whispered. "The not knowing is worse than anything you can do to me."

There was a moment of hesitation before he was striding forward. Before Shay knew what was about to occur, she felt herself being tossed onto the center of the soft bed.

Her eyes flew open as she landed, but not in time to prevent him from following her downward and covering her body with his much heavier frame.

"Very well." His head angled downward until his lips were pressed to her throat and the silken silver hair brushed her face. "I want you in my bed beneath me, screaming out my name as you come in pleasure," he murmured, his mouth moving against her skin to send a thousand tingles of delight through her body. "I want to drink deeply of your blood and bathe in your heat. I want to wrap myself in you until I can get you to stop haunting my dreams. Is that what you wanted to know?"

Her eyes slid shut as she battled the urge to wrap her legs around his waist and beg to be taken exactly as he described.

He wasn't the only one haunted.

"Not really," she rasped.

"Don't worry, pet. I don't force myself on women. We have an eternity to sate my hungers." His mouth shifted so she could feel the sharpness of his fangs. "Both our hungers."

She shivered even as she shook her head in denial. "You know nothing of my hungers."

"I intend to learn."

A sharp, poignant sadness swept through her, helping to

dispel the seductive madness that this vampire could infect with such terrifying ease.

"What I desire you can't offer."

Easily sensing her withdrawal Viper pulled back to regard her with a fierce expression.

"Never doubt me, Shay. I am a vampire of amazing skills." He kissed her with a swift, but shocking intimacy before he was pressing himself fluidly to his feet. A smile touched his lips as he regarded her sprawled on the soft quilt, as if the sight of her lying there somehow pleased him. "Rest well."

Unbelievably, he turned and walked out of the room.

He hadn't chained her to the bed.

He hadn't locked her in the closet.

He hadn't even closed the door.

Cautiously pressing herself upright Shay gave a shake of her head.

What the hell was going on?

Viper made his way through the dark house to his private study. It was close to dawn but he still had a few details to tidy up before seeking his bed.

A pity one of those details wasn't the beautiful Shalott alone in her room, he acknowledged with a rueful sigh. His body still ached with the effort it had taken to leave her alone on that bed.

His mind might assure him that she would soon enough be offering herself without hesitation, but his frustrated desire insisted that it couldn't possibly be soon enough.

Five minutes from now couldn't be soon enough.

Entering the book-lined room he moved straight to the door hidden behind the walnut paneling. Pressing the lever that would let him into the security room beyond, Viper stepped inside and regarded the bank of monitors with a faint sense of pride.

Unlike many of his kind he had never shied from embracing the latest technology. It went beyond arrogant to downright stupid to ignore the ever-changing world.

Besides, if he were perfectly honest, he would admit that he was like any man. He had to have the coolest, the shiniest, most expensive toys with which to play.

At his entrance a small, redheaded vampire watching the monitors was on his feet with his fangs fully extended.

Viper raised a calming hand. "Be at ease."

Realizing who had snuck up on him, the vampire offered a deep bow. "Master."

"Have there been any disturbances?"

"No. It has been very quiet." The green eyes narrowed. "Are you expecting trouble?"

"There is the possibility that I was followed tonight," Viper said. "I want the guards doubled and everyone on full alert."

"Of course, master."

Viper smiled at the swift obedience. No questions. No arguments. No lethal glares.

His employees were far better trained than his new slave.

"Who is on duty after you?"

The vampire glanced toward the list that was set by one of the monitors. "Santiago."

"Good." Viper gave a nod. Santiago was still a young vampire, but he was well-trained and capable of thinking on his feet. Nothing would be allowed to slip past him. "I want you to warn him to keep a close watch on the grounds."

The redheaded vampire regarded him with a curious expression. "Should he keep a close watch for anything in particular?"

"I have a guest staying with me," Viper confessed with a smile that refused to go away. "A very special guest. I fear she might decide to wander off while I sleep."

"Ah. You want to have her captured and returned?"

Viper gave a slow shake of his head. "No. If she is seen trying to leave, I am to be awakened immediately."

The vampire gave a surprised lift of his brows. "You don't want her halted?"

"Not unless Santiago suspects there might be something dangerous lurking nearby." Viper glanced toward the monitors.

"I think it might be interesting to discover just where my guest decides to go."

It shouldn't have been surprising that Shay overslept.

She had paced the floor of her bedroom for over an hour before she had at last accepted Viper was not coming back. That there wasn't going to be any torture, or tormenting, or rape.

At least not yet.

She wasn't nearly ready to believe that it wasn't in her future.

Still it was a shock when she at last awakened and realized that it was already past five in the afternoon.

Good God. She had not only slept, but her sleep had been deep and utterly free of nightmares.

It was unheard of.

It had to be the soft, feather mattress. Or the silence that drenched the estate, she reassured herself as she muttered a few choice curses and scrambled to the bathroom to toss water on her face. It certainly couldn't be that she felt at peace in the home of a vampire.

That would be beyond ridiculous.

She managed to find a new toothbrush and toothpaste in the attached bathroom, as well as a hairbrush that she used to smooth her long hair before she braided it and hurried down to the kitchen.

With no change of clothing, she was forced to remain in the harem pants and glittering top, but as she moved toward the back door she noticed the heavy velvet cloak that Viper had tossed aside the evening before.

She was not as sensitive to the brisk fall air as a normal human, but she didn't possess the ability of a true Shalott to ignore the elements.

Neither one nor the other.

A mongrel.

The story of her life.

Gathering the soft material around her Shay ignored the tantalizing scent that was so uniquely Viper. She had a promise to keep, and no time to allow herself to be distracted. Especially not by her annoying reaction to a damn vampire.

Leaving the house with a silence that few could match she managed to elude the guards that Viper had mentioned patrolled the grounds. Once at the high gates that protected the estate she paused to toss the cloak over before easily climbing the smooth bricks and landing on the other side.

It was her last barrier and gathering the cloak about her she took off at a steady run that would lead her back to the city and the auction house.

Settling into a swift trot she could maintain for hours if necessary, she headed south. In the distance she could see the looming skyline of Chicago and she kept her gaze fixed on the Sears Tower as she crossed the rural fields that lay well outside the sprawling city.

She did take one detour to collect the bag she had hidden when she had first felt the compulsion to return to Evor. She hadn't known then what she might need, she had only wanted to have a few surprises tucked away in case she would have the opportunity to use them.

Now was the perfect opportunity.

Dusk had painted a canvas of pinks and pale violet across the sky when she neared the auction house. Had she been free of the curse, she would have crawled atop one of the towering buildings to watch the wash of color spread over Lake Michigan. There was nothing quite so soothing as being near the water and allowing its power to spread through her.

Her steps never halted, however, and it was still early enough that most of the trolls would be sleeping when she arrived at the auction house.

Unfortunately, more than just trolls and vamps waited for full dark before rising and silently sneaking to the lower basement she discovered Levet still in statue form.

"Levet, wake up," she hissed, silently praying it was long enough past sunset for him to hear her. "Dammit, wake up."

For long moments there was nothing but the scrambling of mice to break the thick silence. Then, there was the faintest crack of rock and the thick stone encasing the gargoyle began to crumble away.

The sight never failed to amaze Shay as the tiny statue shed its skin like a snake molting to reveal the demon beneath.

A shower of dust briefly blinded the small gargoyle and Shay moved closer to the iron bars.

"Levet."

"Eeek." With a loud shriek, Levet scurried to the dark corner of the cell.

"For God's sake, be quiet," Shay hissed.

"Shay?"

"Yes, it's Shay."

Levet slowly crept from the shadows, as if half expecting her to be a figment of his imagination.

"What are you doing here? *Mon dieu,* have you been returned already?"

Shay reluctantly smiled. She didn't blame the gargoyle for jumping to the conclusion her newest master had kicked her out after only a few hours.

She was not exactly slave material.

She hated taking orders. She was short-tempered. Overly proud. Skilled in the most deadly arts. And inclined to battle against fate rather than accept it with grace.

There might be worse slaves than herself.

But not many.

"I told you that I would come back for you. I don't make promises I don't intend to keep."

Levet stilled. As if he had returned to his statue form. "You came back? For . . . me?"

"Yes."

He slowly sank to his knees, his flippant manner lost in a surge of bone-deep relief.

"Oh, thank God." His voice echoed through the empty cavern. "Thank God."

"Sssh." Shay gave an anxious wave of her hand as she

glanced toward the nearby stairs. "We have to get you out of here before Evor awakens."

"How? You can't touch the bars and I'm not strong enough to bend them."

Shay reached beneath her cloak to pull out the small ceramic pot. With great care, she pulled out the stopper.

"Stand back."

Levet rose to his feet and slowly backed away. "What are you going to do?"

The smoke was already beginning to rise from the pot. Never a good sign.

"Dammit, Levet, just get in the corner."

With a flap of his gossamer wings, he was scurrying to the back of the cell even as Shay tossed the pot directly at the iron bars.

There was an evil hiss and an acrid cloud of mist as the liquid from the pot rapidly ate its way through the metal.

"*Sacrebleu.* What is that stuff?" Levet breathed in shock.

"A potion I stole from the witches."

"You stole it?"

"Yes."

The gargoyle delicately inched his way forward. "Um, Shay?"

"What?"

"Next time you want to rescue me could you just steal the key?" He deliberately regarded the large, dripping hole in the center of the bars before his gaze lowered to the stones that were being slowly eaten away. "I'm not really certain you should be allowed to have potions."

Shay slammed her hands on her hips. She had been saving that particular potion for Evor. One day he would push her too far and she fully intended to enjoy watching him melt into a troll-puddle. Even if it did mean her own death.

"Are you going to stand there and criticize my jail-breaking techniques or are you coming with me?"

"I'm coming, I'm coming." Using his wings to carry him

over the dangerous vitriol still pooled on the ground, he darted through the hole and landed beside her.

Shay caught her breath at the beauty of those gossamer wings he always kept so closely guarded against his body. Even in the shadows she could detect the shimmering reds and blues veined with pure gold. Had he been a wood sprite he would have displayed those wings with all the pride of a strutting peacock. As it was they were nothing more than a source of embarrassment.

Shifting her gaze to keep from staring at the beautiful wings and ruffling Levet's tender pride, Shay gathered the cloak closer about her.

"I can't sense the trolls near but we must hurry. It won't be long until they are preparing for the night."

"Wait." Levet caught her arm even as she turned toward the stairs and pointed toward a small opening at the back of the dungeons. "This way."

"That only takes us deeper into the dungeons," she protested with a shudder. She didn't want to know what Evor hid in those damp chambers.

"There is a hidden door."

"A hidden door?" Shay frowned. "How do you know?"

"I can feel the night." Levet leaned back his head to sniff the air, a faint shiver rippling over his gray skin. "It speaks to me."

Shay wasn't about to argue with a gargoyle who could smell the night. She might be stubborn, but she wasn't entirely stupid.

"Fine, you lead the way."

Without a backward glance the small demon was hurrying into the narrow opening. Shay swallowed a sigh as she followed closely behind him.

As she had expected the walls were lined with heavy iron doors that hid rooms where the most powerful of demons could be caged. Without windows in the doors it was impossible to determine what was locked in the dark, but she could catch a musty, snake scent of a reptilian demon followed by the spicy, almost herbal scent of a powerful imp. There were other smells that were fainter, as if the demons were beginning to fade behind those thick, ruthless doors.

She battled the urge to pound her fists against the thick iron. No matter what sort of demons might be lurking behind the doors none of them deserved to be in Evor's power.

The sound of her companion's hurried steps brought her back to her senses.

No. She could do nothing tonight.

Not without risking Levet.

The remaining demons were a worry for another night.

They traveled in silence through the spiderweb of tunnels. Levet never hesitated as he angled through the various passageways. Shay found herself having to bend nearly double more than once, but at last the gargoyle turned and began to climb a narrow set of stairs carved into the stone.

As they made their way upward even Shay could begin to sense the brush of fresh air. Within minutes they were squeezing through the narrowest of openings and were standing on the vast grounds that surrounded the auction house.

She blew out a breath she hadn't even known she was holding.

Holy crap, they had made it.

Even when she had been plotting to rescue Levet she hadn't truly thought she could pull it off.

Not with Evor and his merry band of trolls so close at hand.

On the point of sharing her rush of joy at their success Shay abruptly froze. A cold prickling was creeping over her skin.

A cold that could only belong to one creature.

"Levet, fly," she commanded as she bent low and prepared for an attack.

She had barely lifted her hands when there was a streak of blackness and she found herself flat on her back with a silver-haired vampire perched on top of her.

"Well, well, pet. Fancy meeting you here."

Her breath had been knocked from her lungs, but not from the swift tackle. Viper had made certain his arms encircling her body had taken the impact.

No. It was nothing so mundane.

Cloaked in his rich scent and surrounded by the cloud of his silver hair she could barely think, let alone breathe. He surrounded her. His body pressing against her a shockingly familiar weight.

Even worse his face was so close their noses were nearly touching. So close that she had only to tilt her chin to press her lips to his.

The very fact that the mere thought brushed through her mind sent a thrill of panic racing through her heart.

"Get off me," she gritted.

His low chuckle brushed against her cheek. "Make me."

She reacted more out of the fear of her response than to his soft challenge.

Smacking her fists into his wide chest she pretended to fight as most women would be expected to fight. He instinctively leaned heavier into her arms, which gave her just enough room to move her leg. Before he could suspect her intention she hooked her leg around his waist and with a fierce motion she had rolled him onto his back.

Just for a moment she was perched on top of him, her legs straddling his waist and a smug smile curving her lips.

His beautiful features were briefly startled, and then a smile curved his own lips.

She braced her legs, expecting him to attempt to roll her back beneath him. Men always preferred to use their greater size to overcome an opponent, not realizing their own strength could be used against them. Once he began to roll she would use his own momentum to end up on top again.

Unfortunately, Viper was a vampire not a man.

His smile widened as he simply lifted her upward, his arms wrapping about her as he flowed to his feet. Shay gritted her teeth as she abruptly bowed backward, throwing her arms over her head and wrapping her legs about his waist.

As she hoped her movement threw him off balance. He stepped forward and she grabbed him around his knees, her flexible back easily able to bend in an impossible curve. Her head turned to sink her teeth into his thigh.

"Oh no, my beauty."

With a soft hiss, Viper once again did the unexpected. Following her movement forward he placed his hands on the ground and with a smooth motion rolled until he was again on his back. This time her legs were trapped beneath him and he was able to reach down and grasp her with enough strength to jerk her up to his chest. His arms lashed about her, pressing her arms to her side so that she was well and truly caught.

Shit.

Chapter Six

Viper couldn't deny a thrill of excitement as he wrestled with the beautiful Shalott.

No doubt he should be furious at her attempted escape. He had, after all, done everything possible to make her comfortable in his presence. From ordering the necessary food, to having her room decorated, to filling her closets with clothing. He had devoted weeks, not to mention a small fortune, to pleasing the ungrateful brat.

To top it off he had behaved as a perfect gentleman when his dark hungers had howled in frustration.

What other demon would have treated her with more consideration?

Oddly, however, he found it was more of a predatory anticipation than fury he felt as he had started in pursuit of his renegade slave.

There were few things that stirred his blood more than a cunning, dangerous woman.

Especially when she happened to be beautiful in the bargain.

Not a bad bonus.

Holding her captive in his arms he slowly smiled into the golden flash of her eyes.

"Do you want to continue, pet, or are we done with our fun and games?"

She held herself so stiff it was a wonder she didn't get a cramp. "What I want is for you to release me."

"Not until we've had a little chat."

She angrily squirmed against him. Viper gave a soft moan. His last few lovers had been vampires and he had nearly forgotten the pleasure of feeling himself drenched in such heat.

"Dammit, Viper, let me up."

"No. You've already tried to run away once tonight." His arms tightened about her. "Once is all you get."

Something that might have been outrage rippled over her delicate features. "I didn't run away."

"You waited until I could not halt you and you slipped from my home. What would you call it?"

Her lips thinned with annoyance. Clearly she disliked being accused of slipping away like a thief in the night.

A demon with a sense of honor.

"I had a few errands to run. Surely I'm allowed some freedom?"

"That depends. What are you doing here?"

"I left something behind."

"Something?"

If her arms had been free, Viper didn't doubt she would have given him a solid punch to the nose. Which was precisely why her arms weren't free.

"A friend," she at last gritted.

Friend? Viper turned his head to regard the small, fluttering gargoyle who was attempting to hide in the branches of a nearby tree. He had spotted the demon when he had come from the tiny opening, but he had dismissed him once he had caught sight of Shay.

She managed to drive most things from his mind when she was near.

A rather dangerous realization.

"You mean the gargoyle?" he demanded with a hint of surprise.

"Yes."

"He belongs to Evor?"

"Yes."

He gave a slow lift of his brows. "If you had requested, I would have bought him last night. There was no need to endanger yourself."

She blinked in astonishment at his soft words. Even her muscles relaxed as if she temporarily forgot he was the enemy.

Viper silently savored the feel of her body pressed close against him.

"Evor has never attempted to auction Levet." Remembered pain flashed through her eyes. "He prefers to leave him as a treat for his goons to torture."

His arms loosened their hold enough to allow his fingers to trace a light pattern up her spine. He didn't like seeing that hurt darken her eyes. It made him want to drain someone.

Beginning with the pasty-faced troll.

"For the right price, Evor would sell his own mother," he growled.

It took a moment before she grudgingly met his steady gaze. "I could hardly be expected to know you would be willing to grant your slave such a favor."

His hand shifted to cup the back of her head. "Why are you so determined to consider yourself a slave when I have yet to do so?"

She blinked at his blunt demand. "What else could I be? You bought me from a slave trader. You possess the amulet that keeps me chained to you regardless of my own desires."

"Would you prefer that I return you to Evor? You would rather possess a different master?"

"Does it matter what I want?"

"Answer the question."

Despite the darkness Viper could easily read the emotions rippling over her face.

Confusion. Embarrassment. And at last a reluctant acceptance.

"No," she whispered so softly that if he hadn't been a vampire he would never have heard her. But he was. And he did. And it was enough to make his hand tighten on the back of her head to press her head downward.

Her breath came in a rush as he captured her lips, captured

the heat of her, and pulled it deep within him. She tasted of warm honey and life. A taste sweet enough for a vampire to drown in.

Thrusting his fingers into her hair Viper allowed his free hand to sweep down to cup her hip. He wanted her here, now. He wanted her with a raw ache that was nearly frightening in its intensity.

Gently parting her lips with his tongue he searched the moist cavern of her mouth. He groaned deep in his throat as her hands clutched at his arms and for a startling moment she returned his kiss with the same frantic need that pulsed within him.

Heat flared between them, and then with a startled gasp Shay was abruptly wrenching her lips from his own, and regarding him with something perilously close to horror.

"Viper."

He swallowed a curse as his body clenched in protest before he was sternly chastising his unruly passions. What the devil was the matter with him?

He was a centuries-old vampire with endless power and sophistication. He did not indulge in public orgies. No matter what the temptation.

"You are right, this is hardly the setting for a romantic tryst," he muttered. "Nor is it the time to be distracted."

She sucked in a deep breath, the motion pressing her small, firm breasts tightly against his chest.

Hell's bells.

"How did you find me?" she demanded.

"I told you that I had the grounds guarded."

Her brows lifted. "I was followed?"

"Yes." Viper deliberately turned to regard the tall, silent vampire that stood in the distant shadows. Not surprisingly Shay stiffened with wary unease.

Santiago was an impressive sight with his leather pants and black T-shirt designed to reveal his thick muscles. His face was narrow with high cheekbones and his eyes the deep brown of his Spanish ancestors.

It took only a glance to know precisely what he was.

A trained warrior who would kill to protect those of his clan.

Shay swallowed heavily. "He's a vampire, he couldn't possibly have been patrolling when I left."

"This isn't the Stone Age, pet," Viper drawled. "The grounds are guarded by a very high-tech system that includes motion sensors, silent alarms, and a series of cameras that are constantly monitored. Santiago was deep underground when he spotted you leaving."

"Why didn't he send someone to try and stop me?"

"I told him not to."

Her gaze snapped back to regard him with open suspicion. "Why?"

"I knew I could easily track you."

"You wanted to spy on me."

"I will admit to some curiosity, but more than that I wanted to prove to you that you are a fool to try and escape."

Her expression abruptly hardened. "I know I can't escape. You don't need a guard. You have only to use the amulet and I will be forced to return."

"That's not the point."

"Then what is?"

His hands shifted to cup her face, his eyes narrowed. "There is a powerful force that has tried to capture you more than once. Until we discover what it is you will not be allowed to travel on your own."

He was prepared for her anger. Slave or not she was not the sort of demon to mildly accept any sort of restrictions. Even those meant to keep her safe.

Astonishingly, however, he could read nothing but a flare of concern in her beautiful eyes.

"You believe I'm still in danger?"

"Don't you?"

She chewed on her bottom lip before at last heaving a sigh. "Okay, point made. I was an idiot to take off on my own. You can let me up now."

Pleased that she seemed capable of allowing logic to overrule her fiercely independent nature, Viper slowly smiled.

"It seems a pity." His hands brushed down to the tempting curve of her throat. "I've thought about having you in this position for a long time. Of course, my fantasies didn't include either of us in clothes, or a hovering gargoyle."

"I told you to—"

Her heated words were brought to an abrupt halt as a soft breeze rippled through the air and Viper was swiftly on his feet pushing Shay behind him.

"Master," Santiago called from the shadows.

"Yes, Santiago, I smell it."

He felt Shay grasp the back of his silk shirt. "Smell what?"

"Blood. Fresh blood."

"Crap."

A shiver raced down Shay's spine as Viper slowly turned to face her. Until the past few moments she had managed to forget the hovering evil that seemed intent on capturing her. She had been so intent on how she could manage to rescue Levet from Evor that she had forgotten she possessed yet another enemy.

Stupid, stupid, stupid.

And embarrassing that Viper had remembered when she had not.

"Did you kill Evor and his trolls?" he demanded.

His tone was merely curious. As if he didn't give a bloody hell if she had slaughtered the trolls.

And probably he didn't.

"No, I didn't even catch sight of them."

"So you saw no one? Heard nothing?"

"No."

His head tilted to one side. "And you did not think that unusual?"

Shay shrugged, thinking back to her swift trip through the auction house. "They rarely enter the auction house before dark. Besides, I used the back entrance and went straight to the dungeons. You think they were attacked?"

"Something was." He glanced back toward the silent building. "Wait here."

Shay watched as Viper collected his vamp and they moved through the darkness. Within a heartbeat they had melded into the shadows, and not even her enhanced vision could make out their silhouettes.

She wrapped the cloak tight about her oddly chilled body as Levet fluttered onto the ground beside her.

"Maybe we should just leave," she muttered.

"Do you think?" Levet slapped his hands on his hips and regarded her with a narrowed gaze. "Oh, wait. Why would we leave when we can linger in the backyard of our enemies and play suck face with whatever vampire happens by? And after that we can douse ourselves with gasoline and play with matches. The fun, as they say, never ends."

Shay felt a ridiculous blush touch her cheeks. She had not played suck face. Well, at least not on purpose.

"Don't push it, Levet."

"Or what? You'll hold me down and kiss me to death?"

"You can be returned to your cell, you know," she growled. *"Sur le corps."*

Over his dead body? Shay gave a lift of her brows. "That could be arranged as well."

Perhaps sensing he had touched her last nerve Levet lifted his hands in a purely continental gesture.

"Now, now, *ma cherie*. There is no need to be testy."

Unconsciously, Shay glanced toward the last spot she had seen Viper. "Actually there seems to be any number of reasons," she muttered.

"Yes, I suppose there is," he murmured softly. "Your new master is an oh-so-hated vampire."

"So it would seem."

"A clan chief."

Shay's attention sharply returned to the gargoyle at her side. "How can you tell?"

"I can smell the mark of CuChulainn upon him."

Shay licked her suddenly dry lips. She had never attended

the gladiator games. Few demons were considered worthy to attend the most elite of competitions. And even fewer allowed to participate.

Those who walked out alive were feared and respected by all.

They were warriors worthy of the title master.

"He has gone through the Battle of Durotriges?"

"And lived to tell the tale. Quite impressive." Levet regarded her with a knowing expression. "A wise demon would not wish to anger such a champion."

The very fact he was right only deepened Shay's frown. Even if she were a pure blood Shalott she could never hope to best a clan chief.

Somehow the knowledge annoyed the hell out of her.

"Thanks, Levet."

He blew her a kiss. "Anything to be of service for you, *ma cherie*."

She rolled her eyes. "Remind me why I bothered to rescue you."

The tiny, oddly lumped face became somber. "Because you cannot bear to see another hurt. Even if it means sacrificing yourself."

Shay shifted with a flare of discomfort. She wasn't a saint. Far from it.

The simple fact was that she had precious few friends. Demons considered her blood tainted and humans considered her some sort of freak. When she did find someone willing to accept her for whom and what she was, she would do a lot more than risk Evor's fury to keep them safe.

Uncertain how to break the uneasy silence, Shay was almost relieved when she felt the cold chill that proceeded Viper's silent return.

Of course, that didn't halt her treacherous heart from giving a lustful leap as the moonlight spilled over his silver hair and perfect profile.

Vamp beauty.

It was a damn pain in the ass.

Giving an unconscious shake of her head she cleared her ridiculous thoughts.

"Did you find Evor?"

His expression was oddly guarded. "Not precisely."

"What do you mean?"

"I think you should see this. Perhaps you can shed some light on what has happened."

Shay hesitated only a moment before following his tall form toward the auction house. She didn't doubt there was something horrible awaiting her. Something that might very well give her nightmares.

But even as she forced her feet forward she couldn't deny a ridiculous flare of warmth. Dammit, she was Viper's slave. His possession. But at every turn he made her feel as if she were something more. Something . . . worthy.

Deep within her she understood that the sensations he stirred were far more dangerous than if he locked her in a cell and beat her every day.

Turning her head to ensure that Levet was safely following behind them, Shay allowed Viper to lead her into the dark auction house and up the stairs to Evor's private quarters. As he threw open the door, she nearly gagged at the overwhelming stench of blood and gruesome death.

She had expected bad, but this went way beyond bad.

Her hand clamped over her mouth as she struggled not to hurl up what was left in her stomach.

The once elegant room was now splattered with bits and pieces of trolls. Blood, limbs, and body parts that should never be seen, were so mixed together it was impossible to even know how many had died in the attack.

Forcing herself to study the nightmare, her disbelieving gaze at last halted on the black marble mantle and the head of the mountain troll that had been stuck there like a trophy.

The red eyes were open and a snarl revealing his open teeth, as if he were damning the soul of his killer.

Whatever he had been doing it hadn't saved him or the other bodyguards. They had been butchered with violent ease.

The nausea rolled through her stomach once again.

"Blessed saints. This is impossible."

Taking her arm Viper gently pulled her from the room and closed the door. Then, as if sensing her weakness, he pressed her into a chair and crouched down before her.

"There are few things that can kill trolls with such savagery, but there is no doubt they have been well and truly slaughtered." He studied her face with a searching gaze. "Do you sense anything that might give a clue to what or who was responsible?"

With an effort, she battled back her crawling horror and forced herself to think with what logic she could muster.

"It wasn't a human. They wouldn't have the strength to rip apart a troll with their bare hands."

"Was it a spell?" Viper demanded.

"No." She took in a deep breath. "There is no magic in the air."

Viper gave a nod of his head. As a vampire he had no ability to sense magic. Which was no doubt one of the reasons why he wanted her along.

"So it had to be a demon that possesses incredible strength, and the ability to mask their presence from a vampire," Viper murmured. "That narrows the list but leaves far too many suspects."

Shay shivered as she wrapped her arms about her. The shock was beginning to recede and the full impact of the savage attack hit her with an alarming force.

"Oh, my God," she whispered.

Viper reached out to grasp her shoulders. His touch was cool but surprisingly comforting.

Perhaps because it had been so incredibly long since anyone had touched her in anything but anger.

"I should not have brought you to see this. Forgive me."

She gave a shake of her head. "No, it's not that. It's Evor."

"Evor? Why . . . ah." Viper slowly nodded. "He's not among the dead."

She gave a short, unsteady laugh. "Obviously not. I think I would know if I had suddenly become a corpse."

"Yes, it's rather hard to miss," he said dryly.

She grimaced, struggling to regain control of her raw nerves. Holy crap, but it had been a close call.

Too close.

"If Evor had been in that room . . ." she breathed.

His fingers tightened. "He's alive, pet, and so are you."

"Yes, but it was a near thing," she rasped. "Too near."

"On that we agree." He glanced toward the door of the blood-drenched room. "We need to discover who did this, and just as importantly where Evor has disappeared to."

Shay grimaced at the thought of the slimy little troll. "No doubt he crawled beneath some rock the moment the trouble started. He's always happy to sacrifice his servants to save his own hide."

"He was here." His gaze was somber as it returned to her face. "His blood is mixed among the others."

"His blood?"

He gave a lift of his shoulder. "Only a small amount, but enough to reveal he was here during the attack."

She pulled from his touch. Of course he could smell Evor's blood. He was a vampire.

Blood was his specialty.

"So someone, or something, came here tonight, killed the mountain trolls and injured Evor?" She gave a shake of her head. "Why?"

"It's possible that it was a demon in search of valuables that was caught off guard by the trolls. Or even one seeking vengeance. Evor is hardly the sort to endear himself to others, and there are many who find the slave trade a disgusting business."

She met his gaze squarely. "It's possible, but you don't think it was a housebreaker or someone seeking vengeance."

"No." His beautiful features were hard in the dim moonlight. "The timing of the attack is too much of a coincidence. I think whoever is hunting you returned to this auction house."

Her throat went dry. "To kill Evor?"

A frown touched his brow. "If they wanted Evor dead, he would already be dead. Either he managed to escape during the battle or they came to take him alive."

"But why?"

"To use as bait." Levet's unexpected voice had both Shay and Viper turning in astonishment.

"What?" Viper demanded.

The gargoyle gave a nervous flutter of his wings. "If they hold the troll then they can threaten to slice his throat open and kill both of them. Shay will have no choice but to do what they want."

Shay felt her heart stutter to a halt. Shit, it was bad enough to be in the power of Evor. Now she had to worry about some mysterious enemy who could rip apart trolls with his bare hands.

Not good.

Not good at all.

"Do you think that's what they want?" she rasped.

"I think it would be foolish to leap to any conclusions until we have more facts," Viper retorted, reaching down to easily scoop her into his arms. "We need to leave here."

It was a testament of just how troubled Shay was by the latest turn of events that she didn't struggle once as Viper carried her from the blood-drenched auction house.

Not one kick. Not one poke in the eye. Not even a curse.

Astonishing.

She came back to herself as Viper slowly lowered her to her feet, and pressed her back to one of the towering oak trees.

"Before we leave are there any other possessions you desire to collect?" he demanded softly.

Not softly enough as Levet gave an angry flap of his wings. "Possessions? *Sacrebleu*. I am a gargoyle. A demon to be feared and respected above all others. I will—"

"Enough, Levet," Shay interrupted the furious words, her gaze never leaving Viper's beautiful face. "There are demons trapped in the dungeons."

He gave a lift of his brows. "They are your friends as well?"

"I don't even know for certain what creatures are behind the doors. I only know that with the trolls dead and Evor missing they might be locked in those cells for eternity. It's worse than torture."

"They may be dangerous."

She didn't doubt for a moment that they were extremely dangerous, and more than likely deadly.

That didn't change her determination to have them rescued.

"We cannot leave them."

"Santiago."

His gaze never left her pale face as he lifted a hand and a shadow detached itself from behind a nearby tree.

"Yes, master?"

"Go to the dungeons and release the prisoners."

"As you wish."

"We will meet you at the car."

There wasn't a moment's hesitation as the vampire silently melded into the dark. Shay grimaced at the mindless obedience. If that was what Viper was expecting from her . . . well, he was in for a major disappointment.

And no doubt she would be in for a number of beatings.

Pride was a hell of a thing.

"You think it's safe for him to go alone?" she demanded.

Viper shrugged. "He is a vampire."

Vamp arrogance. It made her teeth clench.

"Fine, then can we go?"

Viper opened his lips, but it was Levet's voice that echoed through the darkness.

"Umm . . . Shay?"

She turned to discover him standing a safe distance from Viper.

"Yes?"

"What of *moi*?"

"Oh . . . I . . ." Her gaze reluctantly returned to the vampire standing way too close. "Viper?"

"Yes, pet?"

She wanted to tell him to back away. Now that she was no longer dazed by Evor's disappearance she found his hovering presence far too distracting. But she held her tongue. She was in the unpleasant position of asking for a favor.

Something she didn't do well under the best of circumstances.

"We cannot simply leave Levet here. He has been cast out of the Guild by the other gargoyles."

His hands slowly lifted until he could place them on the tree on either side of her head.

"Are you requesting that I take him under my protection? That I offer him shelter?"

She ignored the unsteady beat of her heart. "Yes."

A worrisome smile curved his lips. "And what is to be my reward for such generosity?"

"Shay, no," Levet hissed.

She ignored his warning, her gaze remaining locked with Viper's dark eyes.

"What would you have of me?"

"Now that is not a question to be answered in haste. There is so much that I want of you," he murmured, leaning ever closer. "Perhaps I should simply require a boon to be given when I have considered more carefully."

Shay licked her dry lips. "You mean I will owe you a favor?"

"You will be in my debt. A debt that I can call due whenever I feel the moment is . . . ripe."

"Don't do it, Shay," Levet commanded. "Never bargain with a vampire."

Shay was well aware of the risks. Every demon knew that a vampire could twist words until they screamed in agony.

But what did she have to lose?

She was already Viper's slave and at his mercy. If he truly wanted to force her to do something, no matter how awful, she had little choice but to comply. After all, the amulet made certain she could not escape.

Why not attempt to make the bargain and keep Levet safe?

Of course, there was nothing to say that she couldn't try and get the better of any deal.

"Can the terms be negotiated?"

"Negotiated?" His gaze drifted to her lips. "That depends. Tell me your offer."

"The debt cannot include blood or sex."

He gave a soft laugh as he lowered his head to bury his face in the curve of her throat. When he spoke, his lips brushed her skin and sent a disturbing rash of shivers down her spine.

"You have just taken away my two deepest desires. What else can you offer?"

She battled to keep her eyes from rolling to the back of her head. "I am a trained fighter."

"I possess many warriors."

"Warriors that can walk in the day?"

"A few." His tongue drew a warm, wet line to the edge of her collarbone. "What else do you offer?"

Her knees felt weak. "I learned to prepare a number of potions while with the witches."

His tongue stroked her racing pulse. "Intriguing, but hardly worthy of a boon."

She paused, her hands unconsciously gripping the rough bark of the tree behind her. It was that or gripping the vampire in front of her.

Perhaps sensing why she hesitated, Levet gave a low hiss.

"Do not, Shay."

Viper pulled back to regard her with a searching curiosity. "What is it, pet?"

"I . . ." Shay swallowed back her unease. "My father was a Lumos, the healer of our tribe. His blood could cure all but death."

His eyes slowly widened. "And you?"

"His . . . blessing was passed to me."

"A rare gift." Something flashed through the dark eyes. Curiosity? "A rare gift, indeed, but hardly necessary for an immortal."

Her hand unconsciously lifted to touch the spot still tingling from his lips.

"Even immortals can be harmed. My mother claimed that

was why my father was killed. His blood was used to save the life of a vampire."

"A vampire?" The curiosity deepened. "You're certain?"

"Yes."

"Strange that I never heard such rumors." He pondered the notion for a moment before seeming to dismiss it from his mind. "So, what precisely is it that you're offering?"

"If . . . if you are injured, I will freely offer my blood to heal you. But only to heal you. No occasional snacking." Her chin tilted. "Do we have a deal?"

His features once again softened with that seductive amusement. "A bargain," he corrected softly.

"No blood unless absolutely necessary, and no sex."

"I do not need to bargain for blood or sex. You will soon give them freely enough."

He bent to sweep his lips over her mouth, allowing her no opportunity to argue. Back and forth, with exquisite care, he rubbed his lips over hers. An electric tingle followed his touch and before she knew what she was doing she had instinctively opened her mouth at his teasing.

Only then did he claim a kiss that was edged with such possessive hunger it branded its way to her very heart.

It was the sort of kiss women dreamed of in their deepest fantasies. Hot, demanding, and utterly consuming. Her hands had actually started to rise to pull him closer when he was stepping back and glancing toward the shadows.

"Ah . . . Santiago has accomplished his task. Perhaps we should leave before whatever he loosened has the opportunity to eat us."

Hard to argue with that logic.

Chapter Seven

Viper's thoughts were distracted as they reached his estate outside Chicago.

And not pleasantly distracted.

He wouldn't have minded a bit of bemusement at the sweet scent of Shay that still clung to his body like a wicked promise. Or the lingering heat that flowed through his body.

It had been far too long since he had enjoyed that sort of distraction.

This distraction came from the darkening certainty that something powerful was hunting his Shalott. Something so dangerous and vicious that it might be more than he could protect her from.

The thought made his heart clench with a fear he could not name.

Still, even with his thoughts clouded, he sensed a presence the moment he stepped through the door into the kitchen.

"Someone is here." Holding out his arm he swept Shay behind him and turned to his guard. "Santiago, search the grounds and make sure we do not have any other unexpected guests."

He waited until the vampire had disappeared before lifting his head and testing the air. Only when he was certain there was no immediate danger did he shift to regard Shay's pale face.

There was pride etched into her beautiful features, and a

grim refusal to reveal the least hint of fear, but not even her staunch will could hide the shadows in her golden eyes. She would stand tall and spit fear in its face. On this night, however, that would not be necessary. She was his. His to protect.

"My dear, I believe it would be best if you return to your rooms and lock the door."

She frowned, her chin jutting to a stubborn angle. It was an expression that was growing familiar to Viper and one he found ridiculously charming.

"Shalotts are warriors. We do not cower behind locked doors."

He allowed a slow smile to curve his lips. "It is not that I doubt your skills in battle, pet, but our intruder is a vampire. I would not wish to be forced to kill a clansman because they find you irresistible."

Her mouth opened and closed before she gave a reluctant nod of her head. She might hate looking like a coward, but she hated the thought of encountering yet another vampire even more.

A small pang shot through his heart as he watched her walk across the kitchen with the gargoyle in tow. She had every reason to hate and distrust vampires. It was a prejudice that would not easily be overcome.

Giving a shake of his head Viper turned to follow the scent of his clansman toward the back of his house. He was not surprised to enter his study and find the tall, raven-haired vampire calmly seated behind his heavy desk.

Of all his clansmen, he was perhaps closest to Dante. They had recently ended the threat of a coven of witches determined to bring an end to all demons and rescued the Phoenix, the Goddess of Light who protected the world from the dark prince.

It was during their efforts that he had first encountered Shay. He didn't know whether to thank his friend or throttle him for having his peaceful world shaken to its very foundation.

He split the difference by moving to the built-in bar and collecting a bottle of blood. It was a poor substitute for the magical power he sensed within Shay's blood, but for now at least it restored his waning strength.

Watching his precise movements Dante allowed a smile to curve his lips. He was one of the few not overawed by Viper's presence.

"Good evening, Viper."

Leaning against the bar Viper folded his arms over his chest. "I see you have made yourself at home despite the fact you are well aware I never allow guests here."

The smile never wavered. "You are fortunate that I am the one sitting here and not my mate. Abby is quite anxious to share her opinion of buying young women at a slave auction." The silver eyes narrowed. "Especially a young woman who saved your life."

Viper didn't doubt for a moment that Dante's mate would readily burn him to a crisp. Despite becoming a goddess she retained her human compassion and was always ready to fight what she thought was injustice.

No demon with the least amount of sense wanted the Phoenix gunning for them.

Still, he was a clan chief. A leader among vampires.

He didn't answer to anyone.

"When I called to tell you that I had purchased the Shalott it was only to request your assistance in discovering what evil hunts her, not to request your opinion of my personal affairs."

Dante shrugged. "You have offered your opinion of my personal affairs often enough."

"Opinions you ignored. Just as I intend to. Now, if that is all . . ."

With a sharp motion Dante was on his feet, his silver eyes glittering in the soft glow of the lamplight.

"Viper, what game are you playing?"

Viper set aside his empty bottle. "There is no game."

"There is something." Dante moved from around the desk, the black leather pants and black silk shirt making him appear a dangerous predator. Which was exactly what he was. "You have condemned any slave trader to death if you discover they have attempted to capture and sell a vampire within your territory."

"Shay is not a vampire."

"That does not alter the fact you detest those who peddle in flesh."

Viper smiled wryly. He possessed any number of pleasure houses. Elegant, expensive establishments where demons and fairies, and even a rare few humans, could come to enjoy whatever delights they could imagine.

"There are some who claim that I peddle in flesh."

Dante frowned. "Never unwilling flesh."

Viper shrugged. He could hardly argue. Those who served him did so at their own choice. He waved a hand toward the bar. "Wine? Or perhaps a taste of my private stock of brandy?"

Dante narrowed his gaze. He was not about to be distracted. "What are you doing with Shay?"

A helluva question. A pity he had no answer.

"What does it matter to you?"

"I can't say it bothers me in the least. Abby, however, will not give me rest until she is assured you mean the demon no harm."

Viper gave a short laugh. "At least you are honest. But tell me, Dante, would your oh-so-beautiful wife have preferred that I had stepped aside and allowed Shay to be bought as a blood whore? Or perhaps a trophy to be hung on the wall of some demon hunter?"

"She would prefer that you set her free."

Allow Shay to slip from his grasp? To disappear like she had done after the battle with the witches?

Over his cold, dead body.

"I did tell you that it is not possible. I hold an amulet that forces her to come when I call, but the curse that binds her is held by a lesser troll named Evor. A troll who has suddenly disappeared."

Dante lifted his brows. "What do you mean?"

As concisely as possible, Viper revealed what they had discovered in the auction house. He was careful to describe the

mutilation of the trolls in great detail. It could be that Dante
would recognize something about the attack that would assist
in tracing the savage culprit.

"You are certain a demon is responsible for the massacre?"
his companion demanded.

"What else?"

"A witch or wizard perhaps."

Viper hid a smile. Who could blame his friend for being suspicious of witches? Having someone try to kill you on several
occasions tended to make you a bit twitchy.

"Shay sensed no magic."

Dante gave a shake of his head. "If it were a demon, you
should be able to track it. There are few who can hide their
scent from a vampire."

"A Hunding, an Irra, perhaps a Napchut."

"Are they powerful enough to tear apart a nest of trolls?"

It was the question that had plagued Viper since he had discovered the various troll parts splattered across the room. Unfortunately, he could only imagine one demon strong enough
to defeat the trolls and yet possess the magical abilities to hide
his scent.

"A Lu warrior would be."

Dante stiffened. Viper didn't blame him. The Lu were the
bogeymen of the demon world. The nightmares that crawled
from the earth to devour whatever was in their path.

"The Lu haven't been seen for centuries," Dante breathed.

"Neither have Shalotts."

"True enough." Dante moved slowly forward, his expression
somber. "A vampire, even a clan chief, would not be strong
enough to battle a Lu. Their teeth are capable of severing the
heads of even immortals."

"I do not intend to allow anything to take a bite out of me."
Viper smiled. "Not unless they happen to be naked in my bed
at the time."

Dante's concern didn't ease. "Your slave has fallen to the attention of a very dangerous enemy. You would be better served
to pass her ownership to another."

"I recall saying precisely the same words to you only a few weeks ago."

"Abby is my true mate. She belongs to me and I would give my life to keep her safe." He regarded Viper with a far too knowing gaze. "Why do you risk yourself for the Shalott?"

Viper battled an unexpected surge of anger. He didn't want to explain his fascination for Shay. Not to Dante. Not to anyone.

Even himself.

"That is my business."

Dante paused as he easily sensed he had pressed Viper's temper as far as he dared. He gave the smallest bow of his head.

"As you wish." A hint of amusement returned to the silver eyes. "I will warn you that Abby will not be satisfied until she has assured herself that Shay is not being mistreated."

Viper gritted his teeth. He was the clan chief. A ruler who held the power over hundreds, no thousands, of vampires and lesser demons. But even he knew better than to try and argue with a woman.

"And how will she be satisfied?"

"She desires to have Shay spend a day with her."

"A day?"

Dante gave a helpless lift of his hands. "She was very specific that the visit be during the day."

"So I cannot interfere?"

"In part." A whimsical smile touched the younger vampire's lips. "But in truth I believe that Abby longs for the companionship of another woman. Despite being a goddess she is still human enough to long for hours shopping at the mall and gossiping over coffee."

Viper shuddered in horror. "By the blood of the saints, why?"

"That, old friend, is a question beyond vampire logic."

He gave an impatient shrug. Blood and bones. He didn't want to share Shay. Not with anyone. Unfortunately, he couldn't make himself forget the shadows deep in her eyes and her fierce determination to save her gargoyle.

She was lonely.

Deeply, heart wrenchingly lonely.

"I will extend Abby's invitation to Shay, whether or not she agrees is up to her."

Dante was swift to pounce on his casual words. "So she is not your slave?"

"She is my . . . guest."

"You knew she would be at the auction when you went there."

Viper's patience came to an abrupt end. If he were going to squabble the night away with someone, he intended it to be Shay.

That was the sort of squabbling a vampire could enjoy.

"I think it is time for you to return to your lovely mate."

Something very close to a smirk curled Dante's mouth. "She captured your attention and you sought her out. Well, well."

"Do not press your luck, my friend."

Dante held up his hands as he gave a small laugh. "I am leaving."

"Good."

The smile vanished as Dante reached out to grasp his shoulder in a tight grip.

"Viper, you are more than my clan chief, you are my friend. If you find yourself in need, I want your promise you will call me."

"And have the Phoenix angry that I put you in danger?" Viper gave a lift of his brows. "I am not entirely stupid."

"No one is more conscious of the debt owed to you than Abby. She will use her own powers if it will keep you safe."

"And considerable powers they are."

Dante's grip tightened. "You will call?"

Viper paused before giving a reluctant nod of his head. Dante was almost as stubborn as himself. He would not leave until he had a promise.

"I will call."

Dante stepped back and offered a surprising bow. "Our pledge is made, master." He straightened, a wicked twinkle in the silver eyes. "Be sure and give your demon a kiss for me and Abby."

A flare of warmth swept through Viper's heart. "Oh no, my friend. When I kiss Shay I assure you it will not be for you."

With a laugh, Dante turned and with one great leap he had disappeared through the window. Left on his own Viper poured himself a large measure of brandy and paced the room.

His friend had spoken the truth.

Shay was being pursued by an enemy that might endanger his very existence. The wisdom he had earned over centuries should have him tossing her and her damnable amulet in the nearest river.

What could possibly be worth the risk of death? And, worse, the deaths of his clansmen?

He sipped the warmed brandy knowing that the answer to his questions might be more frightening than any lurking demon.

It was nearly two hours later when Viper slowly climbed the steps that led to the second floor.

It had been two hours of hell as he had tried to distract his thoughts from the beautiful woman who filled the entire house with her sweet scent.

He had tried searching his library for clues as to the demon that had attacked the trolls. He had called his various businesses to ensure there had been no unexpected problems. He had even made a swift inspection of the grounds to speak with his guards and assure himself that all was quiet.

At last he could deny the pounding need within him no longer.

He wanted to see Shay.

To hear her voice and touch her soft skin.

To just be near her.

It was downright pathetic.

Reaching the landing Viper paused as he regarded the small gargoyle curled on the floor next to Shay's door. Obviously the temperamental beast was playing guardian. A thought that might have been humorous if Viper wasn't well aware that love and loyalty counted far more than any amount of strength.

He would rather battle a fierce warrior than a friend protecting his comrade.

Someone willing to die for another made him a dangerous enemy indeed.

Moving forward Viper watched as the gargoyle scrambled to his feet and leaned against the wall in a negligent manner. He might not possess the size of most gargoyles but he had all of their towering pride.

Strolling forward Viper halted directly before Levet. Oddly he didn't feel the expected flare of annoyance at the intrusion of this uninvited guest. Instead he felt something closely akin to respect. Perhaps because he had revealed that Shay's welfare was as important to him as it was to Viper.

"There are any number of fine bedrooms," he murmured. "Most of which I am certain would be more comfortable for a gargoyle than this hallway."

"I will seek a room when dawn arrives. Until then I will remain here."

"Ah. You are on sentry duty?"

His tone was mild but the small, undeniably ugly face hardened with offended pride.

"You believe I cannot protect Shay?"

"On the contrary, I believe you would prove to be a most dangerous adversary. Thankfully, there is no need for your concern this night. My guest is gone and the grounds are secured."

"You remain."

Viper gave a lift of his brows. There were few demons, no matter what their size that would dare confront him directly.

"I am no threat, my small warrior."

"You suggest she is safe in your hands?"

"I paid a great deal of money for Shay." He pointed out in reasonable tones. "I am a good enough businessman not to toss away a near fortune on something I intend to injure."

The gray eyes narrowed. "I asked if she would be safe."

Viper slowly smiled. For all his fussing Levet was male enough to sense the hunger that flowed through Viper's blood.

"She is under my protection. I would never offer her harm, nor allow anyone else to harm her as long as it is within my power to keep her safe."

The gargoyle considered his words a long moment, perhaps pondering whether he could force a more specific promise from Viper. At last he gave a slow nod.

"You would offer your pledge to that?"

His demand caught Viper off guard. "You would accept the pledge of a vampire?"

"I would accept the pledge of a clan chief."

Unconsciously, Viper touched the dragon tattooed across his chest. He had forgotten that gargoyles were so sensitive to demon marks.

"Then you have it."

"Good." The long tail gave a sharp twitch. "Then I shall leave her in your care and find myself something to eat."

"There is ample food in the kitchen."

"Bah." Levet grimaced in disgust. "I have had my fill of human food."

Viper regarded him steadily. "You intend to hunt?"

"Of course. It has been too long."

"I would suggest you remain near the estate until we can determine what is stalking Shay."

The gargoyle shrugged. "It is too close to dawn to go far."

"And no humans or vampires on the menu," Viper warned in stern tones.

The gray eyes widened. "*Sacrebleu.* Do I look like I often eat humans or vampires?"

Viper hid a smile as he glanced down at the tiny demon. "I prefer the rules to be clear."

With a flutter of his pretty wings, Levet turned on his heels and stomped toward the nearby stairs. Muttered curses floated behind him, most of them in French, but clear enough for Viper to realize he was being unflatteringly compared to a jackass.

Ah well.

He gave a shrug as he turned toward the door leading to Shay's rooms. He had been called worse. And probably would be again.

No doubt from the woman awaiting him behind the door.

Shay paced her room for over an hour before she felt comfortable that they weren't under attack. Obviously the waiting vampire had dropped by for a late-night chat, not a late-night snack.

Thank God.

She had had quite enough bloodbaths for one day.

Confident that Viper was properly distracted she had stripped off her clothes and climbed into the shower. She felt an overwhelming need to scrub away the ghastly images of dead trolls.

Shay sighed deeply as the hot water cascaded over her knotted muscles. She sighed even deeper as she discovered the large stash of soaps and oils that lined the glass shelves in the back of the shower.

It had been far too long since she had been able to indulge in such luxury, she acknowledged as she washed her long hair in a flowery scented shampoo.

Too long?

A wry smile touched her lips.

Closer to never.

Lingering until her skin was wrinkled and scrubbed pink, she at last reluctantly wrapped a towel about herself and returned to her bedroom.

She had expected to discover Levet on her bed awaiting her return. He had been oddly reluctant to leave her side since they had arrived at the house.

But what she discovered wasn't Levet.

It wasn't even a gargoyle.

Instead it was a tall, silver-haired, midnight-eyed vampire who made her breath catch in her throat and strange things flutter in the pit of her stomach.

Damn, damn, and double damn.

Clutching the towel tight about her naked body she glared into those sinful eyes.

"What do you want?"

With an elegant motion Viper rose to his feet, his gaze taking a full, blatant inventory of her slender form.

"I thought you might wish to know that my guest has left."

His voice held a smooth darkness that slithered straight down her spine. The flutters beat all the harder.

"Is that all?"

"My housekeeper has left dinner for you in the kitchen."

"Oh . . . thank you." She licked her lips. "I'll go down later."

His gaze once again roamed downward, lingering upon the small swell of her breasts. His smile slowly widened as if he could sense her nipples tighten in response.

Freaking hell.

"Surely you must be hungry?" he drawled softly. "I know you possess a healthy appetite."

With an abrupt motion, she turned her back to him. He might be able to seduce her with a glance, but she didn't have to let him witness his power.

"I can hardly go as I am."

He gave a smoky laugh. "Why not? I assure you I don't mind."

"I do."

"Very well." She heard him walk across the carpet and the sound of a door opening. Just for a moment she thought he had left the room and she struggled to deny the faint flare of disappointment that stabbed through her. Then, without warning, there was a prickling chill that raced over her skin and Viper was standing at her side. "Here."

Turning her head she regarded the crimson silk robe he held in his slender fingers. She frowned as she slowly reached to take the robe, absently rubbing the expensive fabric between her fingers.

"You said you never had guests here."

He waved his hand toward the still open closet that revealed a number of obviously feminine outfits.

"I don't."

"These are yours?" Shay blinked in surprise. "I knew vampires had exotic tastes . . . but I would never have suspected."

"They are for you."

"Me?"

His brows lifted at her blank disbelief. "Did you think I intended to keep you chained naked in a cell?"

"I . . ." She gave a slow shake of her head as she slowly walked to peer into the closet. There were casual jeans and T-shirts, khakis, soft sweaters, and sophisticated gowns that made her mouth water. Never in her life had she possessed so many clothes. And certainly none so expensive. "I didn't expect you to buy me a new wardrobe."

"Hardly a wardrobe. Just a few things to tide you over until you can go shopping for yourself." He paused before giving a small sigh. "Speaking of which, Abby wishes to drag you to the nearest mall to indulge in some female bonding."

Still reeling from the thought that Viper would have gone to such trouble for her she turned to regard him with uncertainty.

"Abby?"

"You met her while we battled the witches."

Shay's confusion only deepened. "You mean the Phoenix?"

"I believe she prefers Abby."

She reached out to touch the edge of the closet door. Her knees felt oddly weak as she struggled to make sense of Viper's words.

"But . . . why? Why would she even remember me?"

He shrugged. "You did help her defeat the witches."

"I did nothing."

"You resisted the witches command to capture her, and instead allowed yourself to be beaten nearly to death for your refusal to assist them. You also stood at her side as she fought Edra." His expression was somber. "She has not forgotten. Neither has Dante."

It was all true enough. She had done what she could to thwart the witches in their bid to use the Phoenix as a tool to kill demons.

Still, she couldn't imagine why the woman would request her presence. Certainly not to go shopping of all things.

"That hardly makes us friends," she muttered.

He smiled wryly. "Tell that to Abby. She seems to think a near-death experience gives her the right to not only call you friend, but to ensure that you are not being horribly mistreated beneath my roof."

Clutching the forgotten robe in her hand Shay moved to perch on the edge of the bed. There was something squeezing deep within her.

Something that felt very much like fear.

"Does she know what I am?" she whispered, her gaze trained on the thick carpet at her feet.

She sensed more than heard him cautiously move to stand close to her. She kept her gaze downward. She didn't want him to see her face. Not when she couldn't control her expression.

"What you are?" he demanded.

"Does she know that I'm a demon?"

He hesitated, as if choosing his words with care. "She is aware you have the blood of a Shalott in you."

"And she wants me to go . . . shopping with her?"

"Only if it's what you want. I'm sure she would be willing to alter her plans if there is something you would rather do." He was suddenly sitting at her side, close but carefully not touching her. "What is it, Shay? Have I said something to upset you?"

"I don't know what she wants with me. I'm a demon."

He gave a soft laugh. "Abby is not precisely human herself anymore."

"No, she is a goddess."

"A goddess, perhaps, but she's also the woman who battled the witches to save all demons and is now mated to a vampire. She has no prejudice against us if that is what you fear."

Was that what she feared?

Shay hunched her shoulders. The truth was she didn't trust this Abby. Not when she offered something so rare as friendship. Her experience had taught her that such offers always came with a cost. Usually one she didn't want to pay.

Feeling the heavy weight of Viper's gaze she at last heaved a sigh.

"I've never had anyone ask me to go shopping before."

"Ah." She felt him shift to reach around her. She stiffened as she thought he meant to draw her into his arms. No way. She didn't want his pity. Not when she was so vulnerable that she might actually break down and cry.

How embarrassing would that be?

He made no effort to touch her, however, and instead he reached to grab the brush that had been left on the nightstand beside the bed. Only when she warily relaxed did he settle himself so he could begin running the brush through the waist-length tangle of her hair.

"You said your mother raised you as a human?"

The warning voice in the back of her head told her to move away. The feel of his soft, soothing touch was far too intimate, far too pleasurable.

Unfortunately, her mind was no longer attached to her body.

"That was long ago," she muttered.

"Did you pass?"

Shay grimaced. There were those demons who could pass, which simply meant being able to move among the human world without detection. Many of them without a drop of mortal blood.

The saints knew that she had tried hard enough. She would have done anything to please her mother. Anything to belong.

"No."

The long brush strokes never hesitated. "You look human enough."

Shay found her lashes resting on her cheeks. She never spoke of her past. Not to anyone. But with the peaceful silence surrounding them, and the tender stroke of the brush she found the words tumbling past her lips before she could halt them.

"But I don't age as a mortal. My mother was forced to move us from place to place to make sure no one noticed that I was not growing older as I should be." The memory of her mother sent a shaft of loss ripping through her heart.

"A difficulty, for certain, but not insurmountable."

"Perhaps not, but my strength and swiftness were. There is nothing human about them."

He lifted another section of hair to pull the brush through. "The other children were afraid of you?"

"Yes."

"They can be very cruel."

Shay clenched her hands in her lap. "Not as cruel as their parents. Over the years we had our houses burned, stones thrown at us, and priests trying to exorcise the devil from me. I was even lynched one night."

"Lynched?"

"A gang of half-wits hauled me from my bed and hung me by my neck from a tree in our backyard. You can't imagine their surprise when I came looking for them the next morning."

There was a long silence, as if Viper were brooding upon her soft words. His touch remained gentle, but Shay could sense a building frustration that smoldered about him.

Strange.

"Why didn't your mother seek out help from the demons?" he at last demanded.

She turned her head, ignoring the tug on her hair as the strands remained firmly held in his hands. "My father had already been murdered by a vampire. She was trying to keep me hidden from demons."

His eyes darkened, as if he didn't want to be reminded she had every reason to hate vampires.

"There are demons that would have given you sanctuary. Not all are vicious animals."

"My mother was human. She didn't know who she could trust." Without warning her eyes filled with tears. "And neither did I."

The brush abruptly dropped from his hands as he cupped her face in his hands.

"Shay."

Chapter Eight

Shay forgot how to breathe as she watched Viper lower his head.

He moved slowly. Slowly enough that she realized he was giving her ample opportunity to say no. For a heartbeat she stiffened and he hovered over her lips, not touching as he waited for her to push him away.

But while her mind was desperately attempting to remind her that this was a vampire touching her with such care, a vampire who owned her as if she were a piece of property, her body remained stubbornly indifferent to common sense.

She needed his touch. No, she craved his touch.

The taste of his lips. The press of his skin to her own. The caress of his hands on her breasts.

She had never understood how a woman could allow herself to be seduced. Either you decided you wanted to have sex with someone, or you didn't.

In this moment, however, she understood the power of simple lust. The stark need to touch and be touched, no matter how many warnings your mind might whisper.

"You must tell me yes, pet," he murmured softly. "I will not be accused of breaking my promise. You must tell me you want this."

His voice should have jerked her back to awareness. Back

to some tiny bit of sense. Instead it poured through her like a fine whiskey.

And just as intoxicating.

"Yes."

He caught the word before it ever left her lips, imprisoning her mouth in a kiss that sent a shock of heat flowing through her blood. She was prepared for pleasure, but the sheer power of it caught her off guard.

Oh, yes, this was precisely what she needed. What her body had ached for since she had first caught sight of Viper all those weeks ago.

She arched forward, drinking of the brandy that clung to his lips, and the cool maleness that was uniquely Viper. Still, she was not close enough. Her hands lifted to his chest, smoothing over the silk of his shirt.

He growled deep in his throat as he reached down to grasp his shirt and with one tug had ripped off the buttons to spread the silk wide.

"Touch me, pet," he whispered against her lips. "Let me feel your hands on me."

Shay moved back. Not in rejection, but quite simply because she wanted to see what she was touching. She had imagined what lay hidden beneath those velvet coats and silk shirts a hundred times. Now she wanted to fully appreciate the sight.

Her eyes widened and her lips parted in a silent sigh.

In the dim light his chest was broad and just as finely muscled as she had dreamed. But her dreams hadn't included the exotic dragon that had been tattooed across the ivory perfection of his skin.

In amazement she traced the golden outline of the mythical creature before brushing over the brilliant crimson wings and dark jade body.

"What is this?" she breathed.

He shuddered beneath her gentle touch, his head lowering to sweep his lips over her cheek.

"It is the mark of CuChulainn."

"Oh." Shay found it growing difficult to think as he kissed his way to the curve of her ear. "Did it hurt?"

"The tattoo?"

"Yes."

His hands trailed up her bare arms sending a rash of excitement shivering over her skin.

"No. I didn't even feel it." He gave a small nip at the lobe of her ear. "It simply appeared after my last battle in the arena."

"It marked you as a clan chief?"

"Yes."

"I . . ."

Whatever she was about to say was lost in a haze of pleasure as his tongue ran a damp path down the line of her jaw.

"What?" he whispered.

"I don't remember."

He gave a soft chuckle as his hands drifted over her shoulders and then determinedly moved downward, pausing at the edge of her towel.

"I need to see you, pet," he murmured as he pressed his lips to the frantic pulse at the base of her neck. "I need to touch you. Say yes."

Shay shuddered as a building pressure settled in the pit of her stomach. She found it oddly erotic to be so firmly in charge of the seduction. It gave her a sense of power that she had rarely experienced. For once she was the one in control and it was as heady as the rarest aphrodisiac.

"Yes."

His fingers briefly tightened, as if he was caught off guard by her ready capitulation, and then with a slow motion he was pulling open the ends of the towel.

She shivered as the cool air hit her skin, the faintest hint of embarrassment touching her cheeks. A thick silence filled the air and at last she lifted her gaze. Any chill was seared away by the smoldering heat that filled his midnight eyes.

"By the blood of the saints," he rasped, tossing the towel aside so his fingers could boldly cup the small firmness of her breasts. "You are . . . perfect."

Shay's head tilted back at the sensation of his thumbs stroking over the hard points of her nipples. She wasn't perfect. She was far from perfect. Too skinny. Her skin too bronzed. Her breasts too small.

But in this moment she felt beautiful.

Beneath his predatory gaze she felt desired.

Growling deep in his throat Viper hauled her against the strength of his chest, his lips kissing a hungry path down her throat to her collarbone. He pressed hard enough for Shay to feel the sharpness of his fangs, but she made no effort to pull away.

In this moment she trusted him.

Trusted that he would not demand more of her than she was willing to offer.

Running her hands over his chest in a restless path she reveled in the satin smoothness of his skin. It was a fascinating contrast to the hardness of the muscles beneath. Like velvet draped over steel.

Intrigued with exploring his body, Shay barely noticed when Viper gently tugged her back onto the soft mattress and pressed her onto her back. Not until he bent over her to capture a nipple between his lips.

She cried out as his tongue swirled over the sensitized tip, teasing it until her back was arched in delight. Freaking hell. It felt so good. So terrifyingly good.

"Dear goddess," she moaned, shivering as his lips traced the curve between the mounds of her breasts before moving to torment her neglected nipple.

Her fingers impatiently tugged at the clasp holding back his hair, allowing the heavy curtain to spill over her in a fragrant cloud. The satin strands brushed her skin, heightening the heat that poured through her blood.

Breathe, Shay, breathe, she fiercely reminded herself, as his hands outlined the curve of her hips and down her thighs. His touch was cool, but she was melting beneath the heat flowing through her veins.

Tugging at her nipple with the edge of his teeth Viper

eased his hand between her legs and sought the moist heat between them.

Her hands shifted to his shoulders, her fingers unwittingly digging into his flesh as his finger stroked over the sweet spot of her pleasure. She was falling into a whirlpool of sensations that were almost overwhelming.

"Viper."

Easily sensing the faint edge of panic in her voice Viper lifted his head to nuzzle his lips just below her ear.

"Sssh . . . pet," he softly soothed. "I will not hurt you."

"I'm not afraid of being hurt," she rasped.

"Then what do you fear?"

She shivered as her hips instinctively lifted to press more firmly to his caressing finger.

"I don't know."

He lifted onto his elbow and peered deep into her wide eyes. "Trust me, Shay."

For a long moment she merely gazed into his beautiful face. With his silver hair tumbled over his shoulders and the muted light playing over his elegant features he looked like a decadent angel who had fallen from heaven.

Don't do it, Shay, a warning voice whispered in the back of her mind. *You can't trust a vampire. Not ever.*

Her lips parted, but *no* was not what tumbled from her lips. Instead her lashes floated downward and her arms encircled his neck in a tight grip.

"Yes."

His mouth covered hers as his hand shifted and his finger pierced her. He swallowed her cry of pleasure as her hips left the mattress and she nearly strangled him with her arms.

He was not her first lover, but nothing could have prepared her for this. Not for the smooth expertise of his talented fingers or the demanding pressure of his mouth.

She was burning from within and she couldn't make herself care. For this one fragile moment she wanted to be consumed. She wanted to be held in the arms of a man and feel what a woman was supposed to feel.

Thrusting his tongue between her willing lips Viper stroked her with an increasing intensity. Shay clutched at him as the building pressure deep inside arched her back.

She was close. So very close.

"Viper."

"I know, pet," he muttered against her mouth, his body pressing against her side until she could feel the hard thrust of his erection against her hip. "Don't fight it."

Her breath came in short gasps as the pleasure tightened and narrowed to one shimmering point. His finger pressed deep within her and at the same moment his thumb caressed over that hub of pleasure and the pressure hit a critical point.

Her entire body tightened and hovered a breathless moment out of time. And then with the force of a small explosion the bliss shattered through her and she was trembling from the un- expected force.

They lay in stunned silence for a long moment, Viper's still hard body pressed against her own. Shay felt as if she were floating. As if she had been tossed into a sea of warm water and been left to gently drift to the shore.

At her side Viper shifted to cradle her face as if she were some fragile treasure he feared to break, his lips brushing soft kisses over her cheek.

Unable to move Shay at last managed to suck in a deep breath as she gathered her shaken thoughts.

"Oh . . . freaking . . . hell . . ."

Viper didn't know why he was smiling as he watched Shay seated across the table from him.

No man in his right mind would be smiling when his body was hard and aching. And when he was facing the distinct pos- sibility his frustrated need was going to be an unwelcome com- panion. At least for the next few hours, perhaps even days.

But even with his body in rigid protest he couldn't halt the smile curving his lips. Perhaps it was the sight of Shay's slen- der form so lovingly caressed by the crimson silk of her robe.

With her raven hair tumbling down her back and bronzed skin glowing against the rich material, she looked like an exotic butterfly.

Or maybe it was the amusement at the three bowls of beef stew she had managed to consume in less time than it took for him to drain his bottle of blood.

Or maybe it was the knowledge that for all of his aching frustration he had managed to breech a wall that she had surrounded about herself. She might have scuttled back behind her defenses, but he now knew that she was not invulnerable.

He had found her weakness and he wasn't about to hesitate in using it to claim her as his own.

His.

An unnerving flare of possessive satisfaction raced through him even as he wondered what the hell was the matter with him.

Devil's balls. He had clearly lost his mind, and he didn't have enough sense left to care.

Glancing up from her now empty bowl of soup Shay sent him a wary frown. "I wish you would quit doing that."

"Doing what?"

"Watching me like I'm dinner."

Viper leaned back in his seat, his gaze traveling over the length of her crimson gown.

"I wouldn't mind a bite or two."

She abruptly stilled, no doubt sensing the hunger that pulsed through his body. A hunger he no longer attempted to disguise.

"We have a bargain. No recreational blood."

"I wasn't thinking about blood."

A swift heat touched her cheeks. Viper's smile widened with a hint of male smugness. She couldn't entirely pretend to forget she had shivered her climax in his arms.

"It's almost dawn, shouldn't you be in your coffin?" she demanded.

He gave a laugh. "It has been several centuries since I was bound to the night. Although I cannot bear the sunlight, I am capable of remaining awake when I choose."

"How old are you?"

"Surely you must know that vampires rarely reveal their age?" he demanded with a lift of his brows. "It is nearly as well guarded a secret as his lair."

She shrugged as she pushed aside her empty bowl. "I've never understood why. When you're immortal it hardly matters how old you are."

"A vampire's power grows with each passing year. To know his age is to know his power."

"So the older you are the more powerful?"

Viper shrugged. He supposed he shouldn't be overly surprised with her lack of knowledge regarding vampires. Her mother had obviously attempted to keep her isolated from the world of demons.

"In theory, although we are like any other race. There will always be those who possess more strength, or even more intelligence than others, regardless of their age."

Her tongue peeked out to touch her lips. Viper swallowed a groan. He could think of several intimate places he would like that tongue to explore.

"Vampires like you?"

Viper struggled to smother the renegade images. He was suffering enough without adding to his misery.

"Yes, vampires like me."

Her features were carefully expressionless. "And that's why you're a clan chief?"

He measured his words. He sensed that any boast of overwhelming power was not going to impress this woman. Not when she was for all practical purposes completely in his control.

"In part."

"What's the other part?"

He smiled blandly. "My charming personality?"

She rolled her eyes. "Not freaking likely."

He regarded her for a long moment. "Shalotts are quite similar to vampires. Do they not choose their leader with a trial by combat?"

"I don't have the least idea." Her voice was casual, but there was a tightness to her expression that Viper didn't miss. "For all I know they pluck them out of thin air."

"Surely your parents must have told you something of your heritage?"

"I was raised as a human. My mother thought the less I was . . . exposed to the demon world the better. After my father's death I wasn't even allowed to mention the word Shalott."

Viper frowned. It was little wonder the poor woman considered herself a mongrel. Her mother had made certain of that.

"A rather narrow-minded view."

She bristled at the implied criticism. "She wanted to protect me."

"Understandable, but to deny you the history of your people was to deny you a part of yourself. Surely you must have possessed some curiosity?"

"Why should I? Having demon blood has caused me nothing but grief."

"The Shalotts are a proud and much respected race," he insisted. "Before following the dark prince in his departure from this world, they were known as the most feared assassins among demons. Even vampires feared their skills."

"That's hardly something I take comfort in."

Viper bit back his impatience. "You think humans are superior? They have a reputation for violence and wars, not to mention outright genocide on occasion. At least Shalotts never kill their own. It is their most sacred law."

A hint of grudging curiosity glinted in her eyes. "Never?"

"Never." He held her gaze. "They believe that to shed the blood of another Shalott is to condemn themselves and all of their family to the fury of their gods. It is a sin that cannot be redeemed. I could only wish vampires possessed the same belief."

Her gaze dropped as she absently toyed with her glass of wine. "Have you known many Shalotts?"

"A few. And before you ask, I did not drain them, enslave them, nor were any of them my lovers."

"Don't tell me they were some sort of demon buddies?" she demanded in disbelief.

His fangs snapped together. If she were deliberately attempting to goad him, she was doing a hell of a job.

Of course, it was more likely that her jabs were self-preservation. If she pretended she didn't care, then nothing could hurt her.

"I happen to have many demons as friends, but the Shalotts were more . . . associates. A clan chief has many enemies."

Her gaze abruptly lifted. "You hired them as assassins?"

"Actually I hired them to train me," he clarified.

"Train you for what?"

"Most Shalott's are thoroughly skilled in the arts of combat and, more importantly, possess intimate knowledge of weapons." He gave a lift of his brows. "Surely your father did?"

The pride she could not completely hide flickered over her face. "Of course."

Viper hid his sudden smile. He wasn't entirely stupid.

"And you?"

"I have some experience with swords and daggers, but my father died before I could be fully trained," she confessed in cautious tones. No doubt she worried she was handing information to the enemy.

"Well, I cannot possibly claim the talent of your father, but if you would like we could train together."

Silence.

The sort of thick silence that assured him that Shay was trying to decide if he were scheming some horrid plot, or simply out of his mind.

Maybe when she figured it out she would tell him.

"Train together?" she repeated with a frown. "Are you joking?"

He shrugged. "Why not? I haven't had a decent sparring partner in years."

"Most owners aren't anxious to teach their slaves how to kill them," she said dryly.

"Do you intend to kill me?"

"It's not a decision I've made one way or another."

He gave a short, startled laugh. "You'll let me know when you do decide?"

"Perhaps."

"Not quite the reassurance I hoped for," he murmured, his gaze brushing over her beautiful features. Now this was a sparring partner that a vampire could truly sink his teeth into. "Well?"

"Well what?"

He reached out to touch her fingers. "Do you wish to train with me?"

She studied him with a guarded expression, but before she could answer the peaceful night was abruptly shattered.

In the distance an unmistakable bay echoed through the air.

They both froze. It could have been a coyote or even a stray dog howling at the fading night, but they both knew it wasn't. No mere animal could make the air shudder in fear.

"Hellhounds," she whispered.

Viper was on his feet and reaching out with his mind to his servants.

"The guards are under attack."

"Why would hellhounds attack your guards? They are no match for vampires."

He gave a sharp shake of his head, distantly sensing the battle occurring near the gates to his estate. At the moment Santiago and his crew were holding their own, but there were far too many hellhounds to kill at once. They were taking wounds that would need the healing of deep earth.

"I don't know." Reaching out he tugged her to her feet. "Come."

Of course she couldn't simply follow his lead. Digging in her feet she regarded him with a worried gaze. "Where are we going?"

"There are tunnels in the basement. They will take us to the garage."

"Surely we are safer here than the garage?"

"There are cars in the garage."

Her eyes widened. "No."

Viper heaved an exasperated sigh. "What is it?"

"For God's sake, Viper, it is almost dawn," she gritted, as if he were almost too stupid to bear. "You can't be traveling around in a car."

"I cannot travel, but you can."

"You want me to leave?" She flashed him a fierce frown. "Alone?"

"I will stay here and make sure that you aren't followed."

"No. We both stay and fight."

It wasn't often that Viper found himself caught off guard. It was difficult to surprise a centuries-old vampire. But he couldn't deny a sense of astonishment.

"Shay, this isn't the time to argue." He regarded her with a stern command. "The hellhounds might not be much of a threat, but I seriously doubt that they are out there alone. Something wants you. They want you bad enough to risk a direct attack. You have to leave now."

Without warning she moved to stand directly before him, her hands on her hips.

"And what if that's what they want?"

He frowned. "What do you mean?"

"What if the hellhounds are only a diversion to make me flee here without you? Whatever is out there might be waiting for me once we're separated."

Viper growled deep in his throat. She was right. The demons might very well be attempting to separate them.

"Dammit to hell. That would explain why they attacked so close to dawn."

"And why they sent the hellhounds first."

"Yes."

He shoved his hands impatiently through his hair. It was not that he feared a fight. Hell, it had been far too long since he had enjoyed a rousing battle. But for the first time in his long life he possessed someone besides himself to worry about.

It was an unnerving sensation.

And one that he wasn't quite certain how to deal with.

Glancing about the room Shay abruptly held a hand to her heart. "Where is Levet?"

"Hunting." Viper gave a distracted shrug. "After the arrival of the hellhounds he is no doubt halfway to Chicago by now."

"Or doing something totally stupid," she muttered as she spun on her heel and headed toward the back door.

It took Viper a beat to realize she actually intended to go out and find the gargoyle. With a blur of speed he was blocking her path, regarding her with disbelief.

She could try the patience of a saint. A mere vampire didn't have a shot in hell.

"You can't go out there," he rasped.

A dangerous spark flared to life in the golden eyes. "Viper—"

"No. The demons have no interest in Levet. He is far safer than you are at this moment."

"We don't know that for sure." Her jaw stuck out in warning. "He's my friend and I won't leave him out there to die."

Viper briefly savored the image of tossing the aggravating woman over his shoulder and being done with it. Oh, she wouldn't go quietly. She was half Shalott and she would put up a furious fight. But he felt certain that in the end he could force her to his will. Unfortunately, such a simple solution was bound to create far more difficulties than it would solve. She was only half Shalott, but she was all woman.

Cursing himself for a fool he gave an impatient shake of his head. "Go to the basement. I will retrieve your missing gargoyle."

As if waiting for the perfect cue, the door was thrust open and the tiny gargoyle waddled into the kitchen.

"There will be no need for heroics, vampire," he drawled. "I am here."

Viper frowned. "What of the hellhounds?"

Levet didn't even attempt to hide his shudder of distaste. "They have been driven off for now, but I do not doubt they will be back."

There was a movement behind the gargoyle and Viper locked gazes with the vampires that had been standing guard.

He growled deep in his throat at the sight of the blood that covered their clothing and the wounds that marred their faces.

He was clan chief. Whoever had sent the hellhounds would soon regret their fatal decision.

"Santiago, gather the other guards and take them to your lair."

The tall vampire stiffened at the command. "We will not leave you."

Viper gave a shake of his head. His guards were still young and bound closely to the night. Once the sun rose they would be unable to protect themselves.

"You are wounded and it is too close to dawn. There is nothing you can do."

Frustration shimmered through the air as the guards were forced to accept the truth of his words.

"Your human servants will soon arrive," Santiago at last muttered.

"They are no match for the demon who hunts us. We must attempt to evade him if we can." Viper laid a hand on Santiago's shoulder. "You must take care of the others, my friend. Now go."

Trapped by Viper's demand to protect the lesser vampires Santiago had little choice but to offer a grudging bow.

"As you command."

He waited until they melted into the darkness, headed for the secret lair that Santiago had built when Viper had brought him here to guard the estate. They would be safe and covered by the healing earth. Which was more than he could say, he wryly acknowledged as the distant baying echoed eerily through the air.

He turned to meet Shay's troubled gaze. "The hellhounds return. We must go."

Chapter Nine

On this occasion Shay didn't protest when Viper grasped her hand and tugged her across the kitchen and through a narrow door that led to the basement.

A small miracle, but at the moment she was far more concerned with whatever was creeping closer to the house than asserting her independence.

With Levet clinging to the back of her robe, they moved in swift silence. She could vaguely make out the dark, secluded bedrooms they passed. No doubt spare bedrooms in the event Viper decided to have a sleepover.

Viper would have a room for himself, but it would not be his lair. At least not his hidden lair.

To prove her point the vampire halted before the paneling at the end of the hall. With a movement of his hand and a whispered word the paneling opened to reveal steps leading farther down into the ground.

"Through here," he whispered, waiting for them to pass so he could close the paneling behind them.

Shay could sense the curses that bound the door. They were powerful, but they wouldn't provide protection from the demon that hunted her. Not if it were truly determined to follow her.

The smell of warm, rich earth surrounded Shay as she cautiously moved down the flight of steps and entered what she assumed was Viper's lair. Once on solid ground she was forced to pause as complete darkness folded around her. Unlike Viper she didn't possess the ability to see through the murky black.

Perhaps sensing her troubles there was a sound in the dark and then the faint bloom of light as Viper held a taper to the tall, silver candelabra.

Shay's eyes slowly adjusted as her breath caught in her throat.

"Holy crap," she breathed, her gaze traveling around the vast cavern that surrounded her. She had never seen so many weapons in one place. Long swords, short swords, daggers, ninja weapons, bows and arrows, handguns, and ancient armor were all carefully stored behind glass cases. There was even a case where she could feel the power of magically blessed weapons. "Where did these come from?"

Taking a key Viper unlocked a case to retrieve an elegant sword that he strapped to his back. He handed a dagger to the oddly silent Levet, and a sword to Shay who held it with the confidence of a woman accustomed to wielding such a weapon.

"It is part of my collection," he answered as he moved to another case and chose a small handgun that he loaded with swift ease.

Moving to stand beside him Shay shot him a glance of disbelief. "Part? Are you intending to invade Canada?"

The midnight gaze lifted to reveal a faint hint of amusement. Shay's breath disappeared at the sheer beauty of his face in the candlelight. It was almost indecent that a man should possess the face of an angel.

The eyes darkened as he felt the fine tremor that ran through her body.

"It's not on the agenda," he huffed, moving to stand far too close. "At least not for today."

There was a disgusted hiss from behind them as Levet gave a vicious tug on Shay's robe.

"I hate to interrupt such a touching scene but those hellhounds are not going to wait for you two to play kissey face. So, unless you intend to nail a chunk of roast beef to my butt and have me run around as a distraction, I would suggest we prepare for battle."

The glare that Viper shot at the small gargoyle should have made Levet turn to stone, but he stepped back from Shay and waved them both toward the back of the room.

"They shouldn't have been capable of breeching my defenses," he muttered. "There is something with them."

Levet gave a small flutter of his wings. "Something bad."

Shay sensed it as well. A dark, creeping dread that filled the air and made it difficult to breathe. It was not yet at the door, but it was close enough to make a shiver inch down her spine.

Close enough to know that she didn't want it any closer.

She didn't want it at all.

Holding the sword in her hand she bent her knees and widened her stance. The robe had parted to reveal the long line of her legs but she barely even noticed.

Modesty was the least of her concerns at this point.

The howling of the hellhounds echoed through the air and she braced herself as they threw themselves at the door. There was a thick thud and then the sickening sound of frenzied eating as the hounds devoured one of their own that had obviously been injured.

The sound of Levet's breathing rasped beside her, but Viper was motionless. Absolutely still. Awaiting death.

Shay wasn't certain if the sight of him was comforting or terrifying.

And in truth it didn't matter as the howls returned and the door shuddered beneath the fresh assault. Wood splintered, cracked, and at last shattered beneath the writhing tide of hellhounds.

There was a moment to prepare as the beasts tried to charge in as a group and became lodged in the narrow opening. For a moment there was nothing but a black knot and the sound of howling fury. Then the dam broke and the demons poured through the doorway with deadly intent.

Bracing herself, Shay watched the first charging hellhound leap in her direction. They were fearsome creatures that stood as large as a pony with crimson eyes and fangs that dripped a corrosive acid. Thankfully, they were nearly as stupid as they were vicious and there was no strategy, no attempt to attack with a cohesive plan as they swarmed through the room.

Holding the sword in two hands she waited for the first demon to impale itself on her weapon. Teeth snapped at her face and hot blood ran down her arms as she smoothly turned and used the beast's own weight to fling it off her sword.

The dead hellhound landed in the middle of the pack and was immediately ripped apart by the rabid animals, but Shay had only a glimpse of the ghastly feeding as she continued to spin. She dipped the sword, down and then up to take off the head of the nearest hound.

Blood and the stench of dying hellhounds filled the air as Shay danced with deadly intent through the swarming mass. It had been years since she had been thrown into a full-fledged fight, but she had practiced her skills every day as she had sworn an oath to her father to do, and she found the sword moving with fluid ease through the attackers.

In the distance she was aware of Levet's grunts and fluent curses as he used his dagger to keep the demons at bay, and the swift precision as Viper waded through the room to leave behind a trail of dying hounds. Her concentration, however, had narrowed to the closest demons who charged without fear or hesitation.

She used short, controlled swings of her sword, managing to keep the beasts from her with the force of her kicks and the deadly blade.

The end came without warning.

One moment she was slicing through the throat of a hound and the next a thick silence filled the lair.

With a sigh, Shay leaned against the wall. She had a bite on the back of her calf and a deep scratch down her arm but she had survived. Never a bad thing.

Her gaze moved to ensure that Levet was still standing before moving on to the tall vampire who was calmly cleaning his sword.

Across the floor the dead and dying demons were beginning to decay to a layer of gray ash. Even the blood on Shay's arms was flaking to drift through the air.

Sliding the long sword in the sheath that was strapped to his back Viper moved to stand before her.

"Are you harmed?" he demanded.

She swallowed a weary laugh. She looked like she had been rolled through a dust pile and he stood there without a damn hair out of place.

"Nothing that won't heal," she muttered, frowning as he knelt down to examine the wound on her leg. His cool fingers sent a flash of heat through her body as they brushed over her skin. She gritted her teeth as she glared down at the gleam of his silver hair. "I'm fine."

He glanced up, his expression unreadable. "Do you heal like a human or a Shalott?"

"I don't know about Shalotts, but I heal far faster than humans."

"Are you immune to infections?"

"Yes."

He returned his attention to the wound that had already stopped bleeding and was beginning to close over. Her inhuman strength wasn't the only reason she had been called a freak over the years. With a faint nod, he rose to his feet.

"Can you sense the demon approaching?"

Shay shivered. "Yes."

"Is it the same demon that attempted to steal you the night of the auction?"

She forced herself to concentrate. A task that would have been a lot easier if Viper had the decency to move to the other side of the room. The cool wash of his power was a distraction that she didn't need.

Sucking in a deep breath she closed her eyes and reluctantly opened herself to the approaching demon. It had taken her years to learn how to put aside her human logic and trust in the delicate senses of her demon blood. She might not understand how she could reach out and feel the essence of another, but she no longer questioned it.

It took a long moment but at last she gave a small shake of her head. There was a sense of cold, looming danger, but it wasn't the same.

"It's not the same demon."

"I don't know whether to be relieved or disappointed." Viper gave a shake of his head before holding out his hand. "Come, we need to get out of here."

Shay widened her gaze. "Wouldn't it be safer to stay?"

"We'd be trapped."

"At least we have weapons," she pointed out.

He shrugged. "We need someplace we can run if things go to hell."

"*If* they go to hell?" she choked in disbelief.

A faint smile curved his lips before he bent down to place a kiss just beneath her ear.

"The fun has just started, pet," he whispered.

Collecting a pair of daggers that he fit into his boots and a small amulet hung on a leather thong Viper led Shay and the gargoyle from the armory.

The hellhounds were dead but that hovering demon remained a distant threat that could not be ignored. He didn't want to be cornered with no means of escape when it finally attacked. Not when he couldn't be entirely confident he was capable of besting the stalking demon.

Choosing a narrow tunnel that led away from the house he moved with a silent urgency that had Shay muttering beneath her breath and the tiny gargoyle stumbling to keep up. He ignored their complaints as he flowed through the darkness and at last came to the stairs he sought.

"This way," he commanded, standing aside so Shay and the gargoyle could pass.

Both halted to regard him with suspicion. He should have

known it would be too much to hope they could simply do as he requested without a prolonged argument.

"Where does this lead?" Shay demanded.

"To a chamber beneath the garage. We will attempt to hold off the demon from there, but if we fail it will give you the opportunity to flee."

Her expression hardened. "You think that I'll leave you . . . I mean, leave Levet to fight off a demon that is obviously after me?"

"We have no choice." Viper reached out to grasp her arm. "Neither the gargoyle nor I can leave these tunnels, not until night has fallen. We can only give you time to escape."

Levet heaved a rasping sigh. "He's right, Shay. You have to go."

"Forget it. I . . ." Shay's words came to a halt as the sound of rumbling came from behind them. "Shit."

"The time to argue is over."

Keeping his grip on Shay's arm he forced her up the steps into the small chamber. Once at the narrow ladder he reached into his pocket to retrieve the small amulet and placed it around her neck.

She glanced down in confusion. "What is that?"

"The amulet holds a spell that will mask your presence from the demon."

A strange expression rippled over her pale face. "Magic?"

"So I have been assured," he muttered. "Forgive me."

"What?" Shay gave a small squeak of pain as he reached up to tug several strands of her hair from her head. "What the hell was that for?"

Viper tucked the hair into his pocket. "At least some scent of you must remain here or the demon will become suspicious. Now you must go."

Expecting another argument Viper was startled when she gave a sharp nod of her head. "Yes."

"Wait until Levet and I have left the chamber before you climb the ladder and push open the trapdoor. The keys to the cars are hung on the wall. Just take one and go as far from here as you can."

"Okay."

Viper didn't trust this sudden compliance. Shay was precisely the sort of woman to insist on going down with the ship. A Joan of Arc just waiting to happen. For God's sake, he had been preparing to physically throw her from the tunnels.

Framing her face with his hands he glared into her wide eyes. "I will have your word that you will leave, Shay."

Annoyance flashed in the golden eyes, but astonishingly she gave a nod of her head. "I will leave."

"Your word?"

"My word."

He gave a growl low in his throat. He didn't doubt her pledge, but he couldn't shake the certainty that she was planning something ridiculously dangerous.

Unfortunately, any lecture he might have given her on foolish bravado was forced from his mind at the sound of cracking timbers and shattering earth.

The demon had lost patience and was forcing his huge bulk through the tunnels.

Devil's balls.

Without hesitation Viper bent his head and pressed a brief, hungry kiss to her lips. "Go, Shay," he whispered softly, and then giving her a gentle push toward the nearby ladder, he headed for the door.

Once again he braced himself for some protest, but with a smooth motion Shay had turned and was sprinting across the room. Viper hurried to leave the chamber and shut the door behind him. He could feel the heavy pressure of dawn already filling the sky. He had no desire to greet it up close and personal.

Back in the tunnel he moved to stand beside an obviously nervous Levet.

"Did she go?" the gargoyle muttered.

"Yes."

"She did?" Levet gave a startled blink. "You didn't hurt her, did you?"

"For once it was not necessary." Viper pulled his sword from its sheath as he prepared for the demon crashing through the tunnel. "She went quite eagerly."

"*Sacrebleu*. It can only mean she is plotting something stupid."

"No doubt," Viper agreed with a grimace. "For the moment, however, she is out of danger. We can only hope to disable the demon before she decides to return."

"Disable the demon, he says," Levet muttered beneath his breath, holding his dagger with an awkward hand. "More likely we are about to become an early morning snack."

Viper smiled with grim anticipation. "Not without a fight, my friend. The demon will discover that vampire meat is not so easy to come by."

The gargoyle gave an aggravated twitch of his tail, but thankfully he held his tongue as a glow began to fill the air and the looming demon thrust into view.

Viper clenched his teeth at the sight of the narrow, scaled head with its long snout and mouthful of razor teeth. Many would confuse the demon with a small dragon, but Viper knew the difference. It was the long-forgotten Lu. A creature feared throughout the demon world. One that was nearly impossible to defeat without magic. And he was fresh out of magic.

"Shit," he breathed.

"Shit, indeed," Levet said at his side. "Now what?"

"Do you possess any spells?"

Levet gave a disgusted snort. "Do you think if I possessed any spells I would still be here? I am not nearly so fond of you, vampire, as to gladly die at your side."

"I thought all gargoyles could use some magic," Viper muttered as he edged to the side and prepared for an attack.

"Oh sure, mock me as I'm about to die," Levet groused.

"You are not about to die, Levet. We are both immortals."

"Fah. We both know that even immortals can die. Usually in horrible ways."

Well, Viper could hardly argue. It was true enough.

"If you prefer, I could simply toss you to the demon and hope he would make your death a swift affair."

Whatever French curses hovered on Levet's lips were drowned out by the hissing rumble of the Lu.

Although the body of the demon was too large to slide through the tunnel without an effort, the serpentine neck allowed the black-scaled head to swing disturbingly close.

"I smell the Shalott." A forked tongue tasted the air. "Where have you hidden her?"

Viper's expression remained impassive as he concealed his relief that the Lu hadn't yet realized his quarry had escaped. There was nothing like centuries of practice to perfect the poker face.

"She is near enough, but I fear she is not overly anxious to meet with you," he drawled. "It seems that the charms of the elusive Lu are highly overrated."

The crimson eyes flashed with fury. Lu's had never been known for their sense of humor.

"You mock me at your peril, vampire."

Viper shifted closer to the wall. The faint, iridescent glow from the demon's scales would become blinding during a battle. He wanted to be in a position to be able to watch that deadly mouth when worst came to worst.

"I doubt my peril has anything to do with whether I mock you or not." He firmly kept the demon's attention on himself and away from the cowering Levet. "You're not here for my sparkling personality."

"True enough." At least the demon didn't try to deny his murderous intent. "Still I am not unreasonable. Hand her over and there is no need for you to die, vampire."

Viper smiled with cold disdain. "Oh, I have no intention of dying. Not by your hands. Or rather, by your teeth."

The angry hiss made the entire tunnel shiver in warning. "Brave words, but unless you have more than a stunted gargoyle to lend you assistance you are no match for me."

There was an angry buzz of wings as Levet took swift exception to the insult.

"Stunted?" the gargoyle huffed. "Why you overgrown worm, I'll—"

"What is your interest in my slave?" Viper forced the Lu's

attention back to himself. Shay would never forgive him if he allowed the tiny pest to end up in the belly of a demon.

The leviathan head turned back to stab him with a smoldering glare. "That is a matter between my master and the Shalott."

"Your master? Since when have the mighty Lu allowed themselves to call another master?"

"You would be surprised, vampire. Surprised, indeed."

The soft, mocking laughter chilled Viper's already cold skin. He didn't like the idea the demon was hiding something from him. Something that was causing the Lu a great deal of pleasure.

"Why speak in riddles? Is your master so cowardly that he must hide in shadows?"

"Ah no, if you desire answers then you must first defeat me."

Viper held out his sword. "That can be arranged."

The crimson eyes narrowed in a dangerous threat. "Foolish, vampire, I will have the Shalott. No piece of steel is going to halt me."

To prove his point, the long snout lashed forward with mind-numbing speed. His teeth bit through Viper's arm before he could leap out of the way. Clenching his teeth Viper stabbed the sword into the exposed throat of the demon. There was a hiss of pain from the Lu before he drew back, leaving deep gouges in Viper's flesh that bled with sluggish pain.

Slammed against the wall it took a moment for Viper to clear his fogged mind. Dammit all. There was more than one means to battle the much larger demon.

"Perhaps steel will not stop you, but there are some forces not even a Lu can battle."

Pointing the sword toward the ground Viper ignored the blood trickling down his numb arm and concentrated his will upon the rich earth beneath their feet. He possessed no magic. No vampire was able to wield spells. Or even to sense them. But they did control ancient powers. Powers that came from the elements themselves.

His fierce will spread from the sword to the ground, churning deep below. The tunnel shook sending a spray of dirt falling from the low ceiling.

"Halt," the demon commanded, his tongue flicking between the sharp teeth. "I will have none of your vampire tricks."

"Unlike you I am my own master and take commands from no demon," Viper gritted.

"Fool."

The Lu struck again but on this occasion Viper managed to slip enough to the side that it was a glancing blow. The teeth raked his shoulder, but he firmly kept the sword pointed toward the now crumbling dirt below the demon's feet.

The earth was moving, but not fast enough, he angrily acknowledged. The power he called on was used by vampires to sink their victims into the soil after a deep feeding. It was never good manners to leave behind corpses to draw attention to a local clan.

Unfortunately, in this day and age most vampires preferred synthetic blood to the dangers of hunting live prey and his skills were rarely called upon anymore. Not to mention the fact that he had never before attempted to bury a creature as large as the Lu.

Still unaware of the ground that was now covering his clawed feet and inching up the thick scales of his legs the Lu gave a hissing growl and struck at Viper's head. It was a killing blow, but jerking back Viper managed to avoid the snapping teeth. His head banged painfully against the wall, a small price to pay for having it still attached.

Grimly clearing his foggy mind he reached down to snatch one of the daggers from his boot. He needed to distract the demon if he wasn't to be shredded into nasty bits.

Never allowing his call upon the earth to waver he drew back his arm and threw the dagger with deadly force. There was a sickening thud and a roar of pain as the dagger sank deep into the Lu's oblong eye.

"You will die for that, vampire," the demon roared, his desperate writhing digging him ever deeper into the ground.

"There is no need for either of us to die," Viper called out, keeping the demon concentrated on him even as he motioned the silent gargoyle back against the wall. If he could manage to trap the Lu, they might survive this relatively intact. He grimaced as he felt the blood soaking through his clothing. Relatively was all he could hope for at this point. "Tell me what you want with the Shalott, and we might make a deal."

"I said you must defeat me if you wish answers, vampire, and I am far from defeated." The serpentine face was a ghastly mask of blood and fury as the Lu glared at Viper with the dagger still stuck in his eye. He made an attempt to lunge forward, only to scream in frustration when he discovered that the ground held him firmly trapped. "Noooo."

"Tell me why you want the Shalott," Viper demanded.

"For this you will die," the Lu snarled.

Lifting his sword Viper prepared to plunge it into the remaining eye when the narrow head jerked upward and slammed into the ceiling. A shower of earth rained downward and Levet gave a squeak of alarm.

"*Mon dieu,* has he gone mad?" the gargoyle squeaked.

It did seem a distinct possibility, Viper conceded, as the demon lowered his head and once again reared up to thrust his head into the dirt above. The Lu demons were always unstable. Inbreeding was never a good thing.

He was in the process of deciding whether the Lu was trapped enough to risk a strategic retreat or to use the opportunity to land a few more blows when the realization hit him. The Lu hadn't gone mad. He was doing precisely what he had warned he was going to do.

Kill him.

The tunnel gave a mighty shake and the earth began to tumble with alarming speed from above. Soon the demon would bring the entire ceiling down upon them. They would be buried beneath the rubble.

But not buried deep enough, he realized as he lifted his eyes upward in alarm. The soil was beginning to split open and when it did it would bring with it the tide of the early morning dawn.

Devil's balls.

"Levet," he called out in warning. The gargoyle would not

be harmed by the sunlight but he would return to his statue form. He would be helpless if the Lu decided to carry him off.

Strangely, however, the small demon paid him no heed. Instead he knelt on the heaving earth and muttered beneath his breath.

Viper opened his mouth to offer another warning when Levet threw his arms upward and cried out.

"I call the night."

The words could barely be heard over the sound of the ceiling collapsing. There was no mistaking, however, the thick cloud of inky black that abruptly shrouded about them.

Viper froze in astonishment, his hands clutching the sword as if uncertain whether the foul cloud was a blessing or a curse.

Not far from him he heard Levet give a startled gasp and then a shout of triumph.

"It worked." His wings stirred the dark air with a flutter of excitement. "By my father's stone balls, it worked."

Chapter Ten

Shay had driven a car before. Not often and not well. But she knew the basic method of moving from one place to another.

She had never, however, had her hands on anything like the sleek Porsche. The barest touch on the accelerator and she was hurtling through the cresting dawn at a horrifying speed.

It was little wonder that she had managed to gather a few dents and one busted headlight by the time she arrived at the auction house and gathered her small store of magical potions she had left behind.

A demon was not intended to travel over a hundred miles an hour without some cost, she assured herself as she returned to the decidedly worse-for-wear car and sped back to Viper's estate. Besides which, the silver-haired vampire was bound to be so furious at her return he wouldn't even notice that she had managed to ruin the expensive automobile.

Adding several more dents, a broken window, and a flat tire as she cut through fields and back roads she squealed to a halt inside the garage.

The trip had been made as swiftly as humanly, or demonly, possible. Still, she couldn't deny a sickening dread that clenched her stomach.

A dread that nearly drove her to her knees as she slipped through the trapdoor and into the chamber below. Across the room she could see the door buckled and torn from its hinges by some unknown force. But that was not what made her blood run cold.

Even from a distance she could see that the tunnel had collapsed and morning sunlight was pouring in.

She was hurtling forward before she could even question why her breath was lodged in her throat and her heart was twisting with pain.

It couldn't be the fact she feared Viper would be dead.

That would just be . . . insane. Wouldn't it?

Refusing to ponder the panic bubbling through her blood Shay carefully cradled the bag to her body and forced her way through the small opening.

She wasn't sure what she expected, but it wasn't the thick cloud of darkness that was nearly tangible in the air.

"Levet?" she called softly. "Viper?"

There was a soft scrape and then the darkness was suddenly pierced by a soft glow. At first she thought someone had managed to light a candle, but as she turned her head she realized the light wasn't a candle.

Not even remotely a candle.

Frozen in horror her gaze ran over the enormous demon with its glowing scales and scarlet eyes. She had never seen anything like it. And never wanted to again.

As she watched, the bloody snout twitched with what she very much feared was a smile of triumph.

Oh . . . shit, shit, shit.

"The Shalott," the beast hissed.

Mesmerized by the fiery gaze it took Shay a long moment to hear the cold, furious voice from deeper in the shadows.

"Goddammit, Shay, I told you to leave. Get the hell out of here."

She grimaced as she came back to herself with a sudden thud. Were all vampires such ungrateful asses, or was Viper a special breed?

The demon standing before her gave a rumbling laugh that echoed through the tunnel. Disturbing. Very, very disturbing.

"There is nowhere you can run that I will not find you, Shalott, but come to me and I will spare the lives of these two," he promised in a rasping voice. Shay sucked in a deep breath as she covertly reached into the bag and closed her fingers around one of the ceramic jugs. "Come to me now," the demon roared.

"I'm coming, I'm coming," she muttered.

"Shay." There was an edge of something that might have been panic in Viper's smooth voice. "The Lu is trapped for the moment, but I can't hold him for long. Get out of here."

"Do what he says, Shay," Levet echoed. "You can't defeat this beast."

The beast in question gave a low hiss toward the gargoyle before attempting to look harmless. A hopeless task, of course.

"I am not your enemy, my dear. I have only come to collect you for my master." The glow rippled eerily over the demon's scales, as if he were in the grip of some fierce emotion. "A master who does not like to be disappointed."

She took a step closer. Not that she wanted to be in biting distance of those sharp teeth. But she had to be near enough to use what weapons she possessed.

"Who is this mysterious master?" she demanded, more to keep him distracted than to discover the truth.

Priorities, priorities.

Get out of this alive, and then worry about who wanted her so desperately.

"A powerful friend, or deadly enemy. The choice is yours."

"You still have yet to give me a name."

"His name is forbidden to speak, but I assure you that I mean you no harm."

Shay rolled her eyes at the typical demon mumbo jumbo. "Somehow I find that hard to believe."

"You have my pledge that I will take you without harm to my master. Does that satisfy you?"

"That all depends on what's going to happen after we arrive." She inched closer. "What does your master want with me?"

"That is a question that he will have to answer."

"You are not exactly inspiring my confidence."

The red eyes flashed with dangerous fire. Or at least one red eye did. The other was currently sporting a heavy dagger. Ick.

"I have no need. Either you go with me willingly, or I take you by force. There are no other options."

Shay sensed Viper slowly edging around the back of the demon, but she dared not take her eyes from the dangerous mouth that hovered all too near. She had no idea if her impetuous plan would work, and it seemed wise to be prepared to duck.

She was rather fond of her head precisely where it was.

"Actually . . ." she murmured, pulling out the ceramic pot. "I have another option."

"Shay, no."

Viper's words came too late as she hastily launched the pot. It busted against the long snout and the demon roared with unmistakable pain.

For a moment Shay was blinded by the sharp glow that rippled over the scales. She hadn't been expecting the flare of light, and her brief vulnerability cost her as the demon lunged forward and used his head to smash her against the wall.

It hadn't been intended to be a killing blow, but that didn't keep it from hurting. With a shake of her head, she painfully forced herself to her feet and watched in horror as Viper threw himself between her and the razor-sharp teeth.

The Lu instantly charged and Shay's heart halted as the vampire raised his long sword to slash at the striking mouth. The ring of steel meeting something much harder than mere metal echoed through the tunnel.

Shay scrambled to retrieve her fallen bag and pulled out another pot. She had to do something before the demon managed to reach Viper.

As she came to her feet, however, she heard a sharp hiss and her eyes widened as Viper's sword slowly began to sink into the thick scales.

"What's happening?" she demanded.

Viper's muscles rippled as he forced the deadly sword ever deeper. "The potion you threw on him has weakened his armor."

The Lu roared in anger and cocking back her arm Shay lofted the pot of nasty witch's brew directly into the bloody wound.

This time she was prepared for the shock of searing light and holding her arm over her eyes she attempted to ignore the high scream of pain.

Shalotts might be renowned warriors, but she had enough human in her to feel compassion for the dying demon. The Lu would no doubt kill all of them without an ounce of remorse, but she couldn't bear to prolong the obvious agony.

Bending down she grasped the last of the potions and prepared to launch it.

"Hold, pet," Viper abruptly commanded as he yanked free the sword that had sunk deep into the demon's skull. With a hiss, the Lu flopped to the ground.

"You cannot mean to leave him like this?" she demanded as she watched the beast twitch in a pool of his own blood.

"He made a bargain with me, did you not mighty Lu?"

The crimson eye slit open. "I do not bargain with vampires," he hissed.

Viper moved forward to place the tip of his sword on top of the demon's head. The scales had already begun to turn to a ghastly liquid.

"You said that if I could defeat you that you would answer my questions." Viper seemed to grow even bigger in the dimming glow of the scales. "You are defeated. Now honor your pledge."

For a moment the air shimmered with the frustrated fury of the dying demon. Then, astonishingly the Lu offered a rasping sigh.

"Ask."

"Why does your master want the Shalott?"

"For her blood."

Shay cringed. Damn her blood. It had a great deal to answer for. It seemed every demon in the world wanted a taste of it for one reason or another.

"Who is he?"

"I told you, I am forbidden from speaking his name."

"Then where can I find him?"

"He was in Chicago, but I feel him traveling farther away. I do not know where he is headed."

Viper gave a low growl, his hands tightening upon the hilt of the sword. "You have no answers for me."

The Lu gave a low, disturbing laugh. "Because you do not ask the right questions, vampire."

"What are the right questions?"

"Ah no, I will not make it that easy."

Shay stepped hastily forward. It didn't take a genius to realize that Viper had taken a giant leap over the edge of his patience. The Lu wouldn't be able to answer any questions once that sword slid through his brain.

"You said the master wanted me for my blood," she directly confronted the demon. "Does he intend to sell it or use it for himself?"

The crimson eye turned in her direction. Shay shivered at the unnerving intelligence that smoldered deep in the glittering depths. She abruptly realized he was far more than a lumbering, deadly beast. Or at least she assumed it was a he. She wasn't about to ask the thing to roll over and check.

"My master has no use for your blood himself," he hissed.

"So he intends to sell me?"

"You are . . . more a means to an end."

Her own temper flared. No wonder he agreed to answer questions. He wasn't revealing a damn thing.

"Does he have Evor?"

Perhaps sensing her annoyance a smile of taunting satisfaction curved his lips.

"The troll is alive and well. For the moment."

Shay blinked in bewilderment. "What do you mean?"

"If you desire an answer to your questions, look to your curse." A horrid, bumbling sound came from the demon's throat and he gave a sudden shudder. "I have fulfilled my pledge, you damnable vampire, now end it."

Viper turned to send her a questioning glance. "Shay?"

There were no doubt a dozen other questions she should ask. Some the demon might even answer. But she couldn't do it.

Her stomach simply wasn't strong enough to watch any creature suffer.

"Yes."

The urge to turn away was nearly overwhelming, but Shay forced herself to witness the killing blow. The demon had been after her, and her alone. It was entirely her fault that Viper and Levet had been attacked at all. The least she could do was stand at his side while he vanquished her enemy.

Raising the sword Viper swung it with a fierce stroke that severed the long head with a clean blow. Like her he seemed intent on putting an end to the demon's suffering.

There was no sound to indicate the Lu was dead, but with a slow pulse the glow of the scales began to fade. Shay sent up a silent prayer. She wasn't sure what deity the Lu prayed to, but her words could surely not go astray.

A heavy silence descended as the darkness became complete. The demon was dead but Shay felt no sense of relief.

There was still something out there that wanted her blood.

The only question was what he would send after her next.

Lost in her brooding thoughts Shay gave a startled shriek as she felt a small hand abruptly tug on the hem of her robe. "Levet?"

"Ah, so you do remember the poor gargoyle forced to battle hellhounds, and demons, and to hold this magnificent spell of darkness even as he is enduring a terrible cramp in his side," Levet muttered in obvious disgust.

A portion of her tension eased at her friend's familiar grumbling. "It is a magnificent spell, Levet, but in case you haven't noticed, I've been rather busy."

"Oui, oui," he snapped with an obvious lack of awe. "Ding dong the demon's dead, now can we admire our delightful handiwork someplace where the ceiling is not about to cave in and your oh-so-handsome vampire is not about to become a dust bunny?"

Good point.

* * *

Attired in nothing more than a pair of black silk boxers, Viper shifted to a more comfortable position on the bed that consumed a large portion of his hidden lair. Beside him Shay was sprawled in a restless slumber, her beautiful curls spread across the black satin pillowcases.

Unable to resist temptation he allowed his fingers to lightly stroke the rich darkness.

He knew he should be resting. After the death of the Lu it had taken him several hours to gather his human servants and put them on watch around the house, and to contact his clan to warn them to be on alert. He didn't truly believe that the mysterious master could launch another attack so swiftly, but he was determined to be prepared.

It was only when he was confident he had done everything in his power to ensure Shay's safety that he had joined her on the bed and allowed himself the luxury of sleep. A sleep that had been disturbed far too early by the feel of a warm body entangled with his own and a heady female scent filling the air.

Well hell, sleep was overrated anyway, he acknowledged as he propped himself on his elbow to study Shay's delicate profile.

With a sense of wonderment, he realized it was the first time in all of his long years that he had actually awoken with a woman in his arms.

A vampire rarely equated sex with a relationship, and while they lived in clans they did not couple until they found their true mate.

Savoring the feel of her satin hair as it trailed over his fingers Viper hid a smile as her lashes fluttered upward.

God, but she was magnificent.

Annoying as hell, but magnificent.

The sleepy golden eyes roamed over his face as if memorizing his every feature before she realized what she was doing and abruptly stiffened.

"Viper. Is something wrong?"

"No." He slowly smiled. "I merely enjoy watching you."

She shifted uneasily on the satin sheets. He was discovering that this woman was oddly shy when it came to intimacy. As if she had little experience with desire.

"What time is it?"

"It is not yet four." Grasping the cover he pulled it down to reveal the slender·form barely covered by her robe. "Do your wounds hurt?"

"No. I'm just stiff." Her breath caught as Viper ran his fingers over the faint pink marks that still marred her bronzed skin. "What are you doing?"

"I wish to assure myself that you are healed."

"You don't have to touch my leg to see that I'm healed."

Viper gave a soft chuckle, his fingers deliberately trailing up her calf to toy with the back of her knee.

"No, but it is a lot more fun than just looking."

Her features tightened with disapproval, but he didn't miss the faint shiver she couldn't completely hide.

"Where is Levet?"

Viper grimaced. "Still in statue form, thank God."

Shay propped herself onto her elbows and glared at him in genuine annoyance.

"You really are an ungrateful toad. Levet saved your life."

Viper shrugged, far more interested in the satin skin beneath his meandering fingers than the sleeping gargoyle.

"That does not mean he couldn't test the patience of a saint. I have met drunken pirates with more pleasant tongues."

A hint of grudging amusement entered her eyes. "He is, perhaps, an acquired taste."

"Like arsenic?"

"I should have let you become toast," she muttered.

"I don't know about becoming toast, but I do know you should never have returned." He held her gaze with the sheer force of his will. "Why?"

"Why what?"

His fingers tightened on her leg. "Don't pretend to be stupid, pet. I'm aware you possess an uncanny intelligence. At least when you choose to use it. Why did you return?"

Her gaze lowered, hiding her eyes behind the thick sweep of her lashes. "I couldn't leave Levet."

"The Lu wouldn't have harmed the gargoyle."

"You don't know that for certain."

He leaned closer. Close enough that her heat washed over his skin and the pulse of her heart was nearly tangible.

It was his turn to shiver.

He was a predator. A creature meant to hunt and capture his prey without mercy. He wanted. He wanted to be deep in this woman. To sate his lust as he drank of her blood.

Thankfully he had had centuries to gain control of his hungers. And to learn to appreciate the lesson that the more difficult the prey to capture the more satisfying the hunt.

"Try again, pet," he murmured, his voice edged with a faint rasp.

Her tongue peeked out to touch her lips. "I don't like the thought of some demon stalking me. It seemed wiser to confront it directly than to have it sneak up on me again."

He shifted his body to press firmly against her curves as his roaming fingers reached the edge of her robe.

"Very logical."

"I think you've more than assured yourself that my leg is healed," she said, her voice not at all steady.

"I prefer to be thorough."

Abruptly she dropped back onto the pillows. He could hear her heart pounding far too fast. "Viper."

He followed her down to hover a breath from her lips. "You came back to save me, didn't you?"

"No."

"Why is it so horrible to admit that you don't want me dead?"

She gave a choked sound as his hand shifted to tug at the belt of her robe, slowly parting it to reveal the stunning beauty beneath.

"Stop that."

His hand reverently brushed over the soft curve of her stomach. "I have never felt such skin. So smooth . . . so warm. I had forgotten the beauty of Shalotts."

Although she was strong enough to toss him across the room, and perhaps even through the heavy door, Shay remained lying beneath him, her face tight with something that was suspiciously close to pain.

"I'm a mongrel, remember?"

"I have forgotten nothing about you, and I can honestly swear that your human blood makes you no less lovely." He deliberately allowed his gaze to skim the delicious length of her body. "In fact it adds a charming hint of fragility."

"I'm not lovely."

Viper stilled as an unfamiliar tenderness swept through his heart. By the blood of the saints, how could this woman not know she could make angels weep in envy?

"Look at me," he commanded, waiting until her lashes reluctantly lifted to reveal her wary eyes. "Do you think it is the Shalotts's blood alone that intoxicates vampires? It has always been their astonishing beauty that captivated us first."

She gave a shake of her head, clearly not willing to believe his words. "What do you want from me?"

Well, that was easy enough.

He leaned his forehead against her own, drinking in her intoxicating scent.

"Touch me," he whispered, his voice thick with need. "Let me feel your hands upon me."

She shivered in response. "Viper, we should—"

He brushed her lips with his own, his hand tracing up to cup her breast. "Please, Shay, just let me feel your touch. That is all that I ask."

For a long, tense moment he thought she meant to deny his plea. However much she might desire him, her defenses were formidable. She didn't want to want him. Perhaps she even feared to want him.

Then with a painful slowness her hand lifted and the tips of her fingers skimmed over his bare chest.

Viper groaned as his entire body clenched in reaction. Christ. She had done no more than brush him with her fingers and yet he was already hard and aching.

And aching, and aching, and aching . . .

His head dipped so he could press his lips to the sensitive skin of her temple.

"Don't stop now," he pleaded softly.

Him. Viper. Ancient vampire. Clan chief. Feared predator. Pleading for the touch of a woman.

Unbelievable.

But what was a desperate man to do?

Nibbling his way down to the curve of her ear, Viper shuddered as her hands pressed more firmly to his skin, smoothing over his chest until she came to his sensitive nipple.

He made a sound deep in his throat at the jolt of excitement. Easily sensing his pleasure, Shay teasingly circled the nipple until it hardened in reaction.

"I didn't know men liked such things," she murmured.

"I don't know about all men, but I like it very much," he rasped.

"Do you like this?"

Shockingly she bent downward to flick her tongue over the clenched peak and Viper gave a muffled shout. The pleasure raced through his entire body, tightening his erection and making him worry for the first time in centuries if he might actually reach climax with nothing more than a touch.

His fingers entangled in her hair, urging her to continue with her delectable caresses.

She did.

Even as his heavy lids slid shut, her delicate fingers trailed a blazing path down his clenched stomach to toy with the edge of his boxers. He jerked in response, a growl coming from his throat.

"Oh, yes."

"Yes, what?" she whispered, clearly taking a perverse enjoyment in driving him to the point of madness.

He spread heated kisses over her face as he shifted to jerk down the offending boxers.

"Are you deliberately attempting to torture me?" he rasped,

his hand moving to cover hers so that he could urge it toward his straining erection. "Or do you simply wish me to beg?"

"Torture and begging? I like the sound of both," she retorted.

Viper laughed softly only to have it end in a broken moan as her fingers stroked the throbbing length of him with a tentative touch.

"Holy hell," he gasped, his back arching as she gently explored him from tip to base and back again.

There was nothing experienced in her touch. It was more as if she were discovering for herself how best to bring the low groans to his throat, but he had never battled so hard to keep himself from thrusting in mindless need and spilling his pleasure.

He buried his face in her hair as she clasped him in a firm grip, careful not to allow her to feel his fully extended fangs. He had no desire to remind her that he was one of the dreaded vampires.

Not now.

Nothing was going to spoil the mood.

Nothing but the sudden pounding on the heavy oak door.

"Shay." The piercing, irritating, utterly unwelcome voice of Levet floated through the air. "Do you intend to lie in bed the entire day? I'm starving out here."

Viper froze, but Shay bolted from the bed as if she had been shot from a cannon. Hastily she wrapped the robe about her shivering body.

The mood was most definitely broken. And if her stricken expression was anything to go by, it wasn't going to be coaxed back to life anytime soon.

With a snarl of frustration, Viper tossed himself on his back and smacked the mattress with his fists.

"I . . . will . . . kill . . . him."

Chapter Eleven

Shay was seated at the kitchen table with Levet polishing off the last of the apple pie set before her. It wasn't that she was starving. Thanks to Viper's housekeeper she had discovered the kitchen overflowing with food. Most of which she had put a credible dent in.

But she had a habit of eating whenever there was something troubling her mind. Especially if that something was a silver-haired, dark-eyed vampire who could turn her into a raging hormone with a mere glance.

My God, she had wanted him so badly. Wanted to feel him shudder beneath her touch, to hear him groan in pleasure, to guide him within her so that she could join him in paradise.

And worse, she couldn't even totally convince herself that it would never happen again.

Or that she didn't want it to happen again.

She was pathetic. Pathetic, pathetic, pathetic.

She scooped another bite of apple pie and stuffed it in her mouth. Thank God Shalotts never had to worry about their weight.

In contrast Viper was not an eater, but a stomper.

Having consumed his bottle of blood in one swig he had begun storming through the house, rallying his troops to ensure that the guards were on duty, and calling in assistance to begin repairing the tunnels. He swirled through the house attired in a pair of black velvet pants that fit tight enough to make Shay choke on her pie and a silver shirt that was left open to reveal his perfect chest. He was delicious enough to tumble to the ground and have her way with him. Except for the unmistakable scowl that marred his handsome features.

In fact it was almost a relief when he muttered something beneath his breath and slammed out the back door.

"I do not know why that vampire is in such a foul mood," Levet muttered, working his way through his fourth bowl of stew. "Thanks to me he was not turned into a pile of dust. And with your swift thinking you managed to defeat the Lu. He should be bowing at our feet in gratitude, not stomping around as if he has a stake stuck up his butt."

Shay sighed as she moved aside the empty pie pan. "I wouldn't push it right now, Levet."

Something in her tone made the gargoyle regard her with a raised brow. "*Cherie,* exactly what did I manage to interrupt?"

A stupid blush touched her cheeks. "I said don't push it."

Levet gave a sudden laugh. "Ah . . . so your hatred of vampires does not extend to the *boudoir*? I cannot fault your taste. He is gorgeous in a cold, arrogant sort of manner."

Shay regarded her friend with a dangerous frown. "You think Viper arrogant? Isn't that the pot calling the kettle black?"

"Pot?" Levet gave a helpless lift of his hands. "I do not know what this black pot is."

Shay rolled her eyes. "Forget it, Levet. You've been in America since the Revolution. Your command of English is better than my own."

"English, bah. Such a foul language. There is no romance, no beauty. Just horrid noises that grate upon my delicate ears."

Attempting to appear casual Shay gave a lift of her brow. Somehow, someway, this ridiculous gargoyle had become an important part of her life. She couldn't bear to think of him being hurt because of her.

"Then why do you remain here? Why not return to France?"

A shudder raced through the small, gray body. "You mean to the loving arms of my family? *Sacrebleu,* I would not survive such a reunion. The last that I heard my brothers were determined to have my head upon a pike."

Shay grimaced. "Yeah, families are a bitch. From all I have discovered most of my extended kin are bloodthirsty assassins who often keep the skins of their kills as trophies."

"Charming."

She tugged on her long braid that was still damp from the shower. "There are places besides France for you to go. I've heard Italy is a beautiful country."

A beat passed as the gargoyle stared at her with growing suspicion. "Are you attempting to be rid of me?"

She hesitated as she tried to come up with a reasonable lie beneath that steady regard. At last she blew out a sigh. Shit. She never could manage to lie worth a crap.

"Levet we both know that I'm not safe to be around. Something out there wants me dead and they don't care who they have to hurt to get to me."

His wings twitched in outrage. "You think me a coward to run from danger? Why do you not just cut off my manhood and be done with it?"

"I have never thought you a coward, but it's stupid to put yourself in danger when there is no need."

Levet ducked his head to finish off the last of his stew. And more importantly to hide his expression from her.

"I have nothing better to do for the moment. I might as well remain and protect you while I await something to catch my fancy."

Shay found herself ridiculously touched. For all his grumpiness the gargoyle did care for her.

"Levet—" About to demand that he find someplace safer to be, Shay was abruptly cut off as a roar split the night air. "What the hell was that?"

Levet hopped off his chair to go to the door and pull it open. "The howls of the damned. Or a very angry vampire. They seem to be coming from the garage."

"The garage . . ." Shay slowly lifted herself to her feet as a sense of dread filled her stomach. "Oh."

"What is it?" Levet demanded.

"I might have had some difficulties with Viper's car."

"What sort of car?"

"A Porsche, I think. What does it matter?"

Levet rolled his eyes heavenward. "Holy mother of God."

Shay frowned as the gargoyle grabbed a loaf of freshly baked bread and headed toward the stairs to the basement.

"Where are you going?"

"To find shelter from the coming storm."

There was another roar and Shay pressed a hand to her cramped stomach. "You just promised you would remain to protect me."

Levet sent her a raspberry. "You wrecked a man's Porsche. You are on your own."

"Traitor," she called after the retreating demon.

Her voice was still ringing through the kitchen when the back door was thrust open and a surge of power rushed over her skin as Viper stepped into the room.

Despite her best intentions Shay discovered herself backing into the nearby counter as he swept forward.

"What did you do?" He came to a halt a few steps away, as if not at all certain he could trust himself to be any closer. Shay clutched the countertop behind her, grudgingly accepting that even in his fury he was fiercely beautiful. It was almost an effort not to reach out and touch him just to remind herself he was real and not just some fantasy from a woman's dream. "Stop by a demolition derby on your way?"

She sternly gathered her thoughts.

Pathetic. Absolutely pathetic.

"I'm not used to driving a stick."

"So you drove it into every tree and ditch you could discover?"

Her lips thinned at his sharp tone. Beautiful or not there were times when he was damn annoying.

"It's not that bad."

"It's a total wreck."

"I'll admit that there are a few scratches and dents, hardly a wreck."

The midnight eyes narrowed. "The drive shaft is beyond repair, the transmission is shot, the—"

"Okay, there are some problems," she interrupted, inwardly wincing as she recalled just how many ditches and trees she had managed to locate. "It's just a car."

"Just a car?" He blinked as if she had spoken a foreign language. "That is saying that a Picasso is just another painting. It is . . . was a masterpiece."

"You were the one who ordered me to take a car and leave."

"I did not realize that I needed to specify that it be returned in one piece."

Enough. Her chin stuck out and she planted her hands on her hips. He had to be the most insensitive, ungrateful, ill-mannered vampire ever to walk the earth.

"What do you want from me? An apology?"

For a moment he continued to glare at her and then without warning his rotten mood seemed to slide away and that dangerous, sinful smile slowly curved his lips.

"Mmm . . . what do I want from you." He moved forward with a sensuous grace. "An intriguing question."

Her heart gave an alarming jolt. All the warning she needed to keep this vampire firmly at arm's length.

"Don't you dare come another step closer."

His soft chuckle trickled down her spine. "Now, pet, you know better than to challenge me."

"Don't do it."

Of course he took that next step. He was a vampire, wasn't he?

Shay allowed instinct to take over. As he reached out to touch her face, she grasped his arm and with a swift motion she was diving to the floor, using his momentary astonishment to pull him down with her. With a hard kick against the floor she had rolled Viper onto his back and was perched on his chest.

It had all happened with such a smooth ease that Shay knew that Viper had done nothing to fight back. A suspicion that was confirmed as she glared into his smoldering eyes.

"Now what do you intend to do with me?" he murmured softly, his hands moving to cup her hips in a suggestive grip.

Thank God for the thickness of jeans. She wasn't sure what would happen if he touched her bare skin again.

Nothing she *should* want.

"Don't tempt me."

"But that is precisely what I want to do." He did something with his chest that rubbed against the juncture between her legs, sending a small shock of pleasure through her. "Are you tempted?"

She gritted her teeth. "To put a stake through your heart."

"Before or after you scream out your pleasure?"

"We don't have time for this nonsense," she muttered, giving a sudden shriek as he lifted himself to his feet in a fluid motion and she was forced to wrap her legs around his waist or be dropped onto her backside.

His arms lashed about her and he bent his head down to steal a fierce, hungry kiss.

A kiss that made her head spin before he pulled back with a sigh.

"Unfortunately you are right." He gently placed her back on her feet. "We must make our plans."

Shay wobbled, but she didn't fall down.

It was something.

"We?" she demanded.

"Whether you like it or not, pet, you still belong to me."

She stiffened before common sense warned her that his provoking words had been deliberate. He wanted to distract her.

The question was why.

"You can't seriously intend to keep me around?" she demanded. "You were almost killed. Why would you want me near when it's bound to endanger your life?"

He shrugged. "It's a break from the monotony. I haven't had anyone try to kill me for a very long time."

It sounded remarkably like Levet's lame excuse. Her eyes narrowed.

"I don't believe you. Why don't you break the amulet and be free of me?"

His features hardened. "Because you belong to me and I take care of what is mine."

Belonged to him? Ugh. "That's not reassuring."

His fingers brushed her cheek. "It should be."

She took a hasty step backward. Dammit, he knew she couldn't think when he was touching her.

"You said something about a plan?" she demanded, accepting that he was going to remain like a thorn in her side no matter how stupid or dangerous it was to be around her.

Men.

"It is obvious we cannot simply hide," he murmured, leaning against the counter to look cool and perfect. "We must decide how best to keep you safe."

"The Lu said that we must look to my curse." Shay furrowed her brow. "What did he mean?"

"I haven't the least notion. What do you know of your curse?"

"Nothing."

"You must know something."

Shay shrugged. "I was very young and I only have vague memories of being in a dark cave and a sharp pain in my shoulder."

"Your shoulder?"

Shay paused before she heaved a sigh and tugged at the neckline of the comfortable sweatshirt she had discovered in her closet. Turning around she revealed the brand that marred the skin of her shoulder blade.

She was prepared for the feel of his finger lightly tracing the perfect circle that enclosed the intricate, strangely drawn symbols. She had studied the brand a thousand times over the years. She knew that in the overhead light it would possess a faint glow, and that it would have an odd translucent quality to it. As if it floated a breath above her skin rather than being a part of her body.

Ever so softly his fingers brushed her skin, as if fascinated by the odd mark.

"Were you alone when you were in the cave?"

Shay shivered. She had no true memory of the cave. Only bits and flashes that would enter her dreams and make her wake with a flare of panic.

"No, but it was too dark for me to see who else was there."

"The symbols are familiar," he murmured.

With a jolt of shock, she turned to regard him with wide eyes. "You recognize them?"

He shrugged, his expression brooding. "I can't read them, but they are witch runes."

"I have seen witch runes. Edra's coven didn't use anything like this."

"Edra was not an elemental witch. She used blood sacrifice for her power, not the earth."

Shay gave a shake of her head. His words made no sense. "Why would a witch curse me?"

"That's the question, isn't it? I think first we should find someone who can tell us precisely what is involved in this particular curse. That might give us a clue as to who cast it."

"Witches." She wrapped her arms about her waist. "Damn."

He smiled wryly. "I'm not overly fond of witches either, but I do know they are not all like Edra."

Shay grimaced. She had spent far too many years in the clutches of the crones not to be a little prejudiced. They had treated her like a feral animal to be leashed and punished upon their whim.

As far as she was concerned the only thing worse than witches was vampires.

"So you think we should seek out a coven?" she grudgingly demanded.

"First I wish to speak with someone I know. She may be able to give me the information I need."

"*You* will speak with her?" Shay narrowed her gaze. "While I'm cowering in some hole? I've told you that I will not be treated like a helpless idiot."

His lips twitched with the amusement he couldn't entirely hide. "Yes, yes, you are a warrior."

He was about to discover just how dangerous a warrior.

A poke in the eye, a fist to the nose, a knee to the groin.

Not necessarily in that order.

"Don't you dare patronize me," she hissed.

As if sensing he was nearing a painful blow, Viper reached out to lightly grasp her shoulders, his expression somber.

"Shay, for the moment we don't know who is after you, or who they might have called upon to assist them. I'm not about to take you into a coven where they could trap us both with one spell. This is not about running from the battle, but using our assets to our best advantage."

It sounded annoyingly sensible.

Shay didn't want sensible. She wanted to charge in and find out the truth. Preferably with force. She most certainly didn't want to hide away and wait for someone else to solve her troubles.

Yuck.

"And if you are trapped?" she demanded.

"Then you can come and rescue me," he promised with a slow smile.

"You're so certain that I would?"

"If I am killed, you will be forced to return to Evor and whoever is holding him."

She hid the sudden chill that inched down her spine. "The Lu said that Evor was alive and well."

"Alive and well, but for how long?" he demanded.

This time she couldn't hide her horror. "Don't."

Without warning his arms were about her and she found herself hauled tightly to his chest. She should have protested, but it just felt so damned good to be held.

Even if it was Viper's arms around her.

"Shay . . . I will protect you," he whispered close to her ear. "That I promise."

Leaning back she was about to say something.

Something that was quite thoroughly forgotten as he leaned forward to cover her lips in a kiss that melted her to her very toes.

* * *

The house in the elegant neighborhood north of Chicago was a testament to conspicuous consumption. Large enough to house a good size army, it was stuffed from basement to attic with rare works of art and priceless treasures.

Still, Shay was rather startled to discover that for all the echoing grandeur and lovely artifacts it managed to possess a sense of warmth.

Well, perhaps not so surprising, she acknowledged as she glanced at the woman walking at her side. There was something very down to earth and comforting about Abby. It was more than her casual jeans and T-shirt, or her ready smile. There was a natural ease about her that managed to thaw even Shay's tension. Not at all what she would have suspected from the Phoenix, a bane of demons everywhere.

Thankfully oblivious to Shay's simmering amazement, Abby pushed open the door to the library and motioned Shay within.

"You should find something here that will tempt you," she murmured.

Shay stepped over the threshold and came to a stunned halt. When Abby had requested to know how she spent her time Shay had casually mentioned her love for books. Of course, Abby had instantly been on her feet to lead Shay to their library. She seemed oddly anxious to please her guest. Especially considering that Viper had so high-handedly dumped her onto the doorstep like a bit of unwanted trash.

"My God, it's beautiful," she breathed.

And it was.

The ceiling towered three stories above with a vast chandelier that cast a muted light on the hundreds and hundreds of leather-bound books. On each floor was a walkway to frame the endless shelves, and in the main room was a heavy walnut desk and matching leather wing chairs set beside a fireplace.

Abby chuckled at her unmistakable awe.

"Believe me, if Dante had his way the entire house would be

overrun with books. It's only with grim determination that I keep most of them confined to this room."

Shay moved forward to better appreciate the scent of aged leather. Ah. It was a little bit of heaven.

"He must have been collecting these a very long time," she murmured.

"Over four hundred years." Abby stepped forward to open a small cabinet set into the shelves. "If you would prefer a magazine you can find them here."

Shay instinctively stepped from her companion. Almost as if she expected a blow. She had spent years being a slave. She didn't know how the hell to be a guest.

"Thank you."

Straightening Abby sent her a curious gaze. "Are you afraid of me because I'm the Phoenix? I promise you I won't hurt you."

Shay twisted her hands together, embarrassed that her discomfort was so obvious.

"I . . . Viper should not have forced me upon you."

"Forced you on me?" Stepping forward Abby took Shay's hands in her own. Her skin was warmer than a normal human's, as if the spirit she carried within her spilled out with a gentle aura. It was the only indication that Abby was not quite normal, unless one counted the startling blue eyes that were the true mark of the Phoenix. With a smile, Abby gave her hands a small squeeze. "Surely Viper told you that I particularly sent Dante over to invite you to visit me? I have been longing to have you here."

Shay ducked her head in confusion. "Why?"

Thankfully, Abby seemed to understand. "As much as I adore Dante, I miss the companionship of another woman."

"You must have friends."

Abby heaved a faint sigh. "No, not really."

Shay abruptly lifted her head, realizing her words had been utterly thoughtless.

"Oh. I'm sorry, I didn't think about you being the Chalice . . ."

"It's not that, although it doesn't help to be considered a goddess by some." Abby smiled wryly. "To be brutally honest, I've never really had any friends."

"All humans have friends."

"Not all." Abby grimaced, as if recalling bad memories. Then, with an obvious effort the smile returned to her lips. "So, no more of this nonsense about being forced on me. I'm delighted to have you here."

The last of Shay's anxiety melted beneath her kindness. It was simply impossible to be self-conscious and awkward with this woman.

"Thank you," she said as a wide, genuine smile curved her lips.

Abby gave a startled blink, stepping back to regard Shay with an oddly bemused expression.

"Good God, no wonder Viper looks as if he has been struck by lightning," she breathed.

"What?"

"You're gorgeous, but then you already know that."

Shay blinked. "You're being ridiculous."

"Have you looked in a mirror? If I weren't already mated, I would be jealous as hell."

Wondering if Abby was teasing her, or if she were simply attempting to be kind, Shay gave a restless shake of her head.

"I'm half demon."

"And Viper and Dante are full demon. Are you going to tell me you don't think they're beautiful?"

Well, hell. That was a loaded question.

Not only would a female have to be deranged not to think the two vampires were all sorts of yummy goodness, but this woman was married to one of them.

Shay had never had many friends, but she did know that it was bad form to imply that there was something less than perfect in their mate.

"Dante is very handsome," she conceded.

Abby gave a lift of her brows. "And Viper?"

"He's a pain in the ass."

"At times," Abby readily agreed. Her head tilted to the side.

"You know I was furious when I discovered that he had bought you from that horrid slave trader. I couldn't believe that he would do such a thing after you had saved his life."

Well, thank freaking God.

At least someone understood her outrage.

"Trust me, neither could I."

"But now, I must admit, I begin to wonder if his intentions were entirely selfish."

"Well, he most certainly didn't do it out of the kindness of his heart," Shay felt compelled to point out.

"Perhaps not entirely. He is after all a vampire." She gave a chuckle. "But, I do think that you intrigued him enough that he felt compelled to seek you out."

Shay gave an unconscious shiver. She agreed that she had intrigued Viper. Just not for the reasons a woman wanted to intrigue a man.

"I'm the last Shalott. Vampires have been hunting us since the beginning of time."

"That might be true, but you don't look like you've been too harshly abused."

Shay could have lied and pointed out that as a demon she healed with remarkable speed, but it would have been grossly unfair.

Viper had treated her with a tenderness that was as unnerving as it was unexpected. And even if she couldn't entirely trust that he wouldn't abruptly become the monster she dreaded, she had no reason for complaints.

"He has made . . . certain promises," she admitted.

"Ah."

What the *ah* meant Shay was never destined to discover as the door to the library was pushed open and a tall, raven-haired vampire entered the room.

"Sorry to intrude, my love, but Viper has returned," Dante murmured with an apologetic smile.

Shay stiffened, her stomach clenching with dread. To have returned so swiftly could only mean he couldn't dig up any information of value.

"Already?"

Dante glanced toward his wife. "He has brought with him a witch."

It was Abby's turn to stiffen. "He brought a witch to this house?"

Dante lifted his hands in a helpless motion. "He swears she is here to help Shay find the truth of her curse."

There was a tense moment before Abby turned to regard Shay with a searching gaze.

"Do you wish to meet with her?"

Shay licked her dry lips. She better than anyone understood Abby's distaste for witches. Nothing like a near-death experience to bring people together.

Still, she had to trust that Viper knew what he was doing.

Dammit.

"I suppose I should."

As if sensing the effort the words had taken, Abby gave her hands a gentle squeeze.

"Don't worry. We'll be with you."

Chapter Twelve

Styx was waiting in the lower caverns when Damocles strolled in through the darkness and moved toward the scrying pool.

As always Styx felt a surge of disgust for the flamboyant imp. Despite the bare rock and muddy floor the fool was attired in a rich, velvet robe that was heavily embroidered with golden thread. Even his hair was carefully arranged and threaded with those ridiculous leaves that filled the air with an annoying sound of bells. But it was more than his frivolous clothes and mocking manner that made Styx grit his teeth. The demon had brought nothing but misery and grief in his wake.

Had he been wise he would have turned the imp away the moment he had appeared. How could they possibly trust a demon who had once been a faithful servant to a vampire the Ravens had been forced to kill?

Unfortunately he had been blind to the danger until too late. Now he was forced to clean up the unfortunate mess as best he was able.

Waiting until the imp was nearly upon him Styx slid silently from the shadows to block his path.

"So you have failed again, imp," he said in cold tones. "We do not have the Shalott, and even the pathetic troll eluded your grasp."

Coming to a halt the imp performed an elaborate bow before rising to regard Styx with a lift of his brows.

"Failed? Such a harsh word. Especially for a poor man who has just lost his most treasured pet." His hands swept down the black velvet of his gown. "Can you not see that I am in mourning?"

Styx bared his fangs. He had been furious when he had learned that Damocles had wakened the Lu and sent him rampaging through Chicago. They might as well have sent an engraved invitation to every one of their enemies.

"All I can see is a treacherous imp who feathers his own nest while serving poison to his master."

Damocles pressed a hand to his chest, his expression one of mocking innocence. "Poison? Whatever do you mean?"

"Do not think that I am unaware of those goblets that you sneak to the master's bedchambers each night."

"It is true that I send a mixture of rare potions to help ease our master's pain." The imp shrugged. "Would you rather watch him suffer, or perhaps waste away entirely?"

"It was your foul concoctions that have brought him so low."

Something flashed in the pale green eyes. Something that was dark and dangerous. Instinctively, Styx slid his hand beneath his robe to touch the hilt of his dagger.

"An evil charge? Can you offer proof?"

"I know that the master was improving greatly after . . ." In spite of himself Styx discovered that he was reluctant to continue.

"After you captured the Shalott's father and offered him up as a sacrificial lamb?" Damocles finished with a smile that made Styx struggle to maintain his icy calm.

By the saints he hated to be reminded of that necessary evil. Even after all these years it possessed the power to strike deep at his conscience.

Strange considering he could drown in the blood he had shed.

"Yes," he gritted.

"I heard that he managed to kill three of your Ravens before you were able to beat him senseless and drag him to this cave."

The desire to sink his teeth deep into the imp's slender throat and drain him dry was nearly overwhelming. Only the commands of his master kept him from being rid of the nasty pest.

"Regardless, the blood of the Shalott had cleansed him of his illness until you arrived with your . . . potions," he accused, his hand still on his dagger.

The imp gave a toss of his golden curls. "I have only done what was commanded of me by my master. Do you question his decisions?"

"I should have sliced off your head the moment you appeared."

"Ah, you would lay the sins of the master at the feet of the servant? Is that your notion of justice, Sir-Holier-Than-Thou?"

Styx gave a low hiss. "If there were any true justice, you would have died alongside your previous master."

"As you would have done?"

"If necessary."

Damocles merely smiled. "We shall see."

"Enough." Styx cursed the realization he allowed himself to become so easily provoked. The past was done. Only the future mattered. "I did not come to bandy empty words with the likes of you. I have convinced the master to allow me to retrieve the Shalott. Once you have revealed to me the location of the demon, you're . . . services will no longer be required."

Predictably Damocles appeared exquisitely indifferent to the threat hanging in the air. With languid movements he circled past Styx to halt beside the scrying pool.

"I must say that I am surprised that you would take on such a task yourself," the imp drawled.

Styx watched the demon with a fierce gaze. "Why?"

"Surely the master must have told you who is holding the Shalott?"

"If you have something to say, imp, then say it."

"It simply seems odd that after all of your tiresome bleating about preserving vampire blood that you would be so eager to spill it now." Damocles waved a slender hand over the scrying pool and motioned Styx closer. "Come."

A cold sense of dread inched down his spine as Styx moved to peer into the murky water.

At first glance he could see only the delicate bronzed face of the Shalott. A face that looked hauntingly like her father's. He was swift to steel himself against any sense of regret at her fate. Her blood was all that stood between peace and chaos.

The water shifted and his attention turned to the man at her side. The dread spread through his body as he caught sight of the familiar silver hair and arrogant features.

"Viper," he rasped in shock.

"A friend of yours?"

"Where are they?"

With a taunting smile Damocles gave another wave of his hand and the image pulled back to reveal an elegant mansion that Styx recognized at once.

Every vampire knew the address of Dante and Abby.

No demon wanted to accidentally stumble across the goddess.

"I will say the Shalott knows how to pick her companions." The imp slid him a pointed glance. "Two vampires, a stunted gargoyle, and the Phoenix."

Styx abruptly straightened. "What of the troll Evor?"

"I fear my meager attempts to discover his whereabouts have gone for naught." Damocles gave a low chuckle. "Perhaps he has disappeared in the proverbial puff of smoke."

"You find this amusing?"

"I find this deliciously ironic."

Styx narrowed his gaze. "Be careful you do not choke on such irony."

"Oh, I shall do my best."

Styx had endured enough. He knew where to locate the Shalott. He had no further need of the aggravating imp.

"Have your bags packed while I am gone, Damocles. When I return I intend to see that you are escorted from the estate."

"As you wish."

Styx ignored the flamboyant bow the imp offered as he turned on his heel and left the chamber. Soon enough Damocles would be thrown from the estate or killed by his own hands. Either way he would no longer be able to spread his poison.

For now, nothing mattered but confronting Viper and somehow convincing him to give up his slave.

Waiting until he was certain that the vampire had left the cavern Damocles gave a soft laugh and moved toward the deep shadows behind the pool. With a wave of his hand the rock abruptly shimmered to reveal a hidden opening.

Damocles slid inside and carefully navigated the narrow stairs that had been chiseled into the ground. His nose wrinkled at the foul smells that filled the air. The smells of unwashed flesh and excrement.

Holding a prisoner was always a messy business.

Still, it did have its rewards.

Coming to a halt at the bottom step he regarded the pudgy troll who hunkered in the corner and glared at him with hatred in his beady red eyes.

"Well, Evor, I see that your imprisonment has not impaired your appetite," Damocles murmured as he pointedly glanced toward the numerous bones that had been stripped clean and tossed over the ground.

The filthy troll gave a rattle of the heavy chains that held him to the wall.

"What else is there to do in this pigsty?"

Damocles gave a low laugh. "Is that any way to speak of your lovely chambers?"

"Bugger off."

"Tsk, tsk. Such language."

The red eyes narrowed with a low cunning. "What do you want of me? Money? Slaves?"

"Nothing so valuable." With a lift of his hand Damocles patted his golden curls. "All I need from you, dear Evor, is your life."

Chapter Thirteen

Viper didn't bother to hide his impatience. Pacing from one vast end of the foyer to the other he kept his gaze trained on the elegant marble staircase.

It wasn't that he was worried for Shay's safety. The devil knew there were few places more secure than at the side of the Phoenix. What demon would risk daring the wrath of a goddess?

No, his impatience was much more personal.

It had been less than an hour and he already felt anxious that she was not at his side. That he couldn't reach out and touch her.

It was a bad sign. A very bad sign for a vampire who had never given a woman a second thought unless she was under the protection of his clan.

Unfortunately, he couldn't seem to find it in his unbeating heart to care that he was in waters far deeper than he had ever tread before.

No doubt another bad sign.

His acute hearing picked up the sound of footsteps long before Dante, Abby, and at last Shay, came into view. Striding forward he allowed the others to pass but, as Shay reached the bottom step, he reached out to pluck her off her feet and planted a thorough kiss upon her startled lips.

Pulling back she regarded him with wide eyes. "Viper."

He ignored her wriggles as he kept her firmly pressed to his chest. "What?"

"We're hardly alone," she hissed.

Brushing his cheek against hers, he savored the scented heat that clouded his senses.

"That could be arranged if you're interested," he whispered against her ear.

"No," she muttered in an outraged breath, but Viper didn't miss the sudden hardening of her nipples.

Hard to miss that.

Nice. Very nice.

"Are you certain?" He tightened his arms about her. "I could show you just how much I missed you."

"You were only gone an hour."

"What can I say? You have bewitched me."

She gave a furtive glance over her shoulder, a hint of pink staining her cheeks.

"Speaking of bewitchment, I think your companion is feeling neglected."

With reluctance Viper lowered Shay to her feet and gave a negligent shrug.

"Natasha has never been my lover."

"Does she want to be?"

He smiled at her tart tone. "She has indicated that she would not be opposed to sharing my bed. Are you jealous?"

"You would like that, wouldn't you?" She folded her arms over her chest, her eyes flashing. "Two women fighting over you?"

"I've never had a taste for angry women, but I would like very much to think you are jealous that another woman wants to be my lover."

She bit her bottom lip as if realizing she had given away far more than she intended to.

"Why is she here?"

Viper allowed his attention to stray toward the door. The young witch was pretty enough with her long black hair and pale skin, but she couldn't hold a candle to Shay's stunning

Alexandra Ivy

beauty. Something Natasha seemed well aware of as a petulant pout settled on her narrow face.

"She promises that she can cast a spell on your marking to help us discover who put it there."

"You're kidding?"

Viper gave a small shrug. "It's worth a try. Come, I think Natasha should explain."

He led the reluctant Shay toward the waiting witch, hiding a smile as the two shared a mutual glare of dislike.

"Let me see the mark," Natasha demanded.

The always stubborn Shalott narrowed her eyes in suspicion. "Why?"

"Shay."

Viper touched her arm and she heaved a sigh.

"Fine." Turning about she pulled down the neckline of her sweatshirt to reveal the brand. "Here."

The witch's hint of childish annoyance faded to be replaced by the concentration of a professional. Holding her hand over the brand Natasha murmured beneath her breath.

Long moments passed before the witch gave a sharp shudder and pulled her hand back.

"A powerful spell, but not evil. It's more a binding than an actual curse."

"Can it be broken?"

"Not without the one who holds the curse. They must be together for the curse to be broken."

Viper frowned. "Can you at least help us discover who was responsible for the curse in the first place?"

Natasha considered a moment before giving a shrug. "I can cast a spell that will give you a trail to the witch. As long as she hasn't managed to cover it with a counterspell."

Shay slowly turned about, her expression wary. "What sort of trail are you talking about?"

"Have you ever played hot and cold?" Natasha demanded.

"No."

"Once the spell is cast the mark will become warmer the

closer you come to the witch who branded you, and colder the farther you go away."

Shay licked her lips. "How long will it last?"

"A day, maybe two."

Viper moved to place a steadying arm about her shoulders. "Do you wish to risk it?"

She glanced up, her eyes oddly vulnerable in the dim light. "We don't really have a choice, do we?"

He wanted to lie. He wanted to assure her that he would take her far away and they would never have to worry about another thing for all eternity. But they both knew that as long as the curse bound her to Evor they would never be safe. No matter how fast or far they ran.

He gave a slow shake of his head. "Not really."

She blew out a heavy sigh. "Then let's do it."

Viper turned to the waiting witch. "What do you need?"

Natasha slowly smiled. "I have brought my supplies."

Of course, it wasn't a simple process. Natasha demanded that she *feel* the house before deciding that the kitchen possessed the best aura for her casting. Only then did she place Shay in a chair and pull a black candle from her bag. With a slow procession she made a counterclockwise circle, and then slowly retraced her steps. Over and over she walked the circle, pausing upon occasion to test its strength before at last giving a satisfied nod. With brisk efficiency she handed the candle to the wary Shay and lit the wick. Holding up her hands she began to chant beneath her breath.

Viper anxiously paced the edge of the kitchen, hating the sense of helplessness as he placed Shay in the hands of this woman.

No vampire felt comfortable around magic.

How did you battle against something that you couldn't see or touch?

Reaching into her pocket the witch pulled out a white feather that she touched to the candle's flame. There was a foul smell that filled the kitchen as Natasha spoke the last of her spell and suddenly Shay slumped over in her seat.

Viper stepped forward, cursing beneath his breath as the enclosed circle held him firmly out.

"Shay, are you all right?"

With a shake of her head she was sitting upright, handing the burning candle to Natasha.

"I'm fine, just a little dizzy."

"What have you done to her?" he demanded of the witch, his expression warning of dire retribution if Shay was harmed.

"Don't worry, it will wear off," Natasha muttered, putting away her candle and kneeling beside Shay. "Can you sense your brand?"

Shay sucked in a deep breath. "It . . . tingles."

Natasha rose to her feet with a triumphant smile. "The spell has worked. You can use it as a compass."

Viper battled back his surge of fear and offered a half bow. "You have done well. Thank you."

The smile became flirtatious as the witch ran a hungry gaze over his body. "I'm always ready to help . . . you."

Shay recovered enough to send him a glittering glare. Viper was wise enough to hide his smile.

"I will see you home," he murmured to Natasha.

In the beat of a heart Shay was on her feet, her expression determined. "I might as well come along. We can begin tracking the witch who did this to me."

"As you like," Viper murmured.

Natasha opened her mouth to protest only to be halted as Dante stepped into the room and gave Viper a sly smile.

"I'll see her home, Viper. You and Shay only have a few hours to find the witch."

He flashed his friend a relieved glance. As much as he enjoyed watching Shay prickle with jealousy, he was far more interested in finding out who was responsible for her curse. Once they were free of the threat he would have all the time in the world to savor his Shalott.

"Thank you."

Without warning Abby suddenly appeared at the side of her

mate and sent Viper a stern frown. "You will return here before dawn?"

"A kind offer," he murmured, "but we would only endanger you."

The goddess smiled with a confidence that she had gained over the past few weeks. "There are few demons who would dare intrude into this estate. Carrying the Phoenix does have a few perks."

He could hardly argue with that. Hell, there were times when she creeped *him* out.

"Still . . ."

"I insist."

Dante gave a sudden chuckle and held his hands up in warning. "Don't bother arguing with her, old friend, I assure you that you are only wasting your breath."

Viper offered a smile. "I thank you."

"We owe you," Abby said simply, reaching out to grab her mate's hand. "We owe you both."

Shay absently rubbed her shoulder as they crawled their way through the south side of Chicago, moving down Maxwell Street to neighborhoods that were considerably different from the elegant estates they had left behind.

Damn the witch, she silently cursed as her shoulder gave another flare of heat.

You can use it as a compass.

Easy for Natasha to say. It wasn't her shoulder burning like someone was poking it with a hot stick.

"Turn here," she commanded, her hands gripping her knees as Viper slowed the black Jag to a mere crawl.

"Do you sense something?" he demanded.

"My shoulder certainly does." Peering out the window Shay studied the passing shops. It was a depressing combination of abandoned buildings, liquor stores, and porno shops that made Shay long for a shower. And plenty of soap. Wincing at the smoldering pain of her brand Shay suddenly stiffened in surprise. "Stop."

Pulling to a stop before the crumbling brick building Viper turned to regard her in surprise. "Here?"

"Yes."

"You're certain?"

Climbing out of the sleek car Shay wrapped her arms around her waist and waited for Viper to join her on the dark street.

"I know this place. We used to live just around the corner."

"It looks like an old store."

Shay struggled to sort through her vague memories. It had been so many years ago. And the neighborhood had changed so much. Still, she was certain she was not mistaken.

"Yes, a bookstore. My father used to bring me here." She grimaced as she gave a shiver. "Damn, my shoulder is burning."

"I suppose we should go look around." Turning Viper took her hands and lifted them to his lips. "Shay . . ."

"What?"

"Promise me you won't do anything stupid."

She jerked her hands from his grasp. Why the . . . ass. As if she were the one who had stayed and tried to fight the Lu with nothing more than a sword. Or stomped and snorted because a ridiculous car had a few dings.

Stupid, indeed.

"Excuse me?"

He grimaced at her cold tone. "Maybe I could have phrased that a little better."

"You think?"

"What I mean to say is that I don't want you taking any risks. The devil only knows what might be waiting for us."

"Do you sense something?"

He glanced toward the darkened shop. "No, and that's what is bothering me."

Shay heaved a sigh. He had a point. Whatever was hunting her was still out there somewhere. Waiting. Biding its time. She would almost prefer another attack to this sense of brooding unease.

"Me too," she softly agreed.

He gently pulled her into his arms and pressed his lips to the top of her head. Down the dark street the muffled sounds of a brisk drug trade and the shrill calls of hookers could be heard, but Shay barely noticed them. She was in the arms of a vampire. Gangs, muggers, or rapists were not a problem.

"We can return to Dante's," he murmured against her ear. "We don't have to go in there."

For a moment she allowed herself to lean against his strength. Saints above, but it would be wonderful to simply hide behind Viper and pretend that he could keep her safe. It had been so damn long since she had been able to depend upon anyone but herself.

Then firmly she was pulling away.

No. She was no weakling to have to cling to another.

Jeez. The day she became so spineless she would toss herself from the nearest bridge.

"Yes we do." Her chin tilted. "At some point we have to go in. It might as well be now."

He studied her for a long beat, as if he could sense her pulling back behind her shields of protection.

At last he offered a wry smile and moved toward the store. Ripping apart the iron grating he pushed open the bolted door with obvious ease.

Show off.

"After you."

"Boy, having a vampire around can be handy," Shay murmured as she swept past him.

Without warning his hand shot out to grasp her arm. He bent close to her ear.

"Pet, if only you would allow me, I could take handy to a whole new level."

Her stomach clenched and she hastily dodged into the darkened shop with far more haste than grace. *Okay. Don't tease dangerous vampires in the future.*

Halting in the center of the uneven floorboards she glanced around with a wrinkle of her nose. The interior was narrow with several shelves still loaded with crumbling books and a collection of strange objects that were impossible to recognize beneath the layers of dust and spider webs.

Toward the far wall there was a long counter with a handful of stools, and behind it another shelf with ceramic pots that looked oddly sinister in the shadowed light.

Or maybe it was just the fact she had learned to distrust those tiny pots, she acknowledged with a tiny shiver. Being at the mercy of witches could do that to a girl.

"It looks like it's been abandoned for years."

Viper stopped at her side. "Yes."

She gave a faint shake of her head. "Why would the mark lead me here?"

"I'm not certain." A frown touched his brow. "Perhaps we should look around. There might be something here to assist us."

Shay swallowed a sigh. She had no desire to poke around the dingy shop. Not only was it filthy, but it made an odd chill prickle over her skin. There were memories here. Memories of her father when he was still alive. Memories she didn't want stirred among the mold and decay of this place. Unfortunately, Viper was right. The pain in her shoulder had led her directly here. There must be something.

Now if she just knew what that vague something was.

Moving toward the shelves she skimmed her fingers over the forlorn books. Nothing there but the usual children's classics and a few philosophers. Not a curse book among them. She shifted to the lumps of odd shapes that consumed the nearby shelves. Her hand reached for something that looked to be a crystal ball only to step back with a muffled scream.

As fast as a strike of lightning Viper was at her side, his hands grasping her shoulders in concern.

"What is it? What happened?"

She swallowed hard as she battled back a shudder of disgust. "A spider."

A beat passed. "A spider?"

"Don't mock, I hate spiders. They're creepy."

The full lips twitched. "Oh yes, very creepy."

She stepped back with a huff. It had been a huge spider. And hairy. Who wouldn't have screamed?

"Fine. Just go back to doing what you were doing," she muttered.

He leaned against the shelves, folding his arms over his chest. "Why don't you tell me what you remember of this place?"

She hesitated, her gaze unwillingly straying toward the distant counter. The stir of ghosts brushed over her skin.

"Not much. I remember sitting at that counter and reading books while my father would talk to the woman who owned the store." Her expression softened. She could almost feel the warm, strong touch of her father's hands as he would lift her onto one of the high stools. "Books in that time were far more rare, and each one was a treasure to me."

"Did you ever speak to the woman?"

Shay had the misty recollection of a round face and kindly smile. "She would sometimes give me candy, but I don't remember any specific conversation."

Viper gave a pointed glance toward the ceramic pots. "Could she have been a witch?"

"It's possible." Shay struggled to dredge up the past she had buried so long ago. "She never seemed to question how . . . different my father or I was. And there were always customers coming in to purchase those small pots. At the time I just thought they were pretty bits of clay."

"Potions," he muttered, moving toward the counter with cautious steps.

"That would be my guess."

"Hmmm . . ."

With a frown, Shay watched as the vampire pushed aside the various pots and began rapping on the wall behind them.

"What are you doing?"

Without turning around Viper continued his strange taps on the wall as he moved down the wall.

"If she was a witch she would have a secure room to perform her spells. A place where she could establish a stable circle and ensure she wouldn't be disturbed." He paused and rapped several times in the same spot. "Ah."

"Viper?"

He ignored her for a long moment. Long enough for her to consider tossing a book at the back of his head. Then, doing something with a small plaque set in the wall, he abruptly turned to flash a smug smile.

"Here it is."

Moving forward Shay realized that a portion of the shelves had slid open to reveal a narrow flight of steps.

"Oh my God."

"Shall we have a look?"

She swallowed before giving a reluctant nod of her head. She would go, but she intended to wait for Viper to take the lead on this occasion. There was a decidedly nasty stench wafting from the lower darkness. She had no desire to step into whatever it was making that smell.

They moved in silence. Well, Viper moved in silence. Shay was not blessed with the same night vision, and managed to stumble on a half dozen occasions before they reached the bottom of the stairs.

Thankfully for the safety of her neck Viper managed to discover a switch that turned on a single bulb hanging from the rafters above. Shay blinked as her eyes adjusted and then she froze in shock.

"Viper . . ."

His hand reached out to grasp hers, his cool touch offering a sense of security that allowed her to breathe again.

"The cave," he murmured, his gaze skimming over the roughly carved dirt walls and the circle clearly chiseled into the floor. "This is where you were cursed."

"Yes. I remember the markings." She gave a shiver. "This is the place."

"So where is the witch?" he murmured.

Taking back her hand Shay forced her feet to carry her toward the circle. The memories were still hazy, but she was absolutely certain that this was the place where she had been taken and given the mark.

Unconsciously, her hand reached out. She wasn't sure what she was reaching for until the tips of her fingers touched the invisible wall of power that surrounded the circle. She gave a faint gasp as the air seemed to shiver, and then without warning, the ground beneath her feet began to shift and she fell to her knees. The spell that had surrounded the circle was broken and suddenly she could see the pile of bones that had been hidden behind the clever shield.

Bones that were unmistakably human.

"I think I found her," she choked in horror.

Viper approached with understandable caution, his gaze trained on the skeleton. "If this is the witch, she's been dead for a considerable length of time."

Shay licked her dry lips, edging forward to get a better look at the gruesome pile. Her breath caught in her throat at the sight of the knife that remained caught between two rib bones.

"Murdered."

"Yes."

She glanced up as Viper bent next to her in the center of the circle. "It was Evor."

His face showed surprise. "Are you certain?"

"He has a blade that matches this one exactly. I would recognize it anywhere."

Reaching out he grasped the knife and pulled it free. "That would explain how he managed to take command of your curse."

Her stomach cramped as she thought of the hideous little troll who had made her life a misery. She certainly wouldn't put cold-blooded murder past Evor. It was practically a hobby with him. But she still had far too many questions unanswered.

"It makes no sense."

"What?"

She gave a restless shrug. "When I was young the mark on my back was just a nuisance. I didn't even know it was a curse until Evor used the binding to force me to him. If the witch was the one who placed the curse on me why didn't she ever allow me to sense the bond?" She pointed toward the bones. "And why didn't I die when she did?"

Viper absently studied the dagger in his hand. "The only explanation would be that Evor managed to force the witch to hand over the curse before he killed her. As to why she never used the mark . . . I do not know."

"Crap." Shay heaved a sigh. "Now what?"

He rose to his feet and glanced about the cramped cellar.

"Dawn is approaching. Unless I am to be trapped here, I must return to Dante's. We can return tomorrow night if you wish."

She grimaced as she began to rise to her feet. She paused as her gaze caught sight of a small box nearly hidden beneath the skeleton.

"What's that?"

"Shay . . ." Viper barked as she reached out to dig the box free.

"I know, I know, don't be stupid," she muttered.

"Touching things that we know once belonged to a witch would come under the category of stupid. There might very well be a trap awaiting an unwary touch."

She flashed him an exasperated glance. "We can't leave it behind. It might have something inside it that will help us."

"Fine." Reaching down he hauled her to her feet, his expression set in hard lines. "But if you try to open that before we're certain it's safe I'll . . ."

She narrowed her gaze. "You'll what?"

His expression remained grim but there was a definite hint of amusement deep in his eyes.

"When I conceive of something hideous enough I'll let you know."

Chapter Fourteen

Viper had been expecting the soft footsteps that crept by his door. He smiled as he slipped on his heavy robe and pulled his hair back with a gold clip. They had returned to Dante's a little over two hours before, but he didn't for a moment expect Shay to meekly crawl into bed and go to sleep.

That would be entirely too sensible.

And while Shay was many wonderful things, sensible was not among them.

Giving her plenty of time to achieve her goal, Viper silently slipped from his room and made his way to the library. He had no fear of encountering anyone else. Dante and Abby were comfortably tucked in their marriage bed, while Levet—who had been sent for earlier—had turned to stone with the crack of dawn. He and Shay were for all intents and purposes alone in the sprawling mansion.

A knowledge that made his blood stir with an excitement that was as dangerous as it was potent.

Entering the library he watched as Shay picked up the witch's box and studied it with a frown. His entire body clenched at the sight of her dressed in nothing more than a thin gown that revealed the slender length of her legs, and hinted nicely at the curves beneath the silk. It was a pity her beautiful hair was in its familiar braid, but on the upside it exposed the vulnerable curve of her neck.

His fangs lengthened and his body hardened.

Damn.

A part of him knew he should return to his chambers. She had stirred his hunger to a fever pitch only a few hours before and his control was dubious at best. A larger part of him, however, knew there was no way in hell he was walking away. They had unfinished business that he had every intention of finishing.

To both their satisfaction.

Moving until he stood directly behind Shay he trailed a finger down the line of her neck.

"Running away, pet?"

There was a sharp squeal as Shay dropped the box back on the desk and whirled to confront him.

"Shit." She gave a sharp tug on her braid as an unmistakable blush crawled beneath her skin. "Don't sneak up on me like that."

He allowed his gaze to sweep over the deep plunge of her neckline. "How would you like me to sneak up on you?"

"Don't sneak at all."

"I didn't realize I was doing so. Should I stomp my feet before approaching you?"

She flashed a sour frown as she folded her arms over her chest. Clearly she didn't appreciate getting caught snooping where she didn't belong.

"You could tie a cowbell around your neck."

"A cowbell? Hardly the fashion statement I was looking for." He smiled as his hand smoothed over the rich fabric of his robe. "What are you doing?"

"I . . . I was getting a glass of water."

"In the library?"

"I always read before I go to bed. Not that it's any of your business."

"Liar." He stepped even closer, his fingers brushing down her bare arms. "You were trying to open the box."

He felt the fine shiver that raced through her body even as she mustered a dark glare.

"Shouldn't you be in your coffin?"

"An excellent point, my dear. I most certainly should be in my coffin, just as you should be in your bed."

With a movement too swift for her to avoid, Viper had Shay scooped off her feet and cradled close to his chest. Turning on his heel he headed toward the door, ignoring her struggles as he left the library.

"Viper." She hit him hard enough that if he had been human it might have broken a rib. As it was it merely brought a small smile to his lips. She growled deep in her throat. "Damn you, put me down."

He gave a click of his tongue. "Really, such language from a lady, pet."

"I'm not a lady, I'm a demon."

Viper moved swiftly through the silent house, anxious to be behind locked doors.

"And a beautiful demon you are," he murmured, turning down the hall and entering one of the numerous vampire-secure rooms that Dante had had the foresight to construct in the mansion.

Crossing the thick white carpeting that nicely contrasted with the black and silver décor he dropped his delicious burden in the center of the vast bed.

"There. Are you satisfied?"

Sprawled on the black silk sheets she struggled to sit up. "No."

"Ah." A smile curved his lips as he smoothly lowered himself to cover her body with his own. "Are you satisfied now?"

Her skin glowed with a bronzed perfection and her wide eyes glittered with pure gold in the flickering candlelight. Viper stilled in wonderment. He had never seen anything so beautiful in his entire existence.

She was perfect. A vision from his dreams that he could not quite believe was real.

Keeping her firmly trapped beneath him, Viper reached for

the offensive braid and began to loosen the silken curls. He wanted to see her hair spread across the pillows. More than that he wanted to have that satin curtain tangled about them as they made hot, sweaty love.

No doubt sensing the sudden heat in the air, she regarded him with wary eyes.

"What are you doing?"

His fingers never hesitated as he tugged her hair loose. "I did warn you that I would punish you if I caught you attempting to open the box."

"I was only looking at it."

He flashed a smile. "I have something far more interesting for you to look at."

As expected a lovely blush stained her cheeks. "Says you," she muttered.

He lifted a strand of hair to deeply inhale her delicate scent. "You seemed to find me interesting enough a few hours ago."

"I was traumatized by my battle with the Lu. I wasn't thinking clearly."

"Traumatized?"

"Yes."

Viper skimmed her lips in a light kiss.

"And now?"

"Now?"

He chuckled softly. "Are you traumatized now?"

The golden eyes darkened with unmistakable desire. "I must be."

"Why? Because you want me?"

"Yes."

Any hope of retreat was lost as Viper cupped her face in his hands and lowered his head.

Hell, any hope of retreat was lost the moment he had first laid eyes on the Shalott.

"Moonlight silk," he murmured as he caught her lower lip between his teeth. "It is no wonder I am bewitched."

"Bewitched?" Her lips moved against his as she spoke. "I thought you didn't like magic?"

He gently outlined her mouth with his tongue. "I like this magic. I like it very, very much."

"Viper . . ."

Her hands lifted as if she would push him away and Viper stifled a curse. Dammit all. It didn't take a thousand years of experience to know that she wanted him. Truly and utterly wanted him. He could feel her desire like a tangible force in the air.

Why the hell did she continue to fight him?

He prepared himself for her rejection, but astonishingly her hands hesitated and then ever so slowly, slipped beneath his robe to smooth over the tense muscles of his chest. If he had a beating heart it would have halted beating.

The touch was light, hesitant. But it was enough to send a jolt of sizzling need through his body.

"Yes," he whispered as he captured her mouth in a kiss that was no longer teasing.

Drinking deeply of her sweetness he at least possessed the sense not to nick her with his fangs. He was consumed enough with physical lust. He wasn't certain what would happen if bloodlust was tossed into the mix.

He might self-combust on the spot.

Impatiently tugging off his robe, Viper tangled his fingers in the silk of her hair and pressed hungry kisses over the line of her cheek. He wanted to feel the heat of her warming his skin. To wrap himself in her smoldering life.

He nipped at the lobe of her ear, murmuring soft endearments in an ancient Slavic tongue as he shifted to tug at the hem of her gown.

"Shay, I need to feel you next to me," he muttered. "I want your skin against my own."

"What are we doing?" she whispered, as he peeled the gown over her head and tossed it onto the floor.

He regarded her with amusement as he allowed his hands to freely explore the slender curves. "If you haven't figured it out yet, I'm doing something wrong."

She sucked in a sharp gasp as his fingers cupped her breast and his thumb gently teased her nipple to a tight bud.

"This is insanity."

"I can't think of a more pleasant madness," Viper murmured as he dipped his head down to close his lips around the tip of her nipple.

Shay moaned as she clutched at his shoulders, her body instinctively arching in silent invitation.

Viper used his teeth and tongue to pleasure her sensitive flesh, his hands clamping on her hips to keep her from rubbing against his straining erection.

He wanted this to last.

A task that was in dire jeopardy with every lift of her hips.

He trailed his tongue along the underside of her breast, planting a kiss in the valley between her breasts before moving to the unexplored nipple.

"Viper . . ."

"Do you like this?" he demanded as he lightly flicked his tongue over her breast.

"God, yes."

"And this?"

Giving a last tug on her nipple he kissed his way down her stomach, pausing to caress the dip of her belly button before seeking the waiting treasure below. Tugging her legs apart he allowed his hands to run a soft line down her inner thighs. Just for a moment he wanted to appreciate the sight of her spread on the black silk.

Lying on the pillows, Shay met his glance with a smoldering golden gaze, her features softened with a passion she was no longer attempting to conceal.

"Viper?"

"You are so beautiful," he said as his head lowered and his mouth moved down the length of her leg. He wanted to explore every satin inch of her. Every precious curve.

He nuzzled the inside of her knee, the line of her calf, and the delicate bones of her ankle. She gave a gasp as he suckled her toes, her hips arching off the bed.

"That tickles," she breathed, although she did nothing to pull away from his lingering touch.

"You're ticklish?" he teased, licking a path down the bottom of her foot.

She gave a soft squeal. "Viper, stop that."

"I want to taste every inch of you," he said.

Her hands clenched the satin sheets. "I'm not sure I can bear it."

"Let's see just how much you can bear."

He grasped her other foot and slowly feasted his way back up her leg. Her amusement faded as a soft moan was wrenched from her throat.

He paused at the smooth line of her thigh, the scent of her blood pulsing beneath the skin nearly overwhelming. His tongue traced the pale blue vein as he battled back the urge to sink his fangs deep into her flesh.

Not tonight.

Not until she was prepared to give of herself utterly.

Unaware of his dark thoughts, Shay shifted restlessly beneath his lingering touch.

"Viper . . . please."

He smiled as he settled between her legs and at last sought out the source of her need.

"Is this what you want, pet?" he asked as his tongue swept through her damp heat.

"Oh . . . shit," she breathed as her fingers reached down to tangle in his hair.

He laughed. "I'll take that as a yes."

He spread her even farther as he stroked the tiny nub hidden in the soft folds. Her breath came in shallow gasps as her hips pressed upward.

The scent of her filled his senses and Viper pressed his hardness into the slick sheets. He was thick and aching and desperate to be deep inside her. But first he wanted to taste her climax on his lips.

Skimming his hands up to find her breasts he tugged at the hardened peaks as his tongue continued its steady pace. Her breath became almost frantic. Her fingers pulled at his hair as her legs encircled his neck.

"Viper . . ." she breathed.

She was close. He could feel her muscles clenching in pleasure, and with one long last stroke he pushed her screaming over the edge.

Moving swiftly he positioned himself above her while she was still trembling with her release, and taking her lips in a possessive kiss he thrust deep. A moan was wrenched from his throat as her hands swept down his back to cup his hips. Her slender body fit perfectly beneath him, and the Shalott pheromones that had lured vampires for centuries were filling the air with a potent force.

So much for making anything last.

With a slow movement he pulled out to his very tip before thrusting back into her silken heat. Saints above, but she was hot and tight and she clutched him as if she had been made just to hold him deep within her.

Scattering kisses over her face Viper rocked his hips over and over, keeping his pace steady as she wrapped her legs around his waist. Her nails bit into his skin deep enough to draw blood. He growled in encouragement, the sharp pain only heightening his pleasure as he buried his face in the curve of her neck. The pressure was building as his hands moved beneath her hips, lifting her up to meet his quickening thrusts more easily.

"Shay, come with me," he urged as he felt her quiver beneath him.

Her head twisted restlessly on the pillow, her eyes squeezed shut. "I don't think I have a choice," she panted.

"Good."

Sealing her lips with his own he plunged within her, feeling her clenching about him before he at last lost himself in the fierce orgasm that shook him to his very soul.

Wow.

It seemed a ridiculous sort of word.

Or at least it had until the past few moments.

Not the sort of word she would ever use.

Now, however, as Shay battled to gather her breath she realized that there really wasn't any other word to actually describe what had just occurred.

Still bathed in sweat and too weak to move, she rested her head on Viper's chest. It wasn't the first time she had found pleasure in a man's arms. But she couldn't fool herself that she had ever felt such raw, unrelenting need.

Or had her body ever responded to a man's touch with such a fierce joy.

Crap, crap, and double crap.

Why the hell did the best sex she had ever enjoyed have to be in the arms of a vampire?

It sucked. Literally.

As if sensing her tangled thoughts, Viper slipped a finger beneath her chin and tilted up her head to meet his searching gaze.

"You're quiet. Are you well?"

Was she well?

Certainly she was sweaty, sated, and stunned.

But well?

The jury was still out on that.

"I thought vampires always took blood when they—"

His brows rose as her words broke off in embarrassment. "Make love?"

"Yes."

He studied her for a long moment, obviously sensing that it was not just the lack of blood donation that was troubling her.

"It's not mandatory, but it's true that our lusts tend to rise together. Does it worry you that I might bite you?"

"I'd be a fool if it didn't."

His expression never altered, but lying so close to him she could feel his body stiffen.

"If you will recall, pet, I offered my word."

Untangling herself from his arms she propped herself on the headboard and tugged the sheets up to her chin. It wasn't so much modesty that made her cover her body, but more the fear that the least touch from Viper and she might not be able to control herself.

God . . . he was just so gorgeous. Lying on the black sheets with his hair tangled in a silver cloud he looked like something that had been dropped from heaven. She swallowed heavily, forcing herself to meet the glittering black gaze.

"Are you angry?" she at last demanded.

The arrogance was in full throttle as he glared at her. "It's not often that my honor is questioned. I'm beginning to wonder what it is I have to do to earn your trust."

She shrugged, too involved with her own confused emotions to pay full attention to the tension humming in the air.

"What does it matter? I'm your slave. I'm forced to obey you regardless of my feelings. Why would you even desire my trust?"

With a blur of speed he was off the bed and regarding her with a cold anger. He seemed utterly indifferent to the fact he was stark naked.

Unfortunately, Shay was not nearly so indifferent. Her entire body clenched in excitement as her gaze traveled helplessly over his alabaster perfection.

Oh . . . sweet heaven.

"Forced to obey?" The edge in his voice brought her gaze back to his cold expression. "Is that why you're in my bed? Because you think you were forced?"

"I . . . no, of course not."

The dark eyes remained hard and unyielding. "There is, *no of course not,* about it."

Shay shivered beneath the sheet. This was a side of Viper she had never seen before.

"Why are you so mad?"

"Oh, I don't know." His mouth twisted in a humorless smile. "Perhaps because you have done what no other woman has done in over a thousand years."

"What's that?"

"Imply that I raped her."

Her breath caught in shock. "I never implied—"

"No? You lay in my arms speaking of being my slave, and attempting to convince yourself that you could not possibly have desired me." His harsh voice rasped over her body in a near tangible punishment. "You would rather believe that I forced myself upon you than to admit that it was your own passions that led to this moment."

Shay dropped her gaze. He was right, of course. Her body had no complications. It wanted Viper. Wanted him with a force that was downright frightening.

But her mind . . . ah, her mind remembered that it had been a vampire who had ruthlessly murdered her father. And vampires who hunted Shalotts like they were animals.

"What do you want from me?"

"The truth."

She reluctantly lifted her gaze. "What truth?"

He narrowed his gaze. "Admit that you want me. Nothing more, just that."

Shay licked her lips. "I'll admit that you're handsome and obviously experienced . . ."

A deep growl rumbled through his throat as he grasped his robe and shoved his arms into the sleeves. "Enough."

Shay watched in shock as he turned toward the door.

"Where are you going?"

He halted, but he refused to turn around. "Anywhere but here. If you can still think of me as a monster after what we just shared, then there is no hope for you."

A flare of guilt clenched at her heart. As much as she might hate to admit it, he was right. She was being utterly unfair. She had wanted him every bit as much as he had wanted her. Hell, maybe even more. And she still wanted him.

Deep inside her she knew that if he walked out that door now his pride would keep him from ever opening himself to her again.

She slipped from the bed and hurried until she was standing directly in front of him. "Wait, Viper."

"What now?" He stabbed her with a cold glare. "You've

already mangled my pride, and my manhood, is there something else you wish to destroy?"

Her lips twitched in spite of herself. She had never seen a vampire in a huff before. And Viper was in a full-blown huff.

"I doubt anyone could mangle your pride, vampire." She reached up to boldly grasp the lapels of his robe, deliberately arching her naked body against him. "God knows you have enough to share with most of Chicago."

He stiffened, his gaze regarding her warily. "And my manhood?" he demanded.

She slowly smiled as she rubbed against him. "It feels in adequate condition."

There was a moment as he battled between his offended pride, and the desire that she could already feel stirring against her.

"Adequate?"

The jut of his erection pressed heavily against her stomach. "Perhaps more than adequate."

He gave a shake of his head as his arms wrapped about her, his hands instinctively lowering to cup her bare bottom.

"Are you attempting to drive me mad? Is that my punishment for having been foolish enough to purchase you from Evor?"

She grimaced as she gazed into his beautiful features. She could tell him that she would try to be a little less of a pain in the ass. But it would be a lie. He was still a vampire. And she was still his slave. And there was still someone, or something, out there who intended to have her blood. Being a pain was almost inevitable.

"I'm not very good at this," she admitted.

He gave a lift of his brow. "Good at what?"

"Relationships."

"Is that what we have?" he demanded. "A relationship?"

Barely aware of what she was doing her hands slipped beneath the heavy robe to stroke over the lines of his chest. She loved his skin. She had never felt anything so smooth. Like cool silk beneath her fingers.

"You're the expert, you tell me."

"You keep that up and I won't be telling you anything, I'll be showing you," he rasped, his eyes dark and his fangs extended.

She shivered with anticipation. She had no idea what sort of relationship she might or might not have with Viper. In truth, she would rather ignore the word relationship altogether. It always made her break out in a rash. But she was beginning to accept that having a lover wasn't such a bad thing. She breathed deeply of his exotic scent.

"I have always preferred action to talk," she murmured.

"You are—" He broke off with a rueful chuckle.

"What?"

"I have yet to decide." He reached down to brush his lips over her brow. "I only know that I should have my head examined for ever showing up at the auction house. You are destined to be a thorn in my side for all of eternity."

Her hands began to trail in a determined path downward when he gave a low groan and abruptly cupped her hips to lift her off the ground. Shay's heart lodged in her throat as her legs instinctively wrapped about his waist.

"Viper."

"You did say you preferred action," he murmured as he positioned her above his erection and thrust inside with one smooth motion.

Shay's head tilted backward as pleasure speared through her body.

"Yes . . . oh, yes."

Chapter Fifteen

Shay woke alone.

Well, not entirely alone.

There was a breakfast tray left on the bedside table, complete with an omelet, bacon, toast, hash browns, a carafe of orange juice, and an entire apple pie. There were also delicate ivory rose petals sprinkled over the sheets to fill the room with their musky scent.

More than a little unnerved by her night of passion in Viper's arms Shay managed to consume every bite on the tray. Then, after jumping in the shower, she attired herself in a pair of comfortable jeans and sweatshirt before losing herself in the vast maze of the mansion.

It wasn't that she was regretting her time with Viper.

Holy moly.

There wasn't a woman, demon, imp, or fairy who would regret being in his arms.

Still, she wasn't sure she was prepared to confront him so soon.

She found it far too difficult to think clearly when he was near. An embarrassing realization, but true. And now seemed a good time to be thinking clearly.

At last stumbling across a small, but lovely solarium she settled herself on a padded bench and breathed in the scent of

rich earth and fresh flowers. There was something very peaceful about nature, she decided. A reminder that there was something far more vast and powerful than her and her troubles.

Allowing the silence to ease the tension that knotted her
muscles Shay leaned her head against the cushions of her seat
and heaved a deep sigh.

It was the sudden chill in the air that warned her that she
was no longer alone. And that the intruder was a vampire. But
not Viper, she acknowledged as she reluctantly straightened.
Her heart wasn't leaping, her mouth hadn't gone dry, and her
skin hadn't grown clammy. All symptoms of one very specific
vampire.

Proving her instincts right Dante strolled around a large
mound of daisies to offer her a charming smile.

"So you found the solarium."

She couldn't help but return his smile. Despite being a vampire there was something very beguiling about the man.

"It's beautiful."

"I'll tell Abby you approve. She is quite adamant that the
only means of enjoying nature is to have it properly civilized
behind glass." His smile widened. "Of course, she's also determined to civilize me as well, but with much less success."

"Civilize you?"

"It has been claimed that I am too much a warrior and not
enough of a poet."

Shay could believe that. He looked like a wicked pirate with
his long black hair and golden hoop earrings. But she was
not so easily fooled.

"You forget, I've seen your library. If anything you're a
scholar."

He gave a lift of his hands. "Good God, don't let that get
around. I far prefer the image of a warrior."

She couldn't help but laugh. "My lips are sealed."

Moving forward he leaned against the edge of the marble
fountain. At a glance he appeared utterly relaxed, but she
didn't miss the sharp, piercing curiosity in the silver eyes.

"You know, I never did thank you for your assistance in helping me to rescue Abby," he said.

"It was fairly self-serving." She didn't bother to hide her shiver. "No one wanted Edra dead more than I did."

"You didn't have to take a spell blast meant for Viper."

Well, hell, wasn't that the truth?

She rolled her eyes. "Believe me, I've regretted that impulsive decision more than once."

His soft chuckle was nearly tangible. Shay had to wonder if vampires practiced their affect on women or if it was just a power that came with the fangs.

"No doubt." He tilted his head to one side, abruptly shifting the conversation. "Is there any reason you're out here alone?"

"Just catching my breath."

"Perfectly understandable. Shalotts have always preferred to be the hunter rather than the hunted. It's not pleasant being on the run from dangerous enemies."

Her hands closed in her lap as the familiar dread clenched at her stomach. "No, it's not."

His expression softened. "At least you are not alone. For all his arrogance, there are few I would rather have standing at my side than Viper."

Was that why he had sought her out? To convince her that Viper was some sort of knight in shining armor?

"If you do not mind, I would rather not discuss Viper."

He regarded her for a long moment. "Is he troubling you?"

With a short, humorless laugh she rose to her feet and paced away from the looming vampire.

"Always."

"Do you wish me to speak with him?"

"No." She abruptly spun about, her hands pressed to her stomach. "I mean . . . crap, I have no idea what I mean."

He was wise enough not to laugh at her bumbling stupidity. "I don't think you are the only one, my dear," he said gently. "I have known Viper for a considerable length of time, and to be honest I have never seen him so . . . unhinged by a woman.

He has a reputation for being aloof even in his most intimate relationships."

"Aloof?" She made a rude sound. "I have never encountered a more meddlesome, pushy, invasive vampire."

"As I said, he is not at all himself." He gave a lift of his shoulders. "I don't know whether to congratulate you or offer my condolences."

Funny, that made two of them.

She gave a shake of her head. "I just don't understand him."

"He does enjoy shrouding himself in mystery."

"Why did he buy me? He doesn't want a slave. He doesn't want to sell my blood. He hasn't even tasted of it." She heaved an exasperated sigh. "What does he want?"

"Does he have to want something?"

She sent him a pointed glance. "He's a vampire."

"True enough." Dante slowly straightened, his hands on his hips. "I suppose the simple answer is that he doesn't know himself why he bought you."

"He's over a thousand years old not sixteen, how can he not know why he bought me?"

He shrugged. "Sometimes living so long tends to make us . . . a bit self-absorbed."

"You think?" she said.

His lips twitched but his expression remained serious. "Even within our own clans we are solitary creatures. There are many vampires that exclude themselves entirely and go decades without contact with others."

"So you are hermits?"

"Of a sort. The world passes while we remain unchanging. It's a natural tendency to withdraw into ourselves until something, or someone, tempts us from our shells."

She grimaced. She hadn't done a thing to lure Viper from his shell. At least not intentionally.

"You do not entirely withdraw." A faint edge entered her voice. She was all too aware that vampires were not harmless hermits. Not by a long shot. "You must still hunt."

"No longer. We have synthetic blood that most prefer to the dangers of the hunt."

"What dangers?" she scoffed. "You're immortal."

The handsome features seemed to close upon themselves, as if he had revealed more than he had intended.

"There are ways to kill us. Why risk a wooden stake through the heart when you can have your meal served from the microwave?" he demanded, his tone almost too casual.

Shay might have pursued her suspicion that Dante was hiding something from her if she hadn't been caught up in the wounds that had never healed.

"I thought vampires enjoyed hunting their victims? The thrill of the kill, and all that."

Dante didn't miss the bitterness in her voice. "Viper told me your father was killed by a vampire. I'm sorry."

Her gaze dropped. "It was a long time ago."

"But never forgotten."

"No, never forgotten."

Without warning the toes of his biker boots came into her view and she lifted her head to discover Dante standing directly before her.

"Shay, Viper didn't kill your father."

She winced at his soft tone. "I know that."

"Do you?" He lightly touched her arm. "Do you truly?"

"Most of the time," she conceded.

"Shay . . ."

"Dante." They both jumped at the sound of the black velvet voice that floated through the air. "For such an intelligent vampire you do like to live dangerously, don't you?"

Turning, Shay watched as Viper strolled in their direction. No, not strolled. Glided. Like a sleek panther sliding through shadow. Her breath caught in her throat as he neared. He was beautiful, as always. Attired in black satin pants and black velvet coat that fell nearly to his knees, his silver hair and ivory skin nearly glowed in contrast. But it was the black eyes that captured and held her attention. There was a smoldering power in them that seemed to stir the very air.

"Ah, Viper." Standing at her side Dante folded his arms over his chest and smiled with a mysterious hint of smugness. "I thought you would put in your appearance sooner or later."

There was a smile on the elegant features, but as Viper halted before them Shay gave a small shiver. His fangs were showing.

Both literally and nonliterally.

"Obviously it should have been sooner," he drawled.

"Oh, I don't know. Shay and I have had no trouble entertaining one another without you," Dante assured him.

The dark eyes narrowed. "You are fortunate that you are mated, old friend."

Dante gave a sudden laugh. "Pull in your fangs, Viper, we were just speaking about you."

The fangs remained very much in evidence. "Actually, that is what I feared."

"Has Abby returned?"

"Yes, she is in the library with the latest witch. Perhaps you should join her."

"An excellent notion." Sending Shay a blatant wink, Dante slapped his friend on the back and disappeared into the shadows.

Ignoring the dark frown that marred Viper's brow as he watched Dante's retreat, Shay stepped in front of him with a frown of her own.

"Natasha is back?" she demanded.

Glancing down at her sour expression Viper's frown was suddenly replaced with a smile.

"No, Abby thought perhaps it would be best to keep Natasha away from you."

"Why?"

"She had muttered something about putting another curse on you when Dante was taking her home."

"Why would . . . oh, I suppose she was jealous?" Shay grimaced, refusing to acknowledge she was relieved the pushy tart hadn't returned. That would mean the witch wasn't the only one jealous, and that would just be . . . stupid.

Moving close enough to make her heart leap into her throat Viper brushed a finger down the line of her jaw.

"There are some females who do not find me utterly offensive."

"You don't have to look so smug. She must have been sniffing too many potions."

The midnight eyes darkened with that dangerous awareness that sent a thrill of excitement whispering over her skin.

"If you doubt my charm, perhaps I could give you a demonstration."

"I think you've given me quite enough demonstrations."

"Never enough," he whispered as his head lowered.

Shay's heart halted as he brushed his lips back and forth over hers. It was the lightest of caresses, but it sent a shock of pleasure through her that nearly brought her to her knees.

Holy crap.

Surely any decent woman would be sated after a bout of marathon sex?

If that was true then she was obviously not a decent woman, she conceded, as her body instinctively arched to press against his hard form.

Viper only had to be near for her to melt with need.

Growling deep in his throat Viper kissed her with a swiftly mounting urgency. Shay cupped his face with her hands as she opened her lips to the press of his tongue. Not even the sharp prick of his fangs could dampen the flare of passion.

It felt so good to be in his arms.

So right.

So deliciously wonderful.

His arms lashed about her, nearly hauling her off her feet. Shay moaned. Pressed so close to him it was impossible to miss the hard thrust of his mounting desire. And even more impossible not to recall the memory of wrapping her legs about his waist as he thrust into her.

That's what she wanted. Right here. Right now.

And the force of that want was what at last shook her back to her senses. They were in the middle of a solarium where anyone could walk in on them. She hadn't lost all sense of decency.

Not yet.

Pulling back she struggled to find her voice. "Viper."

Denied her lips Viper contented himself with scattering kisses over her upturned face.

"What?"

"Why is there a witch in the library?"

"She's here to make sure there are no nasty spells on the box."

Shay pressed her hands to his chest, refusing to be distracted as he nuzzled just below her ear.

"Then shouldn't we be in there?"

He gave her ear a sharp nip. "We have plenty of time. You know how witches love to create a sense of melodrama when they are about to cast a spell. It will take her an hour to set her circle and place her candles, and all the other mumbo jumbo they insist upon."

She shivered. "I still think we should be there. I don't want to miss anything."

Just for a moment his arms tightened about her as if he intended to wipe away any thought of witches and boxes and curses. Then, with a sigh, he reluctantly loosened his grip and regarded her with an expression of sorrow.

"Oh, pet, you are brutal upon my pride. Do you have no romance in your soul at all?"

Shay stepped back and smoothed her sweatshirt back in place. She wished it were so easy to smooth the embarrassing hormones raging through her body.

"Very little," she conceded.

"It seems that I shall have to teach you the pleasures of seduction."

"You can teach me later." Unable to resist she reached to place a swift kiss on his cheek before moving toward the door. "Right now I want to find out what's in that box."

* * *

"Sacrebleu." With his stunning lack of anything resembling tact, Levet stomped into the library. "What is that stench?"

The gray-haired witch pointed a gnarled finger in the demon's direction, never lifting her head from her task of lighting the circle of candles.

"Hold your tongue, gargoyle, or I shall stick it to the roof of your mouth," she warned.

With a hiss, Levet glared at the elderly woman. "Eeek. A hag. Who invited her?"

For a moment Viper leaned against the wall and waited in pleasure for the witch to turn the annoying gargoyle into a newt, or a tomato, or anything that couldn't speak. As much as he disliked witches they occasionally had their uses. But one glance at Shay's worried expression and he was grudgingly moving forward to grasp the creature by his ridiculous tail and tugging him out of the fray. Shay had enough on her mind without concern that her pet gargoyle was about to become a toad.

"I would suggest you either close your mouth or take it somewhere else, Levet," Viper drawled, once again leaning against the wall, his gaze returning to Shay's delicate profile. "The witch does not seem to have much patience."

"What is she doing?"

"Attempting to open the box on the table."

"Open a box?" Levet threw his hands up and started forward. *"Mon dieu.* I can do that."

"Hold." Viper grabbed the twitching tail and hauled the gargoyle back. "We are not yet certain if it is warded."

"Oh." There was a moment of blessed silence before Levet was shifting impatiently. "What's in the box?"

"Obviously, we don't know yet."

"Is it going to take long?"

"It will take as long as it takes."

"Are we having snacks?"

Viper's hands clenched at his sides. It was that or throttling the demon.

"Levet, shut up."

"Well, if we have to wait around for the entire night they could at least serve snacks."

"If you're hungry, why don't you go to the kitchen and find something for yourself?"

The gargoyle shuddered. "There's nothing there but blood and some green gunk."

"Then order out."

"Pizza? Greek?" The gray eyes lit with excitement. "Oh, oh, I know, how about—"

Bending down Viper grasped Levet by the horns and pulled him until they were nose to nose.

"Get a phone, order the food, gargoyle, and be assured that if you step foot back in this room I will personally rip off those wings."

Wisely backing toward the door the gargoyle gave a lift of his hands.

"Jeez, there's no need for the attitude. Vampires are always so testy."

The gargoyle had no idea, Viper acknowledged as he firmly turned back to Shay.

Testy didn't begin to cover his mood.

Watching Shay hovering so anxiously beside the witch made his unbeating heart clench with pain.

However brave and defiant she might pretend to be beneath all the bluster, she was heartbreakingly fragile. The mere thought that she might be further hurt made him long to smash everything in sight.

Dammit. He should have locked them both in the solarium. They could even now be soaring to the heights of pleasure, rather than standing in this damnably hot room watching a witch do her endless hocus-pocus.

Shifting irritably Viper ignored Dante's concerned glance and crossed his arms over his chest.

Oh, yes, they should definitely be in the solarium . . .

"I am done." With a dramatic motion the witch waved her hand and the candles were snuffed out. "The box is now safe to open."

Viper straightened as Shay reached for the delicately carved wooden box. He didn't miss the fine tremor of her hand, or the tightening of her features.

Instinctively he stepped forward, longing to pull her into his arms and add his strength to her own. Only the knowledge that she would detest him revealing that she was anything but utterly confident kept him rooted to his spot.

The very air seemed to still as Shay slowly lifted the lid and pulled out a crumpled envelope.

"It's addressed to me," she whispered in the thick silence. Lifting her head she glanced around the room, sucking in a deep breath. "If you'll excuse me, I think I should read this in private."

She turned and headed for the door. Without thought Viper was on her heels. He didn't want her alone. Not when they didn't yet know what was in the letter. It was Dante's hand on his arm that brought him to an abrupt halt.

"Viper, I think you should respect her wishes," his friend murmured in tones only Viper could hear. "She won't thank you for intruding when she wants to be alone."

"It's too dangerous for—"

"She is safe enough here. The house is well warded against demons, and there are alarms for the more human intruders."

Viper gave a low hiss. "I don't like feeling helpless."

Dante gave a wry chuckle. "Get used to it, old friend. Women have a tendency to do that to a man."

Viper narrowed his gaze. "You're not helping."

"Just give her a few moments. Nothing will happen to her while she's in this house."

"Fine, but only a few."

Pulling from the vampire's grasp he paced across the vast library. Damn Dante and his annoying logic. He didn't want to be sensible. He didn't want to give Shay the privacy she desired.

Hell, he might as well be honest. He didn't want her out of his sight for even a moment. He gave an unconscious shake of his head. Devil's balls. He was a fool. A stark, raving fool.

Unable to hold still, he continued his pacing as time slowly crawled past. He was distantly aware that Dante had left to take the witch back to her coven, and that Abby had brought a tray of warmed blood and silently placed it on the desk, but they had no ability to intrude into his dark brooding.

Where the devil was Shay?

Why hadn't she returned?

There had to be something wrong. He felt it in the very depths of his soul.

After an hour he had had enough. Bursting from the library in a flurry of power, he swept through the mansion in search of his missing Shalott. In truth he hadn't expected it to be much of a search. The two obvious places were her rooms or the solarium. Where else could she be assured of relative privacy?

It took only moments to discover she was in neither.

Bloody hell.

And another handful of moments to discover that she was nowhere else in the house.

Thoroughly alarmed Viper returned to his own rooms and withdrew the tiny amulet from his pocket. He didn't doubt for a moment Shay would be furious to be called to him like a dog on a leash. He would be furious in her place. But for now Viper was content to deal with her anger. As long as she was near, and he was convinced she was safe, she could rant and rave all she liked.

Closing his fingers about the amulet he felt it grow warm against his skin. Ten minutes later Shay stormed through the door, her expression defiant but her eyes swollen and red from crying.

"Damn you, Viper," she hissed. "Let me go."

"No." Pocketing the amulet Viper moved forward to regard her with open concern. "It's too dangerous for you to be running off."

She wrapped her arms about herself. "I'm not stupid. I have no intention of running off while there is still someone out there hunting me. I just want to be alone."

"Talk to me, pet," he urged. "Tell me what was in the letter."

There was a long moment when Viper feared she would refuse to answer him. She had been alone for so long. Too long. She no longer knew how to trust others.

"It's from my father."

Chapter Sixteen

Shay had every intention of being furious with Viper. For all his promises not to treat her as a slave he had been swift enough to use the leash that held her to him.

He was no better than the witches, she had told herself.

She had wanted to be alone. She had wanted to battle through her maze of raw emotions before she was forced to face him. He had no right to yank her to his side against her will. And yet the moment she was standing before him she found her anger melting. In fact, she discovered herself longing to lean against that hard body, as if being in his arms would make everything better.

Dammit. The knowledge should be terrifying. Unfortunately she was simply too overwhelmed at the moment to conjure the proper horror. Instead she wrapped her own arms about herself and watched as the inevitable shock rippled over his pale face.

"Your . . . father?"

"Yes."

He seemed to carefully consider his response, as if he were dealing with a nut. And maybe he was.

"Surely that should please you?"

She swallowed past the thick lump lodged in her throat. "He had the curse placed upon me."

He reached up to cup her face, his cool touch ridiculously easing a portion of the pain clutching at her heart.

"You cannot be certain, Shay. This could be a trick."

"No. It's no trick. The letter says that he did it to protect me."

His fingers tightened to a near painful level. "What?"

"He knew that he was being stalked, although he didn't know who or what was chasing him. He says that the curse is intended to hide me from his enemies."

"Hide you?"

"The curse was like a barrier that kept me shielded from most demons."

He considered for a long moment. "Yes, I suppose it has managed to do that. There hasn't been even the whisper of a Shalott in over a century. Still, it was a rather dangerous and desperate gamble. He left you at the mercy of Evor."

Shay pulled from his touch. Just having him so near was distraction enough.

"He never intended to leave me at the mercy of anyone," she said. More to convince herself than Viper. "Once the danger was passed the witch was pledged to break the curse and reveal the truth to me."

His beautiful features were unreadable. "But she was killed before she could do so?"

"Yes."

A beat passed. A beat where Shay had no idea what was going through his mind. A vampire was a master at hiding his emotions when he wanted to.

"He was only attempting to protect you, Shay," he at last said softly.

The stupid tears she had been stemming for the past hour burned hot in her eyes as she abruptly turned to hide her distress.

"I know that, it's just . . ."

With a speed she could never match, he had moved to stand directly before her.

"What?"

She blew out a heavy sigh, accepting there was no way to hide from him.

"All these years I've blamed my rotten fate on whatever horrible monster had put this curse on me. Now I discover it was my own father."

"He obviously did it with the best of intentions."

"That doesn't change the fact that I've spent over eighty years as a slave." Her teeth clenched as the memories threatened to rise up. Memories she kept locked away so they didn't drown her. "I've been beaten, chained, and sold like an animal."

"I know it's been difficult—"

"Difficult?" She gave a short, humorless laugh. "There hasn't been a moment when I haven't been at the mercy of some master. Not a moment when I didn't fear what the next hour might bring. Not a moment when I haven't struggled just to survive."

"Shay."

The pity on his face had her angrily swiping at the tears. "I'm sorry. I'm not usually a whiner."

His eyes darkened. "Don't be sorry." He lightly touched the dampness that lingered on her cheeks. "I only met the witches briefly, but I don't doubt they made your life a living hell."

"Hell is right," her voice held a bitter edge. "When Edra was displeased she would lock me in a cellar. More than once she left me down there for years. There was no light, no food except for the bugs and rats I could find crawling around me. There were times when I didn't think I would ever get out. I thought . . ." Her voice broke and she was forced to clear her throat before she could continue. "I thought I would be stuck in the dark for an eternity."

His expression was carefully neutral, as if he sensed that she would close down at the first hint of pity.

"That's why you insisted that those demons be loosened at the auction house?"

"Yes. Nothing deserves such torture." She forced herself to meet his gaze squarely. "But you know Edra wasn't the worst of it."

"What was?"

"The knowledge that I'll always be in the power of someone.

That I can never be strong enough, or fast enough, or smart enough to escape, because there is no escape."

His features tightened, no doubt sensing that a part of her frustration reached out to include him. With that smooth elegance he turned to pace toward the bed before turning and regarding her from a distance.

"Actually, I know precisely how you feel."

"You?" She gave a disbelieving snort. "How could you possibly understand?"

He remained shrouded in the shadows, reminding her of the aloof vampire who had first arrived at the auction house to bid on her.

"I was not always a clan chief," he said, his tone low and oddly rough. "There were many years after I was first turned that I was at the mercy of whatever vampire wished to claim me."

Shay felt a stab of shock. It was impossible to imagine this arrogant, ruthless man at the mercy of anyone. Certainly not another vampire. He seemed . . . impervious. Invulnerable.

"You were a slave?"

"A slave and worse."

"What could be worse?"

"You do not truly want to know, pet."

She bit her tongue. He was right. However bad the witches had been there could always be worse. Much, much worse.

She gave a slow shake of her head. "I thought that clans protected their own?"

Viper gave a graceful shrug. "Times have thankfully changed and we have grown more civilized."

"Civilized? You think vampires are civilized?"

"Compared to the past. There was a time when the clans were merely wandering bands of warriors. To become a part of the clan a newly awakened vampire had to . . . submit to their demands no matter how twisted or depraved they might be."

Shay frowned. "Then why would you wish to be a part of a clan?"

"To be alone was to die."

"They would have killed you?"

"The strong survived and the weak were merely prey."

"And you were prey?"

Her skin prickled as his power flared through the room. "Until I became strong enough to battle back."

"But you did become strong enough," she said softly.

There was a moment as he battled his own inner demons, and Shay abruptly understood the reason for the vast armory of weapons that Viper had hidden beneath his house. Whatever power he might now possess there would always be the knowledge that there were monsters lurking in the dark. He had surrounded himself with the sort of beautiful, lethal objects that were not only a collectors dream, but an unconscious sense of security.

With those gliding steps he was once again standing before her, his hand reaching out to trace the curve of her neck.

"I became strong, but like you the memories remain."

Shay didn't pull away from his cool touch. There was nothing to be read on his beautiful features, but she knew that he had endured horrors that would no doubt give anyone nightmares for centuries. Even more amazing he had managed to maintain a sense of honor and integrity that had kept him from becoming one of the animals that had tortured him. Still, she could not completely dismiss her petty envy. Not as long as she remained bound by her curse.

"You survived and now you are free."

His lips twisted at her words. "Never free, pet. There are . . . powers that even I must answer to."

Her brows lifted in surprise. "You're a clan chief. What powers could you possibly have to answer to?"

"They are forbidden to speak of."

And that was that.

There was no mistaking his tone of voice. It warned her that she could spend the rest of eternity badgering him for an explanation and he would never yield. Which of course only made her all the more curious.

She grimaced. "Am I supposed to be comforted?"

Without warning a smile curved his lips. That sinful smile

that always tugged at something deep within her, and made the hovering darkness a bit less dark.

"We will discover where Evor has been hidden, Shay." His hand shifted to the back of her neck, his fingers lightly brushing up and down her sensitive nape. "And then we will break the curse once and for all."

Her mouth went dry and her toes began to curl in her shoes. It was insanity. A few moments before and she had been sunk in despair. A despair that had felt so thick and heavy she wasn't sure she would ever be rid of it. Now her entire body was tingling and her heart nearly leaping from her chest. It didn't seem possible that a mere touch could so utterly alter her emotions.

Licking her suddenly dry lips she gazed into his beautiful face. "Do you truly believe that?"

The disturbing fingers continued a path down her arching spine. "I would not have said it if I did not believe."

Shay struggled to breathe. "You know, if we do break the curse I will no longer be your slave?"

His smile widened as he shifted to scoop her into his arms. Without missing a beat, he turned and moved toward the bed.

"I do not need an amulet to make a woman my slave," he assured her.

Shay rolled her eyes. "Your arrogance is nothing short of stunning, vampire. If you were half as good as you think—"

Her brave words were cut short as she found herself being tossed onto the mattress and Viper's hard form covering her with obvious intent.

Taking swift advantage Viper lowered his head to nuzzle at her neck.

"You were saying, pet?" he murmured with a hint of amusement.

She shivered as his tongue ran a path to the hollow of her shoulder.

"You aren't playing fair," she accused even as her hands lifted to tug the clip from his hair and plunge her fingers into the silver satin.

His chuckle brushed over her skin as he shifted to tug the sweatshirt over her head. Her bra swiftly followed.

"I'm a vampire. I only play to win."

There was no doubt a perfectly reasonable moral objection to his claim, but as his mouth found the tip of her breast Shay couldn't begin to think that clearly. Instead she moaned and held his head even closer while the pleasure rushed through her in a searing wave.

"What is it you intend to win?" she breathed.

He drew back to stab her with a smoldering gaze. "I have already won precisely what I desired. Now it is a matter of pleasing my prize to the point she never wishes to leave my side."

Shay swallowed a moan. "I'm not sure if you please me any more that I'll survive."

His gaze lowered to sweep over her exposed breasts. "I have every faith in your ability to survive, pet. It is one thing we have in common." His thumb brushed her tightened nipple. "Of course it's not the only thing."

Her eyes rolled back in her head as he lowered his head to kiss her with a raw yearning that clenched at her stomach. They most certainly had this in common, she acknowledged as she felt his fingers fumble with the snap on her jeans. Whatever it was . . . lust, passion, or some darker obsession, it had her in its grip.

She wasn't certain she would ever have enough of this vampire.

Tugging impatiently at his shirt, Shay lifted her hips so he could slip the jeans from her legs. With their lips still locked together she ran her hands over his bare chest, reveling in the feel of his silken skin.

It was so smooth, so perfect.

She needed more.

Viper had explored every inch of her. Touched every curve, stroked and tasted her from head to toe.

It was surely her turn?

Not giving herself time to debate the wisdom of necking with a vampire she had locked her leg around Viper's and with a sharp push had him flat on his back. In the same motion she rolled on top of him, straddling his waist as she straightened to regard him with a fierce hunger.

"My turn," she rasped, as her fingers trailed over his chest to lightly brush his nipples.

Viper's hands clutched at the black sheets beneath him as his body reacted to her touch.

"Your turn for what?" he breathed.

Electric excitement raced through her.

"My turn for this."

Bending downward she scattered kisses over his chest, giving each nipple a flick of her tongue before trailing a wet path down the center of his stomach to the waistband of his pants.

For a moment she nibbled and nipped at the clenched muscles of his stomach. Her tongue traced the swell and dip of his washboard perfection. She explored his belly button. The jut of his hip bone. She easily felt the hard thrust of his erection, but she refused to give in to his silent urging.

At last his hands reached up to clutch at her arms, his eyes as black as midnight as his fangs fully extended.

"For God's sake, pet, put me out of my misery."

A smug smile curved her lips as she slowly unfastened the button. She pulled down the zipper and tugged off his slacks. He growled low in his throat, his fingers digging into her flesh as she gently kissed him through the silk of his boxers.

She ignored his bruising grasp as she traced him with her tongue from top to bottom and then back again. He gave a muffled shout as his hips jerked upward.

Pulling back she allowed her gaze to fully appreciate the sight of his ivory beauty. Contrasted against the black sheets he might have been a statue carved from marble.

Except for the eyes. Those midnight eyes burned with a need that sent an answering jolt of yearning through her body.

With a breathless wonder she reached to pull the silky boxers off his body. She had seen it all before, but she suspected that she would never truly become accustomed to such flawless beauty.

Dropping the boxers onto the floor Shay ran her hands slowly up the length of his legs, following the path with tiny kisses that brought wrenching groans from the man beneath her.

At last reaching his pelvis she reached to encircle his erection, exploring the hard length with fascination. Silk and steel. An erotic combination that made her lower stomach quiver with a building ache.

Kissing her way over his hip she at last pulled him between her lips, using her tongue to taste him as she had longed to do.

His hands clutched at her head, clearly torn between urging her to continue her caresses and halting her before he reached that unstoppable peak.

"Shay . . ."

With a last lingering lick Shay moved her way back up his body, nibbling over his stomach and then his chest before at last finding his mouth with her own.

His hands smoothed down her back, grasping the satin of her panties and ripping them off her with one impatient tug. With that same impatient haste, he parted her thighs and rubbed himself along her wetness.

He turned his head to bury his face in her neck.

"I can't wait, pet," he groaned as he positioned the tip of himself at her entrance. "I'm sorry."

"Don't be sorry, just do it," Shay gasped, her body already wet and ready for his thrust.

Clutching her thighs he plunged himself inside her, halting only when he was buried as deep as he could go.

"Yes . . . God, yes," Viper rasped.

He remained still a breathless moment as they both absorbed the sheer bliss of being so intimately joined. Surely there was nothing that could compare to such intense pleasure? Nothing that could bind two people closer together?

Opening her eyes Shay met the dark, glittering gaze as Viper began to move gently inside her.

Something seemed to shift within her as she fell into the dark heat of his eyes.

Something vast and terrifying and wondrous.

Something that might have sent her running from the room if his movements hadn't become more demanding and her rising climax hadn't wiped her mind of everything but reaching for that shimmering, golden bliss.

Viper paced the library with a frustration he made no attempt to conceal. It had been a week since he and Shay had arrived at Dante's house. A glorious week, of course. How could it not be when he had devoted the vast majority of his nights to pleasing and being pleased by the woman who had become such an essential part of his life?

And it had not just been sex. Which was bloody well fabulous, if he did say so himself. But having her near, hearing her voice, feeling her light touch when they sat on the bed. They were moments that he oddly savored.

Still, for all his delight in exploring the woman who had whirled into his life like a Tasmanian devil, he had never forgotten for a moment that the danger lurked just out of sight. There was something or someone out there who intended to take Shay from him. To use her for their own purpose. He would go to hell and back before he would let that happen.

Spinning on his heel Viper regarded Santiago with a smoldering impatience. The vampire was his best lieutenant. Intelligent, courageous, loyal beyond measure, and, most of all, capable of powerful compulsion over humans and lesser demons.

If there was information to be learned, Santiago would discover it.

"I'm sorry, master." Santiago's dark face was expressionless but there was no missing the hint of tension in his broad shoulders. Like any good servant, he could easily sense his master's annoyance. "I can find no talk on the streets of the Shalotts."

Viper swallowed his low growl. "You can't have searched everywhere. There must be someone who knows who is hunting a Shalott."

Santiago gave a lift of his hands. "Most refuse to believe she is anything more than a myth. Very few Shalott have walked this world for centuries."

"Shay is no myth."

"No, but her presence has never been sensed, even among the most powerful of demons."

"Of course not, the curse masked her presence."

"Even from those who might have been able to assist us." The vampire shrugged. "There are no whispers, no rumors that I can find, nothing that speaks of the Shalott. Not even those familiar with Evor were aware he possessed her."

Viper clenched his hands, forcing back the surge of anger. Dammit. He never lost his temper. Never. "Continue with your search."

"Of course, master."

"And do not limit yourself to Chicago. The truth is out there. We must find it."

"As you wish."

With a bow, the vampire turned and silently retreated from the library. Viper watched him leave before turning to slam his fist onto the wooden desk.

There was a faint stir of air before he felt Dante's hand settle on his shoulder.

"Easy, Viper, we will get to the bottom of this mystery."

"Whoever it is that holds Evor is out there plotting to capture her. I can't just wait for another attack. Not when we can't be sure we can defeat whatever it is they send next."

"I understand your frustration, but we're doing all that we can."

Viper slowly turned to face his friend. "Your contacts have turned up nothing?"

Dante stepped back with a shrug. "I fear not."

"Damn."

With restless motions Viper resumed his pacing. He didn't want to be in this library. He didn't want to be fretting over some mysterious danger that he couldn't feel or touch or battle. He wanted to be down in his rooms where he knew Shay would be rising from their bed. He wanted to be holding her in his arms and pretending that nothing could harm them.

Unfortunately, his every instinct warned him that they were running out of time. If he didn't manage to discover who was hunting Shay, then the hunter would find them. He couldn't allow them to be trapped again.

"You do know you're courting danger, old friend, do you not?" Dante drawled from behind.

Viper halted, his expression far from friendly as he regarded his companion.

"You expect me to toss Shay aside because she brings danger with her?"

"I meant that Shay is the danger."

"Dante—"

"No, I will have my say." The younger vampire insisted, his arms folded over his chest. "I have known you for centuries and you have never shown such an interest in a female before."

"I must beg to disagree. I have shown inordinate interest in females. Quite often interest in dozens of them at a time."

"You've had lovers not companions," Dante corrected. "You have never allowed one in your life as you have this one."

Viper narrowed his gaze. He didn't like the direction this conversation was taking. Perhaps he even feared it.

"What are you implying?" he grudgingly demanded.

Dante had the balls to smile. "I'm not implying anything, Viper. I'm warning you flat out that you are showing every symptom of a vampire who has discovered his true mate."

There. He knew he wasn't going to like it, and he didn't. Why the hell did friends always believe they could bring up subjects a wise vampire would never broach? He turned to grasp one of the endless shelves, his entire body stiff with annoyance.

"My relationship with Shay is none of your concern."

"If you feel like throwing something, I wish you would choose that hideous vase on the desk. The books are irreplaceable."

Viper glared over his shoulder. "You're not amusing, Dante."

"Surely I'm a little amusing?" he teased.

Viper was pondering the pleasure of tossing at least one of the irreplaceable books when the door to the library was abruptly flung open and Levet scrambled in with his wings flapping.

"*Sacrebleu*, there you are," he breathed as he regarded Viper with his usual expression of disgust.

Viper held up a restraining hand. His temper was being held by a thread. A thread the gargoyle was certain to snap.

"Not now, Levet, I do not possess the patience to endure your griping at the moment."

Levet managed to look shocked. "Griping? *Moi?* Why—"

"Out." Viper pointed at the door. "Get out now."

"Non." Levet bravely, or stupidly, held his ground. "Can you not feel the air?"

"What?"

"Hold, Viper." Dante stepped forward, his head tilted back as he spread his powers outward. "He's right."

In the distance there was the sudden sound of an alarm ringing and Viper felt his entire body clench in dread.

"Shit. Levet get Shay and bring her here."

"No." Dante halted them both with a commanding tone. "Take her to the escape tunnels in the basement."

Levet slid a glance toward Viper who gave a sharp nod. "Go."

The gargoyle rushed from the room and Dante moved to stand directly before Viper.

"You go as well."

Viper frowned. "I can't leave you here—"

"You must protect Shay." Dante offered a wry smile. "Besides, as much as I admire your strength and courage I have my own protection."

Viper was momentarily puzzled until a prickling heat slowly began to fill the air. Abby had sensed the danger and already her power was crawling through the house.

"The Chalice," he said.

"Exactly. We'll be fine." Dante gave him a firm shove. "Now go."

Moving toward the door Viper paused to toss his friend a final glance.

"Thank you, Dante. You've done more than I can ever repay."

Dante shrugged. "Actually I was in your debt, so now we can say we're even."

"Never."

The pale, handsome face became uncommonly somber. "Viper, take care, and if you have need . . ."

"You will be the first I call," Viper promised before slipping through the door and heading for his chambers. There were a few dozen weapons he intended to grab before joining Shay in the basement.

Chapter Seventeen

The bathroom connected to Viper's rooms was straight out of a fantasy.

A vast expanse of black and gold it boasted a shower large enough to facilitate a small army, a glass cabinet that heated the fluffy towels, and a line of lighted vanities that were of little use to vampires. It was the tub, however, that enchanted Shay. Sunken into the marble floor, it was perfectly curved to soak in its scented waters for hours at a time. A rare luxury for a slave who had more often than not been forced to scrub herself clean with what little water was passed through the bars of her cell.

She found it the perfect way to begin an evening.

Well, perhaps not the most perfect way to begin the evening.

A sudden flush stained her cheeks as she pulled on the jeans and sweatshirt that she had borrowed from Abby.

Crap.

She promised herself that when she had crawled from the bed exhausted and content from Viper's body that she wouldn't lay in the tub and wallow in the memories of his touch. As pleasurable a pastime as it might be, it was disgustingly mushy. Like she was an acne-plagued adolescent mooning over her latest sweetie.

It was enough to make a sensible, mature woman gag.

Brushing out her long hair, she neatly pulled it back in its usual braid and returned to the bedroom. She knew that Abby would be waiting for her in the solarium with a breakfast tray. They would chat and laugh and moan over the numerous faults of vampires. It was a routine that Shay cherished deep in her heart.

Abby was not only kind and generous, but she offered an unconditional friendship that had slowly started to fill an emptiness that Shay had carried with her for far too long.

A friend.

Something so simple, but so precious.

Slipping on her running shoes Shay moved toward the door. Not usually a dangerous task, but this evening she was barely allowed to touch the knob when she was knocked backward as Levet thrust through the door.

"Shay," he panted, his gray skin more pale than usual.

"Good God, Levet, have you never heard of knocking?" she demanded as she lifted herself upright.

"Viper sent me to fetch you."

"Fetch me?" Her brows drew together in warning. It sounded far too much like calling a dog. "Why didn't he come himself?"

"He's waiting for us. We have to go now."

Shay regarded her companion with a growing sense of alarm. Something was wrong. Very wrong.

"What's happened, Levet?"

"There are demons approaching. Enough demons to make me squirm." Levet gave a shudder. "We have to get out of here."

She lost any urge to argue as she allowed Levet to lead her from the room and down the hallway.

"Where are we going?"

"Dante has tunnels built beneath the estate."

Shay recalled the tunnels that Viper had constructed beneath his own house. It seemed to be a theme.

"Of course he does."

Using his wings to give him speed Levet never turned his head. "Vampires have never been known for being stupid, Shay. Or careless."

"No, I suppose not," she readily agreed.

Reaching the stairs she hesitated as Levet headed downward. From above she could feel the faint tingle of power being wielded. An oddly familiar power.

"*Mon Dieu*. Not that way," the gargoyle gasped.

"The demons?"

Levet grimaced. "Worse . . . the Phoenix."

"Ah." Shay had a vivid image of being trapped in a cellar with Abby as she had transformed into the Phoenix. She had managed to scorch the evil witch trying to kill them into a tiny bit of cinder. She didn't really want an encore performance. Especially since the goddess's powers weren't always particular about which demon was going to get fried. "That would explain the heat."

"Yes. Come on."

"I'm coming." Taking the narrow flight of stairs that led to the lower basement Shay halted on the last step. She was going to hurt herself if she continued to stumble forward. "Damn, it's dark. Is there a light switch?"

"We have no need for something so mundane. Not when I possess magic." Levet halted and began to mutter beneath his breath.

"Levet, no—"

Shay's plea came a moment too late as there was a sudden explosion that sent them both tumbling to the ground.

"Light, I said light," Levet muttered as they struggled to their feet and brushed off the ash that had filled the air.

"I appreciate the effort, Levet, but maybe we should stick with the more traditional methods," she muttered.

"Fine." Levet threw up his hands as he disappeared into the thick shadows. "But when those demons are about to . . . how do you say . . . make you lunch, do not come crying to me for some powerful spell to rescue you."

Shay couldn't help but smile despite the disturbing imagery. "I'll keep that in mind."

Shay and Levet were awaiting Viper when he reached the lower basement. A flare of relief raced through him. He had expected to have to go in search of Shay. Hell, he had expected to have to carry her down here kicking and screaming. For such an intelligent woman she could be stunningly stubborn. It would be just like her to flat out refuse to flee regardless of the danger.

Moving directly toward the back wall Viper adjusted the sword strapped to his back and set aside the heavy bag of weapons before he pulled off the vent that concealed the entrance to the tunnel. It was there just as Dante promised and he waved his hand toward the two that hovered in the shadows.

"This way," he whispered, motioning for Levet to go first.

He entered behind the gargoyle and held his hand out toward Shay who hesitated at the opening.

"Shay?"

She bit her bottom lip as she regarded him with wide eyes. "I know, I know . . . we have to go."

For a moment his temper threatened to flare. Damn, they couldn't afford to linger. Certainly not out of some ridiculous misplaced sense of bravado. Then he peered into her pale features and he realized that her reluctance had nothing to do with bluster or pride. The witches had obviously made a habit of locking her in small, dark places. Not to mention Evor and his dungeons. Who could blame her for being a bit squirrelly at the thought of entering the cramped tunnel?

"I'm here, Shay, and I'm not going anywhere without you." He shifted enough to take her hand. Her fingers were as cold as his. "You won't ever be alone in the dark again."

"Maybe that's what I'm scared of," she tossed back, although she couldn't hide the strain in her voice.

"Trust me."

Viper watched in silence as her gaze dropped to their clasped hands and she struggled to swallow.

He grimly ignored the way his entire body vibrated with the need to sweep her off her feet and haul her to safety. Damn, the very air pulsed with the approaching danger. Still, he knew that this was not the moment to press Shay. He needed her faith in him. He needed it if they were both to survive. And just as importantly he needed it for himself.

Could she ever truly offer her trust to anyone?

Could she offer it to a vampire?

At last her fingers tightened on his and she stepped into the tunnel. Inside a flare of triumph raced through him, but Viper was wise enough to keep his expression carefully neutral as he pulled her down the tunnel. He wouldn't give her any excuse to balk now.

Keeping her close at his side Viper reached out with his senses. He could feel the faint prickle that warned there was something other than humans nearby. Unfortunately, he couldn't determine precisely what that something other was. They were still too far away for him to pick up their scent, and he had never possessed Dante's keen ability to determine different species just by their power. Still he knew enough to realize they didn't want to meet up with whatever was chasing them. Not until he could ensure Shay was safe and he had nothing to concentrate on but killing. When he didn't have distractions he was very, very good at it.

The tunnel led them well away from the house, but as they reached the end Viper held back his companions as he cautiously stepped into the chilled night breeze. For a moment it seemed they might actually manage to slip away unnoted. A stroke of fortune that seemed too good to be true.

It was, of course.

Viper stiffened as the familiar stench of hellhounds reached him.

Devil's balls.

The hounds were more an annoyance than a danger. They couldn't kill a vampire, or even a Shalott, but they would remain on their scent no matter how far or fast they ran. If they were going to escape, he needed to keep them off his trail.

"Levet," he called softly.

"What?"

"Come here." There was a long pause before the gargoyle at last climbed out of the tunnel to stand beside him. Viper put a hand on his shoulder. "There are hellhounds near. We're going to need a distraction."

"A distraction?" Levet looked wary. Smart demon. "What sort of distraction?"

"You."

Levet struggled against Viper's grip. "Oh no, do not dare think I will battle those horrid beasts. They smell worse than hell itself."

"You are the only one of us that can fly."

Pulling two amulets out of his bag he placed them about the gargoyle's neck. They carried the scent of both him and Shay. Hopefully enough of a scent to distract the hellhounds long enough for them to escape.

"You listen to me, vampire, I am not some—"

"Sorry, I don't have time to argue," Viper apologized as he gave a heave and launched the gargoyle into the air.

The tiny demon glared down and offered a finger that wasn't precisely a compliment.

"You'll pay for this, vampire," he vowed as he turned and flapped off into the night.

Appearing at his side, Shay regarded him with a dark frown. "What have you done to Levet?"

Picking up his bag Viper turned and tossed Shay over his shoulder. They only had a few moments before the hellhounds realized that Levet was not only inaccessible, but very much alone. Then they would be on their heels.

"I don't have time to argue with you, either," he muttered as he took off toward the nearby streets.

"Dammit, put me down." She smacked the middle of his back with her fists. "I can't fight like this."

She couldn't fight? Her punch would have been enough to break a rib and puncture a lung if he hadn't been a vampire.

"We're not going to fight, we're going to run."

"Levet . . ."

"The hellhounds can't reach the gargoyle. Besides he is immortal. We can't be certain you are."

His blunt words managed to steal at least a portion of her

anger. A rare event and one that Viper was swift to take advantage of as he flowed down the darkened streets. He had managed to put a considerable distance between them and the hellhounds before she heaved a frustrated sigh.

"Can I at least know where we're running to?" she demanded.

"I have several businesses on the south side. If we can reach one of them, my clan will protect us."

"Your clan?" She gave a choked noise of disbelief. "Are you kidding me?"

"Not at all."

"You intend to surround me with a bunch of hungry vampires? Why don't you just leave me for the hellhounds and be done with it? At least I have a shot against them."

Viper never slowed his pace although his grip on her instinctively tightened. He wouldn't put it past her to make a sudden bid for freedom despite his assurances. She possessed a prejudice against vampires that went way beyond logic.

"You will not be harmed," he assured her.

"And how can you be so certain?"

"Because you are mine. They will obey my commands."

He could actually hear her teeth grinding at his offhand arrogance. Of course, that was preferable to the alternative. Having her hanging over his shoulder ensured her feet were dangling perilously close to his more sensitive body parts. Even a vampire could be brought to his knees by a well placed kick.

"Oh, right. Like I have ever encountered a vampire who obeys anyone," she muttered. "If they decide to make me a tasty smorgasbord, there's not a damn thing either of us can do to stop them."

Viper angled through the shadows of an empty office building as he considered his response. Vampires rarely revealed the inner workings of their culture. Not even to other demons. The Secret Service had nothing on them. Unfortunately, he would have to give Shay some reassurance or she was bound to fight him the entire way.

"I'll agree that vampires can be independent, but I am a clan chief," he at last said.

"And?"

"And to challenge my authority is to challenge me."

He wanted that to be the end of the conversation, but of course it wasn't.

"What does that mean?"

"It means that they must either confront me one on one, in direct combat, or leave the clan," he grudgingly confessed. "There are few who would dare either fate."

"They're that frightened of you?"

He paused at a corner, carefully surveying their surroundings. It was late enough that most humans were tucked in their beds leaving behind a shadowed landscape of silence. Prime hunting ground for all sorts of demons. Some that might not be interested in a vampire and a Shalott unless they were stupid enough to stumble over them.

Assured the way was clear he headed swiftly toward the closest alley.

He felt her fist punch him in the middle of his back. "Answer the question or put me down," she commanded.

His own teeth did a bit of grinding. "Being clan chief has given me . . . powers beyond most vampires."

"What sort of powers?"

"It is individual for each chief and never spoken of."

She made a rude noise at his response, but for once accepted he would reveal no more.

"What if one of them wanted to become clan chief themselves?" she instead pressed.

"They must first enter the Battle of Durotriges. If they survive, they can establish their own clan as I did, or challenge another chief to the death."

"Have you ever been challenged?"

"It has been several centuries."

"I take it that you defeated them?"

"Yes."

"So now you're a major badass that no one wants to challenge?"

Viper gave a choked laugh. He had been called many things

over the years, but he wasn't sure that badass had ever been among them.

"I can be a . . . badass when necessary, but in truth most in the clan are simply content." He weaved through the narrow alleys, his swift speed taking them into the less savory neighborhoods. "I am not an overly demanding master and unlike many I have no wish to acquire more power. They do not fear being tossed onto the bloody frontlines of a clan war."

"A benevolent dictator?" she muttered.

He resisted the urge to give her backside a smack. He didn't want to risk a revolt at this point.

"You sound disapproving. Would you rather I was a tyrant?"

"I'm just saying."

"Just saying what?"

"If it looks like a duck, and quacks like a duck, it's a . . . shit."

Viper didn't hesitate as he came to a halt and lowered Shay to her feet. He had caught the scent at the same moment as his companion.

Trolls.

With fluid motions he pulled the sword from its scabbard and tossed it to Shay. With the same ease he retrieved two long daggers from his bag before dropping it to the ground.

A troll possessed skin too thick to be pierced by a bullet. Only a magically enhanced blade would have a chance.

"Aim at the lower stomach," he commanded in clipped tones. "It's the only place the blade can pierce and there is an artery there that can be severed."

Shay instinctively moved to place her back to his own. The best means for them to fight as one smooth unit.

"You don't have to tell me how to kill trolls," she said in bitter tones. "It was the first thing I learned after Evor forced me to his side."

"I don't doubt you, pet, but I smell more than mere fear on these trolls. They are desperate and there is no enemy more dangerous than one ready and willing to die rather than be defeated."

She gave a short humorless laugh. "They can't be anymore desperate than I am."

Viper could hardly argue with her logic. And in truth there was no time as the darker shadows shifted and five large mountain trolls came into view. It would be easy to presume that their slow, lumbering movements meant an equally slow and lumbering mind. A mistake that could lead to a swift death. They may not be intelligent, but they possessed a bloodthirsty cunning that made them dangerous in a battle.

Only a fool would underestimate them.

A dead fool.

Keeping the daggers hidden, Viper carefully studied their approach. As expected they fanned out to surround them, but they did not attack at once. Each herd was held by a fierce hierarchy, and the leaders would send in the weakest first to determine the skill of his opponent. A waste of soldiers, but a good means to discover how best to be victorious.

Eying the smallest of the trolls, Viper was prepared as the troll gave a rumbling roar before awkwardly charging forward. He could hear the same sound coming from behind, but he trusted Shay to hold up her end of the battle. There were few demons beyond vampires that could hope to best a Shalott.

Even a half-human Shalott.

Holding his position Viper ignored the head that the troll lowered as he came forward. It was a deliberately tempting target, but he was well aware that the skull was the thickest part of a troll. The demon could put his head through a steel wall and never blink.

Waiting until the beast was nearly upon him Viper at last raised his hands, using one dagger to make a motion toward the red eyes. As expected the troll instinctively flinched back and Viper used the opening to smoothly thrust the other dagger in the lower right of his stomach.

There was a startled grunt from the troll as the enchanted blade slid through the thick skin and found the soft tissue beneath. Viper didn't hesitate as he twisted the dagger until the putrid smell of spilling blood filled the air. Just for a moment the troll continued to struggle forward, as if he weren't yet aware he was dead. Then with a rattled breath he slowly began to sink to his knees.

Viper was quick to jerk the dagger free and kick the carcass to the side. He didn't want to be hampered during the next attack.

Not daring to cast a glance over his shoulder to make sure that Shay was coping, he squared his shoulders.

At the moment she was still on her feet.

That had to be enough, as the next two trolls realized the danger of attempting a single attack, and charged together. They were also smart enough to keep their heads lowered and their arms protectively held in front of their stomachs.

Realizing that the charge was bound to throw him backward into Shay, and perhaps knock her off balance at a critical moment, Viper smoothly moved to the side, luring the beasts with him. At the same moment he pointed at the ground, murmuring beneath his breath.

There was a sharp crack as the dirt beneath the pavement abruptly bulged upward. It was nothing dramatic, but enough to trip up the first troll who went down with a startled growl. The second fell over the legs of the first and ended up on his knees.

Viper was moving before the troll hit the ground and had his dagger shoved into his stomach while the troll blinked at him in amazement. He even had the decency to fall forward to trap his brethren beneath his twitching body.

Good troll.

With a moment to spare, Viper allowed his gaze to dart toward his companion.

Shay already had her first troll dead on the ground, and was circling the second with a sinuous grace. The sword was too long, and the balance wrong for her, but she moved it like an extension of her own arm. The mark of a true swordsman.

Or woman.

A taunting smile curved her lips as she baited the increasingly frustrated troll. Over and over she slipped close enough for him to take a swipe at her with his massive hands, and over and over she managed to dart away untouched. There were growls and rasps and sounds that were no doubt curses coming from the troll as he began to swing with an increasing careless-ness. More importantly his fury and frustration was bringing him ever closer to the sword held in Shay's hand.

The troll at Viper's feet began to struggle from beneath his dead companion and never allowing his gaze to stray from Shay he planted his foot on the thick skull. He had more im-portant matters on his mind at the moment.

Unaware of his fascination Shay made one last feint and danced backward. The troll stumbled after her, his arms out-stretched. It was all Shay needed as she held the sword high, and then swept it downward in a motion too fast for the troll to counter. He was still moving forward as she plunged the blade deep into his stomach and gave it a deadly twist. There was a grunt of surprise as the troll gazed down in disbelief at the wound. Then he was falling forward to hit the ground with a resounding thud.

Bending down Shay efficiently wiped her sword on the troll's tattered tunic before straightening to regard him with a lift of her brows.

"Are you going to play with that troll all night or are you going to finish it?" she demanded.

Chapter Eighteen

Shay was relieved when Viper dispatched the troll with swift ease and turned to lead her through the dark street without comment. It was too much to hope that he hadn't noticed the dark bruise already forming on her cheek. The first troll had only managed a glancing blow, but it was enough to prick her pride and was no doubt the reason he had halted his own attack to watch her so intently.

He had to be thinking she was a rank amateur, damn him.

Why it mattered that he should consider her a warrior worthy of respect didn't bear thinking about.

At least not now.

With an effort she speeded her steps so she could walk beside Viper rather than behind him.

She didn't hide behind anyone. Not ever.

Ignoring his sidelong glance she forced her gaze to take in their surroundings, determined to be prepared for whatever might leap from the heavy shadows.

And anything might leap in this neighborhood, she acknowledged with a faint grimace. They had left the elegant mansions and trendy businesses behind, replacing them with narrow buildings and empty lots that carried the stench of decay. Even the streets were beginning to crumble and she jumped over potholes that were capable of swallowing a small car whole. This part of the city was dying a slow death, conveniently forgotten by all but those forced to live among the rubble.

Oddly saddened by the sight Shay briefly assumed that the cold chill prickling over her skin was merely a reaction to her surroundings.

It was only when Viper came to a sharp halt that she realized the truth.

"Vampires," he breathed.

"Damn." She instinctively reached to give her braid a nervous tug. "I don't suppose that they're *your* vampires?"

"No."

Of course not.

It seemed the night for unpleasant surprises. And what could be a more unpleasant surprise than encountering vampires on a dark street?

"Maybe they're just passing through?"

He gave a shake of his head, his features hardened to that chilling mask that reminded her precisely of what and who he was.

"None would dare to enter Chicago without my permission. Not unless they were declaring war."

She swallowed heavily. "How many?"

"Six." He tilted his head back, sniffing the air. "And one is a chief."

"So we're screwed?"

Viper cursed beneath his breath as he searched the shadows for the hidden vamps. Not a good sign. She didn't want to see him worried. Not now. She wanted that arrogant, superior, utterly confident man who set her teeth on edge.

"Dammit it all, I've been a fool. A stupid fool," he muttered.

"Not that I intend to argue, but what have you been a fool about on this occasion?" she demanded in low tones.

"The hellhounds and trolls were merely a ruse to flush us from Dante's mansion." He gave a low growl. "We walked straight into their trap."

Shay froze, recalling the chaotic panic that had set in when they had sensed the approaching trouble. He was right. My God, they had been fools. If they had any sense at all, they

would have waited until they were certain that the danger
behind them was worse than the danger before them.

Of course, in all fairness, who wouldn't flee in panic after
the Lu? The thing had scared the bejeezus out of her.

"Do we run or fight?" she muttered.

"I know this vampire," he rasped, reaching out to grasp her
hand. "We run."

It sounded like a damn fine idea to Shay. The best warriors
always knew the wisdom of a strategic retreat. Holding the
sword to the side so it didn't trip her, Shay allowed Viper to pull
her down the dark street. She didn't know where they were
headed, but anyplace had to be better than here. Or at least she
hoped so.

Never losing stride Viper darted down a side alley and smoothly
grasped her about the waist as he vaulted over the looming security fence. Shay swallowed her gasp of shock as they landed on the
other side and turned toward an abandoned warehouse.

She could run fast and jump higher than humans but . . .
damn. She almost felt as if they were flying.

Entering the warehouse Viper slowed his pace, his head
tilted as if he were sniffing the air.

"What are you . . ."

"Shhh." He pressed a finger over her lips before tugging her
toward the back of the building. "This way."

They rounded a towering stack of rusting barrels before
Viper lowered himself to his knees and tugged her down beside
him.

"Why are we stopping here?" she demanded.

"We can't outrun all of them." He turned his head to regard
her with a somber expression. "They've already surrounded us."

Shay's heart skipped, jerked, and came to a stuttering halt.
"Damn."

"If we can't outrun them, then we must outwit them," he
whispered softly.

"You have a plan?"

He gave a slow nod. "Yes."

Shay studied the exquisite features in the muted light. There was a grim determination that made her narrow her eyes in suspicion.

"Why do I have a feeling that I'm not going to like this plan?"

His lips curved in a faint smile. "Because you're stubborn and pigheaded, no doubt."

She reached up to poke her finger into his chest. "Just tell me."

There was a pause before he reached up to grasp her hand. "There is a manhole just behind you. I want you to use it to escape while I distract the vampires."

"No, absolutely not."

"Shay, listen to me—"

His words were cut short by the unmistakable sound of approaching footsteps.

"Viper, you might as well reveal yourself. We have the warehouse surrounded. There is no escape."

Shay gave a small jump at the dark, oddly compelling voice that seemed to wrap about her. Turning her head she peered between the barrels. The shadows shifted and a vampire walked across the floor toward them.

Holy shit.

He was tall. As tall as Viper and much broader through the shoulders and chest. The impression of size was only emphasized by the long black robe that draped him from neck to toe. But it was not his towering strength that stole her breath and widened her eyes. As he neared she was able to see the golden shade of his skin. It was the first vampire she had ever seen without the white paleness that usually marked them.

His hair was as black as a raven's wing and fell past his waist. The heavy curtain was pulled back and held in a tight queue by a series of bronze bands that glinted in the meager light. The severe style emphasized the sharp planes of his face that included the high cheekbones and hawkish thrust of his nose. Throw in the oblong eyes that smoldered with a liquid darkness and the image of an Aztec prince was complete.

Yikes.

"Holy cow," she breathed. "Who is he?"

"Styx."

Shay's eyes widened as her stomach clenched in dread. There was something quietly implacable about the vamp. The sense he would not be swerved from his purpose no matter what.

"Styx?"

"He was named for leaving a river of dead in his wake," Viper said, his gaze never leaving the man relentlessly moving toward them. "He is our most famous of warriors."

"Lovely." She forced herself to swallow the lump in her throat. "A friend of yours?"

"At one time."

"So why is he chasing us? Is he the one who wants my blood?"

"I intend to find that out." Viper turned his head to stab her with a fierce gaze. "But not until you're out of here."

"Viper . . ."

"No. Not now." His grip on her fingers tightened to a near painful level as he relentlessly tugged her backward. He halted only when they had reached the iron grate set in the floor. Loosening his grasp he leaned over the grate and with astonishing strength pulled it off without the faintest scrape to give them away. Setting it aside he cupped Shay's face in his hands. "Styx possesses a fierce measure of loyalty toward vampires. He will not intentionally harm me. You, however, are at great risk. You must flee if either of us is to survive."

Shay gritted her teeth. It was downright insulting to ask her to slink away like the worst sort of coward while he remained behind to play the role of hero. Even worse she was supposed to slink through what smelled suspiciously like a toxic waste dump.

Unfortunately, her pride could not overcome sheer common sense. If she remained then Viper would fight to the death to protect her. And clan chief or not he wouldn't be a match against six vampires determined to have her blood. Even if he fled with her they were bound to be overrun and forced back into this precise situation. The best she could hope for was that she could escape and find help before Viper did something utterly stupid.

Cursing beneath her breath she leaned forward until they were nose to nose. "If you get yourself killed I'll—"

His swift kiss stole her words. "You'll never be rid of me, pet. Now go."

Her heart gave a painful wrench as she lightly touched her fingertips to his cheek before tossing her sword down the dark tunnel and preparing to leap after it. She was halted as Viper abruptly caught her arm.

"Leave your shirt," he whispered so softly she almost missed his words.

Her eyes widened. "What?"

He leaned close to her ear. "Your scent must remain or Styx will know you are no longer in the warehouse. The ruse will not last long, but hopefully long enough for you to escape."

Well, poop.

It wasn't bad enough that she had to flee through a tunnel of smelly waste. Now she had to do it half naked and freezing. Still, the sooner she left, the sooner she could find Dante and return to rescue Viper. Tugging off her sweatshirt she tossed it aside and holding her hand over her nose she jumped into the stinky dark. She landed in a thick goop she could only pray was mud before she was wading forward. Perfect. Just perfect. If she came out of the tunnel glowing green, she was going to stake the damn vampire herself.

"I am in no humor to play hide-and-seek, Viper, show yourself," Styx commanded.

Viper silently replaced the grate over the drainage tunnel before rising to his feet and stepping from behind the barrels. He could sense Shay moving farther away, but the scent of her still hung thick in the air.

Hopefully thick enough to fool the surrounding vampires.

Squaring his shoulders he regarded his one-time friend and companion with a cold gaze.

"And I am in no humor to be spoken to as if I am some

groveling servant, old friend. You seem to have forgotten I am a clan chief."

Styx regarded him with an expression more somber than arrogant. "I have not forgotten your powers, Viper, nor your position."

"So it is simply your manners that you have forgotten?"

The dark head gave a slight nod. "You are right to chastise me. This is not how I would wish to meet once again. Unfortunately my need outweighs any other consideration."

Viper stiffened in anger. He didn't understand as of yet why his former friend and companion was involved in the hunt for Shay, but Styx's sudden presence was too much for mere coincidence. His Shalott had been quite right to fear vampires.

"And what need is that, Styx?"

"All your questions will be answered in time. For now I only ask that you call for your companion and come with me."

Viper folded his arms over his chest. "That's a little vague, I fear. You'll forgive me if I want a few more reassurances before we go anywhere."

Styx regarded him for a long measure, his expression never changing. "We have known each other for centuries. What further reassurance do you desire?"

"You can tell me why you're standing in this nasty warehouse on such a chill night."

"Obviously searching for you."

"Why?"

"This is not the place for such a conversation, Viper. If you and your companion will come with me—"

"And if I refuse?" Viper overrode his smooth words.

"That would be . . . most unfortunate."

Viper narrowed his gaze, his fangs lengthening in warning. "You will take me against my will? Against all the laws that govern us? Tell me, Styx, has the vampire that I admired above all others now become no better than those he once fought against?"

"Enough." The dark voice never altered, but Viper could feel the flare of power that swirled through the air. "You know nothing of the troubles we face."

"I know that we do not enter the territory of clans without requesting safe passage from the chief," he said, his own power flaring strong enough to make Styx wince. "Or compel demons and dark wizards to do our bidding. Or command the murder of another vampire. Tell me why you are here, Styx."

For the first time those golden features held a genuine expression. Disapproval.

"We will not discuss this in public like squabbling trolls. I expected better of you, my old companion in arms."

Viper took a threatening step forward. "Perhaps if I didn't have a knife stuck in my back you would have gotten better. You have broken our treaty and proclaimed yourself an enemy of my clan."

There was a sudden stir in the shadows and five large vampires moved forward with fluid speed. Like Styx they were covered in heavy black robes, although they had their hoods up making it impossible to determine more than the fact that they were big.

Very big.

Viper prepared to confront the charging vampires even as he felt a flare of relief. The Ravens had remained, which meant that they had yet to detect that their prey was slipping from their grasp. Pulling out his daggers Viper tensed for the attack. If he died, he died, but he intended to take more than a few with him.

The vampires, however, were brought to a sharp halt as Styx gave a lift of his hand.

"Hold," he commanded, his gaze remaining on Viper's furious expression. "I am here at the command of my master, which places me above treaties as you well know. Still, there is no reason we cannot deal reasonably together."

"Reasonably?" Viper sneered. "I'm well past reasonable. If you wish a dignified discussion, then we will return to Dante's and we can put an end to this there."

Astonishingly, something that might have been a smile touched the golden features.

"As charming as I am certain Dante's new mate might be I

have no wish to share tea with the Phoenix." The smile vanished as swiftly as it had arrived and the stark somberness returned. With a motion of his slender hand Styx commanded the hovering vampires to surround them. "Forgive me, old friend, but the time grows short. Call for your companion or I will put her in the hands of my Ravens."

The soft words hung in the air and Viper's fingers instinctively tightened around the hilt of the daggers. It was barely a twitch. A movement that would have gone unnoticed by most. But not Styx. The trained warrior was instantly pointing toward one of the hovering vampires.

"DeAngelo, bring me the Shalott," he rasped.

There was the soft swish of fabric as the vampire moved behind the barrels, and then the sharp sound of the grate being pulled from the entrance to the drainage pipe. Within the blink of an eye the vampire had returned holding Shay's sweatshirt in his hand.

"The demon escaped down a tunnel," he intoned. "Shall I follow her?"

Styx regarded Viper with frozen fury. "No. She will not get far. Viper possesses the amulet that will call her to his side."

Viper narrowed his gaze. "I will never call her."

"You will call her, or you will die. The choice is yours."

Levet was wise enough to hover above the narrow streets. There were all sorts of nasty piles of rotting food, rotting clothes, rotting junk, and rotting things that he didn't want to look at, let alone touch. It wasn't the first slums he had ventured into. He was a three-foot gargoyle. He had spent most of his life hiding among the filth and squalor just to survive.

Still, he had come to America in the hope of bettering his lot. There were far fewer demons to plague him here, and enough space to find a bit of land and live in peace.

Or that had been his intention. Of course, his good intentions inevitably led him to some sort of disaster or another, he acknowledged with a sigh.

Following behind Dante he gave a shudder as the stench swirled upward in a stray breeze.

"Such smells," he muttered in disgust. "How do humans bear it?"

The vampire shot him an impatient glance. Dante had argued fiercely against Levet coming with him to track Viper and Shay. For some reason he had been convinced that Levet would prove to be more a help than a hindrance.

Stupid vampire.

It had only been Levet's threat to follow him on his own that had at last brought an end to the short, ugly battle.

"Despair always possesses a stench whether it is human or demon," he at last said.

Levet regarded him in surprise. Attired in black with two swords crossed over his back, a handgun on his hip, and at least one dagger hidden beneath his clothing, he looked ready to take on a small army.

"I thought Viper was the philosopher and you the warrior?"

Bending low Dante sniffed the air like a bloodhound.

"For the past three hundred years I was held prisoner to a clan of witches. Being a slave gives you a considerable insight into despair."

"Yes." Levet gave another shudder. His time with Evor was not forgotten. It would never be truly forgotten. "Yes, it does."

Astonishingly Dante straightened and reached up to touch his arm.

"Slaves no longer."

Levet met the steady gaze and gave a nod. "And never again."

They shared a brief moment of remembered pain, and then Dante was once again on the scent as they weaved their way through the increasingly narrow streets.

Narrow, stinky streets.

Levet found his fear for Shay growing with every block they traveled. Did Viper have no wits at all? It was bad enough that they were fleeing trolls and hellhounds. Did he have to drag her through the dregs of the demon world as well? Stewing with resentment toward the silver-haired vampire Levet was caught off guard when Dante reached up to bar his path.

"Wait," he hissed.

Levet gave an angry twitch of his tail. "*Sacrebleu,* why do we wait? We are at last gaining on them."

The irritating vamp gave a lift of one dark brow. "You sound anxious, gargoyle. I didn't know you cared."

"That vampire tossed me to the wolves, or more precisely hellhounds." Levet crossed his arms over his chest. "No one is allowed to kill him but me."

A knowing smirk touched the pale features. "And that is all?"

He glared at his companion. Blood and smoke. If he didn't need the vamp to help rescue Shay, he would turn him to dust where he stood.

"And it could be that I have some small attachment to the Shalott," he grudgingly acknowledged. "Very, very small, you understand?"

"Ah, yes, I understand."

"So why have we stopped?"

"Trolls have passed by here."

It was Levet's turn to smirk. "Surely you do not fear trolls?"

"Not these." Dante smiled wryly. "They are all dead."

"Shay," Levet murmured with more than a bit of pride.

"Not alone, gargoyle," Dante returned. "Viper stood at her side."

Levet shrugged. "If the beasts are dead then let's go."

He gave a shake of his head. "Trolls are not the only thing to have passed here. There have been vampires."

Levet gave a growl deep in his throat. It would have to be vampires, of course. They seemed to be wading neck deep in them lately.

"How many?"

"Six." There was a tense pause. "And none of our clan."

"Not of your clan?" Levet's heart gave a painful squeeze. "That can only mean . . ."

Dante's pale face hardened to a stark mask. "They are here to kill Viper."

Whatever their intention Shay was in danger, and that was all that mattered.

He was nothing if not focused.

"We cannot wait. We must go to them."

"And be caught in the trap ourselves?" Dante was looking distinctly fangy as he scowled at Levet. "It will help no one."

"And how will it help to hide in the shadows while they are slaughtered?"

The silver eyes flashed with frustrated fury. "Be quiet and let me think or I shall clip those wings of yours, gargoyle."

Levet offered a raspberry as he flapped his wings to rise higher. "Fine, you cower in the shadows. I shall discover what is occurring."

"Dammit, Levet . . ."

Too late the vampire made a grab toward Levet's dangling legs, his expression warning of dire retribution.

Levet blithely ignored his muttered curses as he lifted himself toward the nearby rooftops, careful to keep out of the stray light that might reveal his shadow. The one thing he did, and did well, was remain hidden from searching eyes.

Landing on the roof he moved in absolute silence to the brick edge and peered downward. He was no longer aware of the filth or stench. Or even the thick silence that cloaked the neighborhood. His attention was centered on the silver-haired Viper who was being slowly forced into a long black limo followed by a very large, very angry vampire.

Even from a distance Levet could sense that violence trembled in the air, but just as he was about to shout for Dante to rush to the rescue he watched as the limo pulled smoothly from the curb followed closely by a second limo.

Was Shay inside the limo? Surely she had to be. He might consider Viper a conceited ass, but he did know that the vampire would fight to the death to keep Shay safe. If he were allowing himself to be taken hostage it could only be because they had already captured Shay.

Watching the automobiles slide down the street he turned and flung himself off the building, landing next to Dante with a heavy thud. He had barely caught his balance, however, when he found himself hauled off his feet by a distinctly annoyed vampire.

"Next time you do that I'll have your heart for dinner, gargoyle," Dante gritted.

Struggling to free himself Levet glared at his companion. "We do not have time for you to play bully. A very large vampire was forcing Viper into a car and driving away."

"What of Shay?"

"I must presume they have her as well."

"And he is allowing himself to be taken captive?"

"He does not look happy, but yes."

Dante nodded, absently stroking the blade of his dagger as he considered Levet's words.

"He must realize that it is impossible to fight," he muttered. "Or they have threatened to harm Shay. In either case, if we blunder in, we might very well make matters worse rather than better."

"Unfortunately, I must agree."

Dante gave an exaggerated blink. "It seems miracles do happen."

Levet resisted the urge to roll his eyes. Vampire humor left a great deal to be desired.

"The limos were moving south. They are very large and very black." He grimaced. "What is it with vampires and black?"

Dante regarded him steadily. "Do you have a point?"

"I will follow them and when they reach their destination I will return and give you directions."

Levet was quite prepared for an argument. An argument he was determined to win. No one was going to stop him from rescuing Shay.

Astonishingly, Dante merely gave a nod of his head. "The vampires will be on their guard. One mistake and you will be killed."

Levet gave a short, humorless laugh as he spread his arms

wide. "Look at me. I am barely three feet tall. I am always on my guard, fool."

Another nod. "I will gather the rest of the clan. We will be prepared when you return."

"Make sure you include a lot of very large, very sharp weapons."

With a surge Levet was once again airborne and on his way to track Shay.

"Bon chance, mon ami," Dante called softly.

Levet allowed himself a small smile. A vampire who could speak French. He couldn't be all bad.

Chapter Nineteen

Shay crawled from the manhole and sucked in a ragged breath of clean air. Well, the relatively clean air.

She was frozen, smelly, and half naked. Just as she had predicted, but amazingly there had been no hint of pursuit from the vampires. Perhaps not so amazingly, she acknowledged grimly, as she shivered in the sharp night air.

The tall, bronzed vampire simply known as Styx did not strike her as a particularly stupid man. Cold, ruthless, and inflexible. But not stupid.

Pausing only long enough to make sure the street was vampire-troll-hellhound free Shay slipped through the shadows, and began retracing her steps to Dante's sprawling mansion. She needed help and she needed it fast.

The thought had barely flashed through her mind when her sensitive nose caught a familiar scent. Coming to a halt she cast a startled glance toward the top of a nearby building, nearly missing the vague shadow that scampered along the roof.

Levet.

Thank God.

With a burst of speed she was across the street and down a narrow alley. The ladder that zigzagged its way up the side of the building was rusty and none too steady, but she barely noticed the drunken sway as she clambered up the steps and landed softly on the flat roof.

The tiny gargoyle had reached the edge of the building, but at the sound of her footfalls he abruptly whirled with his hands outstretched as if to toss a spell in her direction.

"No . . . Levet, it's me," she hastily whispered.

"Shay?"

"Yes."

"Holy mother of God. You nearly gave me a heart attack," the gargoyle breathed as he swiftly waddled to join her. A few steps away he came to an abrupt halt, his nose wrinkled in disgust. "Gak. What is that stench? Where is your shirt? Did you . . ."

Shay lifted an impatient hand. "Shhh. Where is Dante?"

"He went charging off to gather the cavalry." Levet planted his hands on his hips. "How did you get loose? I thought those vampires had you for sure."

She shivered, and not just from the cold.

Vampires. Why did it have to be vampires?

"I used a drainage pipe to escape the warehouse, but Viper is still stuck in there."

"Not any longer."

She reached out to grasp his arm. "What do you mean?"

"They tossed him into a very long limo and took off."

Her heart gave a painful jerk. Shit. It was precisely what she feared the most.

"Damn." She licked her dry lips and battled back the flare of fear. Panic, bad. Thinking, good. "We have to go after him."

Levet gave a twitch of his tail. "That's what I was in the process of doing when you came leaping behind me."

"Fine, let's go."

The gargoyle moved just enough to block her path, his expression concerned.

"Shay?"

"What?"

"Do you really think it's a good idea for you to come with me? It's you they're after. If you get anywhere close . . ."

Shay reached out to grasp his shoulder, shivering as a cold breeze brushed over her skin.

Damn. She needed to find some clothes.

And a cross.

And several very, very large stakes.

"I'm coming Levet."

"Ouch. No need to pinch the wings." Pulling free the gargoyle gave a flutter of his delicate wings. "If you want to plunge into danger and get the rest of us killed, then so be it."

Shay wrapped her arms about herself. "I'm already in danger."

"Not if you return to the Phoenix. There's not a demon around who would dare to piss her off."

"Not even Abby can protect me now."

"Of course she can. She's a goddess, isn't she?"

"Think, Levet," she commanded. "They have Viper."

"Are you drunk? I know they have Viper. I just told *you* that."

Her teeth gritted as she resisted the urge to give him a good shake. "They have Viper and I'm Viper's slave. He holds my amulet."

"And . . . oh." The gray face managed to become downright white. "Oh. No, you truly must be drunk if you think Viper will deliberately call you into the hands of your enemies. I might think him an arrogant pain in the ass, but he would never allow you to be harmed."

This time her shiver was not from the cold. "Not intentionally."

Levet frowned. "Shay?"

She hunched her shoulders as old memories rose up like nasty bile.

"Levet, we have both been at the mercy of enemies. We know what it is to be tortured," she said in raw tones. "All that blathering about glorious honor and loyalty is for fairy tales, not reality. In truth a person can be forced to do anything. Even if it goes against everything they hold dear."

He flinched, as his hand instinctively lifted to touch the scars that marred his chest. The trolls had found it loads of fun to use a miniature gargoyle as target practice. At least until Shay had arrived and threatened to cut off their manhood. Amazing how that threat managed to transcend race, culture, and species.

"No." Levet gave a shake of his head. "Not Viper. The amulet must be freely given and he will never do that."

It was what she feared the most, she abruptly realized. Not that he would break beneath the torture, but that he wouldn't. Viper was just stubborn enough to allow himself to die before he would call her to his side.

It was a sacrifice that would break her as nothing else could.

"Then they will kill him and I will still be at their mercy," she rasped.

Levet lifted his hands to rub his temples. "You are giving me a headache. What do you mean?"

"If they hold Evor then killing Viper will still force me into their clutches. I cannot escape the curse."

Levet muttered a string of French curses as he at last understood her head was directly beneath the guillotine.

"*Sacrebleu,* when you tumble into a quagmire you really tumble, don't you?"

That was one way of putting it.

"We have to rescue him, Levet. And we have to do it now."

Chapter Twenty

Viper decided that the black limo could hardly compare to his own.

Although suitably large and boasting soft leather seats, it offered few other luxuries. No soothing music, no plasma TV, no champagne cooling on ice.

Of course, he had to concede, his own limo didn't have any silver shackles hanging from the ceiling that could conveniently hold even the most furious vampire captive. An oversight he would have corrected if he ever managed to get out of this damnable mess.

Ignoring the silver that burned into his wrists, he gave another futile tug on the chains that bound him. Anything was better than brooding on the traitor who sat on the seat opposite him, or worse, the knowledge that Shay was out there alone.

With a click of his tongue, Styx pulled off his cape to reveal the black leather pants and thick sweater that covered his large form.

"Your struggles are futile and will only hurt you, Viper," he said.

Lowering his gaze Viper glared at the man who had once stood at his side. Whatever their friendship in the past he would never forgive Styx for this.

And never was a very long time for immortals.

"You think I will go to my death without some struggle, no matter how futile?" he demanded.

The cold features never altered. "I am trying very hard to ensure that you do not face death."

"Not face death?" Viper gave a humorless laugh, as furious with himself as the man across from him. Devil's balls, but he had been an idiot. "I've been chased across Chicago by dark wizards, hellhounds, and now trolls."

"Merely distractions."

"And the Lu?" Viper demanded. "I assure you he was more than a mere distraction. He damn well nearly took off my head."

Astonishingly, something that might have been unease rippled over the bronzed features. It wasn't much but it was enough to give Viper a faint hope that the man possessed some regret.

"That was . . . not of my doing."

"Your master?" Viper carefully probed.

"You know better than to ask," Styx chided, his arms folded over his chest. "Tell me of the Shalott."

Viper gritted his teeth. "She is about five foot seven, one hundred and twenty pounds, which is shocking considering she eats like a horse . . ."

Styx gave an impatient hiss. "Now is not the time for levity, Viper. If I am to save you, I must have your cooperation."

Viper wanted to tell him what he could do with his cooperation. He would put a stake in his own heart before he would help them harm Shay.

Thankfully, he came to his senses enough to realize that for the moment he was helpless to attempt an escape. Perhaps if he could encourage Styx to talk he might reveal something of what lay ahead.

"And what does this cooperation involve?"

"For the moment I wish to know of your relationship with the demon."

Viper met his gaze squarely. "She is my slave."

"More than that, I think. You have risked your life over and over to save her. Why?"

"You know why."

The dark eyes studied him for a long moment. "You have feelings for her?"

Viper shrugged. It wouldn't help to try and deny his feelings for Shay. They were obvious enough for even a simpleton to notice.

"Yes."

"A dangerous luxury for a vampire," Styx murmured, the dark shadows playing over his face. "And even more dangerous for a clan chief."

Viper gave an unconscious yank on the chains. "What is your interest in my relationship with Shay?"

Styx was silent so long that Viper feared he might refuse to answer. Then slowly leaning forward the elder vampire stabbed him with a fierce gaze.

"It would be best if you cut your connections to the demon and walk away. Give me the power over the amulet that binds her to you, and I will halt the car and not trouble you again."

Viper was wise enough not to laugh at the ridiculous suggestion.

"And if I don't?"

"Eventually you will be convinced to do as you're told, and I very much fear that you will not enjoy the process."

Viper narrowed his eyes. "Torture has been forbidden, even for the Anasso," he said, referring to the leader of all vampires. The master that Styx and the Ravens served as personal guards.

"Necessity at times demands unpleasant sacrifices."

"Me being the sacrifice?" Viper demanded.

"I very much hope not."

Viper gave a slow shake of his head. "This is not like you, Styx. For all of your battles you have always held your honor most dear."

With a smooth motion Styx was leaning back in his seat, but Viper didn't miss the small flinch at his sharp accusation.

"And my duty even more dear," he retorted, his voice carefully bland. As if he feared revealing more than he desired.

Viper studied the features that had once been so familiar to him. He had not aged, of course. In fact his features were precisely the same as they had been centuries ago. But there was no mistaking the hint of tension that tightened his body. Or the bleak somberness that dulled his eyes. As if the years had stolen something precious from him.

"Duty to the Anasso?"

"Duty to all vampires. Our very existence depends upon this."

Viper gave a lift of his brows. "You're being very melodramatic for a vampire who has chosen the existence of a monk. What could possibly be so dire?"

"Can you not simply trust me?"

"No."

Styx lifted a slender hand to touch the small medallion that hung about his neck. It was an ancient Aztec symbol that he was never without.

"You are making this far more difficult than it need be."

Viper made a rude noise. "I have hardly been the one making this difficult, Styx. I was perfectly content to remain peacefully in my lair with Shay, not bothering a soul. You were the one to drag me into this mess."

The coldness deepened around Styx. "The Anasso has spoken. That is all that matters."

The hell it did.

Viper stirred impatiently on the seat, biting back a curse as the silver dug into his flesh. The pain was reaching a level where it was nearly impossible to ignore.

"Did you capture the troll who holds Shay's curse?"

"No, he has managed to elude us."

Viper frowned. Styx might evade or simply refuse to answer a question, but he wouldn't lie. So where the hell was Evor?

Devil's balls.

Viper struggled to make sense of the past few days. All he knew was that it had been the Anasso who had been determined to get his hands on Shay from the beginning. Which was worth a whole lot of nothing.

"What do you want of Shay? Is it her blood?"

Styx turned to gaze out the window. "Her blood is life."

A cold chill clutched at Viper. "Life? Life for who?"

"Enough, Viper." At last Styx turned back, his expression grim. "I have said all that I intend to."

There was no mistaking the finality in his tone and Viper bit back his frustration. At the moment he was in no position to make demands or enforce his will.

He had every confidence that would change. And when it did . . . well, he would have his pound of flesh. Quite literally.

Forced to change his tactics he turned his attention to the brief flare of weakness he had noticed earlier.

"I never did understand why you would pledge yourself to the Anasso," he said in offhand tones, as if he were merely passing the time. "You were always so fiercely independent."

Styx gave a shrug. "I discovered as the years and then centuries passed that I needed more than a mere existence to satisfy me."

"It was hardly a mere existence," Viper pointed out. "Not only were you a feared warrior but you were once the chief of the largest clan of vampires ever gathered. A feat envied by many."

The dark eyes abruptly flashed with anger.

Ridiculously, Viper discovered himself pleased by the rare display of emotion. It proved that something of the Styx he had known and loved still existed.

"Oh, yes, envied so much that every fool with dreams of glory arrived upon my doorstep to lay down a challenge," he said with an edge of bitterness. "There was rarely a year that passed that I was not forced into battle."

"The cost of leadership," Viper retorted. "It was never meant to be easy."

"I do not mind a difficult path; indeed, I welcome it. But I no longer desire a bloody one. I grew weary of killing brethren."

Viper felt a grudging flare of sympathy. He better than anyone understood the regret of having blood on his hands. A helluva lot of blood. Still, Styx had once been an outsider like himself. A vampire without clan and open prey until he had grown strong enough to defend himself. How could he put himself back at the mercy of another?

"As do I. But that still does not explain why you have chosen to bind yourself to another."

"We all serve the Anasso. He is the master of all."

Viper gave a shake of his head. "Not as his personal guard. You have sold your soul."

"No." The word was barely a whisper. "I am attempting to reclaim it."

"Your soul?" Viper demanded with a frown.

"Call it what you will." Styx gave an impatient wave of his hand. "A meaning to life. A sense of purpose."

Viper regarded his friend for a long moment. The last thing he had expected was a debate on philosophy while he was being held prisoner. Of course, it shouldn't have been. This was Styx, after all.

"You sound remarkably human," he at last drawled. "Aren't they the ones always scrambling to discover a fate beyond themselves?"

"Are they wrong?" Styx countered. "Should we not all strive to create a legacy that will enrich our brethren?"

Viper gave a pointed glance toward the silver shackles that were burning ever deeper into his flesh.

"And you believe that is what you are doing? Enriching our brethren?"

The older vampire possessed the decency to grimace although his voice remained smooth.

"You seem to forget that it was the Anasso who led the battle to civilize our clans. It was his strength that allowed us to defeat those who wished to maintain the ancient ways. And his presence that keeps anarchy from returning. I would think you, Viper, of all people, would hold that a worthy goal."

Viper hadn't forgotten the past. Or the brutal, bloody battles that had been waged. Or even the fact that it had been the Anasso who had led the charge. No doubt without his efforts they would still be living as savages. He had also not forgotten that those wars had killed those ancients who had stood

above the Anasso, leaving him the eldest and the most powerful of all.

"And so the end justifies any means, eh Styx?"

"Do you mock me, Viper?"

A wry smile touched Viper's lips. "No, in fact I understand.
I have found satisfaction as a chief, but as you say, there is
more to life than power. It is only now that I have found the
purpose in my life that you seek."

Styx regarded him curiously. "And what is that?"

"Shay," he retorted simply. "And no matter what your dire
predictions I will do whatever I must to keep her safe." He
leaned forward to bare his fangs. "I will condemn the entire
race of vampires to hell if I have to."

Styx clenched his hand around the tiny medallion. "You had
better hope you come to your senses and call for the Shalott,
Viper, or you might just have accomplished that."

Not surprisingly, that brought a short end to the conversation.

The inner caves looked more like the chambers of a me-
dieval castle than damp holes in the ground. The walls and even
the ceilings were hidden behind rich tapestries, the floors covered by thick fur carpets, and the darkness driven back by tall,
bronze candelabras that each held dozens of flickering candles.

There was also the sort of heavy, ornately carved furnishings
that made Styx long for a match and a canister of gasoline.
Whatever his vows he was a warrior through and through, and
he understood the danger of cluttering his lair with such foolish
things. It would be impossible to defend these chambers against
attack. A warrior was as likely to trip over an ottoman and break
his neck as to stab his opponent.

Still, the Anasso had never asked his opinion when it came
to his choice in decorating his chambers, and Styx was wise
enough not to mention his concerns. Over the past hundred
years his master had become increasingly unpredictable in his

moods. More than one servant had met an unpleasant demise when speaking out of turn.

Styx found his steps slowing as he reached the large bedroom. So much had changed over the past hundred years. Too much.

The dark illness that plagued his master. Damocles, who filled the caves with his filthy presence. The ever deepening deceptions that he was forced to endure for the sake of all.

Not for the first time he questioned his decision to remain. He had made a vow. And his word was his honor. But these days his honor was feeling decidedly tarnished.

"Styx?"

The soft rasping voice filled the air and unconsciously squaring his shoulders, Styx forced his feet to carry him into the room dominated by the vast four-poster bed.

The heat from the roaring fire was enough to make his skin prickle and the stench of rotting flesh nearly overwhelming, but Styx never allowed his steps to falter as he moved to the bed and gazed down at the vampire he had sworn as his master. He didn't look like a master.

Not anymore.

Once a large, towering figure he was now so shrunken and shriveled that he appeared more like a mummy than the most powerful vampire to walk the earth. Even his hair was falling out to reveal the growing lesions that marred his flesh. He had the look and smell of death, but only a fool would believe that he was weak. The glittering black eyes revealed the cunning and dangerous power that still smoldered within him.

Halting beside the bed Styx offered a deep bow. "My lord, you wished to see me?"

A faint smile touched the gaunt, hollow face. "Ah Styx, I hear you have brought me Viper, and that soon he will call my Shalott."

"Yes, my lord."

"I would prefer to have the demon in my grasp, but you have done well. Of course, you always do."

"Unfortunately my best does not seem to always be enough."

He knew his voice was stiff, but there was nothing to be done about it.

"Such modesty. And something else in your voice." Those dark eyes regarded him with a piercing intelligence. "Surely it is not regret?"

"I do not like harming a friend."

"I presume you are referring to Viper?" he asked softly.

Styx clenched his hands at his side. When he had been commanded to capture Viper along with the Shalott he had argued long and hard against it. Surely they had battled to bring an end to precisely this sort of treachery among vampires?

"Yes. He is an honorable man. He does not deserve to be treated in such a manner."

The Anasso heaved a faint sigh. "My old friend, you know that I would gladly welcome him as a brother if he will use the amulet to bring us his slave. Has he done so?"

"No." Styx grimaced. "He . . . possesses feelings for the Shalott."

"A pity." The elder vampire stroked the crimson velvet of his robe as if in deep thought, but Styx didn't miss the dark gaze that carefully measured his expression. "Like you I have no taste for causing injury to my brethren. Unfortunately we cannot afford to waver now. The Shalott is almost in our grasp. He must use the amulet."

"And if he won't?"

"I possess full faith that the Ravens will convince him."

"You have given commands to have him tortured?"

"It was your decision, not mine, Styx," the Anasso reminded him gently. "I preferred a far less . . . messy solution."

Styx stiffened, his face hardening with distaste. "To have Viper murdered and the demon taken by force?"

Something flashed through the dark eyes before the vampire was deliberately smoothing his features to an expression of weary patience.

"A harsh accusation, my son."

"What would you call it?"

A thin, gnarled hand lifted in a helpless motion. "An unfortunate sacrifice for the greater cause."

Styx gave a shake of his head. "Pretty words do not make it any less despicable."

"Do you think I have no regrets, my son? That I would not alter the past if possible? I hold myself entirely to blame for the circumstances we find ourselves in."

As well he should, Styx acknowledged. It had been his weakness that had led to this moment. His lust for the forbidden that might very well kill a noble vampire.

"I am aware of that, my lord."

Easily hearing the distaste in his tone the Anasso offered a faint frown.

"Perhaps you believe I should allow Viper and the Shalott to walk away? Without her I am certain to die."

"There must be some other means."

"I have sought every means possible, even taking those vile concoctions that the imp is forever thrusting upon me." The elder vampire sharply interrupted. "There is nothing to halt the disease but the blood of the Shalott."

"Shay," Styx said softly.

"What?"

"The Shalott's name is Shay."

"Yes, of course." There was a long pause as the elder vampire studied him in thoughtful silence. "Styx?"

"Yes, my lord?"

"If you have changed your mind, I understand. I have put you in an untenable position and for that I am deeply sorry." He weakly reached up to touch Styx's arm. "You must know that your faith and loyalty mean more to me than life itself."

A tightness clutched at Styx's chest. "You are very kind, my lord."

"Not kind." A faint smile touched the decaying lips. "Do you recall when we first met?"

"I was battling a pack of werewolves, as I recall."

A soft chuckle disturbed the thick air. "You informed me that I would have to wait for my turn to be killed."

Styx grimaced. "I was still young and brash."

"Do you remember what I said?"

Styx slowly turned to watch the blazing flames in the marble fireplace. He was not entirely stupid. He realized that the Anasso was deliberately reminding him of the day he had offered his pledge. And perhaps, just as importantly, reminding him of the cause that had bound them together.

A cause that went beyond either of them.

"You said that you intended to stop the flow of blood," he said in an empty voice. "To write the destiny of the vampire race in the stars. To band us together and meld greatness out of chaos. And then you asked me to walk at your side."

"At my side, Styx. Never behind." There was a strategic pause. "I want this to be your decision, my son. If you believe it is best to release Viper and allow the Shalott to roam free then that is what we will do."

"No, my lord." Turning Styx regarded the frail man with a sharp pang of horror. "I cannot—"

The vampire lifted his hand to halt his refusal. "Think upon it, Styx, but think quickly. We do not have much time left."

Chapter Twenty-One

Dawn was hovering just over the horizon as Levet scoured the sharply carved bluffs. Below them the charming farmhouse was nestled in a shadowed slumber while the mighty Mississippi River slid by in silent grandeur.

Hardly the setting for a band of dark vampires intent on murder, mayhem, and good old-fashioned bloodletting. Of course, it might have been a little difficult to hide a gothic castle complete with bats and creepy servants in the middle of the heartland. That was the sort of thing people tended to notice.

Leaning against a tree as the gargoyle pulled aside bushes and fallen rocks Shay absently rubbed the muscles of her legs. She had run full out for over six hours as she had tracked the limo through the back roads of Illinois. There had been no means of keeping pace with the automobile, but the scent of so many vampires had been enough for her and Levet to follow.

And follow, and follow, and follow . . .

Her stamina was well beyond a human's but that didn't keep her muscles from cramping into knots the size of Mount Rushmore. Or her feet from feeling as if they had been put through a meat grinder more than once.

At least the pang in her side had stopped throbbing and her breathing was almost back to normal. And even more importantly she had managed to make a short detour to a nearby farmhouse so she could borrow a thick flannel shirt that protected her from the crisp night air. Borrowing sounded so much nicer than stealing.

Glancing toward the sky she cleared her throat. "Levet, the clock is ticking."

"I know, I know," he muttered, pulling and tugging at a pile of thick brush. "It is here. I smell it." There were a few more grunts and then the gargoyle was abruptly straightening. *"Voila."*

"Voila? What the heck is that supposed to mean?" she demanded as she moved forward to study the narrow crack in the rock.

Levet gave a sniff as he squeezed through the opening. "It is a crime against nature that not all people are French. Are you coming?"

She sucked in a deep breath as her palms began to sweat. Saint's blood. Another dark and dank hole. She had sworn that once she was free of the witch's coven she would never enter another one.

You won't ever be alone in the dark again.

Viper's voice seemed to whisper through the back of her mind, easing the flare of fear that had threatened to overwhelm her. She was not alone. She had Levet at her side, and Viper waiting for her to rescue him.

"I'm coming," she said in firm tones, pushing herself through the opening and into the wide tunnel beyond. Wide but not tall she discovered as she banged her head on the low hanging ceiling. "Ouch. Dammit, Levet. You could have warned me."

"You should not be so tall," Levet muttered from the dark. "We need light."

"No." Shay reached out blindly, desperate to halt her friend from creating disaster. Amazingly, however, there were no explosions, no sudden ash in the air. Just a small ball of light hovering over Levet's grinning face. She breathed out a shaky sigh as she rubbed her throbbing head. "Shit, Levet, you could have blown us both to tiny bits."

Levet stuck out his tongue. "Bah."

Returning her attention to more important matters Shay

glanced about the tunnel, sniffing the musty air that held no trace of humans or demons.

"No one has passed through this tunnel for years," she murmured.

Levet pointed toward the large crack that ran along the wall. "It's unsteady."

A chill inched down her spine. "How unsteady?"

The gargoyle gave a small shrug. "It is sound enough for the moment, although I would suggest that you avoid setting off a stick of dynamite."

"I'll keep that in mind."

Smiling gently at her forced attempt at humor Levet moved to take her hand in his own. "The sun comes and I would have your promise before I am forced to slumber."

She gave his fingers a gentle squeeze. "What promise is that?"

"I can't stop you from going in search of Viper, but I want your word that you won't do anything stupid."

Shay rolled her eyes in exasperation. "Why do people keep saying that to me?"

"Because you are rash, and impulsive, and you let your heart lead your path. Just be careful."

"I will, I promise."

She bent down to give his cheek a kiss just as the cave was lit with the first glow of dawn. By the time she had straightened, or had straightened as much as she could without smacking her head, the gargoyle had turned to stone.

With a last pat on Levet's head she turned and walked deeper into the tunnel.

Although immortality had a number of benefits, there were a handful of downsides to living forever.

The endless tedium of the Dark Ages.

The ghastly fashions of the sixties.

The annoyance of learning new technology.

And, worst of all, surviving even the most brutal torture.

And surviving, and surviving, and surviving.

Viper had long since lost track of how much time had passed since he had been hauled down to the dank cavern. Somehow hanging from the ceiling by silver chains and having his flesh sliced open by whips was proving a helluva distraction.

He did know that it was long enough that far too much of his blood had pooled onto the rough stone floor. And that it was increasingly difficult to hold up his head.

With a brutal rhythm the whips cracked through the air, never pausing, never quickening, never altering. A slow, steady rhythm that was ruthlessly shredding his back and legs. The end came without warning. One moment the whip was biting deep into his back and the next the silent Ravens were filing from the shadowed cavern.

He might have groaned his relief if he hadn't sensed Styx step into the room and cross to stand directly before him. He would chug holy water before he would allow his captor to witness any hint of weakness.

Easily able to read his dark thoughts the tall vampire made an impatient sound even as his hand reached out to gently touch one of the gashes that ribboned Viper's back.

"Why must you be so stubborn, Viper? It serves you nothing. All you need do is call the Shalott and you will be released and healed."

Ignoring the agony of even the smallest movement Viper lifted his head to glare at his one time friend.

"The moment you release me I will kill you."

The bronzed face might have been carved from granite. "I am not your enemy."

"So this is how you treat your friends?" Viper spit at his feet. "Then I can only say that your hospitality sucks."

"You know I would never see you harmed. I would never wish harm upon any of my brothers." Styx lifted his hand from Viper's back and frowned at the blood that stained his fingers. "I seek to save us all from chaos and ruin."

"No," Viper hissed. "You seek to sacrifice a young, innocent woman to save a vampire who brought about his own ruin. Or do you deny the weakness of the Anasso?"

Styx clenched his hands at his sides. His loyalty to his master was without question, but not even he could entirely hide his dislike for the illness that had ravaged the once powerful vampire.

It was a closely held secret that vampires could be affected by taking the blood of those who were addicted to drugs. And an even more closely held secret that vampires themselves could be chained to the addiction. The tainted blood would slowly, but ruthlessly destroy any vampire.

Even the Anasso.

"That is all in the past," Styx retorted in frigid tones.

"You mean after he was cured by Shay's father?"

"Yes."

Viper gritted his teeth as a fresh wave of pain shot down his arms. Vampires were not meant to hang from ceilings by silver shackles. Of course, they were not intended to be kidnapped by companions they had once called friend, or whipped like a savage dog.

"If it is in the past why is he ill once again?" he demanded.

To his surprise Styx turned to pace across the damp floor, his flowing black robe unable to hide the tightness that clenched at his shoulders. Slowly he bent his head, almost as if he were in prayer.

"Does it matter?"

Viper's pain was forgotten as a violent fury surged through him.

"Considering you intend to murder the woman I love, then yes, it matters a great deal."

Styx visibly flinched, as if Viper had actually reached out to strike him.

"I . . . regret the necessity. You cannot know how much, Viper, but you must think what will occur if the Anasso dies." Slowly turning the vampire regarded Viper with a haunted expression. "Vampire will rise up against vampire. Some to claim dominion over us, and others simply to return to the days before peace. The blood of the clans will drown us all while the jackals wait to return to their place of glory."

"Jackals?" Viper frowned. "You mean the weres?"

"They are banded together beneath a new king. A young and fierce werewolf who dreams of the day when they rule the night," Styx retorted, his voice dark with concern. "It is only fear of the Anasso that keeps them from howling at our doorstep."

Viper gave a slow shake of his head. By the blood of the saints. Was Styx truly so blind? Had he been rattling around these dark caves for so long that he had no idea what was going on in the world?

"You are a fool, Styx," he growled.

The dark eyes narrowed. "No doubt many would agree with you, but never to my face."

As if a handful of insults would make a spit's worth of difference, Viper thought with a humorless smile. He was already being tortured. What the hell else could they do to him?

"Open your eyes, old companion," he rasped. "It is not the Anasso who keeps the vampires from ripping one another apart. Or even who holds the werewolves at bay."

Styx managed to look as if Viper had just muttered blasphemy. And perhaps it was to him. He had devoted his existence to the Anasso. He could obviously not see beyond that.

"Of course it is," Styx insisted. "He is the one who led us all to glory."

"Perhaps he did lead us, but no one has actually seen or spoken with the Anasso in centuries. He is little more than a vague shadow remembered for past deeds."

"They fear him. They fear the power he wields."

"No, they fear you, Styx. You and your Ravens. You are the ones who rule the vampires whether you will it or not."

Styx stiffened, his features tight with shock. "That is treason."

"It is the simple truth." Viper grimaced, barely capable of keeping his head lifted. His strength was draining away with his blood. "Leave this place and walk among the clans if you desire the truth, Styx. Your loyalty has blinded you."

Styx gave a low hiss. "I came here in the hope you could be made to see sense. Obviously your madness runs deeper than I had feared." His slender hand reached to touch the medallion at his neck. "When you are prepared to call for the Shalott I will return."

Turning on his heel the vampire left Viper to the pain and darkness.

Not that Viper truly minded. As the silver chains bit into his flesh and his muscles clenched in fiery agony, he could swear that he could smell the sweet scent of Shay.

The tunnels that honeycombed the bluff proved to be a bewildering maze that more often than not led to dead ends, or worse, circled back to the precise spot she started from. Within a half hour of fruitless searching she was lost and muttering a string of French curses. She didn't know what half of them meant, but they seemed somehow perfect as she stumbled and squeezed her way through the thick darkness.

She muttered them again as she smacked her head on a half dozen occasions and once nearly fell into a gaping hole in the floor. The place was obviously a deathtrap. A moldy, damp, and smelly deathtrap, which no doubt harbored any number of nasty, creepy spiders. Inching ever deeper beneath the bluffs she at last caught the unmistakable scent of vampires.

Oh, thank freaking heaven.

She would rather battle a herd of ravaging vampires than spend another moment trapped alone in the moldy tunnels.

Smelling vampires, however, and actually finding them proved to be two different things.

There didn't seem to be one tunnel that actually went in a straight line. Damn tunnels. And she was forced to circle through half of Illinois before she at last began to discover torches set in the walls, and occasional rugs and tapestries that revealed she was nearing the hidden lairs.

Coming to a fork she paused to take a deep breath. The vampires were most definitely to the right. At least seven of them.

But to the left there was the smell of humans. A whole flock of humans who smelled of fear and sickness. There was also more. A faint odor of imp and . . . troll?

Her heart gave a brief leap. Could it be Evor? Was he close enough for her to capture once she rescued Viper? It had to be worth a try.

Shay turned firmly in the direction of the vampires and put all thoughts of Evor from her mind. All that mattered at the moment was finding Viper.

This tunnel was wider and obviously more often traveled, but oddly deserted. With her current string of ill luck she half expected to trip over vampires around every curve. Instead there was not a one to be found as she caught the distinctive scent of Viper.

"Viper?" she whispered softly. A frown touched her brow when there was no answer. No matter how soft her voice, he should hear it. Unless . . . no, no, no. She wouldn't even think it.

Swallowing the lump that remained valiantly lodged in her throat she paused long enough to grasp one of the burning torches from a bracket and forced her feet forward. Just ahead there was a narrow opening.

Viper.

He was there.

She could feel it in every beat of her heart.

Careful not to singe her hair, or any other significant part of her body, she squeezed through the narrow opening. Once in the small cavern she held the torch outward to battle the inky darkness. What she found made her heart clench with a sharp, wrenching pain.

Viper was there all right.

Strung by his wrists to the ceiling he had been whipped until his back and legs were sliced open to the bone in some places. Blood was everywhere, turning his silver hair a sickening shade of crimson, and marring the perfection of his ivory face.

"Viper . . . oh shit, what did they do to you?" she whimpered, freezing in horror. The torch dropped to the floor before she took command of her senses. Dammit, the last thing Viper needed was a hysterical fool flapping her hands and oh-my-mying. She claimed to be a warrior. It was damn well time she started acting like one.

She swallowed again and deliberately turned her trembling fear into a grim, determined fury. The vampires had chained, beaten, and tortured Viper as if he were no more than an animal. And for no better cause than to capture her.

She intended to see them in hell.

Just as soon as she managed to get Viper to safety.

It was a task that proved to be easier said than done as she moved to struggle with the heavy chain that held Viper swinging from the ceiling. At least it was silver and not iron, she acknowledged, although she doubted that Viper shared her relief.

She could smell the stench of the metal burning into his flesh, and she knew that it must be as painful as all the ghastly wounds put together.

Tugging, pulling, cussing, and wrenching she at last managed to free the chain from the clasp set in the wall of the cavern. Of course her success did come with a cost as Viper dropped heavily to the ground, the chain landing on top of him.

Shay rushed forward, sweeping the chains off his body before grasping the shackles and jerking them off Viper's wrists.

For years she had cursed the demon strength that set her apart from humans. She had been a freak. A creature to be mocked by children and feared by adults. Now for the first time she truly appreciated the gifts she had been given.

Cradling Viper's head in her lap, she wiped the blood from his face with a shaking hand.

"Viper. Viper, can you hear me?"

There was no response for a frightening beat, and then he stirred in her arms.

"Shay?"

She leaned over to whisper in his ear. "Don't move, I'm here."

"Is this a dream?"

She choked back a hysterical laugh. "Surely you must have better dreams than this?"

"I have been dreaming of you for months. No, I've been dreaming of you for an eternity." His hands reached up to weakly grasp her arms, his eyes opening with a painful effort. "I thought I would never find you, but I did. I couldn't let you go. Not when I needed you so desperately. I will never let you go."

Her breath caught as ridiculous tears stung her eyes. He was no doubt delirious and completely out of his mind with pain. But no one had ever said anything that had touched her so deeply.

She was forced to clear her throat as she gently stroked his hair. "As if you could possibly get rid of me now. We're stuck together like . . ."

"Day-old rice?" he said.

"Refrigerated leftovers are not quite the romantic metaphor I was searching for." A frown touched her brow as his eyes slid shut. "Viper." She gave him a small shake. "Viper you must wake."

With an obvious effort he struggled back to consciousness. "You shouldn't be here. It's dangerous."

Dangerous? A cave full of vampires desperate to drain her blood? Nah.

"Don't worry, I'm leaving," she soothed.

"Yes." His hand squeezed her arm. "Leave now."

"We're both leaving." She gently freed her arm from his tight grasp to place her wrist against his lips. "But first you must drink."

She could feel his entire body tighten at her words. "Shay, no. You don't want me taking your blood."

She gave an impatient click of her tongue. Could the man do anything without an argument?

And he called her stubborn.

"We had a deal, Viper. Blood to heal you. Do you think a Shalott ever reneges on a deal?"

He gave a shake of his head. "Shay, go. They will kill you."

She shrugged. "First they have to catch me."

A weary smile touched his lips. "You aren't nearly so tough as you like to think you are."

"I'm going to show you just how tough I am if you don't drink," she warned, pressing her arm to his lips. "You have to do this now or we're both dead."

His dark eyes searched her set expression for a long, silent moment.

"Stubborn," he at last breathed.

"I learned from a master," she muttered. "Now bite."

He did.

Shay's eyes widened and her entire body shuddered in shock as his fangs slid easily through the skin of her wrist. It wasn't from pain. She almost wished it was. That would have been easy to battle. The saints above knew she had enough experience. But how did she battle the shocking flare of pleasure that raced through her body? Or the heat pooling in the pit of her stomach?

Flat out . . . she didn't.

Her teeth clenched as her lower body tightened with a familiar excitement. Oh, she knew where this was heading, she acknowledged as her breath came in shallow pants. With every tug of his mouth she could feel the pleasure mounting, as if he were deep inside her stroking her most intimate places.

Her eyes threatened to roll back in her head as her free hand clenched in his hair. In a tiny, very tiny, corner of her mind she recognized that Viper's strength was rapidly returning. It was obvious in the fierce sucking at her wrist, and the hand that clutched at her arm.

She was a little too preoccupied at the moment, however, to fully appreciate the knowledge her blood was working its magic.

Go figure.

The sweet pressure reached a critical mass and burying her face in Viper's hair Shay bit back her cry of fulfillment. Holy crap. She was dizzy and weak from the powerful release. And quite frankly more than a little embarrassed. It was hardly the time or place for such a private interlude. Not that her body seemed to mind. It was utterly content as Viper stirred to life and shifted so that he could sit upright and cradle her in his arms.

"Shay?" His hand smoothed back the hair that had strayed from her braid. "Shay, speak to me."

"Yow," she breathed, forcing herself to meet his worried gaze.

Not the most articulate response, but it was a step above a grunt.

Viper frowned. "Did I hurt you?"

"Not exactly."

He searched her expression for a long moment before comprehension at last flared through the dark eyes.

"Are you blushing, pet?"

"I didn't . . ." She gave a shake of her head before she pulled back enough to study him with a worried gaze. "Do you feel well enough to get out of here?"

A smile curled his lips as he glanced down at his blood-soaked body.

"I'm healed. Completely healed," he murmured in amazement. "It's little wonder that the Anasso is so anxious to get his hands upon you."

Shay grimaced as she studied the pinprick fang marks still visible on her wrist. "Actually, I don't think it's his hands he wants to get on me."

He dropped a kiss on the top of her head. "Don't underestimate those pheromones of yours. They are potent enough to seduce any vampire."

"Is that supposed to make me feel better?" she demanded.

Viper rose smoothly to his feet with a soft chuckle. "No, I suppose it wouldn't." With great care he set her on her feet and placed his hands on her shoulders. His expression settled into somber lines as his thumbs absently stroked the line of her collarbone. "Shay, you have given me a great gift. One that I will not forget."

She shifted in discomfort. "A promise is a promise. I gave you the blood-debt, nothing more."

He smiled ruefully. "Be quiet, pet. In just a moment I intend to tell you in no uncertain terms just how stupid it was to follow me and put yourself at risk. For now I simply want you to know that you bring honor to your Shalott ancestors. I have never met anyone, whether it's vampire, demon, or human, who possesses your courage or your loyalty. You are a warrior your father would have been proud of."

A hot blush stained her cheeks. Dang it, she wasn't good at this mushy stuff. Give her a demon to fight, or a witch to outwit, and she was in her element. Give her a compliment and she floundered and fluttered as if she didn't have a lick of sense to her name.

"Maybe we should be thinking about getting out of here," she muttered.

His lips twitched. "There are times when I despair of you, pet, I truly do." He brushed a soft kiss over her brow. "But on this occasion you're right. We need to get out of here. The sooner the better."

Chapter Twenty-Two

Viper was grumpy.

There was really no better way to describe his mood.

Oh, it wasn't that he wasn't grateful. He didn't enjoy being tortured any better than the next vampire. Probably less than most. And he wasn't indifferent to the knowledge that Shay had revealed the secrets of her heart that she wasn't yet prepared to confess. No woman followed a man for hours and risked her life out of simple loyalty. Not even his stubborn, utterly obstinate Shalott. And certainly they did not offer up their precious blood without possessing some feelings.

But as much as the display of her affection warmed his cold heart, he couldn't put aside the maddening knowledge that he had failed. Failed to realize the truth of who was hunting Shay. Failed to capture the damnable Evor and put an end to the curse. Failed to keep Shay from rushing headlong into danger.

It had pretty much been one big stinking heap of failure.

Dammit all.

Behind him Shay remained thankfully oblivious to his silent self-flagellation.

Not surprising.

To her the tunnels were a spiderweb of inky blackness. Even holding tightly onto his hand she was stumbling over the uneven ground as he led her away from the occupied caves.

"Ow," she muttered, nearly going to her knees as she tripped over a stray rock.

Coming to a halt he turned to study her pale face. "Are you all right?"

"No, I'm not all right." She reached down to rub her toe. "I can't see a damn thing in this dark."

"Don't worry there's really not much to see. Some dirt, some rocks, a few spiders," he said dryly.

She straightened. The better to glare at him. "That is so not funny."

"Neither is the fact that you risked yourself to come here," he retorted, his voice edged with his smoldering frustration. "How did you even find me?"

She shrugged. "When I escaped from the warehouse I ran across Levet. He was already following you."

"The gargoyle?" He gave a lift of his brows. "I didn't know he cared."

"He thought that I was with you."

"Ah." Viper frowned. "What of Dante?"

"He is gathering your clan. Once the sun sets Levet will return to Chicago and lead them here."

He cupped her chin in his hand. "And it never occurred to you to wait for Dante?"

Her eyes narrowed. Never a good sign. "You might very well have been dead."

"But you would have been safe," he growled. "Dammit, Shay, I will not have you risking yourself—"

"No." She jerked her chin from his grasp. "You might hold my amulet, but you have promised that I am not your slave."

He gave a hiss of exasperation. "Of course you're not."

"Then I'm free to make my own decisions. And if that means coming here to rescue you then that's exactly what I'll do."

It was without a doubt the most ridiculous argument that Viper had ever heard. And he had heard a lot of them over the centuries.

He gave a disbelieving shake of his head. "Even if it means being captured and drained?" he demanded harshly. "That's exactly what will happen if we're caught. You should have returned to Abby. You would have been safe there."

Indifferent to his dangerous mood she boldly poked him in the chest. Poked *him.* One of the most feared predators in all of Chicago. No. In all the world.

"No, I would not have been safe," she said.

He took a step back. The poking didn't hurt, but it did little to help his wounded pride.

"Shay, not even Styx and the Ravens would dare attack the Phoenix. That's exactly why he lured us out of her house in the first place."

"He might not attack the Phoenix, but it doesn't matter how many goddesses I surround myself with if they decide to kill Evor."

Viper's muscles tensed. "Evor? You know where he is?"

"I think he's here."

"No." Viper gave an adamant shake of his head. "Styx said that they never managed to get their hands on the troll."

Shay gave a short, humorless laugh. "And you believed him after he captured and tortured you? Did he also have some swampland to buy?"

His lips thinned. He fully intended to deal with his old friend. But not now.

"Styx might torture me, he might even kill me, but he would never lie. Not intentionally."

"Charming."

Realizing that it would be impossible to explain Styx's complex morals, he turned his attention to her startling claim.

"Why do you believe he holds Evor?"

"Because I smelled troll when I came through the caves."

A cold chill arrowed down his spine. "You're certain?"

Her eyes narrowed. She didn't call him thick-skulled, but it was implied.

"It's a fairly unique odor."

And one Shay would be all too familiar with.

Viper clenched his fists as he paced across the narrow tunnel. He couldn't begin to guess how Evor could be close by without Styx knowing, but he had to at least search for the rotten troll.

"Damn."

"What is it?" she demanded.

"Where's Levet?"

She regarded him suspiciously. "Playing statue in a cave that leads out of the bluffs. Why?"

"I don't suppose I can convince you to join him while I go in search of this mysterious troll?"

"No."

"Shay . . ."

"No, no, no." She moved to stand directly in front of him, although there was thankfully no more poking. "I'm not some helpless idiot that has to be shooed out of the way whenever there happens to be a bit of danger."

"A bit of danger?" He deliberately flashed his fangs. "These caves are crawling with the most dangerous vampires to walk the earth."

"And for now they are all safely tucked in their coffins."

"You want to risk your life on that?" he rasped.

"It's my life to risk. Not yours."

He closed his eyes and battled back the urge to howl in frustration. Devil's balls, but the woman was destined to drive him to his grave.

"The Ravens should take lessons from you, pet. They're amateurs when it comes to torturing a man."

"Are you going to sulk or are we going to find Evor?" she demanded as she marched blindly down the tunnel.

Viper was in swift pursuit. A fortunate thing as she suddenly halted and nearly fell to her knees.

With a blinding speed he moved forward to wrap her in his arms. "Shay?"

She gave a shake of her head. "I'm sorry. I just suddenly felt dizzy."

Viper's brows snapped together in sharp concern. Even in the darkness he could detect her sudden pallor and the thin film of damp sweat that coated her skin. She was obviously ill.

And just as obviously attempting to hide just how bad she was feeling. It took him a stupid moment before he realized what was plaguing the woman.

"Damn, I'm a fool," he gritted as he plucked her off her feet and cradled her against his chest. Using his senses he searched for an empty cave nearby and headed down the tunnel.

She squirmed in his arms. "Viper."

"Shh, hold still for a moment."

"What are you doing?"

"We need someplace to rest."

"We can't rest now," she protested in shock.

His arms tightened. "We can and we will."

Viper heard her breath rasp between clenched teeth. "You are annoyingly fond of handing out orders."

"No, I'm annoyingly fond of you, pet, and I should be staked for not having realized how weak you must be."

His blunt words momentarily stole her annoyance. A rare trick and Viper was swift to use the distraction to turn into a low, side tunnel. From the number of cobwebs brushing against his face he was confident that no one had been this way for years.

"I told you I'm just dizzy," she at last managed to mutter although her voice had lost some of its sting.

"Shay, you've spent the night dodging demons, fighting trolls, and tracking me across half the state. Put on top of that donating a great deal of blood to a wounded vampire it's a wonder you're even on your feet." He touched his lips to the top of her head. "Even the most powerful warriors must occasionally recover their strength."

"But we have to get out of here."

Viper ducked as the tunnel became even more cramped. "We have time. As you pointed out the vampires will be in their coffins, and I cannot leave the caves until the sun has set."

There was a pause before she heaved a reluctant sigh. "Maybe we could find someplace to rest for a few minutes."

"An excellent notion."

She nudged him with her elbow. "Don't be patronizing."

"Me?" His expression was pure innocence. "Patronizing?"
"Drop it."

"Whatever you command, pet." At last coming to the end of the tunnel Viper glanced about the small cave. It was rocky and damp and seemingly created for discomfort. But it had the benefit of being remote from the other caves with only one entrance. No one would be able to sneak up on them.

Setting her onto the hard ground Viper moved to settle beside her and pulled her into his arms.

"Close your eyes and rest, Shay," he murmured. "I will keep watch."

As a testament to just how weak she truly was Shay didn't even attempt an argument. Settling her head on his shoulder she gave a small sigh and promptly fell asleep.

Levet might not be hideously large, or blessed with the sort of frightening power of his ancestors, but he had more than his fair share of intelligence. Not a bad trade-off, all things considered. Which was why he wasn't particularly surprised when he awoke to discover Shay missing in action.

Whatever her pledge of being careful he had known quite well she wouldn't wait hours to rescue her oh-so-delectable vampire. What few wits she had once possessed were now evaporated to the mists of oblivion. She would happily charge into any danger to rescue Viper.

Gak.

It was enough to make any decent gargoyle want to hurl.

Still, he wasn't about to let her fall into the hands of evil vampires just because she was stupid enough to fall in love. He didn't have many friends. Okay, he'd never had *any* friends until Shay. He couldn't afford to lose her.

Shaking off the bits of stone that clung to his skin Levet carefully unfolded his wings and made his way to the nearby opening. He had to get into contact with Dante, and quickly. They hadn't expected Viper to be hauled so far from the city. Even if they left this moment it would take hours for the clan to make their way to the isolated farmhouse. He couldn't afford to lose time in trekking all the way back to Chicago to give directions.

Once out of the cave he crept along the line of the bluff, his tail twitching as he easily caught sight of the vampire standing guard in the shadows of the farmhouse. He had to get to the river, but he preferred to do it without having a herd of angry vampires on his heels.

Stealth for the moment trumped speed.

Remaining in the deepest shadows Levet moved with near painful slowness. Vampires were near perfect predators. They could use all of their senses to detect prey. It would take only one stray pebble being dislodged, or one wayward breeze blowing his scent the wrong direction and his head would be decorating the farmhouse wall.

Not the most pleasant fate.

He traveled almost a half mile from the vampires before angling his path toward the vast river. Even then he remained low to the ground and prepared to go into flight at the least hint of trouble.

His pace quickened as he crossed a narrow highway that meandered beside the river, and then down a sharp incline that was overgrown with thick brush and choking moss. He slipped and stumbled more than once, but thankfully his blundering was relatively silent.

At last he reached the edge of the river and knelt in the thick mud. Around him the world was alive. Insects, fish, curious raccoons, and wary opossums. But Levet ignored them as he peered into waves that lapped toward him.

Waiting until he could at last see his reflection in the murky water he waved a gnarled hand and spoke the harsh words of magic in a low voice. There was a shimmer of faint light before his reflection disappeared and a black emptiness took its place.

This, of course, was the tricky part.

Although he would rather have his tongue cut out than to admit the truth, his magic wasn't always as predictable as it could be. Okay, most of the time it was nothing more than a wing and a prayer that resulted in small fires, an occasional explosion, and once a painful nosebleed that had lasted for almost twenty years.

He couldn't afford any disasters this evening.

Carefully constructing the image of a dark haired vampire in his mind, he projected the thought into the dark water.

Long moments passed before at last he could detect the fuzzy outline of the familiar countenance.

"Dante. Dante can you hear me?" he hissed.

In the depths of the water the vampire seemed to frown and glance about, as if uncertain if he had heard a voice or not.

Stupid vampires.

"Dante, it is Levet," he growled.

"Levet?" The raven brows snapped together. "Where the hell are you?"

"If you will clear your mind I will show you."

"What?"

Levet muttered a few choice curses. He kept them low enough so that the vampire couldn't hear. He wasn't completely suicidal, but they made him feel better.

"Just clear your mind, I will do the rest."

Dante didn't look happy, but he closed his eyes and obviously made an attempt to empty his mind. Levet didn't waste any time as he thrust his memories of the long journey to the farmhouse through the water.

There was a sharp hiss as Dante wrenched open his eyes and gave a shake of his head.

"It is much farther than I thought. Even taking cars it will be hours before we can arrive."

Levet shrugged. Nothing could be done to make the vampires arrive any sooner.

"I will wait for you near the entrance to the cave," Levet promised.

"What of Viper and Shay?"

"I don't know."

Dante grimaced. "We'll be there."

"Hurry."

With a wave of his hand, Levet closed the portal. Or at least he attempted to close the portal. Dante's image was gone, but the swirling darkness remained. With a frown he leaned forward only to give a sudden squawk as a beautiful face swam into view. Falling back into the mud he watched in horror as the woman pushed through the portal to stand before him.

Not that he didn't appreciate the sight of a lovely woman.

He might be small, but he was all male and no man could deny that the small, curvaceous woman with her pure white skin, slanted blue eyes, and pale green hair was a sight to behold. Quite, quite a sight to behold.

Oh, and it didn't help that she was butt naked beneath the sheer toga.

"Holy mother of . . ." Struggling against the thick, grasping mud Levet glared at the woman who stood only a foot taller than him. "Don't do that."

The woman gave a bat of her lashes, her smile vacant. "Do what?"

At last on his feet he shook the slimy moss from his wings. "Pop up like a . . . a . . . thing that annoyingly pops."

"I didn't pop."

"You most certainly did. Do you have no manners, whatsoever?" Levet gave a shake of his head. "Of course not, what am I saying. You are a water sprite."

"And you're a gargoyle, although I've never seen one so tiny. Did you get shrunk by a spell?"

Levet rolled his eyes as he turned and began stomping away from the river. Water sprites might be visions of loveliness, but they rarely possessed enough brains to fill a thimble.

"No, I did not get shrunk by a spell. This is the size I have always been."

She fluttered at his side, skimming over the rocks and bushes with annoying ease.

"It's not very impressive."

"Shut up and go away you ridiculous pest."

"I'm not a pest, and I can't leave."

"Of course you can." Levet gave a flick of his hand, careful to keep his eyes trained on the ground before him. As a demon he couldn't be bespelled by the sprite, but he wasn't completely immune to temptation. Now was not the time for such a delicious distraction. "Swim away with the nasty fishes."

"You summoned me, little gargoyle," she purred.

"I most certainly did not."

"Yes, you did."

"Did not."

"Did so."

"Did . . ." Coming to a halt Levet threw his hands in the air. "*Sacrebleu,* this is absurd. Why will you not go away?"

She gave a toss of her long curls. "I told you, you summoned me. I am bound to you until the spell is broken."

"Fine, I break it. You are unsummoned. Go away."

A pout touched her full lips. "You don't know much for a gargoyle."

His wings gave an angry buzz. Beautiful or not the woman was a pain in the ass.

"Fine, tell me what I must do to make you disappear."

The pout became a downright sulk. "You do not think me lovely?"

"I think giraffes are lovely but that doesn't mean I want one trailing behind me. Especially one that can't seem to keep its mouth shut."

"You are not a very nice gargoyle." Her skin slowly began to shimmer in the faint moonlight. It was a shimmer that had lured sailors to their doom for centuries. "You should tell me I'm beautiful and long to be with me."

"The only thing I long for is some peace," Levet growled. "I wish you to be quiet."

The blue eyes widened and her lips parted but astonishingly there was nothing but blissful silence.

Levet frowned. Did she actually obey his command? No, it hadn't been a command. It had been a wish.

A sly smile touched his lips. "Ah ha. That is it. You give me three wishes and then you must return to the waters."

Her arms folded over her ample bosom as she glared at him

in frustration. Obviously she had hoped to keep him too befuddled and bewitched to reason the manner of being rid of her. As long as she owed him wishes she was free of her watery prison.

And best of all he was a demon. Which meant that when she returned to the waters she couldn't force him to join her.

Tapping a thick claw on his chin Levet carefully considered what was to be done with his sudden stroke of fortune.

He had used one wish on her silence.

A wish well used, if he did say so himself.

But he had two left.

He must decide precisely just how they should be used.

Dante swayed and reached out a hand to grasp the edge of a nearby table as the contact with the gargoyle was abruptly brought to an end.

Damn the stunted demon. It was disconcerting to have someone wrench themselves from his mind with such haste.

"Dante, what is it? What's happening?"

Giving a shake of his head Dante turned to regard the dark, muscular vampire who had entered the room. Santiago appeared distinctly out of place in the opulent splendor of Viper's private club. Like Dante he preferred a plain black shirt and leather pants.

Of course they were both warriors. It was Viper who possessed the elegant sophistication to feel comfortable among such grandeur.

"The gargoyle," he said in abrupt tones.

Santiago gave a swift glance about the empty lobby. "He's returned?"

"No, he managed to contact me through a portal."

"A portal? I didn't realize gargoyles possessed such powers."

Dante smiled with grim humor. In spite of himself he couldn't help but like the annoying gargoyle.

"The little one seems full of surprises."

"Has he found the master?"

"Yes. They have traveled across the state. We must leave at once."

The vampire touched the heavy sword that was sheathed at his hip. "The clan awaits your command."

Taking a step toward the nearby stairs Dante came to a sudden halt. Shit. He had almost forgotten the most important thing.

"Santiago, I need someone to return to my estate and tell Abby what is happening. I can't have her fretting over my absence."

The vampire took a sharp step back, his eyes widening with horror.

"Are you mad?"

Dante frowned. "What?"

"You want someone to confront the goddess and tell her that her mate is charging off to risk his life against dangerous enemies?" Santiago regarded him with an expression of martyrdom. "I may be young by your standard, Dante, but I'm not stupid."

"Abby would never harm you."

"She might not intend to harm me, but I have no intention of being around a woman who has a history of setting things on fire when she loses her temper."

Dante's lips twitched. His mate was a beautiful, intelligent, extraordinarily kind woman, but there had been moments when her control of the Phoenix was not completely perfect.

Over the past months she had managed to singe a demon or two in public, which had unfortunately lingered in the minds of many.

"She almost never sets things on fire anymore," he protested.

"Almost, is not never, my friend." The dark eyes narrowed. "And when she discovers that you have slipped out of town without her . . . well, you must understand my concern. Have the gargoyle use the portal to contact her. I don't think that gargoyles are flammable."

Dante gave a snort. "Coward."

Santiago shuddered. "Oh yes."

"Fine." Reaching for the cloak he had thrown over a delicate satinwood chair Dante swept it around his shoulders. "Take the clan to the edge of Rockford and I will meet you there."

Santiago gave a choked cough. "You intend to tell the Phoenix yourself?"

"I intend to pick her up and take her with us," he said dryly. "Not even I am stupid enough to tell her that she must stay behind."

Santiago gave a sudden laugh. "Age really does bring wisdom."

"Pathetic," Dante muttered as he marched from the room.

Chapter Twenty-Three

Shay struggled to crawl her way out of the clinging darkness. Not a pleasant task as she realized there was a crick in her neck and every muscle was cramped from sleeping on the hard, damp floor.

Of course it wasn't all bad, she had to concede. Nothing could be truly terrible when her head was resting on Viper's shoulder and his strong arms were wrapped about her.

Allowing herself a moment to simply drink in the scent of his skin and the feel of his body next to her own, Shay at last forced open her eyes.

"What time is it?" she demanded in a husky voice.

"A half hour past dark."

The cobwebs were wrenched from her mind as she abruptly sat upright. Below her Viper remained stretched on the hard rock, his beautiful ivory face and long silver hair the only thing visible in the darkness.

"Why didn't you wake me?"

"I did try on several occasions, but you refused to obey," he murmured. "In fact you called me a number of quite disturbing names and threatened to stake me."

She narrowed her eyes. "I don't believe you."

His lips twitched. "Very well, if you want the truth I was enjoying watching you sleep."

"Ew. Don't do that."

He gave a lift of his brows. "Do what?"

"Watch me sleep. It creeps me out."

"Why?"

"Because I know I must be drooling."

"Only a little and it was very cute."

A reluctant smile touched her mouth. "Stop that."

Viper slowly lifted to sit beside her. He reached to cup her face in his hands.

"Shay, it wouldn't matter what you do in your sleep. Having you in my arms, feeling your warmth, is a joy that I treasure. Surely by now you know that I would sacrifice everything for you?"

Her breath caught and the mere chore of breathing became difficult. "Viper?"

The dark, mesmerizing gaze flared over her face, his expression impossible to read.

"Am I frightening you?" he asked.

Her mouth was dry and her heart lodged somewhere in her throat. But frightened?

Naw.

"If you haven't noticed, I'm not that easily frightened," she forced herself to say.

His fingers tightened. "I've noticed that you are annoyingly eager to risk your life, but you are much more cautious when it comes to your heart."

Her gaze lowered to the full, sensual curve of his mouth. "The wounds of the heart are far more difficult to heal than wounds of the body."

He pressed his forehead to hers. "I would never hurt you, Shay."

His lips whispered over her skin sending a tingle of magic down her spine. She wanted to kiss him and show him precisely what burned in her heart. To softly run her hands over his hard, muscular body. To offer herself without reservation.

That was a simple thing.

It was getting the words past her lips that was proving to be the problem.

She just felt so . . . sappy.

"What do you want of me?" she at last demanded.

"Your trust, your love, your very soul. I want all of you."

Her laugh came out as a breathy whisper. "You don't ask for much."

"It is what all vampires demand of their mates."

She pulled back, her eyes wide. "Mate?"

He studied her deer-in-the-headlights expression with a faint smile.

"Yes. You are my mate, Shay. You are the woman destined to be at my side for all eternity."

"But . . ." She floundered to discover a reasonable thought floating around her brain. "We don't even know if I have an eternity."

"None of us can say precisely how long we have. Fate is fickle even to immortals," he said softly. "But for whatever days and nights we have I want you to share them with me."

She lowered her eyes as a surge of emotion threatened to make her bawl like a baby.

"This is hardly the time or place for such a discussion."

"Perhaps not, but I need to hear the words from you, pet." He smoothed a stray curl behind her ear. "I need you to tell me that you care for me."

She squirmed with unease. It was stupid. Beyond stupid. But she would rather face the Lu before admitting the truth etched across her heart.

"You know that I do."

"The words, pet," he urged. "Can you not say them?"

"It's not easy for me."

There was a long, painful pause before he heaved a sigh and pulled back. "No, it's not easy. Come, we should not linger."

As if to prove just how stupid she truly was, a flare of panic raced through her. This was the most important moment in her entire life and she was blowing it. Blowing it with glorious, stunning success.

And all because she was a flat-out coward.

Tough to admit, but there it was.

Reaching out she grasped the shredded fabric of his shirt. "Viper?"

Stilling beneath her touch he regarded her with a guarded expression. "What is it?"

"I . . ."

"Shay?"

You can do this, Shay. And if you can't, then you damn well don't deserve this man.

End of story.

She moved until she was pressed tight against him, her expression grim with determination.

"I love you."

There was a shocked silence as he absorbed her abrupt words. They hadn't been elegant, or particularly original, but they were sincere.

That had to count for something.

At last a smile curved his lips. A slow, beautiful smile that sent a warm rush of pleasure through her entire body.

"As I love you, pet." Lowering his head he kissed her with a fierce, hungry possession before pulling back to study her with glittering eyes. "I thought by buying you from Evor and bringing you into my home I would rid myself of my obsession with you. I was not nearly so clever as I thought."

"Not nearly," she whispered.

He touched her cheek softly, as if he were touching the most delicate object.

"Of course there are a few compensations," he murmured.

"I'm afraid to ask."

He assumed his most arrogant expression. "I will never again be plagued with those pesky women who are desperate to have me in their bed. Or enter nightclubs through the back door for fear of causing a riot. Or have blood junkies trailing behind me pleading for a bite."

Shay rolled her eyes. "It's a pity that no one is willing to pay for bullshit. I would be rich."

His soft chuckle brushed over her skin. Her lower body clenched in delicious response.

Yummy.

"Ah, but you are rich," he breathed into her ear.

She pulled back with a grimace. "Don't remind me. For the moment that's something I would rather not consider."

The dark eyes flashed with amusement. Not surprising. What woman would ever complain of too much wealth?

It was like being too thin. Or too beautiful. There just wasn't any such thing.

"You would rather live in a squalid ruin and struggle to survive?"

"It's what I've done all my life," she retorted with a hint of defiance.

"No longer." His own tone was firm. "I intend to shower you with luxury."

Shay gave a tug on her braid. A sure sign of her discomfort. "That's what scares me."

Viper shook his head. "You are the strangest creature."

Strange? Her?

Ha. That was certainly the pot calling the kettle black. Or something like that.

She narrowed her gaze. "We aren't mated yet, vampire."

His expression abruptly softened with a tenderness that brought a small ache to the center of her chest.

"Not yet, but soon. Very, very soon." He swooped forward to steal a heart-wrenching kiss before pulling back with a rueful reluctance. "Now we truly must be on our way."

Being on her way was the last thing Shay wanted. Not with her lips tingling from his touch, and her heart thundering against his chest.

Thankfully, she wasn't entirely lost to reason and when Viper rose to his feet and held out his hand, she readily allowed him to tug her upright.

"Yow." She sucked in a sharp breath as her entire body clenched in protest at the sudden motion. "I must have been more tired than I realized."

Concern touched his expression. "You were weakened and in sore need of rest. How do you feel?"

She rubbed her aching neck. "Like I've been sleeping on a bunch of rocks."

He slipped a finger beneath her chin. "Besides that?"

"I'm fine."

"You're certain?"

She knew he was still worried about the amount of blood he had taken from her, and she took his hand to gently kiss his fingers.

"Yes, I'm certain."

He squeezed her fingers. "Then let's get out of here."

She allowed him to take the lead since she had only a fuzzy memory of being carried into the narrow cave. A testament to how weak she had actually been.

They moved in silence, both sharply aware that with the fall of night the vampires would be out of their coffins and swiftly in search of their missing captive. No matter how vast the catacombs it wouldn't take them that long to track them down.

As it turned out, Shay was so intent on trying to move with the same quiet grace of Viper that she nearly missed the narrow tunnel where she had first caught the scent of humans.

Giving a tug on his hand she forced him to a halt. "Wait, Viper, we must go this way."

"No. It goes too close to the occupied caves."

"That's where I smelled the troll."

His features tightened. He wanted to haul her from the caves. He wanted to hide her in some deep hole where no bad monsters could get their hands on her. She could read it in every stiff line of his body.

Thankfully, he was wise enough to realize they could no longer simply run and hide.

"Do you still smell him?" he grudgingly demanded.

She sucked in a deep breath. "It's faint, but yes, it's there."

"I can detect nothing."

Sensing his smoldering frustration Shay moved down the

tunnel. The scent of troll was definitely stronger. She wasn't imagining it.

"There must be a glamour disguising his presence."

Viper followed close on her heels. "Styx would never allow witches in these caves. They would be a danger to the Anasso."

"There are demons capable of performing rudimentary magic."

"True enough," he conceded, although she could still feel the tension that hummed about his large body. "But why would they be in these caves and why would they hide the scent of the troll?"

They were questions Shay had no answer for so she simply kept moving forward.

Not a bad strategy until they rounded a corner and there was nothing ahead but rocks.

"Not that I doubt your tracking skills, pet, but this looks very much like a dead end," he murmured at her shoulder.

Shay studied the smooth rock blocking the path with a frown. "A troll has come through here and not that long ago."

"Styx did use trolls to lure us from the protection of the Phoenix. It doesn't necessarily mean that Evor is here."

"No, but we have to check." She battled back a sudden flare of fear. The tunnel was cramped and thick with darkness. A choking darkness that threatened to hold her for an eternity. Instinctively, she reached back to grasp Viper's hand. The moment she touched his cool flesh the flutters of panic vanished. She couldn't waver. Not now. "We can't leave him behind if they have captured him."

"Damn." He gave her fingers a tight, near painful squeeze before accepting the inevitable. "Can you find a way through?"

"I can try." Moving forward she smoothed her hands over the rock. It took only a few passes to at last discover the tingling sensation that warned of a spell. Pressing her hand forward it appeared to sink through the stone wall. "Here. A glamour. It's very faint and not very well done."

Viper made a small sound in his throat. Vampires possessed a great distrust of magic. Any magic.

"But effective," he muttered.

She turned with a faint smile. "Only against vampires, or humans who can't sense magic."

"The question remains who and why."

"There's only one way to find out."

His eyes briefly closed as he gave a shake of his head. "I don't like this."

"Neither do I, but to be honest I hope Evor is down there. I want this to be over with." She reached out to lightly touch his arm. Beneath her fingers his muscles were coiled as hard as steel. "I'm tired of being scared, Viper. I'm tired of running."

Without warning Shay was tightly wrapped in Viper's arms, her head pressed to his chest as he touched his lips to her forehead.

"I know, pet. Just promise me . . ."

Despite the undoubted joy of being in his arms Shay stiffened at his words.

"If you say not to do anything stupid, I really will stake you."

He heaved a resigned sigh. "Wouldn't dream of it."

Pulling back she offered him a glare. "Men."

Styx had just risen when the knock echoed through his narrow, barren room.

For a moment he longed to ignore the vampire he sensed standing on the other side of the door. He was troubled. Troubled deep in his heart and no amount of brooding seemed capable of easing his sense of restless anger.

This was not how it was supposed to be.

He had put behind his past of savage violence. He was no longer ruled by his lust to conquer and destroy any who stood in his way.

If the vampires were to prosper in this ever more dangerous world, then they had to have peace. They could not survive if they were so busy killing one another that they lost sight of their enemies.

It was a belief that he held as dear as his own life.

But, was that peace worth any sacrifice?

That was the question that now confronted him. And one that he had no answer for.

The knock sounded again. More insistent.

With a sigh Styx touched the medallion that hung around his neck before crossing the room and pulling open the door.

As expected a Raven stood in the tunnel beyond. Although the vampire was hidden by the heavy robe with his hood pulled over his head, Styx could see a glimpse of his pale face. A face marred by a troubled expression.

An expression that was becoming all too familiar among his brothers.

He was not the only one disturbed by the unmistakable illness of the Anasso. And the suspicions that went unspoken.

The vampire offered a small bow. "Master."

"Yes, DeAngelo, what is it?"

"The prisoner."

Styx reached out to grip the edge of the door. If he possessed a heartbeat it would have halted.

"Viper? He isn't . . . he still lives?"

"Yes, master."

His teeth clenched at the fierce relief that raced through him. "What has happened?"

"He has escaped."

It was not at all what Styx had expected.

"Impossible," he growled, sweeping past the vampire and charging down the dark tunnel.

Viper had been gravely injured. There was no possibility of him being healed enough to have escaped. Even if someone had come to rescue him it would have been gruesome cruelty to move him while he was in such pain.

Unless . . .

His pace became a near blur as he glided through the tunnels to the lower caves that held Viper.

He halted only when he had entered the cave and discovered it empty and the silver shackles shattered.

Sniffing the air he gave a growl deep in his throat. "The Shalott."

DeAngelo stepped to stand at his side. "Yes."

It had to be, of course. Only the precious blood of the Shalott would have healed Viper enough for escape.

"Do you have someone tracking them?"

There was a surprising pause before his companion at last bowed his head, as if in silent apology.

"No, master. We thought it best to wait for your commands."

Styx absorbed the low words, well aware that far more was being said.

The Ravens were trained to obey without question and with absolute loyalty. The mere fact that DeAngelo had not been in hot pursuit of Viper the moment he discovered the prisoner missing revealed just how shaken his faith had become.

Styx swallowed a sigh. "Block the exits to ensure they are not allowed to leave the caves, but do not approach them." His expression held a hint of warning. "I do not want blood shed unless you are attacked. Do you understand?"

"Of course, master."

The relief was tangible in the air as DeAngelo offered a deep bow and turned to leave the cave.

Once alone Styx bent down to touch the blood still pooled on the floor.

The Shalott was here. And soon enough the Ravens would track her down.

Time had just run out.

There were few who would accuse Levet of an overabundance of patience. Most who knew him would claim that his temperament was downright snarky.

At the moment he was as snarky as hell.

Halting at the edge of the bluffs he turned to cast a baleful glare at the woman who was flinging her arms and contorting her face until he thought her eyes might pop out.

He had thought nothing could be worse than her flapping tongue. Her ridiculous attempt at charades had proved him wrong.

"Oh, stop that. You're going to put an eye out," he snarled, his wings flapping in annoyance. "*Sacrebleu,* you can speak."

Nearly quivering with rage she stomped her foot. "That was a horrid thing to do. You are an evil, evil gargoyle."

He narrowed his gaze. "Don't forget, I still have two wishes left," he warned. He waited until the sulky pout returned to her face. "What is your name?"

"Bella."

Levet rolled his eyes. There wasn't a sprite born that didn't have the name that somehow meant beautiful.

"Stunningly original."

A hint of confusion touched her face. "Not really. My six sisters are all named Bella."

"And your mother?"

"Bella."

"Of course."

Batting her lashes the sprite regarded him with wide eyes. "Do you not like the name Bella?"

"*Mon dieu,* never mind."

Turning on his heel Levet moved to enter the narrow opening.

Astonishingly, the headache-inducing sprite wasn't tromping on his tail or pestering his wings in her haste to keep up with him. In fact, a glance over his shoulder revealed she had dug in her heels and planted her hands on her hips.

The typical pose for a woman about to be ridiculously stubborn.

"We're not going in there, are we?" she demanded.

"Do you fear vampires?"

"Certainly not, but I don't like imps." She wrinkled her pretty nose. "Nasty, smelly creatures."

"Imps?" Levet demanded.

"Yes. There is one who lives here."

A frown touched Levet's brow. Surprises were never a good thing.

"What would vampires be doing with an imp?"

"He steals humans."

Well, that cleared up precisely nothing.

"A vampire clan hardly needs the help of an imp if they wanted a few humans for a snack."

"Only one vampire drinks of the humans, and only very special humans."

"Special? What do you mean special?"

With a huff of impatience, Bella turned to march toward a patch of trees that clung tenaciously to the rocky ground. She pointed to the ground as Levet moved to join her.

"The humans who come to stick those needles in themselves."

Levet took a hasty step back. He wasn't an expert on humans, but he knew enough to recognize the hypodermic needles scattered over the ground, and to know they were used for some sort of odd drug.

"Damn."

"Can we go someplace and kiss now?" Bella demanded, her hands reaching out to lightly touch his horns. "I'm much more fun than those stupid vampires. I'll play with your wings."

"Not now . . ." Levet's growling words trailed to a soft sigh as her clever fingers stroked down his neck and feathered over his wings. "Oh."

"I'm very good."

She was. His wings quivered beneath the soft exploration. Few realized just how sensitive a gargoyle's wings could be.

His eyes began to flutter shut before he was grimly thrusting aside the seductive pleasure.

Shay might very well be in danger.

He didn't have time for such distractions.

Dammit all.

"*Non, non.* I want you to tell me of your powers."

That familiar pout returned as she continued to toy with his wings. "I'm attempting to show them to you."

"Your magical powers." Levet impatiently batted her hands away. "Precisely what sort of wishes can you grant?"

She heaved a weary sigh. "Anything you desire. Wealth, beauty, love."

An idea began to form in Levet's mind. "Actually, I was thinking of something a bit more exotic."

Her expression filled with suspicion at his words. Perhaps she was a bit brighter than he thought.

"Exotic?"

"I can't just sit here waiting like Godot, hoping that Shay can survive until the cavalry arrives. I have to do something now, and you're going to help me."

Chapter Twenty-Four

Somehow the hidden caves managed to be even more miserable than even Viper had feared.

Brackish water oozed down the walls, puddles dotted the stone floor, and the heavy scent of death and decay hung in the air.

Viper's every instinct prickled with warning.

He was a fool to allow Shay to remain in this place. Any moment Styx would discover them and the Anasso would drain her without a flicker of remorse. He should toss her over his shoulder and run away as fast and as far as possible.

Unfortunately, he couldn't deny that it would be even more foolish to flee before discovering if Evor was being held by the Ravens.

If they did have him in their grasp . . . not all the running in the world would keep Shay safe.

Devil's freaking balls.

Staying on the scent of the troll Viper paused as they neared a large cave. He could sense the mortals that huddled in the darkness. He could smell their decaying desperation.

For a moment he hesitated, revolted at the thought of forcing Shay to bear witness to such misery. His hesitation, however, merely gave the stubborn Shalott the opportunity to sweep past him, her own heightened sense of smell leading her directly to the disgusting cave.

"Humans," she muttered, her body stiffening as she glanced into the shadows to truly see the emaciated bodies huddled together on the damp floor. "Christ, why don't they run?"

Viper grimaced before pointing toward the floor littered with needles. "Look closer, pet."

"Drugs." She turned to frown at him in confusion. "They're drug addicts?"

"Yes."

"But . . . what are they doing here?"

His fangs lengthened as the unwelcome truth slammed into him. Even when he had suspected why the Anasso needed Shay's blood he hadn't wanted to believe it. A part of him had still clung to a hope that their leader wouldn't haven fallen so low.

His gaze flickered over the half-dozen mortals that smelled of rotting death. That lingering hope was gone.

The Anasso was beyond redemption.

He would see him dead before allowing him to remain in power.

"They are destroying a once great vampire," he admitted, his tone weary. Betrayal hung heavy in his heart. "This is why you are being hunted, Shay. Our . . . leader has become addicted, just as these humans are addicted, and their blood is killing him."

"Killing him?" The shock on her face might have been amusing if the situation hadn't been so dire. "I didn't even know it was possible."

"We haven't been overly anxious to reveal such weaknesses to others," he said dryly. "It's one of those need-to-know-basis things."

She dismissed his flippant words. "So, if you drink of humans who take drugs you become addicted yourself?"

"It is a dangerous possibility," he conceded. "One that rarely occurs since it is one of our few crimes punishable by death."

"But, if the vampire is destined to die anyway, why kill him?" she demanded.

"Because they go mad before death. Only last century a vampire managed to ravage and slaughter an entire village in

China before killing three of the vampires sent to capture him. Now they are slain the moment they are discovered."

She studied his somber expression before giving a slow shake of her head. "Obviously not all are slain."

Viper flinched at the accusation. "No."

Wrapping her arms about her waist she gave a visible shudder. "I still don't understand what this has to do with me. My blood isn't contaminated with that filth."

"Just the opposite."

"I don't understand."

"It possesses a cure." He clutched his hands at his side. He wanted his fingers around someone's throat. Preferably that of the Anasso. "You said it yourself, pet. Your blood can heal anything but death. Just as your father, you are to be sacrificed."

She paled as she realized the true extent of the danger that surrounded her.

She alone could save the existence of a legendary leader.

What vampire wouldn't drown the world in blood to offer her up as a sacrifice?

Her lips parted but before she could speak a familiar tingle raced over Viper's skin and with a smooth motion he had pushed her behind him and turned to face the approaching vampire.

"He's right, of course," Styx murmured, his cold expression revealing nothing of his emotions. "Your blood is quite priceless."

"I thought I smelled your stench," Viper growled.

"There's no need to be offensive, Viper," Styx softly chided.

Without warning Shay was pushing her way past Viper, her face flushed with fury.

"No need . . . why you slimy, treacherous, sorry piece of crap . . ."

"Shay, no," Viper shouted.

Grasping her about the waist he managed to keep her from attacking the dangerous vampire.

Damn the woman, what did she think she was doing? She was no match for a clan chief. Especially not this particular clan chief.

Nearly growling in annoyance Viper put his body in front of the rash woman only to stiffen in surprise as he felt her slide a dagger into his hand.

Well . . . hell. She had deliberately distracted Styx so that she could sneak him her hidden weapon. One of these days he was going to have to stop underestimating his dangerous beauty.

At least he possessed enough sense to keep the dagger hidden by his leg as Styx stepped forward and regarded Shay with a small, almost sad smile.

"Spirited and beautiful," he said. "It is little wonder you have become so attached to her, old companion."

"It is rather more than a mere attachment," Viper corrected. "Where are the Ravens?"

Styx halted too far away for Viper to strike without warning. The elder vampire had never been known for reckless stupidity.

His guard would never be fully lowered.

"I have posted guards to ensure that you do not slip out of the caves," Styx said.

Viper gave a lift of his brows. "You came to take Shay away by yourself? How exquisitely insulting of you."

Something that might have been regret flashed over the bronzed features even as the warrior smoothly pulled his sword from its sheath.

"I do not wish to fight, Viper."

"I can't say that I'm overly eager for battle either, Styx, but I am not one of your Ravens. I do not obey without question."

Moving to the middle of the tunnel so he would have plenty of space to swing his deadly sword Styx eyed him with an unreadable expression.

"How did you find this tunnel?"

"The glamour is only effective against vampires. You should have thought of that when you were hiding the pathetic humans."

With blinding speed he dodged forward, plunging his dagger toward Styx's sword arm. Styx easily countered, but as he blocked the dagger with his sword Viper shifted to plant a solid kick in the stomach of his opponent.

Styx grunted but managed to stay on his feet, his sword slicing through the air to force Viper backward.

"The glamour was effective against me as well, old companion," he said as he kept careful watch on Viper.

Viper edged to one side. "You claim to have no knowledge of this cesspit?"

"Knowledge, no." The dark eyes flashed with frustration. "Suspicions? Fears? Yes."

Viper made another feint, more to keep Styx off guard than a true attempt to harm him. Any thirst for revenge at being tortured was forgotten in the need to protect Shay.

Somehow he had to get them out of here.

With all their body parts still intact.

The odds weren't good.

"And yet you still pretend that the Anasso can be restored to his former glory." He gave a sharp motion toward the humans that were sleeping in their drug haze. "He is beyond salvation, Styx. Even if he is healed there is no means to save him from himself. Can you deny it?"

Styx hissed softly. "No. No longer."

Viper blinked, not at all certain he had heard correctly. "You admit that your cause is hopeless?"

The dark eyes shifted with obvious reluctance toward the humans. "I admit that I have been deceived and manipulated. And that I can no longer hold on to the trust that has sustained me."

"Speak clearly, Styx," Viper rasped, the dagger clutched in his hands. "I will not have misunderstandings between us."

The sword slowly lowered as Styx heaved a weary sigh. "I will not halt you from taking your Shalott and leaving these caves."

"What of your Ravens?" he demanded.

"I . . ." Styx stiffened at the thick, swirling foulness that filled the air.

Viper crouched to prepare for an attack. He didn't need

Styx's frightened expression to tell him that they were under attack. The dark power prickling over his skin was warning enough.

The problem was that he could feel the heavy evil, but he couldn't see a bloody thing.

He shot a frown toward Styx. "What is it?"

"The Anasso. He has sensed the Shalott."

"Shit. We must leave here."

Viper turned toward Shay even as the darkness closed around her.

Her eyes widened as her hand reached toward Viper who was already rushing in her direction.

"Viper?" she whispered and then her head bowed backward as a scream was wrenched from her throat.

"No." He reached her side just as she collapsed into his arms. Scooping her off her feet he studied her pale face with a flare of terrified panic. He could sense the steady beat of her heart, but her skin was pale and clammy, and she refused to awaken. "Shay. Speak to me."

Styx crossed the narrow space to stand at his shoulder. "She is in the power of the Anasso."

Cold dread clutched at Viper's heart. He had known that the elder vampire possessed powers beyond any of them, but he hadn't realized that he could reach out and physically touch others at a distance.

Viper clutched Shay to his chest, her long braid trailing over his arm.

"How do I save her?"

"We must take her to him," Styx said softly.

Lifting his head Viper glared at his companion with sharp fury. "Never."

"Only the Anasso can release her from his power."

Viper stepped backward, his fangs extended. "You have tricked me."

Holding up his hands Styx attempted to appear unthreatening. A gesture that was spoiled as the long, deadly blade shimmered in the glow of the torchlight.

Not that he wouldn't have been just as lethal without the sword.

"No, Viper, this is no trick," he protested, his eyes shimmering with a fierce, unreadable emotion. "I did not realize that he still possessed such strength."

"How do I halt him?"

"You cannot." Styx allowed his gaze to move toward the delicate woman in Viper's arms. Something that might be regret rippled over his face. "You must take her to the Anasso."

"I have told you no," Viper rasped.

"You have no choice. He will kill her."

Viper narrowed his gaze. "He cannot kill her. He needs her blood to survive."

"He is not . . . entirely stable in his thinking."

The cold dread deepened as it spread throughout his body. "He is going mad?"

Styx paused. He had spent near a century disguising the slow, relentless decay of his master. It had been a thankless duty he had performed with grim loyalty.

Now he battled with the inner demon of uncertainty that tortured him.

"Mad enough," he grudgingly conceded.

Viper lowered his head until he could bury his face in the sweet silk of Shay's hair. He cursed the fate that had brought them to this time and place.

"Damn you, Styx. Damn you to hell."

Watching the two vampires carry the unconscious woman from the tunnel Damocles slowly stepped from the shadows. A faint smile touched his lips.

"Well, well. I thought I smelled Shalott."

There was a rattle of chains from the cramped cave behind him. Slowly he turned to regard the disgusting troll who was huddled in a distant corner.

"Shay?" Evor demanded, his eyes flashing red. "She's here?"

Damocles gave a soft laugh as he traced his way across the cave. "Do you think she has come to rescue you, sweet Evor? I fear she is a little too unconscious to give you much thought. Still, her arrival does alter my schedule." Moving across the cave he cast a rueful glance down at the rather plain robe he had chosen. "I wish I had worn the gold. This green really is not festive enough."

Evor licked his lips. He was smart enough to know that whatever was about to happen couldn't be good.

At least not for him.

"What are you going to do?"

Damocles's smile widened as a glorious sense of justice washed through him. Soon he would watch his enemy destroyed by his own hands. And even more satisfying his plot would make the entire race of vampires howl in pain.

Events had not unfolded precisely as he had planned, but the end would be the same.

The Anasso would be dead, and he would have the peace that had eluded him for untold centuries.

Reaching up Damocles unlocked the chains from the cave wall. With a tug, he pulled the terrified troll from his corner.

"You, my friend, are about to witness my most triumphant moment. A culmination of brilliant plotting and flawless execution."

Evor tugged against the shackles that held him, but he was no match for a determined imp. For a moment his round face flushed and his pointed teeth clenched in fury.

Then, like any good coward he dropped to his knees and bowed his head in a silent plea for mercy.

"Good master, I think it better that I remain here. I'm not much in the mood for triumphant moments."

Damocles's smile faded as he reached down to lightly stroke the profusely sweating face.

"Ah, but you're a vital part of my celebration. You can't possibly remain behind."

"I would really prefer . . ."

The words came to a strangled moan as Damocles clutched his fingers around the fat throat and easily jerked the troll off his feet.

Dangling him in the air Damocles watched with cold distaste as the round face turned a strange shade of puce.

"Don't annoy me, ugly troll, or I'll cut out your tongue. I wish to savor this victory without listening to your flapping lips." He gave the troll a small shake. "Do you understand?"

It took several tries before Evor managed to get the words past the crushing hold on his throat.

"I understand."

Opening his fingers Damocles allowed the troll to fall back to the floor. His smile returned.

"I knew you'd see things my way. Now let's go have some fun."

Viper would never recall the agonizing trek through the dark tunnels to the lair of the Anasso. Oh, there were vague flashes of progressively more lavish tapestries, and elegant candelabras that offered a flickering light. And overall a pervasive scent of depraved self-indulgence.

His attention, however, was consumed with a simmering panic for the woman in his arms.

He would not allow her to die.

Not if it meant killing every vampire, troll, and human in the caves.

At last following Styx into a cavern that was dominated by a vast bed and a roaring fire, Viper came to a halt to study the frail vampire that was propped among a pile of satin pillows.

Although he was prepared for a change in the once powerful leader, Viper still experienced a flare of shock at the sight of the frail, almost corpselike reality.

By the blood of the saints, he appeared more dead than alive. An unnerving sight even for a vampire.

How the hell could he still possess such powers? It seemed impossible until Viper met the hectic glitter in the sunken eyes.

The Anasso might literally be upon the verge of extinction, but he would battle to the bitter end.

Reading his thoughts with ease, the Anasso offered a smile that sent a flare of fear through Viper's heart.

"Ah, I knew you would come to me, Viper," the ancient vampire rasped.

Clutching Shay protectively to his chest Viper glared into the gaunt face.

"You made sure I would have no choice."

"So angry." The elder vampire heaved a faint sigh. "Do you have no sympathy for your master, my son? Do you possess no loyalty to one who has sacrificed all for the race of vampires?"

"I see a fading shadow of a once great vampire who has been lost to his own weaknesses."

The frail features tightened, but the Anasso kept his voice soft and persuasive. It was a voice that had once lured hundreds of vampires to battle.

"Yes. I have been weak. And a fool. Once I am healed I can promise you that I shall never again be prey to such failings. I will restore myself and all of my followers to the glory that is our due."

Viper gave a slow shake of his head. Styx and his Ravens might accept such a pledge. To him it rang with a hollow lack of conviction.

He had seen the humans trapped below.

"You have made such promises before, master."

This time the vampire didn't try to hide his anger. "Do not think to judge me, Viper. You cannot know what I have suffered to bring peace to us all," he said, his voice sending a flare of pain over Viper's skin.

Viper clenched his teeth. Damn, that hurt. And with nothing more than a thought.

"We all know what you have done for us," he gritted.

The pain ripped through the air once again. "How could you possibly know? How could you possibly understand the cost?" The Anasso pointed a thin finger in Viper's direction. "There is not a night that I am not haunted by the faces of friends and loved ones that I was forced to kill because they would not accept change. Not a night that I do not hear the cries of my kin as they died beneath my hands. Can you truly hold me to blame for seeking to escape the ghosts that plague me?"

Viper had to concede that when it came to battle tactics the elder vampire was a master. A combination of subtle manipulation with the hovering threat of further pain. And all with seeming ease.

Viper might have been impressed if he hadn't been at the receiving end of that clever strategy.

"And what of the ghost of Shay's father?" he demanded. "Does he haunt you as well?"

"He was a necessary casualty."

"Just as Shay will be?"

There was not even the faintest flicker of remorse. "Yes."

Viper's arms instinctively tightened around Shay as he allowed his own power to begin to fill the air. He might not possess the strength of the elder vampire, but he was not helpless.

"What is to occur when all the Shalott blood is gone?" He deliberately allowed the scorn to fill his voice. "Who will you sacrifice then?"

The gloves were definitely off as the vampire lifted himself from the pillows, his face a stark mask of anger.

"Enough of this. Come to me now, Viper."

With a pang of regret Viper lowered Shay to the floor. As much as he desired to have her close to him, he couldn't take the risk that the Anasso might strike without warning.

"I will not surrender the woman I love," he swore, pulling the dagger from his boot. "Not for any reason."

"You dare to deny your master?"

"You halted being my master when you chose to poison your body with tainted blood. The penalty for such a sin is death."

A thick spittle formed on the lips of the Anasso as he struggled to untangle himself from the heavy covers. "Styx," he called sharply.

Viper shifted to keep a wary gaze upon the silent vampire who stepped forward with a bow.

"Master?"

"Bring me the Shalott."

Styx slowly straightened, his face a harsh mask. "The woman is to be Viper's mate. It is against our law to harm her."

Viper barely managed to disguise his shock at the bald challenge.

A shock that was echoed on the face of the Anasso.

"So I am to be betrayed on all sides." With a low hiss the elder vampire managed to struggle from the bed. Holding on to a thick bedpost he lifted a threatening hand in Viper's direction. "I will have her. Bring her to me, Viper, or watch her die on the floor."

Viper deliberately shifted to stand between Shay and the furious demon.

"She would rather die than be drained by you."

Power whipped through the air, stirring Viper's hair and blowing out the candles set about the cavern.

"Do you think I am helpless?" The Anasso moved forward with slow, but steady steps. "Do you believe you can best me, boy?"

Viper was not above a sharp flare of fear.

Not for himself.

He would readily give his life to protect Shay. But if he were to die then there would be no one to rescue her from the Anasso.

That he couldn't bear.

Drawing in as much of his power as he could hold, Viper grimly prepared for battle.

"I am willing to pit my strength against yours," he gritted.

"Even if it means your death?" the advancing vampire demanded, a thick darkness swirling about him.

"Yes."

"Fool." With a motion the Anasso sent the darkness hurtling toward Viper.

Viper held out his hands to deflect the coming blow, but even as his muscles tensed there was a blur of movement and Styx was abruptly standing before him.

"Master . . . no."

The darkness struck Styx and with a muffled cry the large vampire crumpled at Viper's feet.

A stunned disbelief filled the air. No one had expected the loyal servant to throw himself in the line of fire. Not after centuries of unquestioning devotion.

Something that might almost have been regret flashed over the gaunt face. Obviously the elder vampire had not gone entirely mad.

Unfortunately, he was mad enough to swiftly push aside his momentary hesitation, and was once again turning his attention to Viper.

Not about to waste the sacrifice Styx had so rashly made, Viper tossed the dagger directly at the chest of the Anasso, and smoothly reached down to retrieve the sword from his fallen friend.

The sword was in his hand even as the dagger struck true. There was a strangled gasp as the Anasso reeled back and glanced down at the blood running down the front of his robe.

Any hope, however, that he had managed to slow the ancient demon was dashed as the vampire reached up to pluck the dagger from his chest and toss it aside. His expression was disdainful as he once again called his power.

"You will howl for death before I am done with you," the vampire gritted as he lifted his hand and once again sent his power flooding across the room.

Viper did howl.

Nothing could prepare him for such shattering pain. It crawled through him with a ruthless force that had him on his knees before he realized what had occurred.

Clutching the sword in his hand Viper battled to keep the darkness at bay.

He could feel the Anasso moving ever closer.

If he only had one shot at killing the demon he intended to make it a good one.

Chapter Twenty-Five

Shay nearly cried in relief when the agonizing pain was abruptly lifted.

Holy shit. She wasn't a stranger to torture. She had been beaten, burned, chained, and even blasted with magical spells. But nothing had managed to make her body burn as if she were being roasted over the fires of hell, or clutch her heart until she feared it might be ripped from her chest.

She didn't know that anyone could actually survive such suffering. It seemed the sort of thing that should put a demon in her grave.

Or at least wish she was there.

Managing to force open her heavy lids she swiftly realized that she was no longer in the damp tunnels. In fact she was lying on a priceless Persian carpet that perfectly matched the rest of the gaudy room.

Arabian nights gone wild.

The next thing she realized was that Viper was close beside her, his large form kneeling on the carpet as he obviously fought some horrid, unseen attack.

Her breath lodged in her throat as she struggled to force her weakened body to move. She didn't have a clue what she could do to help the suffering vampire, but the need to touch him was overwhelming.

She managed to actually lift her head from the carpet when a sudden shadow fell across her and she stiffened in alarm.

There was no mistaking the dark evil that simmered in the air, or the prickle of revulsion that crawled over her skin.

The same evil she had felt in the auction house and again when Styx and his Ravens had hunted them through the streets of Chicago.

The Anasso.

It could be no other.

Slowly turning her head Shay couldn't halt the sharp gasp of shock at the thin, ravaged face poised just above her. He looked more like an extra from a bad horror flick than the most powerful vampire to walk the earth.

Looks, however, were far too often deceiving and Shay wasn't stupid enough to underestimate the demon that had caused her enough pain to wish herself dead.

Bracing herself for the inevitable attack Shay was caught off guard when he slowly knelt beside her and touched her cheek with a gentle hand.

"My Shalott." His voice was low and gravelly, but rich with a force that could no doubt enthrall demons and humans alike. "I knew you would come to me."

Shrugging aside the compulsion to fall into that voice Shay sucked in a deep breath.

"What have you done to Viper?"

An expression of profound sorrow touched the skeletal face. An expression that in no way matched the hectic glitter in the dark eyes.

"I had no choice. He refused to understand."

"Understand what?"

"That I must survive. That without me the vampires will return to nothing more than savages." His fangs glistened in the light of the flames. "I am the Anasso. I must be eternal."

"No matter how many of your own you must kill?"

His fingers tightened on her face making her wince in pain. "I stand above all."

A flare of fury raced through Shay. This vampire had already taken her father, and now he threatened the man she loved. And all because of some delusional belief in his own glorious legend.

"You're a raving loon," she hissed.

He jerked her face sharply forward. So close she could feel his foul breath brushing her skin.

"So stubborn, just like your father."

"You bastard." Even knowing it was futile, she struggled against his grasp. "You murdered my father."

"He fulfilled his purpose in life, my dear. His blood was meant as a gift. A gift of healing for me. And now you shall be allowed to fulfill your own destiny."

She clutched at his thin wrist, squeezing with all of her strength.

"My only destiny is to watch you die."

He laughed at her feeble threat. "I fear not."

"Actually, the lovely lady is partially right," a new voice drawled from behind the looming vampire. "You will die, old master, and she will be here. Unfortunately, I'm not certain she will survive long enough to watch her destiny unfold."

Shay was released with an abruptness that nearly had her falling on her face. Catching herself with her hands she watched the vampire rise to his feet and turn toward the nearby opening.

Huddled on the floor Shay resisted the urge to crawl into a ball of fear. Instead she forced herself to regard the newest threat.

A flare of shock raced through her at the sight of the tall, golden-haired demon that stood in the entrance.

An imp?

What the devil would an imp be doing in a cave of vampires? And perhaps more importantly, what was on the end of that chain that disappeared into the darkness of the tunnel behind him?

Clearly unhappy to have been interrupted during his dinner hour, the Anasso offered a low hiss in way of greeting.

"Damocles. I did not call for you."

"Yes, I know, and I must say I'm extremely wounded." The

imp gave a toss of his golden curls. "How could you possibly have a party and not invite your most beloved servant?"

"Beloved?" The vampire gave another hiss. "Hardly that."

The imp smiled and Shay found herself instinctively inching closer to Viper. There was nothing pleasant in that smile.

"Tsk, tsk. After all I have done for you, my lord."

The Anasso thankfully appeared to forget the woman behind him as he stiffened in anger. Which suited Shay just fine. Especially when she felt Viper painfully lift his arm to wrap it around her waist.

She glanced toward him in fierce relief, but his stern expression warned her to do nothing that might attract attention.

Once again, that was fine by her.

"And what have you done for me, Damocles, beyond luring me to weakness?" The elder vampire was demanding. "I once allowed myself to be blinded by your lies, but no longer. You have brought nothing but ruin and betrayal in your wake."

The imp chuckled with delight. "Yes, and I did it so very well."

The Anasso seemed as startled as Shay by the blunt confession. "You admit your sins?"

"Of course. I want you to know just how simple it was to bring you to your knees." The imp allowed his faux smile to fade, revealing an expression of overwhelming hatred. "You call yourself the Anasso. You claim to be nothing less than a god for your people. But in truth you are a pathetic, cowardly fool who would condemn your entire race to the grave if it would save your worthless hide."

The Anasso took an unsteady step forward. "You came here to destroy me?"

"Yes."

"Why?"

The imp touched the small medallion that hung about his neck. "I did tell you that you were not the first demon that I served. Once I proudly stood at the side of a truly great vampire."

"Who was this vampire?"

"You are not fit to speak his name. Not after you lied and deceived him so that you could bait him into your treacherous trap."

A charged silence descended as the two glared at each other. Shay felt Viper's arm tighten around her as the thick air swirled with danger. It was no longer a matter of whether there would be violence, only when it would strike.

The Anasso straightened to an arrogant pose. "*I* brought the clans together. *I* ended the tide of bloodshed. *I* brought peace to those who never had peace. *I* achieved what no other could."

The imp sneered at the proud claims. "No, you devised the one sure method of rallying vampires to your cause so that you could kill those more ancient and worthy than yourself and take control of all. A clever plot, I'll admit. But never pretend to me that it was anything more than a greedy grasp for power."

At her side Viper sucked in a sharp breath at the accusation, but Shay didn't allow her gaze to stray from the gaunt form of the elder vampire.

He seemed the sort to take offense at being branded a power-hungry psycho.

Enough offense to get them all killed.

"You have no right to judge me, imp," the Anasso rasped harshly.

"Ah, but I am not the one to judge you, am I?" The imp waved a dramatic hand toward the unconscious Styx. "It is your own vampires who have at last smelled the stench of your corruption. Who have seen through your pretense of glory to reveal the spineless creature you truly are."

With a terrifying growl the Anasso lifted his clawlike hands and pointed them toward the imp. Viper gave a low curse before pushing Shay behind his kneeling body. The violence was about to explode.

"Brave words for a lesser demon. I will teach you to attempt to rise above your station," the vampire promised in an awful voice.

Astonishingly, the imp merely laughed. "Hardly a lesser demon. I single-handedly managed to bring the glorious Anasso to his knees."

"Lies and tricks," the vampire snarled. "Will you pit your strength against my own?"

"Oh, I don't think that will be necessary. It will be far more fun just to kill you."

The green eyes glittered with an insane amusement as the imp gave a firm tug on the chain. Still shielded behind Viper, Shay clutched at his back. There was a sudden, familiar scent in the air.

One she knew all too well.

"Evor," she breathed even as the troll stumbled into the room and fell to his knees.

Viper stiffened. "Devil's balls."

Shay silently echoed the sentiment. Even suspecting that the troll was in the caves the sight of him still made her heart squeeze with fear.

He looked terrible.

The thin, balding hair was matted to his skull, his face was pale and coated with dirt, and his thousand-dollar suit looked like something from the local garbage dump. Not at all the oily, elegant Evor she knew and hated.

"You think this pathetic half troll can harm me?" The Anasso demanded in arrogant disbelief.

Pulling the troll close to his knee like a leashed dog, the imp ran a hand over Evor's head.

"This is a very special troll. You see, he carries with him a curse. A curse that is about to kill your precious Shalott."

There was a shocked beat as the elder vampire at last realized the true depth of his danger. He had to have Shay's blood to survive, but no vampire could drink the blood of a corpse. Shay had to be alive to offer him his cure.

Expecting the furious vampire to launch toward the smirking imp, Shay gave a small scream when he instead turned and flowed directly toward her.

Clearly he hoped to drain enough blood before Evor could be killed.

Not a bad idea, except for the fact that he underestimated the vampire kneeling before her.

With a fluid motion Viper was on his feet, his sword slicing toward the vampire without hesitation. The Anasso was forced to jerk backward or be decapitated.

"Shay . . . get the troll," Viper rasped as he moved forward, the sword a mere blur of silver as he grimly pressed his advantage.

She wavered as the elder vampire lifted his hands and prepared to strike Viper with that crippling pain. She knew firsthand that such pain was impossible to fight. Viper would be completely at the mercy of the ruthless vampire.

As if sensing her hesitation Viper performed another vast swing with the sword that the demon was forced to dodge.

"Shay, go or you'll get us both killed," he gritted, never taking his eyes from the gaunt figure in front of him.

Well, that was blunt enough.

And probably not far wrong.

By lingering her presence was more distracting than beneficial to Viper.

With a shake of her head she was turning to discover that the imp had lost no time. Already the imp had forced Evor onto the floor and he was lifting a knife over his heart.

Shit.

She instinctively leaped forward, but logic warned her that she could never reach him in time.

Evor was about to die.

And she was going to die with him.

Viper sensed when Shay left his side although he didn't spare a glance in her direction.

He didn't dare.

The Anasso might be weakened, but his power was still greater than Viper's own. His only hope was keeping the older vampire on defense long enough to land a lucky strike.

Not the best of battle plans but the only one he possessed at the moment.

Keeping the sword in constant movement he continued to inch forward. The vampire hissed at him in frustration, desperate to get past him. Once again the thin hand lifted to strike and Viper altered his swing to slice through the thin bones of his wrists.

A howl of pain ripped through the air as the hand fell to the floor and the Anasso clutched the bloody stump to his chest.

"I am your master," he rasped. "You cannot allow me to die."

Viper ignored the command. He wouldn't allow his concentration to waver.

The one smart choice he made all night, as it turned out.

Cradling his wounded arm the Anasso tilted back his head and called on the forces that he had honed for a millennium. On cue the darkness began to form around him.

Viper didn't hesitate. With a fierce battle cry, he lunged forward.

He wouldn't survive another attack. His only hope was killing the elder vampire.

Now.

Stepping to one side he feigned a blow toward the vampire's heart. The Anasso easily dodged the strike and even the next blow that was aimed at his maimed arm. The darkness thickened and Viper began to feel the first prickles of pain.

His sword flashed through the air, swinging low in a well-known movement that would traditionally be followed by an upward slash. As he hoped the elder vampire instinctively arched back to avoid the blow.

Viper altered his swing in mid-motion to cut across the unprotected legs. It wasn't a killing blow, but it was enough to make the vampire stagger. The Anasso snarled as the blood flowed from a deep slice in his thigh.

The darkness briefly faltered and Viper was swift to take advantage. With a sharp turn he circled the frail form, his sword biting deep into the narrow back before his foe could follow his movement.

This time the Anasso fell to his knees.

Viper moved in for the kill.

Sensing his near demise the vampire turned his head to regard Viper with a desperate expression.

"I am the Anasso. The vampires cannot survive without me," he pleaded. "You condemn them all to death."

Viper paused with his sword held high. Almost surprisingly he felt nothing at ending the life of a once noble commander. Whatever the Anasso had once been he was now no more than a rabid animal.

"I condemn only you."

The sword arced downward with a flash of steel. The Anasso lifted his remaining hand as if to halt the blow but it was too late.

The years of decay had left him vulnerable and far too mortal.

With a smooth ease the razor edge slid through his neck and with a gurgling sigh the ancient warrior was dead.

Levet's nerves were scraped raw.

Not so surprising.

What three-foot gargoyle creeping through a maze of tunnels while trying to dodge a herd of hungry vampires wouldn't be a bit skittish?

But perhaps for the first time in his very, very long life he refused to allow his cowardly heart to overrule his fragile courage.

With every step he could sense himself drawing closer to Shay and he wouldn't waver. No matter how many damn vampires were lurking in the shadows.

Of course it did help that while he could detect the scent of over a dozen vampires, he had yet to actually run across one of the beasts.

Courage was always better when it wasn't directly tested.

Sniffing the air with a healthy dose of wariness Levet turned toward the richly decorated tunnels. He sensed they were coming to the lair of the Head Honcho, something that seemed better avoided, but there was no mistaking that Shay had come this way. And recently.

He inched forward until he at last reached the mouth of a vast cavern. There he stopped and sucked in a deep breath.

Predictably the woman trailing behind him managed to ram

painfully into his wings and stomp on his tail before she realized he was no longer moving.

With a low hiss, he turned to glare into her petulant face.

"My wings are not your personal air bag," he muttered in low tones. "Could you please attempt to remember that?"

She sniffed, oblivious to his chastisement. "Why did you stop?"

"Shay is in there."

"What is it with this Shay? Is she your lover?"

"I have told you, she's my friend."

"Pooh." Bella ran her hands suggestively over her lush curves. "I could be a much better friend if only you would wish for me to be at your side always."

At his side always? Levet shuddered at the mere thought. He was male enough to appreciate a beautiful woman, but he would lop off his own head before being condemned to an eternity with the flighty sprite.

"What do you know of friendship?" he demanded as he turned back toward the opening.

He felt her fingers lightly trace the edge of his wings. "I could be whatever you want. I could satisfy your deepest fantasies."

Levet gave a twitch of his wings to dislodge her hand. "I don't need a friend for that. Just enough money and a local brothel."

"I would do whatever you asked. No matter what it was. No matter how . . . difficult."

"That isn't what a friend does."

"Then what is a friend?"

He turned his head to stab her with an impatient glare.

"Someone who cares about you, even if you don't deserve to be cared about."

"That doesn't make any sense," she protested.

His annoyance faded as the memories of Shay rolled through his mind.

Shay stepping between him and the tormenting trolls. Shay threatening Evor with castration, and worse. Shay returning to the auction house to rescue him.

"No," he said softly. "And that's the beauty of it."

She opened her mouth to continue her ruthless badgering, but with a sharp motion of his hand Levet returned his attention to the cavern.

Shay was definitely close. But there were also three vampires, the imp that Bella had warned lived in the caves, and . . . Evor.

"Damn." This was bad. Really, really bad. Reaching behind his back he grabbed the sprite's arm and pulled her to his side. "How long will this magic take?"

"You wish it and it happens," she grudgingly conceded.

"Good."

Levet sucked in a deep breath as she hurriedly pressed her fingers to his lips.

"Don't do this. Wish for me to be with you. I will rescue your stupid friend . . ."

"I wish I were the size of the King of Gargoyles," he growled.

He wasn't sure what he expected. A bit of tingling. A puff of smoke.

Fireworks and a Sousa band.

What he got instead was a sharp blow to the head as he was suddenly far too large for the tunnel.

"Ouch." He rubbed the rising lump and glanced down at his body that was three times the size it had been.

His wish had worked. He was now large enough to rescue Shay from anyone and anything that might stand in his way.

A fortunate thing considering he had barely blinked when the sound of a high, piercing scream abruptly shattered the air.

"*Sacrebleu.* Shay."

Chapter Twenty-Six

It was like one of those horrible nightmares that used to plague her. The one where she was trying to flee from the witches, but her feet were relentlessly sinking into a thick mud. No matter how hard she tried to flee she just kept going slower and slower.

She could see Damocles with his dagger gleaming in the light. She could see Evor struggling as his life flashed before his eyes. She could see the short distance she had to cross to halt the relentless blow.

But no matter how fast she traveled she couldn't reach the imp before the dagger was plunged into the troll's treacherous heart.

A scream of fury and fear was wrenched from her throat.

Evor wasn't the only one to see his life passing before his eyes, and it was all so brutally unfair.

For so many years she had taken her life for granted. She had even cursed the miserable existence given to her. Certainly she had never wakened with a fierce desire to leap from her bed and discover what the day might bring.

Now she at last had that. She had Viper. And the thought of dying now filled her with unbearable despair.

. Continuing to run despite the futility of it all, Shay abruptly felt the earth buckle beneath her feet. She fell to her knees even as the stone around the entrance burst inward to shower her in a cloud of pebbles.

Not at all certain what had happened, she cleared her eyes and peered through the cloud of dust.

What she saw was a very large, very terrifying gargoyle. A gargoyle who reached out to bat the imp across the room.

With a sickening thud the imp hit the far wall and crumpled onto the floor. Even from a distance it was easy to detect the unnatural angle of his neck and the wide eyes that were blank with death.

Holy freaking cow.

Too stunned to even appreciate the fact that Damocles had miraculously been killed, Shay began to scoot backward as the looming demon reached down to pluck the screaming Evor off the floor and hold him in his claws.

She was alive for the moment, but the gargoyle that now held the troll didn't look in any mood to hear her pleas. In fact, he looked large and fierce and entirely capable of swallowing them all whole.

The gargoyle took a step forward and she gave a small shriek. To hell with courage. This thing was scaring the crap out of her.

The demon halted, and then shockingly he held up his free hand in a motion of peace.

"Shay, it is I," he rumbled. Then, as she continued to regard him with open horror, he gave a click of his tongue. "It is Levet."

"Levet?" Shay slowly rose to her feet, her gaze belatedly taking in the beautiful wings that were now as large as a small car. "What . . . what have you done?"

He smiled revealing teeth that could snap her in two. "It appears that I have rescued you once again from your own foolishness."

Rescued. Blessed saints. She was rescued. The relief flooded through her. Or at least it started to flare through her. It hadn't gone very far when it was replaced by a flare of fear.

Viper.

Spinning about she turned just in time to watch the beautiful, silver-haired vampire take the head off the Anasso.

This time the relief went unchecked. It was over. Truly, truly over.

She took a step forward to rush to Viper's side. She wanted to throw herself in his arms and shout for joy. She wanted to run her hands through his hair and kiss him until they both could forget the horror of the past hours.

Her steps halted, however, as Viper slowly slid to his knees and an expression of deep sorrow touched his face.

He had just been forced to kill a leader he had obviously respected for centuries. He deserved a few moments to reconcile himself to the painful death.

With an effort she slowly turned back to the waiting demon behind her. He didn't look at all like her beloved Levet. Well, except for the eyes. They could never change.

A shaky smile touched her lips. "I didn't know you could alter your shape."

Levet shrugged. "Oh, we all have our little secrets . . ."

"He didn't do it. I did," a female voice firmly interrupted.

Shay's eyes widened as a curvaceous woman attired in a sheer bit of cloth stepped from behind the looming demon.

"A water sprite?" Shay regarded the gargoyle with a lift of her brows. "Good grief, Levet, you have been a busy boy."

"It looks as if you've been a little busy yourself. That one is still alive." He pointed a claw toward Styx who was beginning to stir on the floor. "Do you want me to squash him?"

Before Shay could answer she felt a comforting arm slip around her shoulder. Her heart gave a small leap as she glanced into the pale face of the vampire at her side.

"Viper?" she questioned softly. This man had just lost his leader. She wouldn't pressure him to also lose a friend.

"No," Viper retorted, his voice firm. "He was only doing what he thought was right. He risked his life to save us."

"Yes, he did," she said softly, her gaze returning to Levet. "No squashing."

"What of this animal?" Levet gave the troll a vicious shake. "Can I kill him?"

Shay lifted a hand. "Not yet. He still holds my curse."

Levet heaved a sigh. "Well, damn. I can't kill the vampire. I can't kill the troll. I hate to waste a good wish. Maybe I should go pillage a nearby village. The local maidens would no doubt appreciate my new, very manly, physique."

Viper chuckled softly. It was one of the best sounds that Shay had ever heard.

"Surely after all these centuries you must know that size doesn't matter to a woman?" he drawled.

"Ha. Easy to say for a six-foot vampire," Levet grumbled.

Reluctantly, Shay left Viper's side to gently take Levet's huge hand and pressed it to her face. She understood just how difficult it must have been for the demon to force himself to charge to her rescue.

"Levet, it isn't the size of the demon that matters, but the size of his heart. And there is no gargoyle in all the world who possesses a heart as large as yours." Her lips touched his rough skin. "You saved my life."

"*Oui, oui.* There is no need to blubber over me." Levet pulled back, a blush staining his gray cheeks. To cover his embarrassment he held out the squirming Evor and gave him another shake. "What do you want me to do with this creature?"

"Put him here." Viper pointed at a spot directly before him.

Holding his arm outward Levet simply allowed the troll to drop from his hand. Evor managed to crumble to the floor before Viper had him by the neck and he was once again on his feet. His eyes bulged and his round face turned red as Viper's fingers dug into his spongy flesh.

"You can't kill me," the troll squeaked. "Not without killing the Shalott."

With a casual motion Viper slapped Evor with enough force to make his head snap back.

"The Shalott has a name."

"Shay," Evor gasped. "Lady Shay."

Viper regarded him as if he were a bug he discovered stuck

to the bottom of his shoe. "What do you want to do with him, pet? We could take him home and have him nailed to the wall as a trophy."

Shay shuddered. "And have to look at that ghastly face every day?"

"Good point. I do have several creatively themed dungeons he might enjoy."

"Creatively themed?"

Viper gave a small shrug. "Traditional torture, ancient torture, high-tech torture . . ."

"No, no. Please." Evor rolled his head toward Shay, his expression desperate. It was an expression she decided she liked on that ugly mug. "I'll do whatever you want."

She stepped closer to the troll, her expression hard. "I want answers."

"Of course." He nervously licked his lips. "What answers?"

"How did you get my curse?"

"I . . ."

Viper's fingers abruptly tightened. "Don't even think of lying to the lady. I can make you pray for death."

"I went to Morgana for a . . . potion," Evor gasped.

"Morgana?" Shay demanded.

"The witch."

"Oh." Shay frowned. She hadn't known that trolls used magical potions. "What sort of potion?"

"It was personal."

"Personal? What does that mean?"

"Trust me, pet, you don't want any more specifics," Viper interrupted.

She grimaced. Viper was no doubt right. The mere thought of what the nasty demon might do in private was enough to give her nightmares.

"Fine. You went to the witch for a potion. How did you end up with my curse?"

"When I arrived the store was closed so I . . . let myself in."

"Meaning you broke into the store," Shay accused.

"I wanted that potion," Evor said in tones that revealed breaking and entering was a common part of his moral code. "I thought the place was empty, but there was a hidden door that had been left open and I could hear voices. One of them was Morgana speaking to a younger witch. Her protégée, I suppose."

Shay frowned, recalling the door that led to the dirt cellar beneath the store.

"What does that have to do with the curse?"

"She was instructing the younger witch on her duties of protecting a young Shalott who was in dire danger. She said that once the curse was passed that she must always be on guard for those who would harm the half demon."

"She was going to pass the curse to another witch?" Shay demanded.

"Yes. Morgana was concerned that she was growing too old to be an adequate guardian."

"Oh." Shay slowly absorbed the words. Perhaps ridiculously she felt a spark of warmth at the witch's concern. Her father had obviously chosen her guardian carefully. It reassured her that he had truly loved her as much as she had once believed. "So she wanted to protect me?"

Evor shrugged. "I suppose."

Always sensitive to her every emotion Viper tightened his grasp on the troll's throat. He would realize just how much she needed to know she hadn't been abandoned by those who claimed to love her.

"And you heard the word Shalott and immediately realized how much she would be worth," he accused in a lethal voice.

Evor squawked, his eyes wide with terror. "I'm a businessman. What would you have me do?"

"You're slime," Shay corrected. "How did you get the curse?"

"I . . ." Evor licked his lips, his eyes warily darting from Viper to Shay. "I slipped down the stairs and waited for the proper moment. Once the curse was being passed I leaped forward to kill the young witch and the spell landed on me."

"Then you murdered Morgana?"

"Yes." A hint of confusion touched the ugly face. "I intended to burn her body, but she seemed to disappear into thin air."

Shay remembered finding the skeleton and small box hidden behind the enchanted circle. Morgana had used her last breath to keep the truth safe for Shay.

"You despicable, coldhearted bastard," she breathed, clutching her hands at her sides to keep from reaching out and throttling the horrid troll.

The creature had made her life a living hell. He had bound her, abused her, and sold her like an animal.

If not for him . . .

If not for him she would never have met Viper, an unwelcome voice whispered in the back of her mind.

The trembling fury slowly faded, and quite unexpectedly she sank to her knees and began to cry.

She wasn't sure why she sobbed.

The utterly senseless loss of her father, perhaps. The horror of her stolen childhood. The years of slavery.

The knowledge that, but for a fluke, she would never have been in the power of Evor.

Or maybe she was simply purging the last of her bitterness so she could put it in the past where it belonged.

Whatever the cause it didn't take long for Viper to be kneeling at her side, his arms wrapped tightly around her.

"Shay, please, my love," he whispered into her hair. "You are breaking my heart."

She sniffed, burrowing into the strength of his chest. "It's over?"

His lips brushed her face, kissing away the wetness of her tears. "It's over. Truly over. We can go home."

"What about Evor?"

"He will go with us. I have enough connections to find us a witch powerful enough to break the curse. After that . . . well, that will be completely up to you, pet."

She tilted her head up to meet the troubled silver eyes. "When we bring an end to the curse, I won't be your slave any longer."

A slow, perfect smile curved his lips. "Maybe not my slave,

but you'll soon be my mate. Which means you're stuck with me for an eternity."

"I haven't said yes, yet," she reminded him softly.

"Good." His lips brushed her mouth. "I want the pleasure of convincing you."

She gave a small shiver. She didn't doubt it would be a pleasure. For both of them.

The sound of Levet clearing his throat echoed eerily through the cavern and Shay glanced up to discover him regarding them with a hint of impatience.

"Not that I wish to be the pooper of the party, but unless we get out of these caves Dante will soon be bringing his army in with guns blazing," he pointed out. "Time is a-ticking."

Viper gave a slow nod. "I hate to agree with the gargoyle, but if Dante is on his way then we must stop him before any further violence." His head turned to regard Styx who was silently gathering the handful of ashes that remained of his master. "There has been enough bloodshed."

Shay lightly touched his face in sympathy before returning her attention to the giant demon. He was quite impressive with his bulging muscles and grotesque features. As terrifying as even the greatest of gargoyles. But she missed her tiny Levet.

"Not that I want to rain on your parade, Levet, but have you given any thought to how you're going to get out of these caves?" she murmured softly.

With a frown of surprise, Levet glanced down at his enlarged body. "Can't I just . . ." He gave a wave of his hands. "Force my way out?"

Viper rose to his feet and pulled Shay to stand close to his side. "Not without bringing most of the bluff down on our heads. And while I appreciate your help, my friend, I have no desire to be trapped in these tunnels with you until we can dig our way out."

Levet gave a testy stomp of his foot, showering them all with chunks of rock from the ceiling.

"This totally blows," he complained. "I finally get to be a

decent size and now I have to give it up before I can even enjoy one good pillaging."

"No." The silent sprite suddenly grasped Levet's arm, her expression pleading. "Don't listen to them. They are trying to deceive you and make you give up your last wish. We can get out of here. I know a way . . ."

"Oh, do shut up," Levet snapped. "It's worth giving up a wish just to be rid of you." He sucked in a deep breath. "I wish I were my normal size."

In the blink of an eye Levet had shrunk to his three-foot stature and, best of all, the wailing water sprite had disappeared.

With a small smile, Shay moved forward to wrap her arms about her dear friend.

"I love you, Levet," she whispered.

He gave a derisive snort at her mushy words, but he didn't try to pull away. With an awkward motion he patted her back with his small hand.

"*Oui, oui.* Now can we go home?"

Home. Yes, she was going home. With her family at her side. No demon could ask for more.

Viper was as good as his word.

He did have the necessary connections to discover a witch willing to break the curse that bound Shay.

Of course, he wasn't pleased with her decision to allow Evor to slink back beneath the rocks he had crawled from. He was fairly straightforward about what he wanted for the troll. A nice, lengthy bout of torture, followed by several hours of being sliced into tiny little pieces.

Shay, however, discovered that her fierce need for revenge was no longer the driving force in her life. Not when she had an eternity to plan with the vampire she loved.

She was free of Evor, and as long as he was being watched by vampires to make sure he didn't hurt any other demon, she was satisfied.

They had quarreled, of course, but in the end she had had her way. And they had both enjoyed the delicious opportunity to kiss and make up.

Now the curse was gone and Shay was able to plan her future for the first time in nearly a century.

With blissful joy she traded her life as a servant for one as a mate.

It had been a beautiful ceremony at Viper's country estate surrounded by hundreds of candles and roses and the sweet scent of freshly baked apple pie floating through the air.

As Viper's fangs had slid into her flesh and he had called the ancient power to bind them as one, Shay thought that there would never be a more perfect moment in her life.

She had been wrong.

As the days had passed she realized that her days were now filled with those perfect moments.

Shopping or just sharing lunch with Abby. Watching Viper teach Levet how to use a sword with deadly accuracy. Late-night dinners with Viper teasing her as she polished off a huge meal left by the housekeeper. The festive gatherings with his clan where the vampires revealed their profound respect and unwavering loyalty to the leader who kept them secure.

They were moments that many would take for granted.

But never her.

Returning to the house after a marathon shopping spree with Abby, Shay silently slipped into the bedroom she shared with Viper, and tossed aside her numerous bags. Until she had fallen in love she had never cared about something so foolish as fashion.

Now, however, she had a very special desire to look her best.

Relieved to discover that Viper was busy in the shower she hurriedly stripped off her clothes and reached into one of the bags to pull out a white nightgown.

It was a beautiful garment.

Shimmering satin with inset lace over her breasts and down her stomach it managed to reveal far more than it concealed.

It seemed custom made to make the most discriminating vampire stand up and take notice.

She had just slipped it over her head when the connecting door to the bathroom opened and Viper stepped in the room.

Just for a moment she struggled to remember how to breathe.

He was just so damn gorgeous.

Wearing a heavy brocade dressing gown and the silken spill of silver hair framing his perfect face, he looked like some decadent fantasy come to life.

Her fantasy.

Coming to an abrupt halt he allowed his eyes to widen as they took a slow, extremely thorough survey of her barely clad body.

Shay hid a smile as she felt the air in the room begin to prickle with the passionate heat that Viper stirred with such ease. It didn't seem to matter how many times he held her in his arms, he was always hungry for more.

His eyes darkened as he paused long enough to ignite the dozens of candles left on the dresser before turning off the overhead light and moving to stand directly before her.

He stood for endless moments, drinking in the sight of her with an expression that was impossible to read. At last Shay heaved an impatient sigh.

"Well?" she prompted.

"Well what?" he demanded, his voice suitably thick.

What was the point in satin and lace if it didn't make a man struggle to speak?

She deliberately ran her hands over the smooth material. "You're supposed to tell me that you think my new gown is beautiful."

His fangs lengthened as he struggled not to simply haul her to the bed and let instinct take over. For all his elegant sophistication there were times when he was utterly male.

"Anything that you wear is beautiful," he murmured.

"I thought you would like it."

Her heart jolted with excitement as his arms slid around her, and she was tugged firmly against his body. The feel and scent of him was enough to make her blood rush and her stomach quiver with anticipation.

"I like it very much, but I'm not certain that it's worth the cost," he said as he dipped his head to gently nuzzle at her cheek.

"Don't tell me that you've become a penny-pincher in your old age?" she protested.

He gave her ear a light nip. "I could care less about the cost, it's the time that you took to shop for the gown that I regret."

Shay shivered as she allowed her arms to wrap around his neck. She knew quite well that Viper was pleased she was forging a friendship with Abby.

He better than anyone understood just how special a bond it was to her.

"I was only gone five hours."

His tongue traced the length of her jaw sending a flare of raw heat racing through her body. Holy guacamole he was good at this.

"Entirely too long," he informed her.

Shay struggled to recall she had a brain. One that usually functioned quite well.

Not an easy task when his hands began to explore the sheer lace that covered her breasts.

"You obviously know nothing of the intricate rituals involved in shopping," she breathed.

His thumbs brushed her nipples, raising them to eager points. "Intricate rituals?"

She obligingly leaned back so he could more easily cover her aching nipples with his talented lips. A sigh slid from her lips as he suckled her with growing insistence.

"Abby is instructing me in the art. It's all very complicated, and very secret."

"Hmm." His tongue stroked the hard tip of her breast until her knees threatened to buckle. "It sounds far too tedious to waste your time upon. You have far more important matters to attend to."

She clutched at his shoulders. "And what matters would those be?"

"Let me see." Before she could sense his intention he had

swept her off her feet and was heading toward the nearby bed. She found herself flat on the mattress with Viper on top of her before she could blink. Not that she minded. It was precisely where she had planned to end up. Although not necessarily with Viper on top. He regarded her with a ridiculously smug expression. "First you should always greet your mate with a kiss."

"Ah." She intended to put a swift end to the smug smile.

Cupping his face in her hands she lifted her head to place her lips against his. At first her touch was gentle. Featherlight kisses, and the brush of her tongue. Viper moaned but she refused to deepen her touch as she nibbled at the corner of his mouth.

She felt his body harden above her, his erection pressing into her thigh with a fierce insistence. Only then did she part his lips with her tongue and allow her restrained hunger to taste him as she desired.

He made a sound deep in his throat as his hands impatiently tugged at her expensive gown.

"Is that how I should kiss you?" she murmured.

"Oh, yes," he said as he wrestled her out of the satin. "That's precisely how you should do it."

"Anything else?"

"You should remove my robe." He smiled as she gave a lift of her brows. "Just to make sure I managed to wash all of the soap off."

"Yeah, right." She chuckled as she obligingly slipped the rich material off his body and tossed it onto the floor. She ran her hands over the rippling muscles of his back. "You wouldn't want any stray soap bubbles."

His eyes were as black as midnight and his hair had spilled like a silk curtain around her. With his fangs fully extended, he looked dangerous and exotic and wholly wicked.

"You really should search more carefully, pet."

"Really?" Angling her head she skimmed her lips down the length of his neck and over his collarbone. She lingered a moment to nibble at the cool, sinfully smooth skin before continuing down to tease his nipple as he had teased her own. "How's that?"

"Perfect," he moaned, his fingers sinking into her hair and tugging it from her tidy braid. "Shay."

With a sharp movement he had pulled her back up to meet his seeking lips. There was no more pretense of gentleness as he captured her mouth in a kiss that demanded full capitulation.

Shay readily parted her lips as his tongue stroked deeply into her mouth. At the same time his hands were roaming over her skin with an urgency that made her heart clench with excitement.

There was nothing quite so delicious as a fully aroused vampire.

Drinking deeply of her desire he scattered demanding kisses over her face before moving to caress the line of her neck. Shay caught her breath, expecting to feel the smooth thrust of his fangs.

The past weeks had taught her that there was nothing to fear in offering Viper the blood he craved. It was an intimate sharing that provided a pleasure beyond all imagination.

His fangs lightly scraped her skin, but he continued to move ever downward, planting a teasing kiss on her breast, her stomach, and the curve of her hip.

Shay's eyes rolled back in her head as he tugged her legs apart and settled himself between them. Oh, she liked this part.

With the patience only an immortal could invoke Viper trailed his lips over the curve of her thigh, his tongue teasing down to her leg to the tips of her toes before returning. Her hips arched off the bed in a silent plea.

"Please . . ." she whispered.

His tongue continued to stroke her inner thigh as he glanced up to meet her glittering gaze. With a deliberate motion he allowed his fangs to pierce the skin, and just as deliberately paused as he waited for her approval.

It was his means of assuring her that he would never take her blood against her will. That she would have the power to deny him at any time.

Her stomach clenched as she studied the sheer beauty of his face.

"If you bite me, I'll never last," she said.

The dark eyes shimmered with pure male satisfaction. She couldn't help but chuckle. He might be a vampire, but there was plenty of testosterone flowing through his body.

She gave a slow nod and gasped as his fangs sank deep into her flesh. Her gasp wasn't from pain. It was pure joy.

Grasping the covers beneath her, Shay rasped in a deep breath as she felt him feed deeply from her body. With every suck, her body writhed in building pleasure. He was touching nothing but her leg but her breath was coming in small pants, and her lower body was clenching with a familiar pressure.

She knew better than to fight the rapidly building climax.

It was as inevitable as a wave crashing against the shore.

"Viper."

Reaching down she tangled her fingers in his hair as the explosion rocked through her body.

Holy . . . freaking . . . cow. Stars shot before her eyes. The earth moved. Time halted.

It was as it always was. Perfect.

Even if she lived an eternity she would never become accustomed to the sheer power of their passions.

With a heartfelt groan she sank into the mattress and with a smooth motion Viper was lifting himself and sliding into her with a fierce thrust.

She clutched at his shoulders, wrapping her legs about his waist as he rode her with swift strokes, his steady motion quickly reigniting her own desire.

"I love you, pet," he rasped as her nails raked down his back. "I love every beautiful inch of you."

Shay smiled as his soft words brushed her cheek. Who would have thought that she would ever hold a vampire in her arms? Or give him the heart she had thought buried forever?

And who would have thought that she would ever come to accept that being half Shalott and half human was a rather wonderful thing to be?

Tightening her grasp on the man who had so profoundly changed her life, Shay allowed the sweeping pleasure to reach its climax just as Viper gave a rasping cry and buried himself deeply inside her.

He collapsed beside her and tugged her into his arms, his lips brushing her tangled curls.

"Sorry about your new nightgown, pet," he murmured.

He didn't sound a bit sorry, she ruefully acknowledged, glancing toward the satin gown that had been ripped beyond repair. In fact he sounded positively pleased with himself.

"Don't worry about it." She snuggled more comfortably against him. "I can always go shopping again tomorrow."

"Tomorrow?" His arms tightened. "You do know that there's a most wonderful invention. It's called online shopping . . ."

Waiting until Shay tumbled into sleep Viper carefully untangled from her arms and slipped on his robe. A smile touched his face as he gazed down at the slender woman who had managed to become the most important thing in the world to him.

Even after weeks of having her in his bed he still found himself waking with a tiny jolt of delight to discover her in his arms.

He had never been so utterly at peace or content in his entire existence, and yet there was a nagging ache that he couldn't completely put out of his mind.

Moving toward the window Viper stared into the dark. Among the trees he could sense Santiago and the other young vampires who diligently patrolled the grounds. The threat to Shay was over, but his position as clan chief ensured that he never took his security for granted.

There would be no more nasty surprises if he could help it.

Lost in his thoughts Viper was caught off guard when a soft voice suddenly intruded into the silence.

"You should go to him, you know."

Turning toward the woman on the bed he gave a lift of his brows. "I thought you were asleep."

Shay smiled lazily, looking entirely too inviting lying naked on the golden cover with her hair spread like a curtain of satin around her.

"Viper, go to him."

"Go to who?" he demanded as he began to walk toward the bed. His body was already responding to the sight of her. He might be technically dead, but he wasn't buried.

A naked woman in his bed was an opportunity not to be missed.

"Styx."

He halted in astonishment. "How did you know?"

"I'm not just another pretty face."

He allowed his gaze to slowly drift over her exposed curves. "Oh, I'm well aware of that," he huffed. "Still, I didn't know you could read minds."

A charming blush touched her cheeks as she tugged the cover over her body. Viper heaved a rueful sigh. Damn. It was a near sin to cover such beauty.

"It doesn't take much skill to realize that you have been troubled since we left the caves," she said. "And that you must hold regrets for what happened there."

Viper grimaced. This woman was beginning to know him far too well.

"It was by my hand that the leader of the vampires is now dead. Styx must take command if we are not to tumble into chaos."

She frowned. "Do you think he will?"

He gave a slow shake of his head. Like all vampires Styx could be stubborn, arrogant, and inclined to retreat within himself when he was troubled.

If he concluded that he was to blame for the Anasso's death, or that he was somehow unsuitable to take command, he would disappear into the mist and no one would be able to find him.

That couldn't be allowed to happen.

Whatever his discomfort or misgivings, Styx was now their leader.

"I suppose that's the question," he said softly.

She regarded him for a long moment, her expression somber. "Go to him."

* * *

In the end it was nearly a week before Viper found himself walking along the high bluffs that framed the Mississippi River. For all his concern for Styx he had his own clan to supervise, and he had neglected his business far too much over the past month.

At last it was Shay's insistent bullying that had sent him to the remote farmhouse. She had claimed that he was making her nuts with his nightly broodings. And that she would banish him to the cellars unless he confronted his old friend and eased his mind.

That was a fate he refused to even contemplate.

Leaving Chicago he had driven through the night and parked his car near the highway. He preferred to walk the narrow path that wound its way through the sparse woods. He still wasn't sure what he intended to say to Styx. Or if the proud vampire would even consent to speak with him.

He was still a distance from the farmhouse when a shadow shifted from behind a tree and he was face-to-face with the looming, raven-haired vampire.

There was nothing to read on the bronzed face, and Viper warily raised his hands in a gesture of peace.

He was technically trespassing on the land of another clan chief. Styx would be quite within his rights to have him executed.

"Is this a welcoming committee, or are you intending to kill me?" he demanded, his tone light but his body clenched to react to any attack.

Styx shrugged, his fingers absently toying with the medallion about his neck.

"I could ask you the same thing. There must be a powerful reason for a newly mated vampire to be so far away from his lair."

"The power of simple friendship and concern for you, old companion," Viper retorted.

"Concern?" The dark eyes narrowed. "Did you fear I might follow in my master's footsteps and develop an addiction to those pathetic humans?"

Viper stepped forward. Around them the night air swirled with an icy breeze, tugging at their cloaks and whispering through the bare trees.

Thankfully, vampires didn't feel the cold.

"My only fear is that you would remain here brooding and blaming yourself for the tragedy of the Anasso." He reached out to lay his hand on a broad shoulder. "I love you like a brother, but you have an unfortunate tendency to believe that you should be infallible."

"Far from infallible." The dark eyes flashed with a guilt so deep that it made Viper flinch. "I nearly allowed your mate to be destroyed."

"Shay is well, and gloriously pleased with her new mate. As am I," he insisted. None of them could afford to have Styx crippled by his sense of failure. They needed him strong and prepared to take command. "The past is done with, Styx. Now it is time to look to the future. The future of us all."

"And that's why you're here?" he demanded.

"You are now our leader. I wish you to know that you have my loyalty, and the loyalty of my clan."

His expression hardened. "It's not a position I ever desired."

Viper couldn't help but smile. "Fate rarely cares about our own desires. It unfolds as it will."

Styx gave a snort of annoyance. "I have always detested philosophers."

"Then let me speak plainly." Viper's hand tightened on his friend's shoulder, his expression somber. "We need you, Styx. It is respect for you and your Ravens that has kept the vampires from open warfare, and, more importantly, it is fear of you that has kept the other demons at bay. If you do not take command then we both know that all we fought for will be lost."

Styx clenched his hands at his side. "Why me? You are perfectly capable of taking command."

Viper slowly shook his head. "If anyone else attempted to take control, then every petty vampire in hope of gaining power would rise up in challenge." He pointed out with irrefutable logic. "No. You are the natural successor, and only you can keep the treaties intact."

"Damn you, Viper," the older vampire breathed.

"I am only saying what you already know."

"That doesn't mean I have to like it."

Viper gave a sudden chuckle. "No, you don't have to like it."

An air of weariness settled about the grim vampire. "Return to your mate, Viper. I will do my duty."

"And you will call if you have need of me?" Viper pressed.

"I will call," he grudgingly conceded.

Content that Styx would indeed do his duty, Viper stepped back and offered a wicked grin.

"You know there are bound to be a few perks to your new position."

Styx frowned. "Perks?"

"There won't be a female vampire around who won't be eager to share the bed of our newest Anasso."

Styx gave a lift of one brow. "I don't need to be the Anasso to have a female in my bed."

Viper laughed as he tossed back his cloak to reveal the intricate tattoo that scrolled along his inner forearm. It was the mark of his mating with Shay.

"Just don't forget that females offer more risk than all the demons put together."

The older vampire regarded Viper as if he feared he had lost his mind.

"That's a risk I need never fear, old companion. There are some of us who are wise enough to avoid such obvious traps," he said with absolute conviction.

Viper merely smiled, remembering his own firm belief that he would never be foolish enough to become mated.

"You do know what they say, my friend. The best laid plans of mice and vampires . . ."

Please turn the page for an exciting sneak peak of
the next Guardians of Eternity novel
DARKNESS EVERLASTING,
coming in May 2008!

Chapter One

As far as nightclubs went, the Viper Pit was by far the most expensive, the most elegant, and the most exclusive in the entire city of Chicago.

Oddly enough, it was also the most obscure.

There was no listing in the phonebook. No gaudy ads on billboards, or flashing neon lights to reveal its location. In fact, the entire building was hidden behind a subtle glamour.

Anyone who was *anyone* knew how to find the place. And those *anyones* didn't include humans.

Moving among the marble pillars and glittering fountains were various demons, all indulging in a variety of nefarious activities. Gambling, drinking, exotic dancing, discrete—and not so discrete—orgies.

All of which cost a small fortune.

Delicious pastimes no doubt, but on this cold December night the vampire known as Styx was not interested in the activities available below the private balcony. Or even in the various demons who paused to perform a deep bow in his direction.

Instead he regarded his companion with a measure of resignation.

At a glance the two of them couldn't have been more different.

Well, that wasn't precisely accurate.

After all, they were both tall and blessed with the muscular bodies of all vampires. And they both possessed dark eyes and the prerequisite fangs. But that's where the similarities ended.

The younger vampire, Viper, had come from the northern Slavic lands and possessed the pale silver hair and even paler skin of his ancestors. Styx, on the other hand, had come from the hot lands of Latin America, and even after his transformation maintained the bronzed skin and proud angular features of the Aztecs.

Tonight he had put aside his traditional robe and chose black leather pants, thigh high boots, and black silk shirt. He had assumed the garb would make him less noticeable as he traveled the streets of Chicago. Unfortunately, there was no way for a six-foot-five vampire with raven hair braided to his knees to go unnoticed. Especially from the mortal women who held no defense against the thrall of vampires.

He had gathered nearly a half dozen adoring females as he had walked through the dark streets. At last he had taken to the rooftops to avoid their persistent attentions.

By the gods, he wished he could have stayed hidden in his caves, he acknowledged with a sigh.

For centuries he had lived the life of a monk as he had protected the Anasso, the leader of all vampires. He had been an enforcer and guardian, rarely leaving the ancient vampire's side.

With the Anasso now dead he was being forced into the role of leader, and he was discovering that he could hide no longer. Not when there was one trouble after another plaguing him.

It was enough to annoy the most patient of demons.

"I am always delighted to have you as my guest, Styx, but, I must warn you that my clan is nervous enough having you among us," Viper drawled. "If you don't stop scowling at me, they are bound to fear they will soon be without a clan chief."

Realizing he had allowed his attention to wander, Styx abruptly straightened in the plush leather chair. By instinct his hand lifted to touch the bone medallion tied around his neck.

It was a symbol of his people.

More than that, it was believed to be a means of passing spirits from one generation to another.

Of course, as a vampire Styx had no tangible memories of his life before rising as a demon. That didn't, however, keep him from holding on to at least a few of his more sacred traditions.

"I am not scowling."

Viper smiled wryly. "You forget, Styx, I have a mate, which means that I am intimately acquainted with every variety of scowl. And you, my friend, are most certainly scowling." The smile faded as the vampire regarded him with an expression of shrewd intelligence. "Why do you not tell me what is troubling you?"

Styx paused before heaving a faint sigh. He had to do this. Even if he would rather be flogged, flayed, and defanged as to admit he needed help.

As clan chief for the territory, Viper was more familiar with Chicago than any other demon of his acquaintance. It would be beyond foolish not to accept his assistance.

"It's the Weres," he said abruptly.

"Weres?" Viper gave a low hiss. Like Cub and Cardinal fans, there was little love lost between vamps and the jackals. "What trouble are they brewing?"

"It has gone beyond mere trouble. They have left their recognized hunting grounds, and I have tracked at least a part of the pack to Chicago." Styx clenched his fists in his lap. "They have already killed several humans, and left them to be discovered by the authorities."

Viper didn't so much as flinch. Of course it would take more than a pack of Weres to rattle the powerful vampire.

"There have been rumors of wild dogs roaming the alleys of Chicago. I did wonder if it might be the Weres."

"They have a new leader. A young Were named Salvatore Giuliani from Rome. A purebred who is far too ambitious for his own good."

"Have you tried to reason with him?"

Styx narrowed his gaze. Whether he wanted the position or

not, he was now leader of the vampires. Which meant that the world of demons bowed to his commands. Including the Weres.

So far, however, the newest pack-master had treated his duty to Styx with nothing more than disdain.

A mistake he would soon learn to regret.

"He refuses to meet with me." Styx's tone was as cold as his expression. "He claims that the Weres will no longer be subservient to other demons, and that any treaties that were made in the past are now void."

Viper lifted his brows, no doubt wondering why Styx hadn't already executed the beast.

"He's either very brave or very stupid."

"Very stupid. I have called for a meeting of the Commission, but it could take days if not weeks before they can be gathered in one place." Styx referred to the council that settled disputes between the various demon races. It was made up of ancient oracles that rarely left their hidden lairs. Unfortunately, they were the only legal means of passing judgment upon the king or leader of another race without retaliation. "In the meantime, the reckless actions of the Weres threaten us all."

"My clan stands ready to offer assistance." A smile of anticipation touched Viper's lips. "If you want this Salvatore dead I'm sure it can be arranged."

Styx could think of few things that would please him more than to order the death of Salvatore Giuliani. Unless it was sinking his own fangs into the mangy dog's throat.

There were times when being a responsible leader was a bitch.

"A tempting offer, but unfortunately the Weres are uncommonly devoted to this man. If he were to suddenly die, I don't doubt that the vampires would be held to blame. I hope to avoid all out warfare for now."

Viper gave a small bow of his head. Whatever his own desires, he would concede to Styx's authority.

"You have a plan?"

"Hardly a plan, but I do hope that I might have discovered a bit of leverage over Salvatore." He pulled a small photo from his pocket and handed it to his companion.

For a moment Viper studied the small, delicate woman in the photo. With her short, spiky blond hair and green eyes far too large for her heart-shaped face she looked like a beautiful urchin.

"Not my type, but certainly eye-catching." He glanced up. "Is she his lover?"

"No, but Salvatore has spent a considerable amount of money and energy in tracking this woman. I believe he has at last discovered her here in Chicago."

"What does he want with her?"

Styx shrugged. The vampires he had commanded to keep track of the unpredictable Were had managed to get their hands on the photo, as well as to follow Salvatore to Chicago. They couldn't, however, get close enough to discover the reasoning behind the man's obsession with the woman.

"I don't have the least idea, but she's obviously very important to him. Important enough that he might be willing to negotiate for her return . . . if I am able to capture her first."

A hint of surprise touched the pale face. "You intend to kidnap her?"

"I intend to keep her as my guest until the Weres can be made to see reason," he corrected, his entire body stiffening as Viper tilted back his head to laugh with rich enjoyment. "What is so amusing?"

Viper pointed at the picture in his hand. "Have you taken a good look at this woman?"

"Of course." Styx frowned. "It was necessary to memorize her features in the event the picture was lost or destroyed."

"And yet you will willingly take her beneath your roof?"

"Is there some reason I should not?" he demanded.

"The obvious reasons."

Styx battled a flare of impatience. If Viper had information about the woman, why did he not just speak it instead of behaving in such a mysterious manner?

"You speak in riddles, old friend. Do you believe the woman might pose some sort of danger?"

Viper held up his hands. "Only in the manner any beautiful woman poses a danger."

Styx narrowed his gaze. By the gods. Did Viper believe he was susceptible to the lures of a mere female? A mortal one at that?

If he wished a woman, he had only to glance over the balcony. The nightclub was filled with females, and more than a few males, who had made their interest flamboyantly clear since he had walked through the door.

"The woman will be my hostage, nothing more," he said coldly.

"Of course."

Sensing Viper's lingering amusement Styx impatiently pointed toward the picture. It was, after all, the reason he had come here in the first place.

"Do you know the location of the establishment she is standing in front of?"

"It's familiar." Pausing a moment Viper gave a nod of his head. "Yes. It's a Goth bar. I'd say four, no wait . . . five, blocks south of here."

"I thank you, old friend." Styx was swiftly on his feet. He reached out to take the picture and returned it to his pocket.

Viper pressed himself to his feet and placed a restraining hand on Styx's arm.

"Wait, Styx."

He swallowed back his surge of impatience. He didn't have time to linger. The sooner he captured the woman, the sooner he would know if she were indeed of importance to the Weres.

"What is it?"

"What are you going to do?"

"I told you. I intend to take the woman."

"Just like that?" Viper demanded.

Styx frowned in confusion. "Yes."

"You cannot go alone. If the Weres are keeping watch they are sure to try and stop you."

"I do not fear a pack of dogs," Styx retorted in scornful tones.

Viper refused to relent. "Styx."

Styx heaved a sigh. "I will have my Ravens near," he promised, referring to the five vampires who had been his constant companions for centuries. They were as much a part of him as his own shadow.

The silver-haired vampire was still not satisfied. "And where will you take her?"

"To my lair."

"Good God." Viper gave a sharp laugh. "You can't take that poor woman to those damp, disgusting caves."

Styx frowned. In truth he hadn't really considered the less than welcoming atmosphere of the caves he inhabited.

To him they were simply a place to remain safely out of the sun.

"Most of the caves are quite comfortable."

"It's bad enough that you're taking the woman hostage. At least take her someplace that has a decent bed and a few amenities."

"What does it matter? She is nothing more than a human."

"It matters because she is a *human*. Christ, they are more fragile than dew fairies." With swift, gliding steps Viper moved toward the desk that consumed a large part of his office behind the balcony. He reached into a drawer and pulled out a sheet of paper. After scribbling a few lines he dug his hand into his pocket and pulled out a small key. Returning to Styx he placed both in his hands. "Here."

"What is this?" Styx demanded.

"A key to my estate north of the city. It's quiet and isolated enough for your purpose, but far more pleasant than your lair." He pointed to the paper. "Those are the directions. I'll alert Santiago and the rest of my staff to expect you."

Styx opened his mouth to protest. Perhaps his lair was not the most elegant or luxurious of places, but it was well protected and more importantly he was familiar with the surrounding landscape.

Still, he supposed there was something to be said for providing a bit of comfort for the woman. As Viper had pointed out, humans were tediously fragile and prone to a puzzling array of illnesses and injury. He needed her alive if she were to be of any worth.

Besides, it would put him in a position to keep an eye on Salvatore.

"Perhaps it would be best to remain close enough to the city to negotiate with the Weres," he admitted.

"And close enough to call for assistance if you need it," Viper insisted.

"Yes." Styx pocketed the key. "Now I must go."

"Take care, old friend."

Styx gave a somber nod of his head. "That I can promise."

Gina, a redheaded, freckle-faced waitress was leaning negligently against the bar when the three men stepped into the Goth nightclub.

"Yowser, stud-alert," she shouted over the head-throbbing bang of the nearby band. "Now that is some grade A prime beef."

Lifting her head from the drink she was mixing, Darcy Smith glanced toward the latest patrons. Her brows lifted in surprise.

As a rule Gina was not overly particular. She considered anything remotely male and standing on two legs as grade A. But on this occasion, well . . . even grading on a curve they reached A status.

Darcy whistled beneath her breath as she studied the two closest to her. Definitely poster-boys for the steroid generation, she acknowledged, eyeing the bulging muscles that looked chiseled from marble beneath their tight T-shirts and fitted jeans. Oddly both had shaved their heads. Maybe to set off the dangerous scowls that marked their handsome faces, or to emphasize the air of coiled violence they carried with them.

It worked.

In contrast, the man standing behind them was built along far slighter lines. Of course, the elegant silk suit couldn't entirely hide the smooth muscles. Nor did the long black curls that brushed his shoulders soften the dark, aquiline features.

With absolute certainty Darcy knew that it was the smaller man who was the most dangerous of the trio. There was a fierce intensity that crackled about him as he led his henchmen toward the thick crowd.

"The one in the suit looks like a mobster," she observed in critical tones.

"A mobster in an Armani suit." Gina flashed a smile. "I've always had a weakness for Armani."

Darcy rolled her eyes. She had never had an interest in designer clothes, or the sort of men who felt it necessary to wear them. A good thing considering men in Armani suits were hardly a dime a dozen in her world.

More like once in a blue moon.

"What's he doing here?" she muttered.

The crowd at the underground bar was the usual mixture. Goths, metal-heads, stonies, and the truly bizarre.

Most came to enjoy the heavy rock bands, and to throw themselves around the cramped dance floor in wild abandon. A few preferred the back rooms that offered a wide variety of illegal pursuits. Hardly the sort of place to attract a more sophisticated clientele.

Gina gave her hair a good fluff before reaching for her tray. "Probably here to stare at the natives. People with money always enjoy rubbing elbows with the riffraff." The woman grimaced, her expression older than her years. "As long as they don't get too dirty in the process."

Darcy watched the waitress efficiently sashay her way through the rowdy crowd with a small smile. She couldn't entirely blame Gina for her cynical nature. Like herself, the waitress was alone in the world, and without the education or resources to hope for a brilliant career.

Darcy, however, refused to allow bitterness to touch her heart. What did it matter if she were forced to take whatever job might come along?

Bartender, pizza delivery, yoga instructor, and occasionally

a nude model for the local art school. Nothing was beneath her.
Pride was highly overrated when a girl had to put food on the
table. Besides, she was saving for something better. One day
she would have her own health food store, and nothing was
going to be allowed to stand in her path.

Certainly not a defeatist attitude.

Kept busy pouring drinks and washing glasses, Darcy didn't
notice when the latest arrivals took a place at the bar. Not until
their glares and flexing muscles had managed to warn off the
rest of the patrons and she found herself virtually alone with
them.

Feeling a strange flare of unease she forced her feet to carry
her toward the waiting men. It was ridiculous, she chastised
herself. There were over a hundred people in the room. The
men couldn't possibly be a threat.

Instinctively halting before the man in the suit, she swallowed a small gasp as she met the golden brown eyes that smoldered with a heat that was nearly tangible.

Yikes.

A wolf in silk clothing.

She wasn't sure where the inane thought came from and she
was quick to squash it. The man was a customer. She was there
to offer him service.

Nothing more, nothing less.

Plastering a smile on her face, she put a small paper coaster
in front of him.

"May I help you?"

A slow smile curved his lips to reveal startling white teeth. "I
most certainly hope so, *cara,*" he drawled with a faint accent.

The hairs on the back of her neck stirred as his golden gaze
made a lazy survey of her black T-shirt and too short miniskirt.

There was a hunger in those eyes that she wasn't certain was
entirely sexual. More like she was a tasty pork chop.

Yikes, indeed.

"Can I get you a drink?" She forced a brisk, professional
edge to her voice. It was a voice she had discovered could wilt
an erection at a hundred paces.

The stranger merely smiled. "A Bloody Mary."

"Spicy?"

"Oh, very."

She resisted the urge to roll her eyes. "And your friends?"

"They are on duty."

Her gaze shot toward the men looming behind their leader with their arms crossed. Frick and Frack, without a brain between them.

"You're the boss." Moving to the back of the bar she mixed the drink, adding a stalk of celery and olive before returning to set it on the coaster. "One Bloody Mary."

She was already turning away when his hand reached out to grasp her arm. "Wait."

She frowned down at the dark, slender fingers on her arm. "What do you want?"

"Keep me company. I hate to drink alone."

Obviously Frick and Frack didn't count. "I'm on duty."

He pointedly glanced around the deserted bar. "No one seems in desperate need of your services. No one, but me."

Darcy heaved a sigh. She disliked being rude. It was bad for her karma. But this man clearly couldn't take a hint.

"If you're looking for companionship, I'm sure that they're any number of women here who would be happy to drink with you."

"I don't want any number of women." Those golden eyes burned into hers. "Just you."

"I'm working."

"You can't work all night."

"No, but when I'm done I'm going home." She jerked her arm from his grasp. "Alone."

Something that might have been annoyance rippled over the fiercely handsome face.

"All I want is to talk to you. Surely you can offer me a few moments of your time?"

"Talk to me about what?"

He cast an impatient glance toward the crowd that was growing rowdier by the moment. He didn't seem to appreciate the enthusiasm of multipierced, leather-drenched teenagers ramming full speed into each other.

"I would prefer that we go someplace a bit more private."

"I don't think so."

His expression hardened. Even more unnerving the golden eyes seemed to suddenly glow with an inner light. As if someone had lit a candle behind them.

"I must speak with you, Darcy. I would prefer that our relationship remain cordial, you are after all a beautiful and tempting young woman, but if you make this difficult, then I am prepared to do whatever is necessary to have my way."

Darcy's heart clenched with a flare of sudden fear. "How did you know my name?"

He leaned forward. "I know a great deal about you."

Okay, this was going from weird to downright creepy. Gorgeous gentlemen in thousand-dollar suits, with their own personal entourage, did not stalk impoverished bartenders. Not unless they intended to kill and mutilate them.

Two things she hoped to avoid.

She took an abrupt step backward. "I think you had better finish your drink, collect your goons, and leave."

"Darcy . . ." His hand reached out as if he would physically force her to join him.

Thankfully his attention seemed to waver and his head turned toward the door.

"We have company," he growled toward Frick and Frack. "Deal with them."

On cue the two thugs were charging toward the door with startling speed. The man rose from the barstool to watch them leave, as if half expecting an army to come charging into the club.

It was enough for Darcy.

She might not be Mensa material, but she did recognize opportunity when it came-a-knocking.

Whatever the man wanted from her it couldn't be good. The more distance she could put between them the better.

Dodging toward the far end of the bar she ignored the man's sudden shout behind her. She didn't even bother glancing toward the crowd for help. A screaming woman in this place was just another part of the show. Instead, she turned toward the back of the club. Just down the hall was a storage room with a sturdy lock. She could hide until one of the bouncers missed her from the bar. They could deal with the crazed stalker.

It was, after all, in their job description.

Concentrating on sounds of pursuit from behind Darcy didn't notice the thick shadows ahead of her. Not until one of the shadows moved to stand directly in her path.

There was a brief glimpse of a beautiful bronzed face and cold black eyes before the strange man spoke a single word and she was falling to the floor as the darkness engulfed her.

Discover the Romances of
Hannah Howell

Nail-Biting Romantic Suspense
from Your Favorite Authors